MURDER
AT THE
MOULIN
ROUGE

MURDER AT THE MOULIN ROUGE

A Blackwell & Watson Time-Travel Mystery

CAROL POULIOT

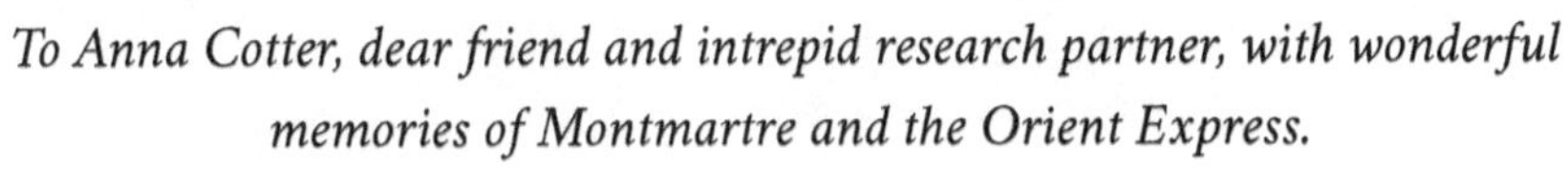

To Anna Cotter, dear friend and intrepid research partner, with wonderful memories of Montmartre and the Orient Express.

To Kyle Adams, whose knowledge, skills, and care have allowed me to sit at the computer for all these years. I'm forever grateful.

Praise for Murder at the Moulin Rouge

"Pouliot's latest entry in the time-traveling Blackwell and Watson mystery series has it all—vivid historical detail, crackling romantic tension, and a twist-filled plot that keeps you guessing to the very end. *Murder at the Moulin Rouge* is a dazzling blend of Belle Epoque glamour and Golden Age sleuthing that fans of historical mysteries will devour."—Jen Collins Moore, author of the Roman Holiday Series

"So happy to see Steven and Olivia return in *Murder at the Moulin Rouge*! This fun historical romp reaches back to Paris in the late 1800's and plunges us into fascinating detail about the artists and dancers of the time while the mystery unfolds. It satisfied both my time travel and cozy mystery cravings!"—Rosanne Limoncelli, author of The Four Queens of Crime mystery series

"In *Murder at the Moulin Rouge*, Carol Pouliot transports us to Paris, 1895. The mystery is set against a glittering backdrop of elegant stages, Impressionist painters, and aristocratic patrons. While investigating the death of a young dancer, time-traveling sleuths Blackwell and Watson uncover deadly secrets hiding behind the glamor. Like the mysterious travel agent who arranges their flight across time and space, Pouliot makes it all look easy. Stories of time travel are as much about the present as they are about alternate eras. *Murder at the Moulin Rouge* cleverly takes that concept one step further. With Toulouse-Lautrec, Degas, and a host of real and fictional characters bringing the story to life, *Murder at the Moulin Rouge* is a vividly rendered historical narrative as well as an exploration of the enduring nature of love and art. *Murder at the Moulin Rouge* guarantees a front row seat—and a first class ticket—to a thrilling tale of deception, murder, and revenge."—Lori Robbins, Amazon bestselling author of the On Pointe and Master Class mystery series

"Carol Pouliot has obviously done her research and her love of French culture—the food, the language, the arts, the joie de vivre—shows on every page of *Murder at the Moulin Rouge*. Through the eyes of 1930s Detective Steven Blackwell and modern-day journalist Olivia Watson, the 19th century streets of Paris come alive in this fun time-travel mystery whodunnit. *Murder at the Moulin Rouge* pits the high life enjoyed by the entitled aristocracy against the tenacious pursuit of the artist's life and the dark, often deadly, secrets that surface when the two clash."—Clara McKenna, USA Today bestselling author of the Stella & Lyndy Mystery series

"The winter of 1895 glitters with opulence and glamour, but the drama breeds deadly consequences in the City of Lights. A young dancer's death prompts a request across time, entangling Steven and Olivia in an investigation involving performers and patrons of the Opéra Garnier Ballet and the Moulin Rouge. Pouliot breathes life into a fascinating cast of fictional and historical characters and keeps the reader en pointe until the final curtain. A twisty, exotic, and engaging story bound to delight mystery fans, armchair travelers, and Francophiles!"—Melissa Westemeier, author of Nun the Wiser Mysteries and host of My Bookcase Slays

Note

French abbreviations before a character's last name are used in conversations throughout the novel. The abbreviations are: M. for Monsieur, Mme for Madame, and Mlle for Mademoiselle.

Cast of Characters

THE SLEUTHS

- **Steven Blackwell** – Depression-era cop who travels back in time to Paris in 1895.
- **Olivia Watson** – Steven's twenty-first-century partner-in-crime. She travels to France with him.
- **Etienne Berthot** – French detective who helps Steven and Olivia.

THE ARTISTS

- **Evangéline Neuilly** – She persuades Steven to investigate a murder on behalf of her friend Henri. She will become Steven's mother in a future time.
- **Henri de Toulouse-Lautrec** – (b. 1864 d. 1901) French post-impressionist artist. Known for his posters of the Moulin Rouge. Friend of Evangéline.
- **Suzanne Valadon** – (b. 1865 d. 1938) Post-impressionist artist and model.
- **Edgar Degas** – (b. 1834 d. 1917) Impressionist artist known for his paintings of ballet dancers. His art holds a dark secret.
- **Alfred Sisley** – (b. 1839 d. 1899) Impressionist artist who comes to Evangéline's rescue.

AT THE OPERA GARNIER BALLET

- **Yvette Caron** – Ballet dancer. Madeleine's roommate and keeper of secrets.
- **MiNou Bordeaux** – Recently deceased ballet dancer. Favorite model of Degas.
- **Pierre Gailhard** – (b. 1848 d. 1918) Director of the Opéra Garnier.
- **Claudine Verlaine** – Ballet dancer. Too young to understand what's going on.
- **Gigi Pantier** – Ballet dancer. Friend of the Marquis de Polignac. She helps Madeleine during her time of crisis.

AT THE MOULIN ROUGE

- **Madeleine Gervaise** – A ballet dancer before she danced the cancan, her young life was cut short.
- **Nini** – She teaches the cancan and keeps a watchful eye on the dancers.
- **Marielle DuPin** – Once a ballerina, she now dances at the Moulin Rouge. She was jealous of Madeleine.
- **Brigitte Allard** and **Joséphine Moreau** – Cancan dancers and friends of Madeleine. They suggest a solution to Madeleine's plight.
- **Charles Zidler** – (b. 1831 d. 1897) Moulin Rouge co-owner and manager.

THE ARISTOCRATS

- **Le Comte de Chamfort (Jean-Claude)** – Patron of the ballet and friend of Madeleine Gervaise.

- **La Comtesse de Chamfort (Nathalie)** – Wife of the Comte de Chamfort.
- **Le Duc de Rochechouart** – Patron of the ballet and friend of Arielle Lambert.
- **Le Marquis de Polignac** – Patron of the ballet and friend of Gigi Pantier.
- **Le Comte de Beauharnais** – Patron of the ballet.

ADDITIONAL CHARACTERS

- **Abel Van der Water** – Time-travel agent.
- **Louis Duclos** – Evangéline's young helper.
- **Bernard Fournier** – Madeleine's former fiancé.
- **Gabriel Glissant** and **Carlos Garcia** – Parisian miscreants.
- **Gaston Visière** – Carriage driver for the Comte de Chamfort.

Chapter One

December 25, 1934

Knightsbridge, New York

"I need you to come to Paris."

"You need *what?*" he asked.

Detective Steven Blackwell stared at the younger version of his mother standing in the room that had been her studio. Jaw dropped, eyes like saucers. He could barely speak.

"I need you—and your friend Olivia, if you like—to come to Paris. There's been a murder and the police aren't doing anything," said Evangéline. "I thought I heard a voice a minute ago. Was that Olivia? Why don't you get her? She's probably wondering what's going on."

In a daze, and feeling like he had no control over his actions, Steven turned away from the vision of his mother and stumbled out into the hallway. He saw Olivia still waiting in the doorway at the end of the hall. Her hand flew to her chest, and she heaved a great sigh. "Oh, my God, you're okay! What's going on? I thought I heard voices. Is somebody here?" As he came closer, she noticed the look on his face. "What's wrong? You look funny."

"It's my mother. My mother's here."

"What?"

"She looks as real as you do, but she's young, around our age. She said she needs me to go to Paris. And you should come too."

"What?" For one terrifying moment, Olivia wondered if a year of grieving had unhinged Steven's mind. How could his mother be here? Evangéline Neuilly Blackwell died last January.

Steven repeated Evangéline's instructions. "She said I should come get you." He held out his hand. Olivia took it and stepped over the threshold into 1934.

They moved slowly down the hall, then paused at the doorway to look at each other. Steven squeezed her hand. Olivia nodded. They both took a deep breath, then entered Evangéline's studio.

There in the shadowy room stood a beautiful woman, shoulder-length copper hair shining in the lamplight. She was slender, taller than average, and wore a stunning emerald dress, the kind French women wore to perfection. A wool coat with a fur collar had been thrown over the back of a chair. She held out her hand toward Olivia.

"Hello. I'm Evangéline Neuilly. I'm so happy to meet you."

Olivia had always wanted to meet Steven's exotic-sounding mother—a famous French artist—but that possibility had died along with Evangéline. Or so she had thought. Olivia told herself to close her mouth, which had fallen open, and shook the woman's hand. "Olivia Watson."

Evangéline looked at Steven. "I can tell you're surprised to see me. I must not have told you about my ability to time travel. Surely, you wondered why you can? And if your father or I also had that ability?"

"Eh, no. Not really."

Evangéline rolled her eyes and gave Olivia a look that said, Men, huh?

Olivia couldn't help grinning.

"Well," Evangéline opened her arms wide, "here's the answer to your unasked question. You got it from me."

Olivia recovered first. "So, Evangéline, you traveled here from… when?"

"1895. And I really need your help. Both of you." She shook her head and waved her hand back and forth. "I know. I know. You have a lot of questions. Let's go downstairs and have something to drink. I'll tell you what has happened."

They trooped down the stairs and into the living room.

"I know I must have lived in this house for some time, and I assume I decorated this room…." Evangéline turned to Steven for confirmation.

"Yes, we lived here about twenty years or so before you…." He swallowed hard.

"Before I died," she whispered, then patted his hand. *"Pauvre chouchou.* Poor sweetheart. I'm so sorry. But, don't tell me. I don't want to know when. Of course, I have an idea. But not the exact date." She opened a door in the sideboard. *"Bon!* A bottle of red." She handed the wine to Steven.

Still dazed, he opened it and poured a glass for each of them. Evangéline curled up in a leather chair. Steven and Olivia sat facing her on the couch.

His mother took a sip and pursed her lips. "Not bad. So, listen, we must act fast. A young girl has been killed, but the police do nothing. They say it was an accident. We know it was not. I want you to find out who killed Madeleine Gervaise."

His cop's instincts kicked in, and Steven found himself intrigued. *Who was Madeleine Gervaise? How did she die? Why do the police think it was an accident? And what was her connection to Evangéline?*

Suddenly, Steven remembered something Sherlock Holmes once said: "When you have eliminated the impossible, whatever remains, however improbable, must be the truth." And with that assurance, he snapped out of his stupor and accepted his mother's bewildering appearance. He leaned forward.

"All right, let's say, for the sake of argument, that I can and will go to Paris. Answer these questions." He ticked them off his fingers. "Why do the police think it was an accident? How do you know it wasn't? When did this happen?"

Evangéline placed her feet on the floor and mirrored him, ticking her answers off her fingers. Olivia almost laughed at the two of them. Talk about a chip off the old block, as her grandfather used to say. "She fell on one of the tall staircases in Montmartre. The police say she slipped on the ice. My friend Henri knows the human body and how it works. He says the…how do you say 'marks of black and blue'?"

"Bruises," Olivia chimed in. "We also say black-and-blue marks."

"Ah! *Bon.* Henri says the bruises prove someone pushed her. It happened late Sunday night, early Monday morning. Today is already Wednesday. That is why we must move fast."

Steven groaned, thinking of the days lost. "Is Henri a doctor?"

"No, an artist. But, believe me, Steven, he *knows* the body. If Henri says she was pushed, she was pushed."

"So, again, if we were to do this, *how* would it work?"

"We must go with all speed. That means we must travel in Olivia's time in one of those fast aeroplanes. That's how I got here so quickly."

"Wait, how do you know about Olivia?"

"*Oh, mon Dieu,* the questions! It is a long story, but if it will help speed this up…last summer, I traveled to 1934, to America, with someone on business that had nothing to do with you or my future. When I was in New York City, I saw a photograph in a newspaper of the painting I'm working on right now. The article said a museum in Chicago had bought it and gave information about me, you, and your father. While my friend was completing his business, I had a couple of days to myself, so I took a train here and came to this house. Naturally, I was curious, so I came in and looked around. You really shouldn't leave your doors unlocked, you know. Anyway, I saw the photograph of Olivia on your dresser. You have her name and the year 2014 written on the back. I realized you had inherited my ability to time travel and that Olivia also had the gift." Evangéline blew out her cheeks. "Can we not return to the problem at hand now?"

Steven grinned. "Yeah, okay. You know, I always thought you learned English when you moved here with Dad. You speak really well."

She rolled her eyes. "As you must know, my father is a professor of English at the Sorbonne. He taught me when I was a child." She took a drink of her wine. "Now, to our *problème*…I went through the portal in Paris, from 1895 to Olivia's time."

"Why did you go into Olivia's time?"

"If you keep interrupting me, we will *never* get anywhere. Just listen." Evangéline took another drink of wine and went on. "Time is of the essence, as it's already been almost three days. We must travel into 2014 and go to New York City as quickly as possible. Someone there will help us with what we need. Tomorrow night, we'll fly to Paris. Once we're there, we'll travel back to 1895."

"You make it sound easy. But I have so many questions," Steven persisted. "How are we going to pay for all this? How do I get a passport fast enough to fly tomorrow? What about other things we might need?"

His mother tilted her head toward the ceiling and sighed. "You think I have come all this way without a plan? Before I left, Henri gave me a sketch. There's a man in New York City—you will soon learn we have travel agents in cities all over the world who help us. This man in New York City, a place called Brooklyn, is selling the sketch for me, so we'll have plenty of money. He'll make a passport and other documents for you, Steven, just as someone in Paris made mine so I could come here." Evangéline turned to Olivia. "Do you have a passport? Do you drive an automobile?"

"Yes. And I have a car."

"Can you take us to New York City tomorrow morning so we can get Steven's documents and the money to buy our tickets for the aeroplane? We *must* leave for Paris tomorrow night."

"Sure. Listen, Evangéline, I'm sorry to hear about your friend Madeleine."

"Thank you. She was lovely—a dancer and one of Henri's favorite models. Such a waste."

"Who is Henri? And why would anybody buy one of his sketches?"

"Henri de Toulouse-Lautrec. I think he is well known in your time, Olivia."

"Toulouse-Lautrec?" Olivia gasped. "He's a friend of yours?"

"Yes, and he's now your employer."

Olivia's jaw dropped.

Evangéline reached out toward Steven with her empty wineglass, then settled back in the chair after he'd refilled it. "Now, let us talk about tomorrow. You must both pack a small bag. Steven, bring any tools or objects you will need to investigate. I don't know what they might be, but that is most important. When we travel to *my* Paris in 1895, you can borrow clothes belonging to my friend Théo. He's away on business right now. His wardrobe is filled with additional items—suits, shirts, collars, and so forth. There's a cloak and hat as well. Olivia, we're about the same size. I'm happy to share my clothes with you. I have plenty of skirts and dresses. I have an extra cloak, too. Just bring your personal things."

Suddenly, Steven realized he had been given a gift. After a long, difficult year of grieving, he had the chance to spend time with the woman who would become his mother. How could he possibly say no?

"I'm sorry, but I have to interrupt again," Steven said, grinning at

Evangéline. "Before it gets too late, I need to call the chief to tell him a family emergency has come up and I need a few days off." He stood and headed for the phone, then stopped. He turned around and walked back to Evangéline. "I know this is going to be weird for you. You don't even know me yet. But I have missed you so much!" And he bent down and kissed his mother's cheek.

Chapter Two

December 26, 2014

New York City, New York

They arrived in Brooklyn shortly after noon.

She'd made good time and, during the drive down, Olivia had let her mind drift back to last winter. It had been a year that changed both of their lives. One night in February, when Steven was still grieving the unexpected and shocking death of his beloved mother, he and Olivia had seen each other across a doorway in the house where they both lived, he in 1934 and she in 2014.

Depression-era cop Steven Blackwell had certainly known nothing about twenty-first-century journalist and researcher Olivia Watson. And she had never heard of him. That night, Olivia told Steven she suspected it was Einstein's theory at work. The physicist had believed that all time happened simultaneously and time could fold over if conditions were right. Olivia thought time had folded over in their house.

Spending his days searching for concrete proof and hard evidence, the detective in Steven was skeptical, but Olivia showed him things that convinced him.

During the months that followed, they learned how to move back and forth into each other's time, grew to be friends, then unofficial partners in Steven's murder investigations. They eventually became a couple. Worries about their future plagued Olivia. She had no idea how they were going to manage a relationship in two different times. One of them would have to give up their present. That didn't make any sense. And it was too much to ask.

* * *

Olivia pulled up to the curb in front of a narrow brownstone, dwarfed by its taller neighbors at only three stories high. She thought if she were ever to move to New York, she'd want to live in a place exactly like this red brick row house. It made her feel like the kids in *The Lion, the Witch, and the Wardrobe*. Exciting things would surely happen in this house.

Evangéline led them up the staircase and rang the bell, discreetly set below a small brass plaque which read *Family Travel. Inquire within.* Moments later, a young woman with purple streaks in her short blonde hair opened the door and bade them enter.

"*Bienvenue*, Evangéline. Welcome back. I see you had a successful journey."

"Yes, thank you. Kayla, this is Steven and Olivia."

The three said hello.

"Grandfather's expecting you. Follow me."

Kayla escorted them down a dark hallway into a large workroom. A small, gnome-like man perched on a stool behind a wooden workbench piled high with notebooks, stacks of paper, leather-bound journals, pots of glue, and an inkwell, as well as modern-day markers and pens of all kinds. His sparse gray hair stuck out at odd angles, creating a halo effect, and his wire-rimmed spectacles seemed about to slide off his long, straight nose. He looked up as they entered.

"Grandpa, Evangéline's here with Steven and his friend Olivia."

"Ah, Evangéline, my dear. I see your trip was fruitful. Congratulations. You'll be happy to know everything is at the ready. And I was able to convince my colleague at Sotheby's to move quickly. I told him it was urgent."

He hopped off the stool and approached Steven and Olivia, his back bent forward, his gnarled hand outstretched. "Abel Van der Water, time-travel agent, at your service." Then he shuffled to a large oak cabinet filled with drawers of varying sizes and extracted a leather folder tied with string. He unwound the string and withdrew a thick cream-colored envelope, a New York State driver's license, and a U.S. passport.

"Kayla, take Steven into the studio and take his photograph so I can finish these for him." The travel agent turned to the women. "Evangéline, here's the money from the sale of the sketch. The documents will be ready in a moment. Olivia, you have everything you need?"

"Yes, I'm all set. Thank you."

While Van der Water put the final touches on the passport and driver's license, Kayla booked three seats on the nine o'clock flight to Paris that evening.

"Remember, if you have any problems, you can always visit my colleague at the Paris agency," Van der Water told them. "This is going to be a tricky undertaking, Steven. Good luck to you."

* * *

On the way to Kennedy International Airport, Olivia cautioned Steven.

"Listen, I need to tell you a few things about going through security.

10

I know you never want to know anything about the future, but this is important. In 2001, terrorists attacked New York City and Washington, D.C. Ever since then, airport security has been very tight and extremely serious. I know everything is going to be exciting, but it would be better if you could hide your interest until after we go through the TSA checks. Most people our age have flown before. Don't give them a reason to pull you out of line and question you. Look like you've done this before. Pretend you're a little bit bored. I'll go first and you'll see what it's like."

She explained the procedures they'd go through, including standing in the X-ray machine. "Watch what I do, then do what they tell you. It'll only take a couple of minutes to actually go through the checkpoint. After that, we can wander around in the terminal, and nobody will pay attention to how excited you are. Everyone else will be the same."

Steven's heart was in his throat.

After the calm of Mr. Van der Water's studio and the quiet in Olivia's car during the drive, the noise inside the terminal at JFK hit Steven like a slap. Crowds of travelers packed the building. Throughout the vast spaces, the air vibrated with people shouting and hurrying. Steven followed Olivia's instructions and watched as she went through security without a hitch. Then it was his turn. His heart was pounding, and his hands were damp with sweat. Did he look like someone who belonged in the twenty-first century? Would they stop him for some unknown reason? Would they ask him a question he didn't know the answer to, then, suspicious of his stammering, haul him off to a room somewhere to be interrogated—without Olivia to help him?

But it all went smoothly and, before he knew it, he was on the other side of the huge machine that had circled his body in a matter of seconds—had it really looked inside him? Now, he was being told to get his belongings and to move along.

As Steven was putting his shoes back on, Olivia and Evangéline joined him. "You did great, Steven! Totally natural," Olivia said.

Steven hardly heard her. He was trying not to gape at the quantity of shops, restaurants, and who knew what else fanning out in front of him for as far as he could see. He was glad there weren't any security people watching here as he tried to keep his eyes from popping and his jaw from dropping. Everywhere he looked, wall-to-wall travelers pulled small rolling suitcases, hurrying in every direction. "It's like an entire city! All inside the airport."

Evangéline wanted a coffee, but Steven preferred to walk around, so they left her in a coffee shop, keeping an eye on their bags and sketching passersby on her artist's pad. They still had several hours to wait.

Chapter Three

Traveling from 2014 to 1895

New York to Paris

As Steven and Olivia strolled through the terminal past souvenir and snack shops, restaurants, bars, and newsstands, Steven grew quiet. At first, it didn't occur to Olivia something might be wrong. She imagined he was taking it all in. Then she realized this wasn't his usual reaction when he traveled into her time. He normally commented on things.

"Steven, are you okay?" she asked, her voice uneasy.

He stopped walking and turned to her. "I don't know. At first, I was excited to see all these new things and fly for the first time and spend time with…" He scrunched up his face. "…a version of my mother. But it's a lot to take in. I was nervous about going through security. Now, there's so much going on, it makes me want to close my eyes and shut it out. Or walk away. And being with Evangéline is just plain confusing. She's my mother, but she's not my mother. She doesn't know me. She looks like she's close to our age, but she talks and acts older. Everything is throwing me for a loop."

Olivia squeezed his hand. "I thought the same thing about her. They say Europeans are more mature for their age than Americans. I suppose this is what that looks like. She's very confident in herself. She seems worldly. Maybe she time travels a lot. Maybe it's because she's an artist. You know, that lifestyle." Something caught Olivia's eye. "Hey, let's go over there." She led him to a quiet space around the side of a shop.

"Steven, this must be overwhelming for you. I can't imagine...." Olivia stepped closer and looked deep into his eyes. "Listen, we don't have to do this. We can go home. Right now. We can go back to Evangéline and apologize, make up a plausible excuse, tell her we're really sorry, but we just can't do it. We'll find a hotel for the night and leave tomorrow morning. The chief thinks you're off on a family emergency. We can hide away at home in my time and relax for a few days. You'll feel like your old self before you know it. I'll make all your favorite meals. We can watch movies in our pajamas. You've been working hard lately. Maybe you just need a break."

He gave her a weak smile. "Thank you for saying all of that." He sighed. "No, I can't go back on my word. Evangéline is counting on us. Her friend Henri is depending on us. I don't want to let them down. I'm sure there'll be fewer people in Paris in 1895 than in this airport right now. It'll be quieter, not so busy. Maybe we can help Evangéline and Henri with the investigation and have a little vacation at the same time. You love Toulouse-Lautrec's posters. Don't you want to meet him?"

"Well, sure, but not at your expense. I certainly don't *need* to meet him." She studied his face. Even at a moment like this, Olivia thought she could look at this face forever. "Are you sure you want to do this?"

He pulled her into a hug. "This is going to sound corny, but as long as we're together, I can do anything."

* * *

They boarded the Air France Airbus A380 and settled into their business-class seats for the trans-Atlantic flight shortly before eight o'clock. Later, when they were enjoying their coffee, Olivia leaned across Steven and said, "Evangéline, is there anything we should know? Like the recent death of a famous person, political upheaval, or an item in the news that we'd know about if we lived in 1895? Anything that would trigger suspicion if we were ignorant of it?"

"Don't worry. I'll be with you all the time. I'm going to be your translator."

"Oh! That's nice of you, but we both speak French," Olivia told her.

"You do?"

They nodded.

"You raised me to be bilingual, Evangéline," Steven said. "And Olivia learned in school. She's pretty good."

"*Formidable*! That's wonderful. I didn't really want to take time off from my painting. Coming back to your questions, Olivia, it'll probably depend on who you're talking to. During the investigation, I'm sure all the conversations will be about the case."

In the end, they agreed that if anything arose, Steven and Olivia could fall back on not understanding what someone said or not having seen it in the newspaper.

Evangéline was quiet during the remainder of the flight, either dozing or lost in her thoughts. Olivia wondered if she had missed spending Christmas with her family and perhaps Théo, whoever he was. Even thinking about a future Christmas without Steven saddened Olivia. She leaned her head on his shoulder and, to her surprise, fell asleep as well, waking only when the cabin lights went on and sounds of the coffee cart rumbling up the aisle brought her out of her dreams.

As they circled Paris an hour later, Olivia wondered who Madeleine

Gervaise had been, and who had hated her so much to have risked everything to kill her.

* * *

March 1894

From the moment she could walk, Madeleine Gervaise danced. She danced across the kitchen, grabbing her mother and twirling her around. She took her sisters' hands and skipped around in a circle, humming music only she heard. Madeleine could not imagine life without dance.

To her great fortune, the ballet master of the Austrian National Ballet Company in Vienna chose to spend his final years in Bar-le-Duc, France. Word of the distinguished new resident spread like wildfire, and when he opened a small studio announcing he would give dance lessons, Madeleine was first in line. It didn't take long for Herr Köenig to recognize her talent. He took her under his wing and tutored her privately until she was eighteen and eager to leave her small town for the bright lights and possibilities of Paris.

Ignoring her father's protests, Madeleine packed a bag and kissed her mother goodbye, promising to write. She carried with her a letter of reference from Herr Köenig to the ballet master of the Paris Opéra Garnier Ballet, asking him to give Madeleine a chance at the competition for a place in the Ballet School. She also brought a reference from a seamstress in town attesting to her sewing skills, in case she needed to find a job before being accepted into the school.

From the moment she stepped off the train, Madeleine loved Paris—the glowing lights, the fancy buildings and statues, even the pervading smells of garlic, cigarettes, and wine. She discovered the Ballet School competition was two months away and secured a job as a seamstress. Then, with luck on her side, in May of 1894, Madeleine Gervaise soared through the dance competition and was awarded a prized place at the Opéra Garnier Ballet and its school.

* * *

When they landed at Charles de Gaulle Airport on the outskirts of Paris, it was late morning. Patches of blue sky showed through drifting clouds, and the temperature hovered at freezing. Olivia reminded Steven to look alert, but a little bored going through immigration and customs.

Out on the curb, they joined the queue for a taxi. They drove on a high-speed, busy highway, then turned onto the *périférique*, the ring road around the capital. Soon, they were climbing the hills of Montmartre.

Olivia grabbed Steven's hand and took a deep breath. "Here we go. Are you ready?"

"As ready as I'll ever be."

Evangéline instructed the driver to let them off at the Place du Tertre, a large square at the top of the *butte*, the hill on which the neighborhood of Montmartre sat. Everywhere they looked, Paris was bursting with life. Around the square, under leafless trees and the icy sky, artists worked. Some stood at their easels, painting landscapes of the neighborhood, holding colorful palettes marked with dabs of oil paint. Others sketched tourists in charcoal, while the object of the portrait sat cold and stiff on a stool.

"We can walk from here," Evangéline said.

She led Steven and Olivia down rue Norvins, past La Mère Catherine, a bright red brasserie with small tables and bistro chairs on the sidewalk. Tall space heaters warmed visitors enjoying lunch in the fresh December air. Laughter and the tinkling of glasses mingled with the sounds of a dozen different languages. Olivia noticed a sign above a door that read *Fondée en 1793*. A waiter in black pants and vest, white shirt, and white apron squeezed around them, carrying a bottle of wine to one of the tables. Behind him came a second waiter carrying two plates. The dishes held a meal sizzling in butter and trailing the mouth-watering aroma of garlic. Olivia realized she was hungry.

Evangéline continued down the narrow, cobble-stoned street, then stopped at a dark green door set in a stone wall. She pushed the round brass doorknob in the center and opened the squeaking wooden door. Steven and Olivia followed her into a hidden courtyard.

"Oh! This is beautiful," Olivia gasped.

The tiny cobbled square was enclosed by three buildings and the wall they'd just passed through. Bicycles leaned against lamp posts. Pots of faded, dead geraniums sat on doorsteps.

Evangéline crossed the patio to the building on the far side and, taking a key from her bag, unlocked the heavy door.

As they entered, Olivia noticed a discreet doorbell next to a small brass plaque that read *Agence de Voyage. Appuyez sur le bouton.* Travel Agency. Push the button. It reminded her of the sign on Mr. Van der Water's brownstone.

The foyer was dark. To the left was a door with gold-tinted panes of glass set in a diamond shape pattern on the top half, and *Agence de Voyage* painted in black block letters below. A narrow hallway led deep into the back of the apartment building, and a curved stone staircase on the right led to the first floor. Evangéline pushed a large, round button on the wall at the foot of the stairs. A light blinked on.

"Follow me and hurry," she told Steven and Olivia. "We don't want to get caught on the stairs in the dark. The light will go off in ten seconds."

At the top of the stairway were two doors. Evangéline unlocked the door on the right. "This is it," she said. "Let me go through first. Wait for me to return to my time, then I'll bring you through like you do at the bedroom door in your house."

Evangéline disappeared through the doorway, then reappeared moments later. She reached out and took Olivia's hand, then Steven's. She stepped back and brought them over the threshold into 1895.

Chapter Four

Friday, December 27, 1895

Paris, France

They stood in a small living area facing a fireplace built into the far wall. Several closed doors on the right led to additional rooms, and a short wall with squares of old, wavy glass on the top half separated it from the large kitchen on the left.

The living room was simply furnished, but had everything one would need. The comfortable-looking sofa, the color of pine trees, was long enough for three people, four if they squeezed together. Two well-worn armchairs upholstered in pale green faced the couch, a low rectangular table between them held a messy pile of magazines and an ashtray. Olivia noticed rings on the surface of the table, likely left by wine glasses or bottles. Between two of the doors on the right stood a small glass-fronted bookcase stuffed with books in rich leather bindings. And scattered throughout the room hung paintings of all sizes and themes: the portrait of a bearded man who resembled Van Gogh, a celebratory street scene with confetti and streamers filling the air, a naked woman reclining on a recamier, and a jug of wine and loaf of bread on a wooden table. Olivia wanted to get close to all these paintings—to read the artists' signatures, to find out who had painted the canvases, and to discover if they were friends of Evangéline's.

"This is swell," Steven said. "Who owns this building? Is it yours, Evangéline?"

"No, it belongs to a university friend of Papa's. It's been in his family for several hundred years. He's the one who noticed something in me when I was about twelve. He took me aside one day and said he suspected I might be one of the few people who had the ability to travel through time and, if I wanted to, we could find out. He taught me everything about traveling. I'm sure you noticed the agency downstairs when we came in? His cousin Jules Duclos runs it. It's crucial to keep the building in the same family. It would be a disaster if we could not access the time portal."

Evangéline turned abruptly and marched to a door in the far right corner, threw it open, and pulled them into her studio.

"*This* is where I live," she said, and spun around with joy. "Isn't it glorious?"

The winter sun shone through three tall windows stretched across one wall, filling Evangéline's studio with light. An easel with a finished painting—sunlight sparkling on the river, a bridge, and the roof and spire of Notre Dame in the background—stood in a corner. Nearby, on a wooden table, was a paint-stained palette, a ceramic jar holding an assortment of brushes, and a small stack of towels and rags. As Olivia approached, she caught a whiff of turpentine, likely in the containers on the floor. To the right of the table, however, a second easel held a secret. A piece of cloth covered what looked like the shape of a stretched canvas. Naturally curious, Olivia longed to see *that* painting.

Stacks of finished canvases leaned against each other along the walls, and in one corner sat a worn leather armchair with a colorful shawl draped over its back. Olivia saw this was truly a comfortable, welcoming place. She felt a moment of envy that her own office, the place where she loved to be, now seemed lacking in comparison. She promised herself she'd redecorate when she and Steven returned home. It would be a good winter project.

Closing the door behind them, Evangéline led them out of her studio and into the kitchen. She grabbed a kettle and filled it with water, then skirted a free-standing wooden cupboard filled with colorful pottery at the end of the counter. She set the kettle on a large, heavy stove, opened a small door on the top, and peered in. *"Bon!* Louis has done his job." She turned to Steven and Olivia. "Louis is Jules's young son. He runs errands, delivers messages, and takes care of things in the *appartement* when I'm away. Keeping the fire going is one of his tasks." She added a few pieces of coal from a bucket on the floor nearby. "He's a wonderful boy. I don't know what I'd do without him."

Looking around, Olivia saw four mismatched wooden chairs circling a table draped with a brightly colored cloth. A bottle of red wine sat near a stack of cotton napkins and a dish holding a block of butter. She had the impression Evangéline used this space more than the living room. It had that friendly, lived-in feeling.

At that moment, a thump drew their attention to the window at the end of the room. Olivia peered out and saw a small blond boy, perhaps ten years old, playing with a ball. Evangéline leaned around Olivia and pushed the window open.

"Bonjour, Louis. Je suis de retour. I'm back," Evangéline called to him. "Will you come up? I have a commission for you."

"Oui, bien sûr! Of course!" the child exclaimed, grinning.

Moments later, there was a light knock on the door, and Louis entered.

Evangéline thrust some coins into his hand. "Go down to the *boulangérie* and get me a baguette. We haven't had any breakfast!"

"Breakfast! It's already lunchtime," the child exclaimed.

Evangéline laughed. "Away with you. I have a second commission when you return. And make sure the bread is fresh."

When the door closed behind the curly blond head, Evangéline turned to Steven and Olivia. "Bring your bags and come with me. I'll show you to your apartment."

"*Our* apartment?" Steven exclaimed. "Aren't we staying with you?"

"There's not enough room, and besides, you're only next door."

Evangéline led them into a similar, though smaller, space. "You'll be more comfortable here. There's plenty of room and you'll have your privacy." She handed the key to Steven. "Leave your belongings here for now. You can settle in, and I'll show you how things work later. First, you need to change your clothes. We're lucky Louis was in and out fast and didn't notice anything. Although, to be honest, some of my artist friends do enjoy dressing in bizarre ways from time to time. Maybe Louis is used to it. When he gets back, we'll have something quick to eat, then you can start your investigation, Steven. Henri is anxious."

They returned to Evangéline's apartment and went into a bedroom behind one of the closed doors. Her friend Théo was close to Steven's size, and his suit fit well enough. At first, Steven wriggled around a bit. The waistcoat felt tight across his middle, and part of the collar lay too heavily on the sensitive spot between his collarbones. But, he liked the cutaway coat and thought he looked dapper in the silk top hat. He was happy to see from the look on Olivia's face that she agreed.

Olivia was the same size as Steven's mother, and Evangéline's clothes fit as though they'd been tailor-made for her. In a nod to the holidays, Evangéline lent her a two-piece outfit in dark green: a tight-fitting jacket and long skirt. The ensemble showed off Olivia's slim figure, had two large ornate buttons on each side at the hip, then widened to a full skirt that brushed the floor. Underneath the jacket, the designer had created the illusion of a white silk blouse. The sleeves were full at the shoulder, like filled balloons, then tapered to the wrists.

* * *

They were finishing the last of their buttered bread with jam, cheese, and fruit, when Louis returned from his second errand, accompanied by a very short, black-bearded man. The man wore black-and-white checked trousers that had obviously been specially made for his childlike height. He set his cane against an empty chair and pulled off his heavy woolen overcoat, which he threw over the back. Leaning towards Evangéline, he kissed her on each cheek. "My dear! Is this our sleuth?" he asked, looking at Steven.

"Henri, I'd like to introduce Detective Steven Blackwell and his assistant, Olivia Watson, from New York. Steven, Olivia, this is Monsieur Henri de Toulouse-Lautrec."

"A girl assistant?" Henri was taken aback. "Is that common in America?"

"It's becoming more so," Steven answered. "We find many occasions where a woman does better than a man."

Henri pursed his thick lips, and his heavy, dark brows flew up, popping his pince-nez out of place. It swung down on a cord.

Olivia had known this moment was coming, yet she hadn't prepared herself. *Really, how could you?* She could hardly find her voice to say, Nice to meet you. Meanwhile, Henri and Steven were moving on, shaking hands, and getting down to business.

"It's been four days now," Henri said. "We must waste no time getting started. I've arranged for you to meet Detective Inspector Etienne Berthot. He's my friend and contact at the Sûreté. He's expecting us. I'll take you to the scene of the crime first, then to the morgue to see Madeleine's body."

"Good. Every day that passes, we lose valuable insights and information," Steven said.

"*C'est logique, ça.*" Then, as if realizing he hadn't said anything yet to Olivia, he turned to her. "A pleasure to make your acquaintance, Mademoiselle. And how do you assist Monsieur Blackwell?"

"I keep notes on everything connected to the investigation. I use my journalist skills to observe. Sometimes I question female witnesses or suspects. It can make a difference in what we learn if a woman talks with them."

Comprehension dawned on his face. "Very sensible. I can see how that might happen. Excellent." Henri smiled at her, then quickly blurted out, "*Bon! On y va.* Let's go." He pulled on his coat, then took some papers from one of the pockets and handed them to Evangéline. "Here are your tickets for tomorrow night. There are four in case Théo returns in time. It's at the Salon Indien du Grand Café. *Vingt heures.* Eight o'clock. I have reserved *une table* for supper at the Moulin de la Galette afterwards." He placed his top hat on his head, picked up his cane, and, without looking back, headed for the door. "*A demain, Evangéline.* See you tomorrow."

Steven and Olivia didn't have time to inquire about the tickets. They threw on the cloaks Evangéline had loaned them and grabbed the writing materials she'd provided. Steven made sure he had his magnifying glass and tape measure, then they followed Henri de Toulouse-Lautrec down the worn stone stairs.

* * *

Four days ago...

It had been a good night, but Madeleine was bone weary. She wished someone had offered her a ride home. It was freezing, and invisible patches of ice made it dangerous to hurry. The wind grabbed her cloak, whipping it around her. One minute, it wrapped her up like a mummy, then a sudden gust would catch it and it would fly around her, getting caught between her legs, causing her to stumble. The simple act of walking posed a challenge tonight.

Madeleine ached all over from a long, busy work week, and her hamstring was killing her. She gave herself a satisfied grin and an imaginary pat on the back. She'd recently begun learning the names of all her muscles. After all, a dancer should know what to be grateful for, right?

Leaving the boulevard de Clichy behind her, Madeleine turned the corner at rue LePic. A sudden sensation of near-complete silence washed over her, as though she'd plunged into the depths of the sea. She no longer heard the quick bursts of Offenbach's cancan music or the conversations and laughter spilling out the door as customers exited the Moulin Rouge. Here, the silence of the night was all-enveloping.

Above the narrow canyon of the street, Madeleine saw the effects of powerful, wild winds racing across the sky, pushing heavy storm clouds that played hide-and-seek with the moon and stars. When a break in the cloud cover revealed a waxing crescent moon, its light would prod the shadows surrounding her, making them move as if they were alive. The moments passed quickly, and darkness enveloped her once again.

After some twenty minutes of struggling along the winding, ever-climbing streets, Madeleine reached a small plateau in the side of the hill. She now faced the most difficult part of her walk home. The soaring staircase loomed like a multi-story building, its top steps disappearing into the darkness as if they didn't exist.

Madeleine began to climb.

As she reached the summit of this concrete Everest, Madeleine found herself breathing harder than usual. I wonder if I'm coming down with something, she thought. The winter had been hard on everyone. Only a couple of weeks ago, the company had grieved when the orchestra leader's six-month-old baby died of pneumonia.

"Hey!"

Madeleine heard a familiar voice call out and carefully turned on the icy top step to see a shadowy figure gripping the railing and moving foolishly fast up the stairs, cloak billowing in the wind like a bird in flight. Although the gas lights along the staircase were either broken or too far away to illuminate the face, she knew the voice.

"What are you doing here? Are you following me?" Madeleine said.

"I've been looking for you."

"Why?"

Her pursuer scrambled up the last five stairs—one hand relying on the wrought-iron railing in the middle—moved around her, and stepped off at the top. "Can we talk for a minute? Would you like to get a cup of tea or a glass of wine? I imagine you've had a few already."

"I don't think so. I'm having trouble with my leg. I need to get off my feet."

"Have a cup of tea with me, then you can go home and sleep until noon."

"Merci, mais non. I'm tired. I'm going to go home, fix a hot water bottle, and curl up in my bed."

"Oh, damn," the other murmured as something fell, tumbling down the stairs in the darkness. The object hit several steps on the long way down, making a metallic clinking sound, pinging shrilly in the quiet night.

Distracted, Madeleine turned to see what it was. The other person took advantage of her being off balance. Holding tightly onto the railing, her assailant lifted a strong, powerful leg and shoved hard. Immediately airborne, Madeleine let out a scream, arms and legs flailing, her skirt billowing out like a parachute. But unlike a parachute, it did not buoy her up. She plummeted to earth, slamming onto the edges of several steps as she tumbled head-over-heels. After what seemed like minutes but was only a matter of seconds, her scream still echoing in the quiet night, Madeleine's broken body landed with a thud at the bottom. The other, ever careful of lurking ice, gripped the handrail and descended the staircase to see if the plan had succeeded.

Madeleine lay crumpled in a heap. Her sightless eyes stared up at the unforgiving sky.

The last word she had uttered was why.

Chapter Five

Outside at the curb in front of Evangéline's apartment stood two magnificent horses hitched to a black carriage. The driver waited nearby, smoking. Spying Henri, he threw his strong-smelling cigarette to the ground and rushed to open the door. While he was arranging a small box to be used as a step, Olivia looked around and was stunned to see that much of the *quartier* she was familiar with was missing. To her astonishment, wooden windmills dotted the hill, their sails turning in the December wind. *I wonder what other surprises are in store for us this week.*

The coachman handed Olivia into the carriage first, then waited as Steven and Henri climbed in.

"We're not going far," Henri told them as they clattered down the narrow, winding street with its buildings set so close it was hard to see where one ended and the next began. "I'll tell you about Madeleine on the way. By the way, did Evangéline tell you Madeleine was one of my models? One of my favorites, actually. She had honey blonde hair and sapphire blue eyes—exquisite to paint. She was petite and had a dancer's wiry body. But muscular, very strong. I always told her she was too skinny, she should eat more—you could see her ribs when she moved—but she just laughed. The last few weeks, she talked about going home for Christmas to see her family. She was very excited. You must discover who did this, Detective Blackwell. He *must* be punished."

Henri coughed and stopped speaking. For a moment, he seemed to fall into a dark place. Olivia noticed a haunted look in his eyes. It was easy to see Madeleine's death had hit him hard.

The carriage continued down the street, creaking and groaning over the uneven cobblestones. The horses snorted, and their breath hung in the crisp air. Olivia, who had visited the artists' quartier of Paris twice before and considered Montmartre her favorite part of the city, peered out the window to read the street signs. She sketched a simple map in her notebook, noting the names so she and Steven could find the crime scene later if they wanted to return.

They reached a corner and made a wide right turn in front of a busy restaurant. They passed a row of small shops, still closed for the two-hour lunch break, the signs in the windows reading *Fermé*. Olivia noticed wooden shelves stacked with dry goods in *une épicerie*. Fresh meat hung in the window of the *boucherie*. And the owner of the *charcuterie* displayed pork products and specialized *pâtés* in his front window. They drove by apartments with their sash windows shut tight against the cold and their green or blue shutters standing open to let in the light. After a couple of blocks, the driver turned left onto rue Vincent and pulled up in front of the legendary Lapin Agile. He jumped down from the box seat and secured the reins around a glossy black post. He opened the carriage door, set the little box back in place, and helped Olivia and Henri down. Steven had no trouble disembarking on his own.

The terra cotta-colored cabaret looked like it was made of adobe and had shutters the color of an evergreen forest. The curious thing about the Lapin Agile, however, was a painting of a large dancing rabbit sporting a red bowtie and cummerbund on the front of the building. Strangely, the bunny had one foot in a pot and carried a bottle of wine in his hand. Olivia made a mental note to Google it when they were back in the twenty-first century.

Henri led them down the steeply sloping street over slippery cobblestones toward a staircase. Olivia used the stone wall along the side to give her added support. Steven reached out his hand. "Be careful. Don't get too close."

Looking down from the top of the soaring staircase, the height of a three-story building, Olivia experienced a moment of dizziness and took a step back. She shivered as she imagined what it must have been like for Madeleine Gervaise. She could hear the dancer screaming and see the young woman's skirts billowing out as she flew, head over heels, hitting steps on her way down. Olivia shuddered, realizing how hard Madeleine must have hit the ground. Then there would have been silence.

Steven and Henri stood well away from the edge of the top step. Steven, who dwarfed the diminutive artist, listened as Henri described the scene Detective Berthot had explained to him after Madeleine was discovered. He sketched it in his notebook as Henri talked.

"Her body was found at the bottom," Henri said. "If only I had stayed at the Moulin Rouge longer and given her a ride home that night! It's my fault. I left early."

"You can't think like that, Monsieur. Don't do that to yourself. It was *not* your fault. It's the fault of the person who killed her, and no one else. Now, tell me, *s'il vous plaît*, how did Madeleine usually get home after the show?"

"She didn't have a routine. Sometimes I gave her a ride. Sometimes other friends offered. And occasionally she walked," Henri said.

"Where is the Moulin Rouge from here?"

"You go down to the bottom of the hill. The streets twist quite a bit, and there are several turns that make up a shortcut. You end up on Girardon, which takes you to a point on rue Lepic. You follow it straight down until you come to the boulevard de Clichy, turn right, *et voilà.* There are staircases on several of those streets."

"How far is it from the Moulin Rouge to her apartment?" Steven asked.

"About two *kilomètres.* But, as I said, there are shortcuts."

"Did she have to use this staircase?" Steven gazed down the towering stairway, picturing someone falling. He hoped Madeleine wasn't conscious the entire time. It was a long way down.

"No, but this is the shortest route. Even though she was probably tired, she was used to climbing the staircases all over the *butte,* and this way would have saved her time."

"Did Madeleine live alone?"

"No, she shared the apartment with a girl named Yvette Caron."

"Does she also dance at the Moulin Rouge?"

"No, she's at the Opéra Garnier Ballet, where Madeleine used to dance."

"Thank you. We'll come back to Mademoiselle Caron later. So, Monsieur…"

"Please, call me Henri." He turned to Olivia. "Both of you. You are friends of Evangéline's, and so am I. That makes us friends. And you have traveled all this way to help me. Besides, we artists aren't so formal. We like to push the system, eh?"

"All right, Henri, thank you." Steven smiled and gave a brief nod as a courtesy. "And we're not formal either. It's Steven and Olivia. So, tell me…what do you think happened? It's my understanding the police ruled it an accident and closed the case. But Evangéline said you're positive it was murder. Why?"

"I saw her body. And when I take you to the morgue, you'll understand. The bruises indicate that my poor Madeleine hit many, many steps extremely hard. I believe someone pushed her quite forcefully. She flew a certain distance, then bounced, striking multiple steps. Think about the difference in the bruising if a person slipped and tumbled down the stairs, falling in close proximity to the steps, versus the pattern of black-and-blue marks of someone who was pushed. That person would be airborne and land hard. Parts of her body would hit the sharp edges of several steps." Henri shuddered. "She was such a sweet little thing. Such a horrible death. And so senseless. *La petite* barely had a chance at life." His face crumbled, his thick lips trembled, and he sighed.

"I see your point. Let me sketch the scene, then we'll go to the morgue. I'm looking forward to meeting your detective friend."

Steven turned to a fresh page in the leather-bound notebook Evangéline had given him and sketched the area from the top of the stairs. Then he grabbed the iron railing and took a step—he needed to draw the scene from the vantage point of the sidewalk below.

"Steven, should I go with you?" Olivia asked. "An extra pair of eyes, you know?"

"Thanks, but no. I doubt I'll find anything after all this time, and it's not worth you taking a chance on these steps. They're too slippery. I won't be long."

Steven carefully descended the staircase. Even though it had been four days, he scoured the area several feet on both sides of the bottom step. There were the expected number of cigarette butts and used matches. He found two soggy tram tickets, one to Vincennes, another to the Gare du Nord, one of the train stations. Steven didn't know enough about the layout of Paris to have any idea what this meant, if anything, but he pocketed the tickets and would ask Evangéline later.

As he was about to turn back and tackle the climb to the top of the staircase, Steven noticed something shining in the weakening sunlight. He stepped to a small patch of coarse, dead grass in a crack between the sidewalk and the foundation of a building and saw a metal key.

The iron key wasn't large, only measuring about three inches long, but it had a distinctive pattern on the biting at the bottom. Steven thought this pattern of notches would be unique to one door in particular. If he could only find it among the thousands of doors in Paris! But then he realized there *was* something that might help him. The key boasted a beautiful quatrefoil design on the head, the part that was held while inserting the key into the lock. The four-leaf cut-out had been covered in what appeared to be gold leaf, although some had worn off. The key was beautifully designed, expertly made. Steven imagined it would open an important door.

Chapter Six

By the time Henri, Steven, and Olivia left Montmartre for the Paris Morgue, the two-hour lunch break had finished, and all manner of vehicles filled the streets. A variety of horse-drawn carriages maneuvered along the boulevards—closed coaches and open ones, broughams pulled by one horse or two, square-shaped and rectangular carriages, as well as simple wagons and carts. Olivia was surprised to see an omnibus pulled by a team of strong horses.

They crossed the boulevard Haussmann and drove through an area that appeared upscale, evidenced by elegant women in fur muffs and sophisticated hats strolling the sidewalks and rich-looking carriages rolling along the wide boulevard. Here, gray stone, multi-story homes, and apartments showcased glossy black doors with shining, round brass door knobs fixed in the center. Their mansard roofs sported rows of gabled dormers along the eaves. Olivia thrilled at the sight of these. She'd always dreamed of living in one of those attic rooms, spending her days writing. It seemed so romantic.

They soon reached the river, busy with boats and barges, and enjoyed a slower ride along the banks, passing the Louvre, which went on for blocks, and Ile-de-la-Cité, where the magnificent Gothic Notre Dame Cathedral dwarfed everything around them. The sky had turned gray again, and the water in the Seine appeared as cold and hard as pewter. While they rode, Henri explained what they were going to see.

"I don't know what it's like in America, but the Paris Morgue is open to the public. People come not only to identify their dead but also to look at the corpses."

"What do you mean?" Steven asked, his brows meeting in a frown.

"Attitudes towards death have changed in recent years. We French accept it as a part of life. People like to look at the bodies."

Olivia's eyes grew large. She couldn't think of a single thing to say.

"However," Henri went on, "I appealed to Etienne to keep Madeleine away from the public eye. I want her to have some privacy. If people found out that a cancan girl was lying in the morgue, we would have to fight the crowds." He turned to Olivia. "I can see you're surprised. It's become our way. It doesn't mean there's any disrespect. People are simply interested."

Henri's driver brought the carriage to the front door of a modern-looking building. The Paris Morgue was a plain, two-story, square structure flanked by one-story wings on either side. The center section sported a roof resembling a small pyramid and was framed by three tall, narrow arches over the entrance.

In the foyer, Henri consulted a gold pocket watch attached to a chain and announced, "*Bon!* We're only twenty minutes late. Etienne will have needed that little rest. He works much too hard."

At that pronouncement, a tall, broad-shouldered man came striding down the hallway. He looked to be in his fifties; his brown hair was mixed with gray, and his weathered face was lined. But it was his eyes that grabbed Olivia's attention. His eyes, so dark they appeared black, looked as though they missed nothing. *What secrets have they uncovered? What sights have they witnessed?* She shuddered.

The two Frenchmen leaned in and performed the quick kiss-on-the-cheek ritual that was ubiquitous in their country. Then, Henri introduced the three of them, using first names for the men, but referring to Olivia as *Mademoiselle.*

"I'm happy to meet you...so, it's all right if I call you Etienne? I'm sorry to say that I'm not as well-versed as I would like to be in French etiquette," Steven said.

"*Mais, oui,*" said the detective. "We will be working together on a sensitive investigation. I think we will become good friends."

"*Merci.* And thank you for taking the time to help me. I'm grateful. I realize you must be very busy," Steven said.

"My friend Henri has not been himself since this tragedy occurred. We miss his crazy antics and sense of humor. We must find the culprit and see justice done," said Etienne. "Come this way."

Henri didn't move. He reached out and touched his friend's sleeve. "Etienne," he said, "I cannot do this. I don't want to see her like this again. I'll take a carriage home and leave mine for you and our friends." Turning to Steven and Olivia, he went on. "My driver will take you to Evangéline's when you finish here—or anywhere Etienne wishes to show you. Tell him what time you require him in the morning, and he will pick you up. He's at your disposal while you're in Paris. However long it takes. I have made other arrangements for myself, so please do not be concerned. I will see you tomorrow night for the showing." He tipped his top hat, gave Olivia a little bow, and left.

The mysterious show tomorrow night. Olivia wondered where they were going and what they would see. This was not the time to ask; however, she would find out soon enough.

After Henri disappeared out the door, Etienne said, "We're all worried about him. Henri is usually the life of the party...when I have the time to join the party." He grimaced. "The crime in Paris is terrible right now. We're drowning in it."

As he talked, Detective Etienne Berthot led them down a long hallway to a spot where the wall became a half-wall and a viewing window occupied the top part. There, in a large room, laid out naked on marble slabs in front of them, were rows of corpses. Olivia gasped.

"Yes, I imagine it takes some getting used to," Etienne said. "People here are interested in death. It's a part of everyone's life, after all."

He moved from the gruesome sight to a door at the end of the corridor, extracted a key, and brought Steven and Olivia into a private space where two hallways branched off at odd angles. Olivia was relieved to see this area was separate from the one with the bodies. She considered herself broad-minded, but she wasn't ready for that.

Etienne took them to a second locked door and, knocking as he inserted a key, called out. *"Jean-Pierre, t'es là?* You here?"

A high-pitched voice emanated from around a corner. *"Etienne, c'est toi? Oui, j'arrive.* Is that you? Yes, I'm coming." A skinny young man in a blue smock appeared. *"Bonjour, mon ami.* How was your Christmas? I hope you didn't have to work."

"No, for once the criminals cooperated. My wife would have killed me if I had left our feast. We had a house full of children and grandchildren. It was wonderful. This is Monsieur Blackwell, the American detective I told you about, and his assistant, Mademoiselle Watson." He turned to Steven and Olivia. "Jean-Pierre takes care of the morgue for us."

The attendant wasted no time. He strode to a large cabinet comprising three rows of five compartments built into the wall. Before he even opened the door, Steven smelled the ammonia and sniffed.

"Yes," Jean-Pierre replied to his unasked question. "We use ammonia to get the temperature low enough to freeze the bodies. It's strong and takes some getting used to, but it works very fast." He swung open the compartment door and pulled out a tray.

Olivia gasped. "She's so young."

"Only twenty," Etienne said.

Madeleine Gervaise looked like a figure in Madame Tussaud's Wax Museum. Like the corpses they had seen through the viewing window, she was naked. Her long blonde hair cradled her head; her eyes were closed. Steven immediately saw the bruises and understood what Henri had explained earlier. This woman had not simply slipped on the ice and tumbled "gently" down the stairs. Deep purple, black, and navy bruises covered her torso, arms, and legs. It was as if she had taken a flying leap and hurled herself down the stairs.

He knew without a doubt she had been pushed—and hard.

"What was the official cause of death?" Steven asked.

"A broken neck," Etienne told him, pointing to his own neck in a kind of reflex. "Both wrists were also broken. Shattered, actually."

"It would have been natural to reach out and try to break her fall," Steven said.

"What's going to happen to her?" asked Olivia, as Steven took out his notebook and pencil and sketched the body, after having received permission from both Etienne and Jean-Pierre.

"We've notified her family. When you finish the investigation, we'll let them know they can take her home for a funeral service and, of course, the burial."

"Do they live in Paris?" Olivia asked.

"No, to the east, in the Meuse." Etienne scowled. "It's officially German now, but we'll get it back."

When Steven looked confused, Etienne explained. "You know, after the war. We had to cede that whole area to the German Empire. I'm furious just thinking about it!"

Steven had no idea what Etienne was talking about, but assumed if he lived in 1895, he would know, so he simply said, "Oh, yes. That was terrible."

He finished drawing the front of Madeleine's battered body and asked if he could see her back. Jean-Pierre nodded, and Etienne helped him turn her over. Steven made a second sketch.

When he'd drawn the last curve, he asked, "What happened to her belongings? I imagine she had a purse or something with her. Maybe a bag with her dance clothes?"

"It's in the *Salle de Sacs* where we keep clothes and belongings. When we're satisfied with an investigation, when it's been resolved, and we no longer need them, we allow the family to take what they want. Perhaps a memento or piece of clothing. After a certain time, if no one claims the victim's possessions, we burn everything," the morgue attendant explained. "Follow me. I'll show you."

Jean-Pierre took them into a room toward the back, where tall wooden shelves lining three walls were filled with bags.

"My goodness," Steven exclaimed, looking at Etienne. "You weren't kidding when you said you were drowning in crime. Do these all represent suspicious deaths?"

"Sadly, yes."

Jean-Pierre removed a bag from one shelf, checked the attached tag to verify they were indeed Madeleine Gervaise's belongings, and set it on a wooden table in the center of the room. He loosened the strap holding the top closed and pushed it over to Steven. "You can look."

Steven turned to Etienne. "Before I contaminate anything, you have all the evidence you need?"

The Frenchman turned up his palms and shrugged in that stoic Gallic way that said quite plainly, "What can you do?"

"What do I need, Steven?" Etienne said. "The powers that be closed the case. It was an accident, they say. No further action, they say. So, there was no need to check for anything since I had no authority to ask anyone to analyze whatever I might have discovered. That's how fast this case was closed down."

Steven made a mental note to ask Etienne, maybe in a few days, when he knew him better, if there was any reason to suspect a police officer was involved. Perhaps the killer was a friend or relative of someone at the Sûreté. Maybe the person they were looking for was a married policeman who'd been having an affair with the victim. Steven had heard French wives accepted the fact that their husbands had mistresses, but the police force might have different standards. Perhaps a policeman himself was the killer. It was worth asking.

Steven opened the large, cream-colored bag and inched his hand inside, not knowing what he might find. He pulled out a navy blue dress that looked of average quality; underclothes that once had been white; a good wool cloak worn in several spots; a pair of leather boots; and a small drawstring bag decorated with colored beads. What caught Steven's eye right away was the high quality of the boots. They seemed too expensive for a dance hall girl to afford, although, since her livelihood was dancing, maybe she spent most of her money on expensive shoes and boots as a means of protecting her most valuable asset—her feet.

Filing that observation away for a later conversation with Olivia, he let go of the large bag and opened the purse. Inside was a small pot of red lip color, a tiny mirror, some hairpins, a cotton handkerchief, several coins, and a wrinkled envelope folded in half. Setting everything else aside, Steven unfolded the envelope and read the front. A messy scrawl addressed the missive to Mlle Madeleine Gervaise, 35 rue des Saules, Montmartre, Paris, France. He carefully slid out a two-page letter.

Ma Chère Madeleine,

It has been over a year and a half since we made our agreement, and you left home to follow your dream of becoming a ballerina in the capital. You know I did not want you to leave, but I thought when you got this fantasy out of your system, you would come home. Papa's health will force him to quit working at the pâtisserie soon, and I will take over. It will be ours, my love! We can get married and raise a family like I always dreamed. The pastry shop will provide a good living for us.

I know from your letters—sadly, too few—that your plan of dancing at the opera house did not work out, and you quit the Garnier Ballet Company. (I'm sorry if that is not the correct name. I do not mean to be insulting.) Now, it seems you are working at the Moulin Rouge. I could not believe my eyes when I read your last letter. A cancan girl! What can you be thinking? What happened to your ballet dreams? After months in Paris working as a seamstress, to finally be accepted in the place of your deepest desire, I can only imagine how thrilled you were. Why did you leave the Opéra Garnier? The Moulin Rouge is so inferior that I cannot find the words. I do not understand how you could put yourself on display every night in front of lecherous men!

But, my darling, we must put all of that behind us now. Everyone makes mistakes. I love you, and I want you to come home where you belong. We can still join our lives together. We will say no more of this pipe dream.

Your mother tells me you are coming home for Christmas. Dare I hope it will be for good?

I will come and get you. I've checked the train schedule and will arrive on Sunday, December 22, at eleven in the morning. We will have plenty of time on the journey home to talk about our future together before you are taken up with your family. I cannot wait to see you, ma chère Madeleine.

Until the 22nd, I am always your

Bernard.

Steven turned the envelope back to the front and read the return address: Bernard Fournier, Pâtisserie Fournier, Bar-le-Duc, France.

"Did anyone talk with this young man, Etienne?"

"*Non.* As I said, the case was shut down before we even had a chance to open it."

"Can I keep this?"

Etienne nodded. "Sure."

Olivia spoke for the first time. "I'm more aware of New York fashions than Parisian, but the dress doesn't seem new, although it's in good condition. And, of course, I see some repairs on the cloak."

"You have an eye, Mademoiselle. The dress looks to be perhaps six or seven years old. I would say that a young dancer—either at the Opéra Garnier or the Moulin Rouge, but less so at the cabaret—cannot afford to replace her clothes too often. She would most likely wear something until it fell apart."

"I have a question, Etienne," Steven said. "I don't understand the references to the Opéra Garnier. Her friend Bernard mentions it in his letter, and you just referred to it. Henri told us that Madeleine was a dancer with the principal ballet company before she went to the Moulin Rouge. What does the ballet have to do with the opera?"

Steven was realizing how much he didn't know about society and culture in the French capital. Thank goodness he had Olivia with him, who always seemed to know about things because of her research. And, of course, he had his mother as a resource. If Evangéline did not know something about life in Paris, it probably wasn't worth knowing.

"Oh, yes, I can see how that would be confusing," Etienne said. "Ballet and theater have gone together for centuries. As a matter of fact, some of Molière's *comédies* were performed with ballet. The Opéra Garnier puts on dance performances by the ballet company, with the orchestra providing the music. They also present operas as the principal attraction, where the ballet supports the story being sung.

"The Opéra Garnier Ballet is one of the top ballet companies in the world, along with the ones in London and St. Petersburg. It's highly competitive. Dancers are accepted only on the condition that they attend the Opera Ballet School—and that's nearly impossible to get into. They hold a fierce competition in the spring. Madeleine must have been exceptional. I can't imagine what caused her to leave."

"Perhaps that will be my first line of inquiry. Can we talk to some people there, Etienne?"

"*Mais oui!* But it's too late now." From a small pocket in his vest, he extracted a gold watch on a chain. "Nearly five o'clock. They'll be getting ready for tonight's performance. We will go tomorrow morning. Perhaps around ten."

"*D'accord.* Oh, before I forget...." Steven rummaged in a deep trousers pocket and pulled out a key. "I found this where Madeleine was killed."

Etienne took the key, turning it over in his hand as he examined it. "This was specially made. Look at the exquisite detail. It could be in a museum. You can see here where the gold leaf has worn off. I'd venture to say that someone who enjoys a great deal of money owns this key. Where exactly did you find it?"

Steven told him.

"That is not an area a wealthy man would frequent, unless, of course, he was following one of the Moulin Rouge dancers, perhaps on her way home," Etienne said. "Hmm. I must think about this. Keep it safe, Detective."

Chapter Seven

Saturday, December 28, 1895

Paris, France

After a breakfast of fresh bread, jam, and butter, Steven and Olivia sat at Evangéline's kitchen table discussing the case and enjoying their *café au lait*—half strong black coffee and half hot whole milk—which they were drinking from traditional French breakfast bowls. Holding the warm bowl in their hands on such a cold morning felt wonderful. Evangéline was at work in her studio, and had been since sunrise. She said the light drove her to get up early every day. "I'm always chasing the light," had been her exact words. The studio door was closed, and Steven and Olivia kept their voices low.

"Evangéline said we could use her camera if we wanted to. I'd like to have photographs, but I think it'll take too long to get them developed to be of any use," Steven said. He made a face. "Olivia, I didn't even realize they had cameras in this time. There's so much I don't know. I have to admit I was nervous yesterday. I was afraid I was going to say something completely wrong and somehow give us away. There are so many chances to make a mistake."

"Steven, how often, when I've been spending time in your 1934, have you told me there's no way someone is going to say *Gee, I think she must be time traveling from the future?* And here we have the advantage of possible problems with the language and coming from a different country to use as excuses. If one of us refers to something that doesn't exist yet, we can say that in New York, we do things differently. Or if we don't know the answer to a question or give the wrong answer, we can say we misunderstood. That our French isn't what we'd like it to be."

"I don't know how you do it when you come into my time. I have a whole new appreciation of how seamlessly you blend in." He leaned over and kissed her cheek.

"Well, thanks." She squeezed his hand. "And that reminds me…we're in Paris, famous for being *the* romantic city…remember, all work and no play—"

He burst out laughing.

"But getting back to the question of pictures…I've seen your sketches, Steven. They're really good. I think that's all we'll need."

"But I never know if I've recorded every detail. More than once, I've been working on a case and noticed something in a photograph that I missed in my drawing. Well," he sighed, "we'll have to work with what we've got."

"What about your murder board? I know how critical it is when you're working on a case. You told me once it might be your most important organizational tool. Maybe we can rig up something like I made at the Great Camp a few weeks ago." She wiped a finger along the edge of her knife and tasted the last bit of jam. "You know, it's great that Evangéline gave us our own apartment. We can keep our notes and observations hidden from any visitors that might show up while we're here."

"Yes, let's ask Etienne if we could stop at a *boucherie.* Maybe we can use butcher paper again. That worked out well." Steven took a sip of his *café au lait*. "The hardest part of this case is knowing everything's already five days old. That's an eternity in an investigation! I can't learn much from the crime scene. Any witnesses will have scattered and, if we *do* find someone, they'll have forgotten important details. Suspects have already had time to concoct alibis, stories, and plausible lies." He sighed again. "Well, I suppose we'll have to do our best and hope it's enough."

"So, what's our plan today? Remember, we have the movie premiere tonight." Olivia's face lit up. "When Evangéline told us last night what the tickets were for, I couldn't believe it. What are the chances we're in Paris on the same day, in the right year, when the Lumière brothers debuted the first-ever motion picture open to the paying public? I'm so excited. I bet there'll be famous people there."

Steven smiled, and for a moment, Olivia got lost in his beautiful brown eyes. "I'm glad we can have these moments alone," he said. "It's nice to see you being yourself." He finished his coffee and pushed the bowl away. "So, for today, if we can interview Madeleine's roommate at the opera house, then talk to some people at the Moulin Rouge, I'll be happy."

"Do you want me to help when you're questioning the dancers?"

"Let's play it by ear. I'll signal if I want you to jump in. I'll introduce you as my assistant, so they won't be surprised if you ask a question."

Olivia rose and put the breakfast dishes in the sink, regretting that she didn't have time to wash and dry them, and promising herself she wouldn't make that mistake again. She wanted to be a respectful guest in Evangéline's home.

There was a loud knock on the door.

Olivia went to answer it. *"Bonjour, M. Berthot. Entrez, s'il vous plaît.* Please, come in."

The detective doffed his hat and entered the apartment. *"Made-*

moiselle, j'espère que vous allez bien ce matin. I hope you're doing well this morning." He gave a little bow, then turned to Steven. *"Bonjour, Steven.* Are you ready? As promised, Henri has given us his carriage and driver for the entire day. We will ride in luxury, my friends."

After telling Evangéline they were leaving—she called out that they needed to be ready to leave tonight by seven—they donned their cloaks, hats, and gloves. While Steven tucked his notebook and pencils into an inside pocket, Olivia stowed two pencils and a red notebook in a small drawstring bag, all provided by Evangéline. Then she led the way down the stairs.

Inside the coach, Etienne pulled several folded pieces of paper from a pocket inside his coat. "I went back to the office last night and organized the few notes I made Monday afternoon when I thought we were going to investigate this case. Here's a list of the dancers at both the Opéra Garnier Ballet and the Moulin Rouge, as well as some of the people who work with them—choreographer, ballet master, and so forth. Tomorrow's Sunday, so we won't be able to do anything official, but I thought you and Olivia might want to visit a couple of the girls in their apartments. You'll see the addresses here. Maybe you can get some preliminary interviews done."

"This is great, Etienne. Thank you. But how is Sunday different? If I'm working on a murder case at home, I usually keep at it on Sunday. Even though stores and businesses are closed, I manage to accomplish something."

"Sometimes I do too, but in France, most people set Sundays aside for church and family. Because the girls at the Moulin Rouge work so late—and they do work Sunday nights, by the way—I imagine you'll find them skipping Mass and sleeping in. Generally, the dancers aren't local girls. Most of them have families in towns and villages far away, so there won't be any Sunday dinners for them. I imagine they'll be home in the morning, resting and relaxing for the show at night.

Perhaps you could go around ten or ten-thirty."

Steven took the proffered papers and scanned the list, Olivia looking over his shoulder.

"Isn't the staircase where Madeleine died on the rue des Saules? I paid attention to street signs when Henri took us around yesterday, and that sounds familiar," Olivia said.

"I see why Steven values your help so much, Mademoiselle. Yes, you're right. Why?"

"Two of the girls live at the same number on that street. I seem to remember it's not far from Evangéline's."

"Then tomorrow, we'll start there," Steven said.

* * *

It was nearly ten o'clock when Steven, Olivia, and Etienne arrived at the famed Paris opera house, the Palais Garnier. Their driver stopped in front of an ornate gate at the back of the majestic building and told them he'd wait as long as they needed. Etienne pushed open the black grill and held out his hand, indicating Steven and Olivia should enter first. They crossed a small area to an entrance in the corner where Etienne opened a door and led the way in. As Olivia stepped into the hallway, she glanced back and saw the driver pull out a copy of a newspaper and settle in on his high seat.

Inside the entrance, an elderly man in rumpled trousers and a knee-length, loose-fitting shirt resembling a blouse sat at a table. Etienne showed his police credentials, and he waved them through.

"Where would I find one of the dancers?" he asked.

"They're getting ready for the morning class, so she'll be in one of the dressing rooms or the rehearsal room. Go straight down this hallway, then take your first right, second left, and second right. That's where the dressing rooms are. If she's not there, someone can direct you to the rehearsal room."

Illuminated gas lamps at long intervals along the hallway created shadows, but Olivia was able to pick out elegant details—pale gray walls with classic-style wainscoting, and touches of gold everywhere she looked. "My goodness, even the corridors are luxurious."

"Yes," Etienne replied. "The architects and designers spared no expense. If we have time, you should go into the theater. It's like no other in the world. And the grand staircase in the lobby defies description. You must see it."

A thin young woman was exiting a dressing room when they arrived.

"Excuse me, Mademoiselle. We're looking for Yvette Caron," Etienne said.

"She's the last one here. Madame is not going to be happy when Yvette arrives late for class…again." And she ran down the hall, leaving the door ajar.

Etienne knocked and stuck his head in the doorway. "Mlle Caron?"

A tall, lithe brunette was hurrying across the room and slid to a halt. "*Oui, c'est moi. Qui êtes-vous?* Yes, that's me. Who are you? What are you doing backstage?"

"Police, Mademoiselle. We need to talk with you about your friend Madeleine Gervaise."

She gasped, and tears filled her bright green eyes; her face fell. She stepped back, allowing Etienne, Steven, and Olivia to enter.

The scent of patchouli filled the crowded dressing room, and Steven sneezed. Olivia wondered how a company of dancers could get ready and dressed in such a cramped space. On the right side of the room, alternating mirrors and lights hung above a polished wooden shelf attached to the wall. All manner of cosmetics were scattered across the countertop. Face powder spilling out of round containers. Tiny pots of lipstick. Small round tins of rouge. Thick black pencils. Brushes of all sizes and purpose. Toward the back of the room, clothing racks held a multitude of costumes, delicate dresses, and tutus with their stiff, short skirts.

"Would you like to sit down, Mademoiselle?" Steven asked.

Yvette walked to a deep plum settee pushed against the wall across from the makeup counter and dropped to the cushion, the full skirt of her white diaphanous dress fanning out around her. The knee-length dress had a low scooped neck and was secured around her waist with a pale blue satin ribbon. She wore white stockings and pointe shoes.

Etienne introduced the three of them, and they sat, Olivia next to Yvette, and Etienne and Steven across from them on mustard-colored chairs that had seen better days.

"Mlle Caron," Steven began, "Madeleine's friend Monsieur Henri de Toulouse-Lautrec has asked us to come all the way from America to find out what happened to her. Will you help us?"

"*Mais oui!* But of course!" Yvette's dark hair was styled into a chignon at the nape of her neck. A square jaw anchored her angular face with its high cheekbones. She sat ramrod straight, shoulders back, long legs tucked against the front of the sofa. She sniffled. "But what can I say? I do not know what happened."

"That's what we're going to find out," Steven said. "As her roommate, you will know things that can help us. For example, did Mademoiselle Gervaise have a routine after her work at the Moulin Rouge? Did she usually stay after the last show? Talk with the patrons? Have a drink, perhaps?"

Yvette shook her head. "*Non,* she didn't really have a routine. The dancers at the Moulin are encouraged to mix with the audience afterwards, but it's not mandatory. Some nights, if she wasn't tired, she would stay awhile. Other times, she'd change her clothes and come right home. I don't know what she would have done Sunday night…oh, wait…." She thought for a moment. "Madeleine had been complaining of a pulled muscle lately. It was giving her a lot of trouble.

She probably would have come right home. Yes. I think so."

"Speaking of home, we'll need to go through her things. I have your address on the rue des Saules, *n'est-ce pas?*"

"Yes, number thirty-five."

"Is there a *concièrge* or landlord who can let us in?"

"Madame is always there. Madame Pommier. She's a widow. Her husband owned the building, but he died last year. She lives above us with her son. We're on the *rez-de-chaussée*, the ground floor."

"Has anyone disturbed her belongings? Have you moved or packed up anything?"

"No, no one has been to the apartment, and I've been busy with performances. Plus, I went to Rouen to spend Christmas with my family."

"*Merci*, Mademoiselle. Now, returning to Madeleine. Had she been upset or worried about anything lately?"

"I don't think so. She was excited about going home for Christmas. She did her holiday shopping and wrapped her gifts. And she started packing."

"How did you and Madeleine meet and come to live together?" Steven asked.

"I was already here at the Garnier when she was accepted last year. My roommate had married, and I needed someone to share the apartment with me. We liked each other and decided to try it. It has been very good, Monsieur. Madeleine is very neat." She made a face and tilted her head in the direction of all the spilled cosmetics. "Not like many of the girls here."

Steven smiled. "That was lucky for you."

Yvette frowned. "Now I have to find someone new to share *l'appartement*. That is not so easy."

"Tell me…we found a letter in Madeleine's bag from a man called Bernard Fournier. Do you know who that is?"

"Yes, her old boyfriend at home."

"Old boyfriend? She wasn't still involved with him? In the letter, he talked about getting married. It sounded like he wanted Mademoiselle Gervaise to return home. Did she talk to you about him or their relationship?"

"Maybe after she first arrived, but not in a long time. I don't think she wanted to get married. She was enjoying freedom. I'm sure she did not want to go home."

"In the note, M. Fournier said he was planning to come to Paris to pick her up. It sounded like they would return home together on the train."

"I don't know anything about that. She never told me she got a letter from him."

"So, he didn't come to your apartment? You didn't meet him?"

"No, Monsieur." Yvette was fidgeting and glancing toward the door. "Monsieur, Madame is going to be furious with me for missing class. It is not allowed under any circumstances."

Etienne stood. "Tell me where the rehearsal room is, and I'll inform Madame what is happening. She cannot punish you for talking with the police."

"*Merci, Monsieur.*" She gave him directions, and he left.

Steven shifted in his chair. "Now, Mademoiselle…Yvette. We're almost finished. Can you tell me if Madeleine had any enemies?"

"Enemies? Of course not."

"I understand the world of ballet can be very…eh, competitive. Was there someone who resented Madeleine when she was here at the Opéra Garnier?"

"*Non, Monsieur.*" She looked away.

"What about at the Moulin Rouge? Were there any disgruntled patrons or dancers who were angry with her for some reason?"

"I don't think so."

"All right, my final question, Yvette, and you can join your class… why did Madeleine leave the Ballet Garnier?"

"I don't know, Monsieur. She never told me why." A delicate hand covered her mouth as she looked down at her ballet slippers.

"Surely, you had an idea? You were friends, roommates. You must have been close. Even if she never said exactly why, you might have guessed her reason. To voluntarily leave such an elite company as the Opéra Garnier Ballet—the National Ballet Company of France!—for a place like the Moulin Rouge, something serious must have happened."

Yvette pinched her lips together, then, hand over her mouth again, shook her head.

Steven knew he wouldn't get any more from her right now. He also knew she had lied to him. Twice.

Chapter Eight

Olivia's reporter skills always served her well when accompanying Steven on a case. She knew as well as he did Yvette had lied to them. But she thought it was a good initial interview. Even lies told you something.

"Steven," she said, "Etienne's taking quite a long time, isn't he?"

"Yeah, let's go look for him." He turned to Yvette. "May we walk with you to the rehearsal hall?"

"*Bien sûr.* Of course."

Two long corridors and three flights of stairs later, Yvette Caron led Steven and Olivia to the morning class of the Paris Opera Ballet School.

Since they'd been inside the Opéra Garnier, the wind had pushed the clouds away and the sky had cleared. Sunbeams streamed through tall windows on the far side of the room, making the chandeliers sparkle. Their light reflected off a wall of mirrors, where several dancers were working at the barre. Despite the brightness of the space, Olivia felt a chill in the air. She pulled her cloak tighter around her and wondered at the fortitude of the scantily clad ballerinas. Then she realized they would be warmed up by the time they'd finished at the barre and would soon be sweating from the strenuous exercise of the class.

The room held perhaps forty young women, all dressed as Yvette was, though with different colored ribbons around their waists. Some were doing *pliés* at the barre, some sat on a raspberry velour bench tying shoes, some were executing *pirouettes* or *jetés* across the floor.

In a far corner, the accompanist was running his fingers up and down the keyboard of a glossy black grand piano.

In another corner of the room, Etienne was talking with an elegant young man who looked like he had just stepped out of a Manet painting. Dressed in the now familiar black cutaway coat and trousers, dark vest, and white shirt and collar, he also sported a bow tie. His silk top hat rested on a nearby chair, along with his woolen cloak. He stood, legs slightly akimbo, holding a cane in front of him with both hands. Tall and slender, his honey blonde hair was short, and he wore a moustache and a trimmed, pointed beard covering his jawline. He was laughing at something Etienne had said.

Yvette Caron joined her fellow dancers at the barre, while Steven and Olivia stayed close to the wall as they navigated their way across the room to the two men.

"Is it just me, or is this floor slanted?" Olivia said.

Etienne turned at the sound of their shoes on the parquet floor. "*Ah, mes amis!* Did you think I'd gotten lost? No, Mademoiselle, the builders angled the floor on purpose. It allows the dancers to become used to the incline. The back portion of the Opéra stage was built slightly higher than the front so everyone in the audience can see all the performers, even those in the last rows." He gestured to the other man. "Meet Monsieur le Comte Jean-Claude de Chamfort. Monsieur le Comte, these are friends from New York, *en Amérique*."

Chamfort shook Steven's hand and bowed to Olivia. "*Enchanté, Mademoiselle.* Pleased to meet you. And what brings you to Paris, M. Blackwell? Celebrating the holidays?"

"Business and pleasure," Steven said. "A friend has asked us to look into the death of Mademoiselle Madeleine Gervaise."

"Oh, the dancer! Yes, I heard. Terrible. Such a waste of a young life."

Chamfort gave Etienne a perplexed glance. "But, surely that was an accident, *non*? What is there to 'look into'?"

"There are still questions to be answered," Etienne replied. "Monsieur Blackwell is a detective. Some friends of Madeleine thought it would be a good idea to know for sure."

At that moment, an older woman entered the room. She tapped a cane on the wooden floor. Every dancer immediately stopped what she was doing. They bowed to her and rushed to form several even rows.

"*Le Maître* was not pleased with your performance last night. Your ballet master has instructed me to work you hard this morning. We will start now."

The pianist began to play a Chopin waltz, and the familiar notes drifted up to the bright ceiling.

* * *

May 1894

Madeleine slid into the routine at the Opéra Garnier Ballet as easily as slipping into a custom-made gown by Worth. She loved everything about it— the early morning warm-ups, the three-hour daily class, the long afternoon of rehearsals, and, most of all, the two-hour performance every evening. As she soared across the rehearsal room executing jeté *after* jeté, *she felt more alive than she'd ever been. Madeleine knew this was what she had been born to do.*

Many people made up a ballet company, some of them more important than others. There was the ballet master, of course, who taught the classes and guided the dancers through rehearsals. Monsieur Ballerat was tough and demanding, but everyone knew it was only because he insisted on drawing the best performance out of each of them. Their choreographer was Monsieur Marius Petipa, on a brief stay from St. Petersburg. Madame was part assistant instructor, part chaperone, part mother. She was always around, no matter what the girls were doing. She kept an eye on everyone and everything. She made sure they arrived on time, warmed up properly before class started, wrapped any strains or sprains tightly so they could continue without serious injury, and took proper care of their pointe shoes. Occasionally, she began the morning class if Monsieur Ballerat was running late.

There was one thing at the Ballet School, however, that confused Madeleine. Throughout the week, several aristocratic young men attended the classes and rehearsals. Elegantly attired in top hats and black morning coats, they seemed to have not a care in the world—and nowhere else to go. They stood and watched. They lounged on the recamiers and settees and observed. Madeleine had no idea who they were or why they were always around, although she noticed they were friendly with some of the dancers.

There were several dozen corps de ballet *dancers, including the principals and soloists, whose ages ranged from a very young thirteen to mid- and late-twenties. Madeleine, having recently turned nineteen, found herself in the middle age-wise, but she was crushed to discover, on her very first day, that she was less experienced than most of the dancers. This was an intolerable and unacceptable condition that she vowed to remedy as quickly as possible.*

On her second day, Madeleine arrived at six-thirty and practiced for an hour before anyone else appeared. Each morning, she pushed herself to the limit, holding poses longer, leaping higher, spinning straighter. She kept up the grueling routine for several months, until one afternoon the ballet master noticed the improvement and complimented her.

However, instead of easing up on herself, Madeleine, driven to perfection, persisted. She practiced until her feet bled, and she fell exhausted into bed at night, but she had never been happier.

* * *

Etienne, Steven, and Olivia slipped out of the rehearsal room, leaving the Comte de Chamfort relaxing on a plush settee.

Back in Henri's carriage, Etienne asked, "Where would you like to go now, Steven? It might still be too early for the Moulin Rouge. Perhaps after *le déjeuner*."

"Could we visit Madeleine and Yvette's apartment first? It's 35 rue des Saules. Do you know where that is?"

"Yes, it's in Montmartre, not far from the Moulin. That makes a logical plan for us. And I know a wonderful restaurant where we can have our lunch before going to the cabaret."

Etienne relayed the instructions to their driver and sat back against the leather seat as they headed back up to the *butte*.

As the carriage rumbled over the cobblestone streets, Etienne thought about how he had become involved in this case with these fascinating Americans and about his unusual friendship with the artist Henri de Toulouse-Lautrec. Henri was a funny little man, though bursting with talent. Etienne wondered what had happened that caused him to be so deformed. It must be hard living his life. The artist had left his aristocratic family and spent his days and nights with the lowest level of society—prostitutes and dancehall girls. But he had to admit, there was something appealing, almost childlike, about the man. There was a sense of freedom about him that Etienne had not seen in any other man, and after spending his days tracking down criminals, there was something appealing about sharing a bottle of wine and talking with this unconventional man.

"Who is the count we just met? And why was he at the dance class?" Olivia asked, interrupting the Frenchman's thoughts.

"He's one of many patrons of the ballet. These are wealthy young men who support the dancers…and the ballet, of course."

Olivia heard a hesitation in the Frenchman's voice. "I detect a measure of suspicion in your answer, Monsieur," she said.

"Very astute, Mademoiselle. There have been rumors."

"What kind of rumors?"

"That at least some of the aristocratic supporters expect a certain behavior—favors, if you like—from the dancers after buying them things or when they intervene on their behalf. Some dancers have suddenly been moved to the front of the *corps de ballet* for no apparent reason, while others have been selected as soloists or principals. But, I hasten to add, these are merely stories that fly around the capital."

He turned to Steven. "Did you learn anything from Mademoiselle Caron after I left?"

"Yes. She seems genuinely saddened by her friend's death. And she's dismayed that she needs to find a new roommate because she can't afford to live by herself. You know, Etienne, I never realized how difficult it must be for these girls. We go to the theater and sit in the audience and only see what's in front of us, never imagining what their lives are like behind the curtain." Steven shook his head. "Life can be hard for some." He thought of the families in his own time who were struggling during the fifth year of the Depression. "Anyway, Yvette said Madeleine didn't tell her about the letter from Bernard. She was aware of who he was, but never met him. I asked if Madeleine had any enemies at the Opéra Garnier Ballet. She said no." Steven leaned forward toward Etienne and raised his brows. "That was the *first* lie I caught her in."

"Ah! I agree it would seem impossible that no one at the Garnier was jealous or resentful of Madeleine. I've heard the world of ballet can be vicious. And as to Bernard, the young man from home, perhaps Madeleine was out when Bernard came to the apartment. Perhaps he was taken with Yvette, and they went to bed together. She's a beautiful young woman. He's a healthy man. This happens. And perhaps later she regretted it, so she said nothing."

"I suppose that's possible. We'll have to wait and see," Steven said, not knowing how to answer this idea. Clearly, Etienne thought nothing of it. Another aspect of French culture that Steven knew nothing about. He'd have to ask Evangéline later. Although maybe not. Did he really want to talk about sex with his mother? Good lord! This investigation was a minefield.

Speaking of Evangéline, Steven thought, who was the man whose clothes he was wearing? Who was this Théo? Did he live in the apartment with Evangéline? What was his relationship with her?

Steven immediately put on the brakes. *No, Blackwell, knock it off. She's not your mother yet. She had a life before she met Dad. Concentrate on the case. And remember what she always taught you...no judgement!*

Etienne was moving on to the next point of interest. "I'm most curious why Madeleine left the prestigious Opéra Garnier Ballet for the lower-class Moulin Rouge. Surely a serious dancer who went through the rigors of a difficult and demanding competition—to say nothing of years of grueling practice—in order to be accepted at the Garnier would hold on to her spot like it was a lifeline."

"I wondered about that too," said Olivia.

"I asked Yvette about it," Steven said. "That was her second lie. She told us she had no idea why Madeleine left."

"Ah ha!" Etienne exclaimed. "Now we're getting somewhere. Something happened at the Garnier. Perhaps a rivalry between Madeleine Gervaise and another dancer. Let's not be fooled by the fact that they look like sweet young things. As I said, the ballet is vicious. Cutthroat! These girls have worked their entire lives to dance at one of the premier ballet companies in the world. No one, I mean, no one, would just give it up. Something serious must have happened."

"I've heard about ballet dancers being ruthless, too," Olivia said. "And I agree with you, Detective. We need to find out what happened.

Although, it might have nothing to do with her death."

"First of all, we should start calling it by what it is—her murder. Because, like Henri said, there's no doubt in my mind that someone murdered Madeleine Gervaise. And second, although it may or may not be tied to her murder, we must find out why she left the Opéra Garnier Ballet," Steven said. "Etienne, do you know if the ballet dancers rehearse on Sundays? You mentioned it's a special day."

"I know there's a performance tomorrow night. And we just heard Madame. The ballet master was not happy. It's possible he'll make them rehearse during the afternoon tomorrow. It's too bad. We French make an effort to spend Sunday with our families." He made a face. "Even though the *Commissaire* seems to forget on a regular basis." He sighed, wishing he could spend more time with his family in front of his hearth, pipe in hand, loving warmth all around him. "I think rather than waste your time on an unlikely gamble tomorrow, we're better off continuing our Opéra Garnier interviews Monday morning."

The carriage was climbing the hill to the top of Montmartre now. The narrow streets curved and turned, then turned back on themselves. Olivia thought you'd have to live here for months, maybe even a year, before you got your bearings. The neighborhood was a maze. Gazing out the carriage window, in the distance, Olivia saw the construction of what would eventually be Sacré Coeur, the beautiful white domed church on the top of the *butte*. Wooden scaffolding surrounded the limestone walls.

Their coach passed a number of restaurants and cafés, tiny stores and, despite the cold weather, sidewalk stalls. Men walked in pairs, talking seriously. Women went in and out of wine shops and corner *tabacs*, picking up cigarettes or tobacco for their husbands. Children played in the streets, jumping back and forth onto the sidewalks when a vehicle approached, sometimes narrowly missing getting hit. It seemed to Olivia that children were the same wherever they were, *whenever* they were.

The kids might be acting the same, but Olivia wondered how Steven was doing, especially after his reaction at the airport the other day. It reminded her of a panic attack she'd had once. She was eager to spend time alone with him tomorrow. She wanted to know how he felt about being here with this different incarnation of his mother, now that he'd had a couple of days to get used to it.

The horses pulled the carriage up to a stairway built flush against the front of a drab-looking building on which a small square blue-and-white tile displayed the number thirty-five.

"I think I'd better come with you, Steven, even though your French is remarkable," Etienne said. "I can show my police credentials to this Madame Pommier. It'll make it easier for her to let us in and look around."

"*D'accord.* Olivia, while we're searching Madeleine's apartment, would you talk with the landlady? Maybe a casual conversation will reveal something about Madeleine."

"Sure, I'll ask if she saw Bernard, too."

They climbed the steps to the first floor, and Etienne rang the bell. The door opened, and a boy of nine or ten stood staring at them. Etienne told him it was the police and to go get his mother. The boy slammed the door, and moments later, a plump middle-aged woman opened it again, apologizing for her son's lack of manners and inviting them in.

"I'm Detective Inspector Etienne Berthot. This is Detective Blackwell and his assistant Mademoiselle Watson from New York—"

"Oh, yes. It's been all around the *butte.* You're investigating Mademoiselle Gervaise's death. Or perhaps, murder?" Madame Pommier ended with raised brows and a whisper.

"Ah. So, you know, eh?"

"Montmartre is a small village, Monsieur. Word gets around quickly." She pulled a man-sized cotton handkerchief from a pocket in her housedress, sniffled, and blew her nose. *"La pauvre petite.* The poor little thing. Madeleine was a lovely girl. How can I help you?"

"Le Détective Blackwell and I need to look through Madeleine's belongings. We spoke with her roommate, Mademoiselle Caron, who gave us her permission to enter the apartment. She said you would have an extra key."

"Of course." Madame Pommier reached behind the door and extracted a key from a hook.

"And while we're in the young ladies' lodgings, Mademoiselle Watson would like to ask you a couple of questions, if that's all right."

"Ah, with pleasure, Mademoiselle." She nodded at Olivia. "I've never talked with an American lady before. Come into the kitchen with me. I must take my son's lunch from the oven."

Although Olivia trailed after the landlady, she could have found her way to the kitchen by the scent alone. A lip-smacking aroma filled the apartment—garlic, onion, cloves, and some kind of meat. Olivia wished they were eating lunch here!

"Madame, that smells heavenly. What is it?"

"Just a simple *cassoulet.* Pork, sausages, carrots, celery…."

"I can smell the garlic and onions."

"Mais oui. And lots of beans. A tasty but hearty winter meal. It's my son's favorite."

"I can see why."

An enormous stove sat against the far wall of the spotless kitchen. Olivia had never seen such an appliance with multiple burners, what appeared to be warming drawers, and two ovens. Madame Pommier opened a door and slid a large casserole dish from the oven. The *cassoulet* was bubbling and steaming. Madame Pommier set the dish on a raised metal plate on the top of the stove and turned to her guest.

"What would you like to ask me, Mademoiselle?"

"How well did you know Madeleine Gervaise?"

"Not very well, but we were friendly. She was a sweet girl. I think she knew I was lonely. I lost my husband last year, you know…."

Olivia nodded. "Yes, I'm so sorry."

"*C'est la vie, eh?*" She gave that very Gallic shrug, but her face was edged with sadness. "What can you do? But, anyway…Madeleine always stopped to talk with me. She was never in too much of a hurry. I appreciated that."

"What did you talk about?"

"She always asked about Nicolas, my son. How he was doing in school. What his latest interests were. What book he was reading. She told me about the ballet her company was performing, the costume she would wear, the part she would play. When she was at the Opéra Garnier, that is. Oh, how she loved it there!"

"Do you know why she left?"

Madame Pommier's mouth fell open and her eyes widened. She stood straight up, hands on her hips. "No, I don't! And I always wondered about that. Why would she leave? She worked so hard to get there. Then to give it all up? It makes no sense."

"Do you think she might have had a fight of some kind with one of the other dancers? Maybe she was…," Olivia struggled for the French word for *fired*. "…maybe they forced her to leave."

"That would explain it, but to tell you the truth, I have no idea at all."

"When was the last time you saw Madeleine?"

Madame Pommier's face fell. "It was the morning she was killed." She sniffed. "She stopped in with a lovely gift for Nico and wished us a *Joyeux Noël et Bonne Année*. I wished her a Merry Christmas and Happy New Year as well, and told her to give my best to her mother. You see, Madeleine was leaving early the next morning for home because she wanted to celebrate not only Christmas Day but also *la*

Veille, Christmas Eve, with her family. And when she said Happy New Year, I guessed her boss had given her the entire week off. I was happy for her to spend so much time with her family."

"I see."

Suddenly, the landlady cried out, "Oh my goodness! Why are we standing here? I'm so sorry. Where are my manners? Would you like to sit?" She indicated the rough wooden table surrounded by four chairs. "I can make some coffee if you'd like?"

"Maybe a glass of water. Thank you." Olivia pulled out a chair and sat on a hand-embroidered cushion. She looked around and realized this was a place she would be happy spending many hours. Cheerful pale yellow walls, blue-and-white curtains, mouth-watering aromas, and a warm and friendly hostess.

Madame Pommier took blue-tinted glasses from a cupboard, poured from a bottle sitting on the table, and joined Olivia.

After they'd both taken a drink, Olivia picked up the interview. "Did Madeleine have many visitors? Girlfriends who came to see her? Boyfriends who visited? Admirers?"

"Sometimes two girls came to visit—I think they danced with her at the Moulin Rouge. But Madeleine worked most of the time. It was admirable, but I worried about her. At the Garnier, she had classes in the morning and rehearsals all afternoon, then they expected her to have the energy to perform in the evening. But, when you're young...." She shrugged again. "I suppose you have that kind of energy, don't you?"

Olivia nodded. "What about men friends? Did she have a beau?" She asked again.

"The only man who ever came here that I know of was someone from her hometown. And that was recently. Now, when was it?" Madame Pommier gazed off for a moment. "Sometime this past week. Sunday! It was right before lunch on Sunday. I remember now because

I had prepared a *coq au vin*. I had just taken it off the stove and heard him banging on Madeleine and Yvette's door."

As if her words had summoned the clamor, a loud crash sounded in the direction of the front door.

"That damn shutter again!" Madame Pommier exclaimed. "Excuse me."

She left Olivia and headed toward the entry. Olivia heard more banging, an exasperated groan, then Madame Pommier returned to the kitchen. "I need to get someone to look at that. For no apparent reason, that shutter gets unhooked and makes such a racket.

"So as I was saying, I couldn't let a strange man keep pounding on the door, could I? I opened *my* front door and demanded who he was and what he thought he was doing, making such a racket. He said he was a friend of Madeleine's from home. That was the way he put it. He seemed angry she wasn't here. I asked if she was expecting him, and he said yes, that he'd sent her a letter. He was annoyed that he'd spent money on a ticket and the whole morning on the train."

"What did you tell him?"

"Well, first I told him to quiet down because it was *Sunday*! Some people were returning from Mass. Others like a peaceful Sunday morning because they work all week, you know? He apologized right away. Once he calmed down, I could tell he was a decent person. He was just upset. So I said Madeleine was probably at the Moulin rehearsing their last show before Christmas. Even that place closes on Christmas Eve and Christmas Day. He asked for directions and that was that."

"Can you tell me what he looked like, Madame?"

"Of course, he was wearing a winter coat like many people in the country wear. Seemed like good quality. He had a tradesman's cap on, so not of the upper classes. He looked about average height for a man and was a bit husky. I think he had brown hair. His beard was brown."

"This is very helpful, Madame. Thank you so much. I have only one more question. When you were explaining that Madeleine might be at the Moulin Rouge, what was his reaction to that?"

"When I mentioned the Moulin, he became angry again."

* * *

While Olivia was gathering a good amount of information, Steven and Etienne weren't having much luck. The small, windowless, lower apartment was clean and tidy, but everything was worn around the edges. In the living area, which was open to a tiny kitchenette on one side, the sofa sagged, and the upholstered armchair showed a dent in the seat. There were two separate bedrooms, however, and it was easy to tell which had been Madeleine's. After only five days, it already had that unlived-in feeling. The covers on her bed had been straightened and one edge turned down as if waiting for her return that night. A small valise sat open on a nearby wooden stool.

"By the way, Steven," Etienne began, "please don't be offended at this question, but how do you know Mademoiselle Watson will ask the right questions?"

Steven chuckled. "She's a trained journalist. She has a university degree in questioning people. She'll do fine."

"Ah." Etienne threw open the two doors of an armoire. The few dresses, skirts, and blouses took up little space and were all ordinary. However, an elegant evening gown stood out. "What have we here? Look, Steven." He held it up.

"I don't know much about fashion, but even I can tell that was expensive. What do you think she was doing with it?" Steven said.

"Well, it's too long to be worn as a costume at the Garnier, so it can't be from a performance. And it's too fine for the Moulin Rouge. Perhaps there was a special event connected to the ballet, and one of the patrons bought her this gown. Maybe other dancers received a special dress as well."

"That makes sense. I've been meaning to ask, Etienne. Do you know anything about her family? I saw the return address on that letter from her friend Bernard—Bar-le-Duc—but that doesn't tell me anything. Might her family be wealthy? Perhaps she brought the dress before she came here. She might have thought she would need something special in the capital."

"I don't know anything specific about this girl, but many of the dancers who come from the provinces are quite poor. Having said that, though, I wouldn't say she was one of the desperately poor ones. These clothes and the ones we saw at the morgue are typical purchases of the *bourgeoisie*. I think my wife might even have the same dress as that blue one. So, to answer your question, I suppose it's possible she brought the gown with her." He fingered the silky material and looked closely at the beading. "No, wait, I don't think so after all, Steven. This looks like couture—Worth or Paquin—although I don't see a label. I'd say someone who has money bought it for her here in Paris."

"What's going to happen to her belongings, Etienne?"

"I was going to talk to you about that. Do you plan to travel to Bar-le-Duc to speak with Madeleine's family and perhaps the young man, Bernard?"

Steven grinned. "You're reading my mind. Yes, I would like to. Henri was generous with our expenses, so there's enough money for Olivia and me to take the train. How far is it? How long would it take?"

"It's in the east. About three hours away. And I happen to know that the *Orient Express* goes to Strasbourg, which isn't far from Bar-le-Duc." Seeing Steven's questioning look, he added, "The *Orient Express* is a fancy train."

"Ah."

"We can visit the company office on Monday and see if there's a stop or a connecting train near Bar-le-Duc. I'm sure Henri wouldn't mind you being comfortable on your journey. It might be a good idea to make a hotel reservation. Your interviews could easily take up an entire day by the time you arrive."

"Thank you. I'll talk with Olivia later."

"So, returning to your question, we could pack Madeleine's belongings and you could take them to her family."

"Yes, I'm sure they'll want her things," Steven said, moving to the valise.

Looking inside, he saw several nights' worth of underclothes, a nice dress—probably intended to be worn on Christmas Day and Christmas Eve as well—and a serviceable skirt and blouse. There were also several small packages wrapped in colorful paper. Seeing the gaily wrapped gifts, Steven felt an unbearable sense of loss, and of sadness. Madeleine's family must have had the worst Christmas of their lives.

While talking, the two policemen had moved around the tiny bedroom, examining what little there was, and only one place remained—the bedside table. On the top sat a black-and-white framed photograph that Steven took to be the dancer's family. There was Madeleine, flowing blonde hair and engaging smile, surrounded by an older man and woman—certainly her parents—and flanked by two younger girls, likely her sisters.

Steven set the photograph on the bed, then opened the drawer. He extracted a packet of letters bound in a satin ribbon. Looking toward the back of the drawer, then feeling with his hand, he found nothing else of interest—no diary, no address book.

"What have you got there?" asked Etienne, who had removed the clothes from the wardrobe, folded them, and piled everything on the bed. He picked up the photograph and added it to the pile. There was not much to show for a life. Even a short one.

Steven opened the topmost envelope and slid out a sheet of pale blue writing paper of good-quality linen. He turned over the page and skipped to the bottom: With all my love, Maman.

"Oh, I bet these are all from her mother. She'll want them back for sure. The poor woman." For the first time since Evangéline had uttered those fateful words *I need you to come to Paris*, since they had traveled back in time to 1895, since they had viewed Madeleine's body in the morgue, even since he had examined the contents of the valise moments ago, Steven felt a profound connection to someone who had been loved. The determination that always burned bright inside him when he was investigating a murder burst into life. He knew at that moment he would not leave Paris until he tracked down the person who'd killed Madeleine Gervaise.

Chapter Nine

It was past noon when they left 35 rue des Saules. The carriage rumbled over the cobbled Montmartre streets and, after several blocks, they pulled up to a restaurant.

Le Consulat was a narrow, three-story building with a red awning over the door and two large windows flanking the entrance. Etienne led Steven and Olivia inside and said *oui* to the waiter's question, *trois personnes?* They followed the young man to a table in the back corner, where a long wooden banquette ran along the wall. The waiter held out his hand toward Olivia for her to select a seat. She chose the upholstered bench, leaving the two chairs for Steven and Etienne.

After ordering a carafe of water and one of red wine, they consulted the menu.

"I'm starved," Olivia said. "It all sounds good. I think I'll order the roasted chicken with *pommes Dauphinoises* and roasted vegetables."

"That sounds good," Steven said. "I'll have that too."

Etienne laughed. "We're going to make it easy for the waiter. That sounds good to me as well." He poured each of them a glass of wine and, still holding the container in his hand, drank half of his own glass, then topped it up before setting the carafe back down on the table.

"So, Etienne, you mentioned earlier that there's a lot of crime in Paris right now. How are you able to leave your duties to help us?" Steven asked.

"My boss feels the same as I do about Mademoiselle Gervaise. He agrees that someone must have pushed her down those stairs. The girl was strong and agile. She was a dancer, for heaven's sake! She would have been smart enough to hold on to the railing. If she had slipped on the ice and hurt herself, her livelihood would have been affected. And those girls earn little enough as it is. Plus, he saw the body." He shook his head. "No. Those bruises didn't come from a simple fall. *Le patron* told me to be discreet and to help you quietly."

"Do you think he suspects the killer is someone at the Sûreté? Could the man who closed down the case be protecting one of his own?"

"*Non.* Of course, anything is possible, but I believe it's because we're so overwhelmed right now—murder, assault, theft. And the city is awash with pickpockets. We're stretched to our limits."

"What happens if we find a strong suspect? What if we find evidence?"

The Frenchman shrugged. "We'll cross that bridge when we come to it."

Their food came, and everyone concentrated on eating for several minutes.

"Detective Berthot, how did you meet the count that we saw this morning? It seemed like you knew each other," Olivia said.

"The same way I met our friend, Henri. Someone burgled both of their homes. I was sent to assess the situation and track down the thief. Of course, the Comte de Chamfort would never socialize with a policeman, even a detective, but Henri has none of those airs. You know he's an aristocrat as well, don't you?"

"Yes, Evangéline mentioned it."

"So, Steven, I'm curious about the methods the American police are using. Has there been anything new that I might not know about?"

At that moment, time froze for Steven, and he fully understood the dilemma Olivia faced when she traveled from her twenty-first-century to his 1934. He had to tread carefully so as not to let slip anything that might be in Etienne's future. *Quick*, he thought. *What doesn't exist yet?* He had no idea about blood typing. He thought fingerprint identification had been around for a while, so he felt safe with that. But what about analyzing poisons? He was on dangerous ground before he even began.

"I don't think we're ahead of you in any way," Steven began cautiously. "Do you have the means to identify fing—?"

Etienne interrupted. "Fingerprints? Yes! It's a most exciting new technique, this system of identification using patterns and shapes. It helped me put several bad characters behind bars this year alone. I've been trying to convince those in charge at the Sûreté that we should keep copies of criminals' fingerprints whenever we arrest them, or even bring them in for questioning. We could build a system of files. It would help tremendously if we found a print at a crime scene. So far, I have not been successful. But I will tell you a secret…" He looked around as though someone might be eavesdropping. "I have started keeping records for myself."

"Good for you," Steven exclaimed, grinning.

"And the new science they're calling toxicology! Has that made its way across the *Atlantique?*"

"Yes," Steven said. "I've relied on blood *and* poison analysis. Our job's getting easier every year, Etienne. Of course, I still use my magnifying glass and powers of observation more than anything."

"Oh, I agree! That's the bedrock of all detecting."

They all refused dessert but ordered tiny cups of strong espresso.

When the check came, Steven snatched it up. "It's our treat," he said. "It's the very least we can do for all your help."

Out at the curb, Etienne consulted his pocket watch. "It's already three o'clock. We may have missed our chance to question the dancers at the Moulin, but you never know."

***

It was clouding over again, and temperatures were falling. Olivia pulled her cloak tighter as they traveled in the cold conveyance.

The coach pulled up in front of an ordinary one-story building with an extraordinary red windmill on the roof. The Moulin Rouge. Home of the famous (notorious?) French cancan. Workplace of Madeleine Gervaise.

Etienne led them to the front entrance. Olivia was nervous about what they would find. Were they walking into a glorified brothel where the show of dancing girls was a front? She knew the cancan had a reputation of being trashy, but didn't know why.

After several minutes of hard pounding on the door, it opened. A skinny, white-haired man stuck out his head. "Ah, M. Berthot. What brings you here during the day? And you brought guests."

Etienne stuck out his hand, and they shook. "Happy Holidays, Marcel. Is Nini here?"

"In her office."

The investigators followed the old man down a dimly lit red hallway to the back of the building, where he knocked twice and opened a door. "Visitors for you, Madame."

A short, plump, busty brunette dashed from behind a battered wooden desk, arms outstretched. *"Monsieur le Détective!* To what do I owe the pleasure?" She grabbed his hands and bussed him on both cheeks, then looked Steven up and down. "And who is this delectable young man?"

Steven blushed. Etienne made the introductions, explaining that Nini was in charge of the dancers and was, in fact, the person responsible for teaching them the cancan at the Moulin.

"Henri brought them all the way from *l'Amérique*, Nini. They're investigating the death of Madeleine Gervaise."

Nini sagged like a balloon that had lost all its air. Her face fell, and her eyes glistened with unshed tears. *"La pauvre petite.* Such promise. So full of life. I loved that girl. She was going places, you know. Here, come sit down so we can talk."

Nini led them to a seating arrangement on one side of the room. Etienne joined her on the wine-colored couch—her rich brown curls bounced as she plopped onto the cushion. Steven and Olivia faced them in comfortable armchairs, one upholstered in a dark gold, the other a rich orange. Olivia thought the room looked like autumn leaves and was pleasantly surprised that Nini's office was so warm and inviting. And *normal.*

"How can I help you? I will do anything to assist in catching the miserable devil."

Etienne signaled Steven to take over.

"Mademoiselle," he began.

Her tinkling laughter filled the room. *"Oh, mon Dieu.* We don't stand on formality here at the Moulin. It's Nini, *mon cher."*

Steven blushed again. "All right, Nini. Can you tell me if Madeleine had been acting different in recent days? Was she upset? Did she seem worried about anything? Was she perhaps afraid of something or someone?"

"She was happy to be going home for the holidays. She's been doing real good here at the Moulin—always on time, always knew her steps and hit her marks, friendly, no temper tantrums, never any trouble. As a kind of reward, I gave her the whole week off to visit her family. She was nervous about seeing her father. She told me he did not want her to leave and come to Paris. He even refused to talk with her the last time she went home. But she thought she could change his mind this time."

"Did Madeleine mention anything about seeing a boyfriend?"

"No, but I bet you're talking about that young man who was banging on our door earlier this week. Marcel said a man came looking for her. Said he was taking her home. I didn't see him, but Marcel can tell you what day it was."

"How did Madeleine get along with the other dancers?"

"Very good. There are always upsets and little rivalries, but that's normal. Small petty things like *You took my lip color, and you didn't ask.* Or *I loaned you my skirt, and you ruined it.* Things like that. It's typical when you get a bunch of women together."

"Was there anyone in particular who had one of these little rivalries with Madeleine?"

"The new girl, Marielle DuPin. She'd be the one you want to talk with." She made a little moue.

Olivia noticed. "*Quoi? Qu'est-ce qu'il y a?* What? What's wrong?"

Nini shook her head. "I don't know. Something's been different with my girls since Marielle came…*l'atmosphère.* They don't seem to be working or dancing together like before. *Bah!* I don't know how to describe it."

She's talking about Marielle not being a team player, Olivia thought. "Do you mean Marielle is out for herself and doesn't work well with the group?"

Nini's hand shot out, and she pointed at Olivia. "*Exactement! C'est ça!* There's the company and there's Marielle. I'm going to give it some more time, but I may have to let her go."

"Can we return to these little rivalries that you mentioned, Nini? How do these problems manifest themselves? The conflicts? The upsets?" Steven asked.

"Ooh, fancy words, eh? *Manifest.*" Nini chuckled. "Weeell…." She drew out the word, leaned forward, and raised her brows, then whispered as though sharing a secret. "I heard that when they were at the Opéra Garnier—"

Olivia interrupted. "Sorry, Madeleine *and* Marielle were both dancers at the Opéra Garnier Ballet?"

"*Oui, bien sûr.* That's how they first met. Anyway, Marielle complained to one of my girls that Madeleine was always picked ahead of her for everything—"

"Excuse me, but you called Marielle 'the new girl.' How long has she worked here?" Steven interrupted.

"Only a couple of weeks." Nini raised her brows, as if asking whether to continue. To Steven's nod, she went on, "So anyway, evidently before Madeleine left, Marielle wasn't happy because Madeleine always moved up in the *corps de ballet* from a back row to one closer to the front while Marielle remained in the back. And there were times when Madeleine danced a more prominent role in a particular ballet. Once or twice, she was even chosen as the principal. I heard Marielle moan to someone the other day that she was sick and tired of always coming in second to Madeleine."

"Did that happen here as well?" Olivia asked.

Nini pursed her lips and gazed lovingly at the enlarged photograph of herself on the wall. "Well, yes, I confess it did. Madeleine was easier to work with, and their talent was pretty much the same, so I often chose her over Marielle. Probably not fair, but Marielle was new. And I needed to watch her to see how she fit in. *C'est la vie.*"

"When did Madeleine begin working here at the Moulin Rouge?" Steven asked.

"About two months ago. Late October, I think. You can check with Marcel if you want the exact date. He keeps all the records."

"Do you know why Madeleine left the Opéra Garnier?" Steven asked.

Nini shook her head, curls bouncing again. "No, she never said. And I didn't like to pry."

"What about Marielle? Did she say why she left?"

"No, but I found out. She was fired."

"Why?"

"She tripped another dancer, and the ballet master saw her. He fired her on the spot."

* * *

Two weeks ago…

Sacré! Damn, damn, damn!! Marielle DuPin was furious with herself.

They were nearly two hours into the afternoon rehearsal. It was a routine movement where the dancers in the two rows of the corps moved the lines into the shape of an X, broke, and circled to the back where the soloist was waiting. Then they opened ranks to reveal her, and she danced forward to the center at the front of the stage. There had been a dozen dancers blocking her from view. She'd been so careful. She'd checked every part of the stage. She'd looked into the wings. She'd glanced down into the pit. She'd even peered out into the theater itself. Where had Ballerat come from? Suddenly, he'd materialized from out of nowhere and seen her trip Pauline.

"Out! Out! How dare you? I'll not have a saboteur in my company. Out, now!" he'd shouted, while everyone gaped at the shame she was drowning in.

Marielle managed to hold her head high as she left the stage. She ran down the hall and flew down the stairs to the dressing room. She hurriedly changed her clothes, stuffed her pointe shoes into her bag, and fled the Opéra Garnier.

Marielle DuPin had always been competitive, though her mother tried endlessly to convince her it was unladylike. Marielle didn't care. She'd known early on she was a dancer. There was simply no other choice for her. She told her mother over and over that she would not—could not—sit and do embroidery, take tea, or make meaningless conversation with women who had no ambition other than to marry and bear children. Her besotted father supported her and arranged ballet lessons. To her parents' surprise, she was a natural. To no one's surprise, she left home at seventeen, won a spot at the Opéra Garnier Ballet School, and began what everyone assumed would be an illustrious career.

Everything went according to Marielle's plan until Madeleine Gervaise was accepted at the school the following year. It was then that Marielle DuPin discovered an endless capacity for hatred.

Chapter Ten

It was dark out when Steven, Olivia, and Etienne left the Moulin Rouge. Etienne consulted his pocket watch and suggested they quit for the day.

"It's already going on five and you need to get ready for the evening," he said. "I'm going to my office for an hour or two. If I return home too early, my wife will think something is wrong."

Steven and Olivia laughed.

"You work too hard, *mon ami*," Steven said. "What time should we start on Monday? I'd like to talk with the dancers at the Opéra Garnier—the girls who knew Madeleine best. And I think we should stop at the ticket office to find out about the train." To Olivia's raised eyebrows, he said, "I'll tell you later."

"Yes, of course," said Etienne. "I'll have Henri's driver pick me up at the Préfecture at nine, then I'll come and get you. By the time we reach the ticket office for the *Orient Express*—Olivia gasped—they should be open. Then we'll go straight to the Opéra."

* * *

"We have a lot to talk about," Olivia told Steven as they were climbing the stairs to Evangéline's apartment. They needed to find out about the plans for tonight and borrow the right clothes before going to their own temporary accommodation.

Steven knocked and opened the door, at the same time calling out his mother's name. *"Evangéline, t'es là?* Are you here?"

There was a blur of copper-colored hair flying and a navy blue dress billowing out around her, as Evangéline ran from the studio to embrace them.

"Mes chers, my darlings, can you ever forgive me for abandoning you this morning?" She hugged them both tightly and kissed their cheeks in the now-familiar French style. "I was so close to finishing my painting…and the light was exquisite…so I had no choice. I couldn't take a chance a cloud might pass over, which, of course, it did later on. I am yours now for the rest of your visit. Starting with tonight. We're going to have a fabulous time."

Steven and Olivia laughed.

"No apology necessary, but now you have to show us the painting," Steven said. "You finished it? Can we see?"

"Mais oui! Venez. Of course! Come with me."

Lamplight cast a warm glow over Evangéline's studio and created shadows in the many nooks and corners. Her easel stood near the tall windows, now showing only darkness outside.

The canvas was vertical, about eighteen-by-twenty-four inches, the size of a small poster.

A little girl in a long, white, rumpled nightgown, long dark hair flowing down her back, stood looking out a tall, paned window. Her chin came up to the sill, though she wasn't leaning on it. Her right hand, with tiny fingers splayed, was flat on the glass as though waving goodbye. Her left arm hung straight down, and in her hand she held a pale pink stuffed rabbit by the ear. The bunny's feet skimmed the floor next to her bare ones. The scene outside the window was cold: a Paris street covered in snow, the sky shrouded in dark storm clouds. A man in a heavy winter cloak and top hat had his back to the window as he walked away.

"Oh, Evangéline! It's so sad. What inspired you to paint such sorrow?"

Evangéline gave a Cheshire-cat grin. "What makes you think it's sad? We can't see her face. Assuming the man is her father, perhaps he just gave her hugs and kisses and is off to work for the day. Perhaps he told her he would bring a treat when he returns home tonight. Perhaps she's smiling. Remember, Olivia, things are not always what they seem."

"Oh, my goodness! You're so right. I should know better. Art makes us think and feel. And everyone doesn't think or feel the same when they look at a painting. Brava, Evangéline! This is brilliant."

The painting sent Olivia's mind soaring back to a time when she was little and *her* chin barely reached the living room windowsill. She remembered standing at the window every day waiting for her father to come home from work—he always came through the kitchen door minutes before five o'clock. Either her mother told her it was getting close to five, or she was able to tell time. Olivia didn't know. She only remembered the anticipation that filled her heart, standing there, looking at every car that turned the corner and drove up the street, eliminating all that were not their family car. She remembered the pure joy that flooded her when that dark blue Chevy came around the corner. She would fly into the kitchen, scooting around her mother, who was finishing getting supper ready. She'd yank open the back door and wait. Moments later, he'd enter the house, say her name, and scoop her up in his strong arms. Olivia sighed inside. That was a really nice memory. She'd have to find the right moment to share it with Evangéline and Steven this week.

A deep sense of missing her parents suddenly swept over Olivia, and she swallowed hard. They had planned on coming to Knightsbridge for Christmas, but had to spend the holiday at home in California because her mother had broken her leg. She hoped they'd be able to come next month. They were getting older, and who knew how much time she had left with them.

"Come, let's have a glass of wine before we get ready for this evening," Evangéline said, leading them into the kitchen. They sat around the table with its colorful red, yellow, and blue Provençal cloth and, as she poured, Evangéline told them about their evening plans. "Everyone is very excited about what we're going to see tonight."

"What exactly *are* we going to see?" Steven asked. "No one has told us anything."

"Have you heard of the Lumière brothers? Auguste and Louis?"

Steven shook his head, but Olivia said, "The name sounds familiar, but I can't quite place it. Something to do with photography?"

"Yes and no," Evangéline said, grinning. "These two men have invented moving pictures. And we're going to the world premiere tonight! You'll be in the room where history is made."

"The first motion picture? The first movie? Wow! That's awesome." Olivia forgot herself for a moment, and this came out in twenty-first-century English. Steven and Evangéline laughed.

"Is it open to the public? Will there be a lot of people?" Steven asked.

"They've invited special guests, and it's open to a small number of people who bought tickets. Henri knows the Lumières—he knows *everyone*—so we're invited." Golden flecks sparkled in Evangéline's deep brown eyes. "Now, the fun part…let's pick out some clothes, Olivia." She stood and headed toward the bedroom door. "Steven, you'll wear Théo's tuxedo. Not many choices for men." She chuckled.

Théo again, Steven thought. *Who is this Théo? And what exactly is his relationship with Evangéline?* Steven suspected Théo either lived with Evangéline or spent a lot of time here. He'd noticed a man's toiletries in the bathroom earlier and, of course, there were the clothes, readily available. He had to keep reminding himself that *this* Evangéline was not his mother. *This* Evangéline hadn't even met his father yet. That was a few years off in the future. But still….

"Steven, are you coming?" *This* Evangéline called from the bedroom, after abandoning him in the kitchen with his bothersome thoughts.

Steven took the expensively cut black tuxedo, waistcoat, crisp white shirt, and collar that she handed him, and returned to their apartment to dress while Olivia stayed to try on evening gowns.

"I'm going to wear this one," Evangéline told her, taking a gold creation from the freestanding wardrobe and holding it out for Olivia to see.

Olivia's jaw dropped, and, at that moment, she felt like a country bumpkin. This woman was so chic, so worldly, so…*French!*

Olivia had traveled to many countries. She had two university degrees, ran her own business, and enjoyed a successful freelance writing career. She owned her own home and had a great social life. But Evangéline emitted a glow of elegant sophistication that seemed impossible to match.

Her gentle laugh filled the warm room. "*Ça te plaît?* You like it?" she asked, throwing the dress on the bed as she stripped. She wore nothing on top. What happened to those boned Victorian corsets Olivia had heard about? What happened to modesty? Olivia wasn't a prude, but the casualness of this, in front of a relative stranger no less, shocked her. She supposed that being an artist and living a bohemian life, Evangéline didn't care about or pay attention to society's mores. Steven had told her his mother was a free spirit. *Guess this is what that looks like.*

Olivia thought about the art community of which Evangéline was a part. What might her group of artist friends be like? Olivia knew there were women in this time, as well as her own, who posed nude for painters and photographers. Obviously, Evangéline wasn't shy about nudity. Maybe she'd even painted someone—man or woman—naked.

Didn't they do that sort of thing in drawing classes? Maybe she had posed herself. Olivia made a decision. This was something she would not share with Steven. He'd only get upset, and for no good reason. Let him keep his illusions about his future mother. He had enough to deal with this week.

Evangéline continued undressing, stripping off her knee-length bloomers. She went to an oaken dresser and pulled a corset from one of the drawers. "With a straight, snug style like this dress, I find I have to put on one of these horrible things." She made a face. "Would you pull the ties in the back for me, Olivia?"

Evangéline slipped the gown over her head, then turned so Olivia could see the front. It was stunning. It had a sweeping square neckline that met translucent gold sleeves, elbow-length and embroidered with metallic beads. Matching silver embroidery graced the front of the fitted bodice. The tapered gown flared out slowly as it flowed down her body and, when it reached the floor, a train swirled around the side and back.

"I'm speechless, Evangéline. I have truly never seen anything so beautiful in my entire life."

Evangéline beamed. "Now, your turn! Come and pick something out. Anything you'd like."

Olivia slid several dresses to the side, then her breath caught as she came to a full-skirted black gown with a garden of pale pink and yellow flowers trailing silver vines from the floor up to the tucked-in waist. Short sleeves in multiple layers of tulle reminded her of ballet dancers' tutus.

"Is this for spring?" she asked.

"No, see, it's made of velvet. You'd look wonderful in this, Olivia. Try it on."

Olivia wasn't sure if she should change right here, but Evangéline spun her around and began undoing the buttons on the back of her dress, which dropped to the floor in a whisper. The petticoat followed, and Olivia stood there in her twenty-first-century bra and bikini underwear.

"Oh! Is that what women wear in your time?" Evangéline asked. "I love it. You must feel so free. The next time I travel, I will buy some for myself. No one here needs to know."

Evangéline helped Olivia with the fastenings, then led her to a tall mirror. "*Voilà*! You look like a princess. Steven will be enchanted."

Chapter Eleven

When Henri, Evangéline, Steven, and Olivia entered Le Salon Indien du Grand Café, Olivia wished she'd thought to smuggle her phone, even though the only people she could show the pictures to would be Liz and Sophie.

The room was smaller than Olivia had thought it would be, but large enough for a hundred people. Satin drapes covered the windows, with matching swags artfully draped above. Potted palm trees were scattered throughout the space, creating an exotic feel. The surprising thing, at least to Olivia, was the seats. They resembled the rickety folding chairs with thin wooden slats that she'd seen in Paris parks, like the Jardin du Luxembourg and the Tuileries.

The room buzzed with excited conversation. Henri waved to a striking young woman escorted by a husky man. His white beard and dark hair mixed with gray and white suggested he might be her father.

There were the ubiquitous cheek kisses, and Henri introduced them to his friends Suzanne Valadon and Edgar Degas. Olivia nearly choked. *Degas? The Degas? Holy crap! I'm going to the first-ever movie with Toulouse-Lautrec and Degas. Look at your life, Olivia.*

When two men strode to the front of the room, everyone hurried to take a seat, and the chatter evaporated. They introduced themselves, for those who didn't know, as Auguste and Louis Lumière. They welcomed everyone and told the audience they were the first people in the world to have purchased tickets to attend a screening of moving pictures. They explained a little about the advances in the machines they'd invented, all of which went over Olivia's head. The brothers told the crowd they were going to see several short films. They hoped everyone would enjoy the show.

Olivia was prepared for uneven, jerky movements and was amazed that the images on the screen moved fluidly for the most part. The first film showed workers leaving a factory at the end of a workday. She guessed they would be men when Auguste had announced the title. *Oops! Don't assume, Olivia.* The vast majority of the workers were women, dressed in simple, floor-length cotton dresses or skirts and blouses. Several men on bicycles slid by them as they exited the building. At the very end came a wagon pulled by two large horses.

The audience went wild, clapping and shouting. Echoes of *Bravo!* filled the room.

Next came *"L'Arroseur Arrosé,"* a man watering his garden with a hose like the ones Olivia had at home. Except for a long apron, this man could have been her next-door neighbor. Nothing about it looked like it was produced in 1895. And it was funny, though predictable, the title being a clue. A teenaged boy snuck up behind the man and stepped on the hose so the water stopped spraying. The perplexed man turned the end of the hose toward his face to see if something was stuck, and, of course, at that moment, the boy lifted his foot off the hose, and the gardener got a face full of water. He then chased the boy out of his yard. The audience roared.

There were films showing several men attempting to mount a horse, a baby trying to catch goldfish in a bowl, a father feeding a baby while the mother poured tea, and young people waving their arms in the air and jumping off a dock into the sea. All were well done.

The film-goers filed out of the *salon* and into the lobby to celebrate the Lumière brothers' success with champagne and hors d'oeuvres.

Crystal chandeliers sparkled. Gowns shimmered. And conversation invited a careful ear. No one wanted to miss a thing that was said on this historic evening.

Steven and Olivia stood on the edge of a growing circle of artists. Henri de Toulouse-Lautrec, their host for the evening, Edgar Degas, and Suzanne Valadon were joined by Alfred Sisley and Paul Cézanne. Sisley and Cézanne were extolling the virtues and joy of landscape painting, while Henri and Degas kept reminding them of the beauty of the human form and the need to showcase it, especially in motion. They kept talking about the muscles and the amazing way everything worked in tandem, creating a beautiful whole.

"Bah! You two and your dancers," Cézanne said to them.

Olivia moved aside to let someone pass and noticed a familiar face. She whispered to Steven that she'd be right back and eased away from the circle.

"Bonsoir, Monsieur le Comte," she said, approaching the elegant Comte de Chamfort.

"Ah, la jeune Américaine. How are you this evening, Mademoiselle?" He gave a little bow as he reached for her hand and kissed the air above it. "Did you enjoy the moving pictures?" He glanced across the room, over the heads of the crowd, and spied Steven, then nodded in acknowledgement.

"Yes, they were wonderful. What did you think?"

"Amusing, but I prefer the theater and works of art hanging in museums...or in my homes."

"Yes, nothing can replace a truly beautiful painting. But, I think this will be a new art form. Something many people will enjoy."

"Perhaps."

"I understand you're a patron of the ballet. That is an art I would love to perform, but unfortunately...." She laughed.

"Yes, ballet takes a special talent and, of course, extreme dedication."

"Did you know the dancer who recently died? Her name was Madeleine Gervaise."

"Ah, sweet Madeleine. Yes, but not well. It is unfortunate you will not be able to see her perform. She danced as though she had wings, floating across the stage like in a dream. It truly was a sight to behold. All the girls at the Opéra Garnier Ballet…they work very hard, and so often at the end of the night they are *épuisées*, exhausted. But who can blame them? They are devoted to the dance."

Again, that Gallic shrug.

"Well, it was nice talking with you, Monsieur le Comte. I just wanted to say hello."

He bowed again.

* * *

Well, well, well. What is this audacious American girl up to, eh? Is she so focused on the investigation into Madeleine's death that she forgets her manners and approaches me, bold as brass? Does she dare think she is my equal? Or is she one of those ignorant foreigners who doesn't bother to learn the customs of the country they're visiting?

Repulsed by Olivia's behavior, the count considered her as she walked away, taking in the exquisite gown and rich dark brown hair shining with auburn highlights, remembering the stunning hazel eyes flecked with gold.

In the end, it doesn't matter. These two—she and the New York policeman, with that annoying detective, Berthot—must be stopped before they stumble onto our arrangement at the ballet. I'll contact Polignac and tell him to send a message right away. Something anonymous, but clear and direct. We cannot allow these Americans to interfere.

Luckily, the four of us will be together tomorrow night. We'll discuss it further and decide what else we should do. We've spent too much time and money to let everything fall apart. To say nothing of the pleasure we take from it.

* * *

Olivia turned from the Comte de Chamfort and made her way across the room to rejoin Steven and their group of happily bickering artists. When she reached them, she saw the lively discussion about an artist's most worthwhile subject matter was ongoing. If they only knew what they would become and how history would honor them!

Soon, Henri informed his party that it was time to leave. He had asked Louis Lumière ahead of time how long the evening would last and had reserved their table at Moulin de la Galette for ten o'clock. Henri told Steven and Olivia that since it was Saturday night, a band would play until the wee hours of the morning, and there would be dancing.

Nothing could have prepared Olivia for the vision she beheld when Henri led them into the famous dance hall and eatery. The room was enormous. Gold-painted circles decorated the pale blue ceiling, and black wrought-iron railings surrounded tables and chairs on a slightly raised dais where people ate and drank. An orchestra seated on a raised platform over a doorway played while people danced. The maître d' led them to a table for six, and Henri ordered Champagne.

Olivia saw a glint in Henri's eyes that she hadn't noticed the other day. She hoped this evening out with friends would help him make some progress through the grieving process and, at least for one night, forget Madeleine Gervaise's sad ending. Although completely eccentric, he seemed like a nice man, and she felt bad for him.

Unfortunately, it wasn't to be.

First, Henri toasted "Good friends," then Degas raised his glass for the second toast. "To Madeleine, may she rest in peace." Setting his glass down in front of him, Degas continued, "You know, Henri, that I understand your sadness. Do you remember MiNou? That little redheaded ballerina I loved to paint? It's already been two months."

Henri solemnly nodded his head. "Yes, I do, *mon ami*. The police dismissed her death as well, didn't they? A heart attack, was it? They said her heart had stopped."

"I always thought that was a particularly stupid thing to say," his friend replied. "Have you ever seen a dead person whose heart was still beating?"

"I'm sorry to interrupt," Steven said, "but are you saying another dancer died recently?"

"Yes, Marie-Hélène Bordeaux. Everyone called her MiNou. She danced in the *corps de ballet* at the Opéra Garnier. I loved painting her. That fiery red hair blooming all around her head and shoulders. Those deep navy blue eyes, like the depths of the sea. And such a funny girl. She always made me laugh," Degas said.

"How awful! What happened?" Olivia asked.

"It was one night after a performance in late October," Degas replied. "After the dancers had taken their final bows and gone backstage to the dressing room, they discovered two boxes of chocolates on the table near the sofa. The *bonbons* were from A la Mère de Famille, one of the oldest and best chocolate shops in Paris. The candies were in the traditional orange boxes with gold diamonds and stars, and the golden helmet in a circle in the center of the lid. There was a handwritten note that said, '*Félicitations. Bon appétit.*' The girls opened both boxes and most enjoyed one or two *chocolats* as a special treat. Two got sick to their stomachs but were able to return home. Marielle DuPin was very ill and spent several hours in the *toilette*. MiNou died. The rest of the girls were fine. The police doctor said the ones who got sick must have had some kind of allergy to an ingredient in the candy. They said MiNou had a heart attack, and it had nothing to do with the chocolates."

"What about poisons? Did they take the candy that was left to be tested for poison? The police have the facilities to do that, don't they?" Steven asked.

"*Mais, oui*," Henri replied. "Etienne has told me he works with an excellent toxicologist. Nothing came of it, so the doctor must have been right, and it was a heart attack."

"How old was this girl?" Steven asked.

"Twenty-one, twenty-two," said Degas. "But consider how demanding the life of a ballerina is. They have class in the morning; the exercises are grueling. They rehearse for several hours in the afternoon, the same steps and movements again and again. Then they dance two hours every night during the performance. They eat little because they must stay thin for the costumes, and to dance the way they do. It's a hard life. Perhaps there was a fatal flaw in her heart. That happens, you know. The police investigated but came up with nothing. In the end, we had to accept it."

"But, two young healthy dancers—athletes, really—dying within weeks of each other," Olivia said. "It seems like too much of a coincidence."

"I don't want to stir up trouble, but I'm going to ask Etienne about it on Monday. I'd like to know the results of the toxicology test," Steven said. "And a little more about that case. I agree with Olivia. I don't like the sound of two dancers dying within such proximity of each other."

Suzanne Valadon had been silent during this discussion, but now she pouted, her full lips puckering up like a silent-movie star from the early twentieth century. "Why all this talk about death and murder?" she complained. "We're supposed to be out having a good time. Henri, *mon cher*, let's order our dinner."

Olivia studied this tall, slender woman, seated across from her, who clung to Henri's arm as if she were staking out ownership. Suzanne Valadon had a straight nose and bold, dark brows over piercing eyes that seemed to miss nothing. She was striking, if not classically beautiful. Her light brown hair, with its auburn highlights, framed a heart-shaped face. Olivia thought she seemed shrewd.

Henri patted Suzanne's arm. "You're absolutely right, my dear. And I'm famished." He called the waiter over and ordered for everyone.

The rest of the evening passed in a blur for Olivia. They ate thin slices of beef that melted in their mouths, whipped potatoes with butter and chives, and a vegetable dish that Olivia swooned over but couldn't identify. The cheese course offered not only brie and camembert but three other types of cheese that Olivia had never tasted before. Finally, the waiter brought tiny cups of espresso and slices of a richly layered torte topped with cream.

After the meal, Steven leaned over and invited Olivia to dance. They glided around the floor with dozens of other couples, losing themselves in the moment. After some time, during the middle of a waltz, she looked up at him and said, "We really do live a magical life, Steven. I can't believe this is real. I'm sitting next to Degas! One of the greatest painters of all time."

"Hey, don't go getting any ideas about intriguing French painters," he joked.

"Ha! No chance."

He squeezed her, then spun them around.

Olivia laughed. "You know, I never told you how wonderful you look in that tux."

"Thank you. You already know how I feel about you in that dress. It's aces."

"Thanks. I could tell by your face when I came out of the bedroom. By the way, I've been thinking…we haven't had any time to talk about things since we got here. When your mother showed up on

Christmas night and asked us to come and help, we didn't think twice. Then we left in such a hurry. Now, we're in the middle of a murder investigation—or maybe two. I feel like I haven't had time to catch my breath. I'm glad we're taking most of tomorrow off. Do you think we can be on our own after we interview the two Moulin Rouge dancers? I don't want to insult Evangéline, but I'd like to be alone with you for a while. Besides, I have a few questions."

"Is something wrong?" His brow furrowed.

"No, I just want to talk about this trip we're on. We've never done anything like it, and I sort of need a debriefing."

"Oh. When you put it that way, I see what you mean. I'd like that too. We'll figure out something so we can have the afternoon together. In the meantime, let's make the most of tonight." And he twirled her around the floor.

Chapter Twelve

Sunday, December 29, 1895

Paris, France

Steven and Olivia were getting used to the French *petit-déjeuner*. The fresh-baked bread not only tasted delicious but smelled like heaven. Along with the rich taste and aroma of the coffee, it was the perfect way to start the day.

"It was lovely, wasn't it?" Evangéline mused. "The food was scrumptious. The orchestra was wonderful, and I think the Lumière brothers have a good idea with their moving pictures. Is that something that has caught on with people in your time, Olivia?"

"Yes, we call them movies, and I don't know anyone who doesn't enjoy going to the movies. Although now, they're about two hours long and tell more involved stories like you'd find in a novel. The people who play the roles are professional actors. And they often become rich and famous."

"Interesting." Evangéline turned to Steven. "So, what are your plans for today? I went out into the courtyard earlier. It's unusually mild for December. I think we're going to have one of those winter days that feels more like early spring. You should take advantage of it and see some of Paris while you're here. You can't work every day." She finished her coffee and set the bowl down. "I have some things I need to do, but we could meet for supper."

"You're reading my mind, Evangéline. That's what we're going to do this afternoon," Steven said. "Etienne gave us a list of the girls who danced with Madeleine at the Moulin Rouge. Two of them live together not far from here. This morning, Olivia and I are going to their apartment. Tomorrow, we'll do our official interviews at both the Opéra Garnier and the Moulin Rouge, but talking with the girls alone at home might encourage them to tell us something they wouldn't when others are around."

"That's smart. I see how that could work," Evangéline said, rising from the table. "I'm going to dress, then I must go out. Is there anything you need?"

"We can walk to the apartment, but how do we get a carriage to take us to other locations?" Olivia asked. "We don't have Henri's coach today."

"You'll find a line of them waiting in certain places around the city. The closest is at the top of the street on the Place du Tertre. Remember? That's the square where you see the artists painting, where we left the cab when we arrived the other day. Tell the driver where you want to go. You can also ask him to wait for you. Some coachmen will accept a fare for several hours—perhaps the morning or an afternoon—waiting for you at each stop, then taking you to the next one. Agree on a price before you start out."

"That sounds easy enough. Thank you," Steven said.

"And don't worry about money," Evangéline added. "Henri gave you enough for everything you could possibly need. But—and this is important—don't flash a handful of bills at once. Divide them up, leave some here, and keep some in different pockets. Remember to look out for pickpockets. They're all over Paris. A lot of them are children, whom you'd never suspect. They'll pretend to run into you or brush up against you, and you'll never feel their little hands grabbing your money. They're trained at a young age, and they're very good." She hugged them both and wished them luck. "Let's meet here around six or seven. I'll prepare supper. Olivia, maybe you'll want to help? Perhaps I can show you some things about French cooking?"

* * *

Back in the privacy of their temporary apartment, Steven said, "Let's set up the murder board before we do anything today. My mind is going in too many directions at once. I need to organize what we know. And I want to *see* it. The board will help me focus on what we've got."

"That's a good idea. I feel the same way. We've been bombarded with so many new and unfamiliar things, I don't know what to think or which way to turn."

"Exactly!" He paused. "I have to tell you it's really strange being with my mother…even though she's not actually my mother yet. It's throwing me for a loop, and it's distracting."

Olivia went to him and pulled him into a big hug. "I think we both feel like the ground under our feet has shifted. I can't imagine how strange and emotional it must be for you. At first, you were so happy to see her after missing her this past year. But, you were right when we talked at the airport. Although Evangéline knew who you were and what kind of work you did because of the newspaper article, she doesn't know *you*. And she doesn't have the feelings she'll eventually have as your mother." Olivia screwed up her face. "That is the weirdest sentence I've ever uttered in my entire life." She shook her head as if to clear it. "But Steven, I think this is the bottom line. You loved and have missed the woman who was your mother. Evangéline isn't that person yet. She doesn't give off those motherly feelings because she's still several years away from actually becoming a mom. I imagine you feel the absence of the warmth that was so natural before, that you always associated with her. But now, although she's friendly, we're still basically strangers."

"That's exactly it! She's polite and welcoming. She's nice and friendly and a good host and all that, but the warmth and love I was used to isn't there. It's strange. And hard to adjust to." He squeezed her, then let go. "You've had a big impact on me, you know. Before I met you, I *never* would have talked like this. I don't know any men who would. But I think it's good. I always feel better after I talk with you." Then, running his fingers through his hair and pretending to pull out clumps with both hands, he said, "But these clothes! Aargh! I can't think in these clothes."

"I'm with you there. You might be choking in those collars, but how would you like to be weighed down with ten pounds of heavy material dragging on the ground everywhere you go? And I have to watch every step I take when we're outside because of all the horse manure in the streets. Yuck! Can you imagine if I got some on the bottom of my dress or skirt? Give me my jeans and my leggings any day. Hey…let's lock the door and change into our own clothes while we put the murder board together. No one's going to come here this morning, and Evangéline already told us she's going out."

"That's a swell idea. Let's do it!"

Moments later, Steven and Olivia, in the comfortable clothes they usually wore, headed into the second bedroom to organize the case.

Steven unrolled a large section of the brown paper, tore it off, and taped it to an open space on the wall.

"Do you think we should add stuff about the other girl's death? The dancer that Degas mentioned last night?" Olivia asked. "I made notes."

"Yes, definitely. We might not find out much since it's been two months, but it could put things in perspective. And, who knows, maybe there's a connection. Madeleine might have been killed for a reason that only had to do with *her*—nothing to do with dancing or art. The other girl, MiNou, could be the same. But, they *were* both dancers and artists' models."

To separate the two investigations, Steven drew a vertical line on the paper, keeping most of the space for notes on Madeleine's murder but leaving enough room for information on MiNou's death. He began with the facts they knew and the suspicions they had, however unlikely. Olivia waited as his mind sifted and sorted what they'd learned in the first thirty-six hours. He wrote, then consulted his notebook and wrote some more. She had her notes available for checking. As he filled part of the paper, Steven began to create a picture of their investigation. Soon, the murder board looked like this:

VICTIM: <u>Madeleine Gervaise</u>

20 years old. 35 rue des Saules. Roommate – Yvette Caron

Dancer at the Moulin Rouge since late October. Formerly at the Opéra Garnier Ballet.

HOW: Broken neck. Pushed down the stairs near the Lapin Agile.

WHEN: Early morning hours, Monday, December 23.

<u>SUSPECTS</u>

<u>Bernard Fournier</u>

Beau from Madeleine's hometown Bar-le-Duc.

Considers himself engaged to marry her.

Works in pastry shop owned by his father. Will soon take over business.

MOTIVE: Jealousy? Anger? Is this a crime of passion?

Wants Madeleine to come home and marry him. Wasn't happy when she went to Paris to dance. Thought she'd get it out of her system. Appalled she left ballet to dance at Moulin Rouge. Seems insistent in his letter. Doesn't consider her feelings, only what he wants.

OPPORTUNITY: He traveled to Paris by train Sunday to bring her home for Christmas. Could have stayed overnight.

MEANS: A man would be strong enough to push her.

Marielle DuPin

Dancer at the Moulin Rouge for 2 weeks. Formerly at the Opéra Garnier Ballet.

Ambitious. (According to Moulin Rouge dance instructor Nini)

Tripped a dancer at the Opéra Garnier and was fired. Ballet master witnessed it and knew it was intentional.

Doesn't blend in well at Moulin. Causes tension, uneasy atmosphere.

MOTIVE: Resented Madeleine always coming in first. Jealous Madeleine got the best spots and parts in dance numbers/shows.

OPPORTUNITY: Could have followed her out of the Moulin Rouge. Could have waited for Madeleine to leave and hung back so not to be seen.

MEANS: She's strong and agile like an athlete. Could have had enough strength fueled by anger and jealousy to push her.

Steven set his pencil down and stepped back. "What do you think?"

"Yup, I agree with all of this so far. And I've got two other people to suggest. First, Suzanne."

"Suzanne?"

"Yes, Suzanne Valadon. The woman we met last night."

"I know who you mean, but what does she have to do with this?"

"Maybe nothing, but did you see the way she was hanging all over Henri? At one point, she was clinging to his arm so tight he could hardly eat his dinner."

"No, I wasn't paying attention to them. I could hardly concentrate on my own food, I was so fascinated looking around."

"Then you probably didn't hear what she said either, did you?"

"I don't know. What did she say?"

"When Degas made his toast, and they started talking about how wonderful Madeleine was, Suzanne muttered under her breath, 'At least I have you all to myself now.'"

"Wow. Who was she referring to? Henri?"

"Yeah, I think so."

"So, we need to find out if Suzanne was or is one of Henri's models—"

"Or if they're having an affair."

Steven looked aghast. "An affair? No, you're on the wrong track there, Olivia. They can't be. She's beautiful, and he's so...."

Olivia nodded. "I know. But you know what they say—love is blind."

"Are you sure she was talking about Henri? I could see her being in love with an older man like Degas. He's a successful painter. He's handsome, intelligent, interesting to be around. That's easy to imagine. And remember, they did arrive together." He shook his head. "Henri? No. They can't be."

"Well, whether or not you can imagine it, we need to find out what their relationship is. You're right about Suzanne being stunning. She'd make a good model, so maybe that's what they are to each other. But I've heard the relationship between an artist and his model can be intense. Who knows? That might generate even stronger emotions than an affair. Let's ask Evangéline later. In the meantime, we have to put her on the list. That was a really callous thing to say, Steven. Even if she didn't mean for anyone to hear it."

"All right." He grabbed the pencil again and, under SUSPECTS, added:

Suzanne Valadon

Artist. Friend of Henri de Toulouse-Lautrec and Edgar Degas.

QUESTION: What's the relationship between her and Henri?

Are they having an affair? Is she his model? Does she want him to paint only her and no one else?

Did she know Madeleine? If so, how well?

MOTIVE: Jealous of the time Madeleine spent with Henri modeling.

Olivia overheard her say, "At least I have you all to myself now." Potentially damning comment.

OPPORTUNITY: She could have attended the show at the Moulin Rouge Sunday night, waited in the cabaret, and followed Madeleine.

MEANS: Not sure. She's tall enough but she's slender. Is she strong enough?

"All right, Olivia, who's your second possibility?"

"This is going to sound terrible, but what about her father?"

"That doesn't sound terrible. I mean, it does, but sadly, it happens. You're thinking of what Nini told us about Madeleine being nervous to see her father again when she went home for Christmas."

"Yes, she said Madeleine's father didn't want her to leave home and go to Paris. And the last time she was home, he refused to talk to her."

"I imagine he'd prefer it if his daughter came home and married the hometown boy, Bernard. I'd also be willing to bet her father was well aware she'd left the ballet and was dancing at the Moulin Rouge. He's probably heard the worst about the cancan, and he's humiliated that his daughter was part of that world. Although, I doubt he knows the management at the Moulin refuses to show the vulgar type of the dance and that it's frequented by aristocrats as well as people of the middle-class."

"Even in my time, Steven, someone says Moulin Rouge and people still think *risqué*. But, anyway, yes, I agree with your thinking about her father."

Steven added Madeleine's father to the list of suspects.

"So, we have two men and two women on our list," Olivia commented.

"And I think after we interview more of the dancers, the list of female suspects is going to grow. By the way, what were you talking about with the Comte de Chamfort last night? That was a bold move to go over there. I'm not sure a woman would do that in this time."

"I thought about that, then I decided I didn't care. He can chalk it up to my being ignorant about the etiquette here. So, listen…since we met him yesterday morning, I've been thinking how strange it was that he was there watching a class. I would have thought the rehearsals and classes were private, that outsiders wouldn't be allowed in. I went over to him last night because I wanted to get a better feel for him."

"I don't think it's so odd. If he's a patron of the ballet, he must have business matters to discuss with people in charge. Maybe he had a meeting with the director, and afterwards he drifted down to the studio to watch for a while."

"Yeah, maybe you're right. But, I don't know, Steven, I got a vibe from him yesterday that made me uncomfortable…no, it was more than that…I felt unsettled."

"You and your *vibes*. I never even heard that word until I met you. Although, I have to say that most of the time you're right. So, tell me more about the *vibe* you had?"

"I was ill at ease. It was a creepy feeling. Like he wasn't enjoying watching the dancers in an innocent or legitimately interested way, like a genuine lover of ballet would. It felt more like the way someone who's stalking a woman would watch her. Or like a Peeping Tom. When we were at the class, I thought, *Now, what's this guy doing here? What's his motive? What does he want here?*"

"Wow! Well, you know I've learned to trust your instincts, Olivia. Maybe we should look at the count as a suspect."

"I'm not saying that yet. But I want to know more about him."

"Fair enough. We can start by asking Evangéline tonight and Etienne tomorrow."

"Good idea. Speaking of Etienne, Steven, why were you guys talking about the *Orient Express*? Somehow, I missed the beginning of that conversation."

"We want to go to Madeleine's hometown, right?"

"Yes, Bar-le-Duc."

"According to Etienne, it's in the eastern part of the country, about three hours from Paris."

"And…?"

"We need to talk with her family and her supposed fiancé. Henri gave us plenty of money for expenses, and going to her hometown is a legitimate part of the investigation. Etienne said there's a train called the *Orient Express* that leaves in the morning, so we could be in Bar-le-Duc before noon. But, because of the long lunch, we won't be able to start our interviews until after two. And we'll need time to question everyone, so we'll have to stay overnight. By the way, I've never heard of the *Orient Express*, but then I haven't traveled in Europe before."

"You didn't read Agatha Christie's book *Murder on the Orient Express?*"

"You know I don't read mysteries."

"Well, never mind. Maybe it hasn't been published yet in your time. Anyway…the *Orient Express* is one of the most famous trains of all time! Super fancy. Oh, my God! Are you telling me we're going to take the *Orient Express?* I don't *believe* I can't use my cell. Damn! No pictures…again!" Olivia moaned. "Okay, regroup, Olivia. Focus. You're actually going on the *Orient Express.* You don't *need* photos."

Steven laughed, then reached over, gave her a hug, and kissed her hard and quick. "It really is good to spend time alone. I miss our evenings together at home." He kissed her again, then turned back to the murder board and made a note of the count. It simply said: Le Comte de Chamfort—Why is he hanging around the ballet practice? Why would he kill Madeleine?

Steven finished by writing the information they had, as well as their questions and observations, about Marie-Hélène Bordeaux, the ballerina known as MiNou. He noted that she danced at the Opéra Garnier and was Degas' model. He added the circumstances of her death, officially a heart attack but suspiciously looking like poison.

He set the pencil down and said, "Done for now. Let's get dressed—"

"Ugh!"

"Yeah, I know. But, let's get dressed and go talk with the dancers who live near the staircase. Then we can be tourists for the rest of the afternoon."

"After a big French lunch." She grinned at him. "You know, Steven, this case feels different from the other ones I helped you with. Maybe because neither of us knew Madeleine. I wonder what she was like."

* * *

September 1894

It took Madeleine three months of hard work to reach the point where she felt confident that, not only were her skills equal to everyone else's, she had surpassed most of the girls at the Opéra Garnier Ballet. And, although she had no idea how to accomplish this and had no plan, she decided it was time to move from the back rows of the corps and dance in the front.

One morning before everyone in the company arrived, Madeleine found herself alone with the ballet master, the choreographer, and the pianist who had come in early to work out some kinks in the new ballet the company would soon be rehearsing.

The men nodded in her direction, then ignored her and went to work. Keeping out of their way, Madeleine continued her usual early morning routine, finishing at the barre, then performing several arabesques, *holding her position as long as possible. With her bosses now sharing the rehearsal hall, she hesitated to continue with the* chassés, pirouettes, *and* jetés *across the floor, but realized there was enough space if she kept to one side of the room.*

Madeleine was concentrating so hard that, at first, she didn't hear Monsieur Ballerat calling her name. As she landed her final jeté, *his voice broke through.*

"Mlle Gervaise!"

Madeleine spun around to face the ballet master. "Oui, Monsieur le Maître."

"Come here, please." He stood at the piano next to Monsieur Petipa. "It's fortuitous that you're here early today."

"I arrive at six-thirty every day to get in some extra practice."

Ballerat exchanged a look with the choreographer. They both nodded.

"Bon. As I said, it's fortuitous that you're here. We need someone to help us practice this new series of movements. I'll partner you while Monsieur Petipa watches." He turned to the choreographer. "Marius, I think the

problem may still lie right at the end of the pas de deux.*"*

The ballet master recited the series of steps and moves, then showed Madeleine, pretending he held a partner.

"Now, let's try it together, Mademoiselle."

Heart pounding, Madeleine said a silent prayer and stepped into his arms.

After several minutes, they parted, and the pianist stopped.

Ballerat stood and stared at Madeleine for several long seconds. He and the choreographer raised their brows and nodded at each other.

"Astounding!" declared the ballet master. "If you can do this on your first try, we just might decide to promote you to soloist for this ballet."

"Oh, thank you!" Madeleine's body tightened in anticipation of their final decision.

"I said might." But he was smiling at her like he had never done before.

Chapter Thirteen

When Steven and Olivia stepped out of Evangéline's apartment building into the courtyard, the sun was shining and the sound of church bells filled the neighborhood. After consulting her notes and the rough map she'd made on Friday, they made their way to number 24 rue des Saules.

The Moulin Rouge dancers lived in a three-story building, which sat along the steep incline near the staircase where Madeleine had died. A pale blue door and shutters brightened the plain white edifice.

"Well, this is strange," Olivia said. "No doorbell, no nameplate, just this pretty door. What should we do?"

"Let's knock and see what happens."

Steven knocked, and they waited. He knocked again, harder this time.

Shutters on the top floor banged open, and a pretty redhead stuck her head out the window. "What the heck is going on? Who are you? What do you want? Some people are still sleeping, you know," she shouted.

Without thinking, Steven said, "Police. We're looking for Joséphine Moreau and Brigitte Allard."

"I'm Brigitte. What do you want with us?"

"We have some questions about Madeleine Gervaise."

"Oh. Wait a minute. I'll come down."

The door was opened by a plump twenty-something with wild, fiery hair. It was obvious the young woman had been sleeping. Pillow creases ran across her creamy, pale complexion. She still wore her nightgown but had wrapped herself in a long, heavy dressing gown, and her feet were bare. "We got in late last night," she said as she led them up a wooden staircase into a tiny apartment. Once there, she disappeared through a door in the back wall.

Looking around the minuscule space, Olivia noted an alcove with a few small kitchen items to the left and two sagging armchairs in the center of the main room.

Brigitte reappeared. "Jojo's coming. I'll be right back. *Toilette*, you know."

When the dancer returned, Olivia could see she had thrown some water on her face.

Brigitte went to a small counter in the alcove where a faucet stuck out from the wall. She filled a glass with water and gulped it down. The bedroom door opened again, and a freckle-faced blonde, also wrapped in a robe, joined them.

"I'm Joséphine Moreau. *J'arrive.* Be right back." She left the apartment, evidently heading to the bathroom down the hall as well.

When the four of them were finally together, they filled the tiny living room. Brigitte told Steven and Olivia to take the chairs, and she and Joséphine perched on wooden stools dragged from the kitchen area. Steven introduced himself and Olivia and began his questioning.

"First of all, let me tell you, this is an unofficial investigation, although we are working with the police. Do you know Monsieur Toulouse-Lautrec?"

"Henri?" they chorused. "Of course. He comes in the Moulin all the time."

"Well, Henri hired us to investigate Madeleine's death."

"I told you!" Brigitte elbowed her roommate.

"What's that, Mademoiselle?" Olivia asked.

"I *never* thought she fell. Madeleine climbed those stairs every day for months. She could have done it blindfolded, in the dark. In her sleep. *Vous comprenez?* You understand? It's impossible that she slipped. We're not stupid. Everyone knows the steps are covered in ice this time of year. We hold on to the railing as though our lives depended on it. Because they do. We hold on hard. We grip *really* tight." She leaned forward as if willing Steven and Olivia to believe her. "None of us can afford to turn an ankle or slip and hurt our back. How would we dance? That's our livelihood."

"Mlle Allard—" Steven began.

"It's Brigitte. Just Brigitte."

"Okay, Brigitte, what do you think happened?

"Somebody pushed her."

"Do you have someone particular in mind?"

"That miserable Marielle. She hated Madeleine."

"Why do you say that?" Steven asked.

"Nini gave Madeleine better parts. She danced in more numbers and got better positions on stage so people could see her."

"Why is that important?" Olivia asked.

"Money, of course."

"What do you mean? Why would she get more money in certain spots?" Steven asked.

"Because of all the men who come in. If they can see you and if they like you, they'll give you tips after the show. They'll buy you drinks. And they might buy dinner too, if they really like you."

The expression on Olivia's face must have betrayed her thoughts because Brigitte quickly added. "And it's not like *that*. Monsieur Zidler would never allow behavior like that. We're not a brothel. We're serious dancers and performers. You should see La Goulue and Jane Avril perform. They're wonderful! And they've worked hard to get where they are."

"Monsieur Zidler's the boss?" Steven asked.

"The owner."

"And what do you think of your friend's ideas, Mademoiselle Joséphine?" Steven asked the other girl.

A giggle emanated from the tower of blankets wrapped around Brigitte's roommate. "Mademoiselle Joséphine," she repeated and laughed again. "It's just Jojo. *Eh bien….*" She pronounced it with a southern twang.

Olivia had once known someone from the south of France and recognized the accent. "Jojo, are you by any chance from Marseille?" she asked.

Jojo's face filled with light and happiness. "Yes! How did you know? *L'accent*? Yes, it's a giveaway." She sighed. "I miss the heat. Paris is too, too cold."

"So, what do you think of Brigitte's ideas about Madeleine's death, Jojo?" Steven asked again.

The dancer sighed a second time, pulling her robe tighter around her. "She's probably right. No dancer would accidentally slip on those steps. Madeleine lived up the street from here. A lot of nights, the three of us walked home together. We're used to the stairs and we're always careful."

"What about that other dancer called Marielle?" Steven asked.

"*Bien* (again, the southern twang), I don't know if Marielle would go as far as pushing someone down a staircase, but she can be really nasty. She's ambitious. She sees nothing but her own desires."

"Did either of you notice when Marielle left the Moulin Sunday night?"

"Not me," Jojo said.

Brigitte shook her head. "Me neither. We were both tired, so we left right after the show for a change. I'm pretty sure Madeleine and

Marielle were still in the cabaret, though."

"What you're saying about Marielle being jealous of Madeleine's good fortune…is this common in your work?" Olivia asked.

Both girls nodded.

"But with Marielle, it's worse than usual," said Brigitte.

"How well did you know Madeleine?" Steven asked. "Beyond walking home together, did you see each other outside of work?"

"Yes, the four of us—including her roommate Yvette—are good friends. We help each other when someone needs something. We borrow things—a scarf, a hat, or maybe a piece of jewelry," said Brigitte.

Jojo rolled her eyes. "I'm always borrowing extra scarves and gloves."

"And when we have a few extra francs, we go out for a drink or a meal together," Brigitte added.

"Did Madeleine ever mention a man named Bernard?"

"The ex-fiancé," Jojo said. "Yes."

"What did she say about him?" asked Olivia.

"She liked him, but she didn't want to get married. She thought he might cause problems," Brigitte said.

"He's stubborn," Jojo said. "Madeleine told us he always gets his own way."

Chapter Fourteen

Steven and Olivia left Brigitte and Jojo to enjoy their Sunday and walked up the rue des Saules until they reached the corner, then turned and continued up the hill to the Place du Tertre. The sun still shone brightly, and a few puffy white winter clouds—the kind that kids liked to imagine were animals—floated gently across the blue sky. The temperature was warm for the end of December. It made a pleasant stroll to the top of the *butte*.

"Look," Olivia cried, pointing to a mass of wooden scaffolding a few blocks beyond the square. "They're building Sacré Coeur. Just when I think I'm getting used to being here, I see something like that and my mind goes off the rails."

"That's what happens every time I look at Evangéline."

The square was bustling with artists as well as Parisians looking for a restaurant where they could enjoy a long lunch. Menus were posted outside each bistro and brasserie. Steven and Olivia stopped to read what was on offer. After checking three or four places, they settled on La Mère Catherine.

The bright red building, its sidewalk filled with tables and iconic rattan bistro chairs, invited them in. Though the day was mild, Steven and Olivia decided it was too cold to sit outside. A short wiry man holding an armful of menus beckoned them to a small table toward the back. Against the wall stretched a long bench upholstered in black leather and running the length of the restaurant. It served as seating for a dozen tables lined up close to each other, each covered in white paper with a bistro chair facing the bench seat.

Steven asked the waiter for a bottle of water, and they read the menu again, more carefully this time.

"Veal sounds good. I'll try the *blanquette de veau à l'ancienne et riz pilaf*. I don't know how it's prepared, but it'll be fun to see. And I like rice pilaf," Olivia said. "What about you?"

"I'll go for the *poulet fermier Mère Catherine et frites*. No idea how the 'farmer' prepares his chicken, but we'll see." Steven chuckled.

"Let's get some *pâté* to start," Olivia suggested.

Steven ordered for both of them and added a carafe of red wine.

"What did you think about Brigitte and Jojo, Steven? I'd say they were telling the truth."

"Me too. I thought they seemed a bit innocent—although I'm not sure how they could be, dancing at the Moulin Rouge—but they seemed genuine. They didn't hesitate in any of their answers, and they seemed happy to talk with us. I caught Yvette in two lies yesterday."

The waiter placed the dish of *pâté* and a baguette on the table. Olivia tore off a piece of bread and spread some *pâté* on it, then handed it to Steven.

"Smells so good," she said as she prepared a serving for herself. "Oh, yum!"

"Mmm, delicious." He took another bite. "So, when Yvette lied…she said she didn't know why Madeleine left the Garnier Ballet, and she wasn't aware of a problem with anyone at the Ballet or the Moulin Rouge." Steven sipped his wine. "Those two questions, especially the one about why Madeleine left the ballet company, seemed to bother her. She started fidgeting."

"I wondered about that at the time. You'd think if Madeleine was upset enough to quit, it would have been building up for some time.

And she would have confided in her roommate. I think Yvette knows why Madeleine left the ballet."

"Or she knows something. Hopefully, we'll find out more when we talk with her again tomorrow. And speaking of learning more, we've got to find a way to talk with the Comte de Chamfort. If he hangs around the ballet, maybe he knows something that would help."

"I never thought of that." Olivia laughed. "I guess I've already decided he's a bad guy."

The waiter brought their food—steaming hot and perfectly seasoned. The delicious aroma wrapped around the table, and they dug in. For several minutes, they enjoyed their food without talking. Then Olivia spoke.

"What's your plan for tomorrow?"

"When Etienne picks us up, I'd like to go to the *Orient Express* office first and get our tickets. I also want to ask him how we go about making a hotel reservation in Bar-le-Duc. Or maybe nowadays they don't make reservations. Maybe people find a place when they get there. I don't know."

"We'll find out. We're getting close to New Year's Eve, you know. That's Tuesday. Then Wednesday's New Year's Day. We're not going to get anything accomplished on a holiday."

"Maybe we should stay in Paris and get more interviews done on Tuesday during the day, then travel on Wednesday."

"Oh, that's a good idea. Let's do that," Olivia said.

They chatted a bit more, then finished their lunch in comfortable silence, each becoming lost in his or her thoughts.

* * *

Steven missed his partner and friend, Will, and his co-worker Jimmy Bou more than he ever imagined he would. He wondered how they were making out back at the station and wished he could pick up a phone and call them. It would be swell to hear their voices. At home, whenever a case was tricky, and he was having trouble getting to the heart of it, Will's solid presence calmed Steven and gave him hope that they would get there in the end. And now that he thought about it, Steven didn't know how he'd get through a day without Jimmy Bou's sense of humor and unshakeable belief that, of course, they would triumph.

But here, Steven felt overwhelmed. First of all, the case was days old, and he hadn't been able to see the crime scene with the body in situ. He trusted Henri's knowledge and Etienne's memory, but it wasn't the same as seeing things for himself. Secondly, he was just a small-town cop. What was he doing trying to solve a murder in one of the world's biggest cities? And in a different century, for crying out loud? Every moment of every day thus far, he'd felt out of his depth.

To make things worse, Steven's whole manner of working was out of kilter. When he investigated a crime, he was used to trusting his instincts and doing the many routine things without thinking. Now, he needed to be careful of everything he said and how he acted towards people—paying attention to unfamiliar rules of etiquette and being extra polite, just in case. And he couldn't assume that any of the policing methods he normally relied on were in use by the French police in 1895.

Then there was the pool of potential suspects. Too many potential suspects! There was a dancer who had already lied to him and an aristocrat he probably shouldn't question. To make it worse, he also had a hunch that the more interviews they did with the ballerinas at the Opéra Garnier and the cancan girls at the Moulin Rouge, the more suspects they would discover. And they hadn't even started on Madeleine's family or the boyfriend from home. Steven hated it when a case felt out of his control. He always worked hard to keep that from happening.

* * *

For her part, Olivia was thinking of her best friends, Liz and Sophie. She tried to picture how they were spending their days as the year drew to a close. She knew Liz and her husband, Joe, were hosting their annual New Year's Eve party. Of course, Sophie and Luc would be there. Olivia regretted that she and Steven were going to miss it. *There's something so appealing about the familiar. Makes you feel warm inside*, she thought.

Since today was Sunday, Olivia imagined Liz would be finishing all the advance preparations for the party, leaving only last-minute things until Tuesday morning. Sophie was likely behind the counter at her bakery. Sophie's *Pâtisserie-Café* was a popular destination for the citizens of Knightsbridge on Sunday mornings.

Whenever she traveled back in time to Steven's 1934, Olivia felt a real physical ache, an ache caused by not being able to stay connected with her two best friends. Olivia's cellphone had always kept her in touch with Liz and Sophie. Even if she didn't *need* to call or text, she knew she *could*. As this past year had proven, Olivia relied on, and sadly had taken for granted, their steadfast support. The love the three friends shared created a safety net that each depended on in good times and in bad. Now, in the *Belle Epoque* that was Paris, Olivia felt the absence of that connection more acutely than ever before.

Olivia sighed. She even missed Mr. Moto. What she wouldn't give right now for a kitty snuggle!

* * *

Focusing again on Steven, Olivia said, "We ought to ask Evangéline about something we could do on New Year's Eve. Maybe she knows someone who's having a party. Maybe we can all go out someplace—the three of us, Henri, Suzanne, and Degas." She burst out laughing. "Oh, my God! Did I just say that?"

They ordered coffee and dessert. Olivia, a *crème brûlée* with orange flower water. "That should be interesting!" And Steven, a *mousse au chocolat*. "You can never go wrong with chocolate."

The temperature had climbed a couple degrees by the time they left the restaurant and stood on the sidewalk at the Place du Tertre. The artists were still painting and doing charcoal portraits of passersby.

"Let's walk around the square before we leave Montmartre," Olivia suggested.

Steven stopped in front of a small, bright blue watercolor listed for sale. Next to it, the artist, a young man who looked like he was still in his teens, stood at his easel working on a new, slightly larger painting they couldn't yet define. It had the same shades of blue as the watercolor.

"Olivia, I really like this little one," he said.

The painting showed a cobalt-blue sky blending into a cerulean sea, which flowed onto pale blue-tinted sand at the shore. Thinly sketched figures, outlined in black, frolicked in the foreground, while to the left stood a bathhouse. Rather than paint within the lines, the artist had allowed the watercolors to flow outside the borders of the figures and building.

"I do too. You know, it reminds me of…" Olivia bent to read the artist's signature. She gasped and turned so the painter couldn't hear her, then whispered to Steven. "This is Dufy! Raoul Dufy. Steven, he's hugely famous. I love his stuff."

"He's awfully young. Looks like he's just starting out. I like his style too. It's different. How much is this one?" He leaned closer to the tiny painting.

Olivia checked the tag and mentioned the price. "That's not much at all." Excitement filled her voice. "I have an idea. I've got some euros from my time back in my suitcase. What if we borrow some of the French francs Henri gave us to buy this? Then we can work out a trade with Evangéline so we can replace Henri's money? I'm sure Monsieur Duclos at the travel agency can help us change money from the different times."

"That's a good idea. Yes, let's do it." He paused a moment. "But, Olivia, if we're buying this together, then at some point when we get home, I want to pay you for my share."

She was quiet for a moment.

"What is it?"

"It's the first thing we're buying together."

They smiled at each other, each lost in the moment and the implications of that idea.

Chapter Fifteen

After purchasing the Dufy watercolor, Steven and Olivia hired a carriage and driver to take them to the Tour Eiffel and to wait while they visited the monument. As they descended the Montmartre hill, then crossed Paris, they marveled at the fact that they were going to see the tower, not even ten years old yet. They'd already heard lively discussions on its merits and shortcomings. At the Lumière brothers' moving picture show last night, Olivia had overheard one man praising the vision and audacity of Gustave Eiffel, while his friend called it a monstrosity and insisted it should be torn down immediately because it ruined the look of the beautiful old city.

They disembarked from the conveyance, then strolled around the giant tower, circling the base, craning their necks, and admiring Eiffel's genius and the exquisite workmanship of the engineers.

Since it was a beautiful day to be outside, Steven and Olivia decided to take advantage of the mild weather. They returned to the coach and told the driver they'd like to go to the famous Champs-Elysées. The coachman dropped them off near the Elysée Palace, and they headed up the boulevard toward the Arc de Triomphe.

The sidewalks were crowded with people, and Olivia thought that, on the surface, they blended in just fine today.

Steven wore the usual cutaway coat, vest, and starched white shirt with collar. Today, his suit was a deep chocolate, which Olivia thought complemented his beautiful brown eyes. Evangéline had loaned Olivia a crimson-colored dress with a wide A-line skirt. The top part resembled a bolero vest over a gold colored "blouse." Similar to the outfit she'd worn on the first day, it gave the illusion of three pieces but, in reality, it was one dress. Steven had expressed his approval when she tried it on earlier that morning.

"You look aces," he'd said.

Strolling along the Champs-Elysées, they passed young men in their top hats and tailcoats—heavy winter garb had been abandoned at home—families with children running slightly ahead of their parents, only to be called back by *Maman*, and couples like them, arm in arm, walking along in the sunshine.

Just when Steven was going to suggest they sit at one of the sidewalk cafés and enjoy a cup of coffee or a glass of wine, an open carriage drawn by two gray dappled horses pulled up to the curb. An exquisite woman sat beside an elegant man, who waved to them.

"*Bonjour*, my American friends. We meet again."

"Monsieur le Comte, what a pleasant surprise," Steven said.

"How are you, Monsieur?" Olivia asked.

The Comte de Chamfort introduced his wife, Madame la Comtesse Nathalie de Chamfort. Steven doffed his top hat and gave a little bow like he'd seen other nineteenth-century gentlemen do. "Would you like to join us?" the count asked. "We're going out to the Bois de Boulogne. Everyone will be there in their carriages. You'll see another side of Paris."

"Thank you. We'd love to," Steven answered, knowing Olivia would agree.

The count instructed his driver to assist Monsieur and Mademoi-selle into the carriage. The dark-haired coachman tipped his top hat in acquiescence, wrapped the reins around a small handle, and jumped down from his high seat to hand them up into the coach. Olivia noticed this luxury carriage had a small step attached.

Steven and Olivia settled on the comfortable leather seat facing their hosts. A lively clip-clop resonated as the horses took off, trotting along the boulevard.

"I was telling the countess only moments ago that I met two Americans from New York yesterday," the Comte de Chamfort said. "What a coincidence that I should see you again."

"Yes," said the countess. "I'm so pleased to meet you. I'm very interested in life in America. Such a large country!" She looked at Olivia. "Tell me, what is it like to shop in New York City? I've always wanted to go there. I'm constantly reminding the count it is one place we must visit."

"I'm sorry to disappoint you, Countess, but I don't really know. We live about three hundred miles north of the city in New York *State*. I don't travel to the city very often."

The countess pouted. "That's a pity."

"I've promised *la Comtesse* we will go soon, but my work often interferes."

"What kind of work is that?" Steven asked, surprised that a member of the aristocracy would have a job. Didn't those types of men go riding and hunting, and spend time in their clubs, while their pampered wives visited with women of the same social status over tea or coffee in palatial homes?

"My family owns vineyards in the Loire Valley. I must keep an eye on things."

While the count talked about growing grapes and making wine, Olivia pretended to listen, but studied his wife. The countess wore a stunning mauve dress trimmed in olive green, under an open sable coat. Perched on her head was a magnificent hat, a fantastic confection with a raised crown, feathers, and a brim that shaded her face from the sun. The Comtesse de Chamfort looked a few years older than her husband, who Olivia suspected was in his early forties. Tiny crow's feet fanned out at the corners of her dark blue eyes, and a few strands of silver threaded through her rich dark brown hair. The countess reminded Olivia of a photograph she'd seen of Marilyn Monroe before the actress had dyed her hair blonde. *Yes, an older Marilyn, but still. It's probably because of the mole near her wide mouth.* Also like Marilyn Monroe, the countess appeared fragile, though Olivia wasn't sure why. The Comtesse de Chamfort intrigued Olivia, and she wanted to know her better.

Olivia turned to her. "Do you share your husband's interest in the ballet, Comtesse?"

"His interest, yes. His passion, no. When there's a new ballet, we attend on opening night. This is something we would do no matter what. We must be seen, you understand. But Jean-Claude is more enthusiastic than I am. He spends a good amount of time at the Opéra Garnier, meeting with the director, sometimes watching a rehearsal. He believes it's important to support the company, but also to look after the girls themselves. He's devoted to them."

"That's wonderful," Olivia said, deliberately misunderstanding the implication. "We have something similar in America. We call those people 'patrons of the arts.' They support not only the ballet, but symphony orchestras, theaters, and even libraries. All cultural organizations."

The Chamforts' coach reached l'Etoile, the large circle named the Star because of the twelve streets that radiated from the center where the Arc de Triomphe stood. The coachman turned onto the avenue du Bois de Boulogne, an even wider, tree-lined street, crowded with carriages. They weren't the only people taking advantage of the lovely weather. Between the row of trees, mere skeletons now without their leaves, and the edge of the road was a wide apron where people strolled, walked their dogs, and rode their horses. Olivia imagined how exquisite this boulevard would be in spring with everything greening and the gardens blooming.

"Oh my goodness," she exclaimed. "I think all of Paris is outside today. How exciting!"

"Yes, the *bois* has become so popular they built this street leading to the park. It's hard to realize it's only been a few years. Jean-Claude and I are already used to taking the carriage and seeing friends and acquaintances on a sunny afternoon. Although not usually in December." The countess laughed.

"Coming back to the ballet, Countess, I'd like to express my condolences to you on the loss of one of the dancers. I understand that a young ballerina died last week."

The Comtesse de Chamfort shuddered. "Oh, it was terrible. The poor thing slipped on the ice and fell down one of those enormous staircases in Montmartre. They're treacherous in the winter. I don't understand why those girls don't take a different way home at night, perhaps use the street instead of the stairs, or get a carriage to take them home. Such a shame!"

"Did you know Madeleine?" Olivia asked.

"Was that her name? No, but I probably met her at an event the Opéra Garnier hosted. There's always a reception or a champagne supper at the start of the season, and they invite the dancers. I imagine my husband knew her. He knows them all. Some girls have come from the provinces with nothing but their dream of dancing. I can't tell you how many times he took one of them to buy a dress or a pair of shoes for a gala or dinner. Sometimes, good leather boots when winter came as well."

They reached the enormous Bois de Boulogne and entered one of the gravel alleyways, joining dozens of other carriages. The horses slowed here, held back by their drivers, who had been instructed by their masters to move at a snail's pace. Everyone wanted to see and be seen. That was the point.

Conversation took on a more general tone as the count and countess nodded at acquaintances and waved and smiled at friends. As welcoming as the couple seemed, it suddenly occurred to Olivia that the count might have had an ulterior motive in inviting her and Steven to join them on their afternoon promenade. They were *the Americans!* All of Paris would be abuzz tonight and tomorrow. Who were they? How did the Comte and Comtesse de Chamfort know the visitors from New York? What were they doing in Paris?

Olivia felt a little like the new kid at school who has to walk the halls to change classes while everyone stared. *Plus ça change* and all that.

* * *

All afternoon, up and down the *allées* in the *bois*, Nathalie watched Olivia. *Who is this woman? This American woman. And what does she want? How long will she be in Paris? Does Jean-Claude think she's exotic and interesting? Will she captivate him if we see them again? Do I need to worry? Perhaps I should find out more.*

* * *

The sun was setting in the late afternoon sky when they left the Bois de Boulogne and headed to the rue du Faubourg St.-Honoré, a street of quiet wealth and elegance. The driver would drop the Comte and Comtesse de Chamfort at their home, then continue across Paris and up the hill to Montmartre, taking Steven and Olivia to Evangéline's apartment. After a lively afternoon, a comfortable silence had descended over the carriage with only the regular clip-clop of the horses' hooves breaking the quiet.

When several moments had passed, the countess leaned over and whispered to Olivia, "I'm sure you must be quite busy this week, Mademoiselle, but I would enjoy talking some more if you have the time. There's still so much I would like to know about living in America."

"I'd like that," Olivia exclaimed. Not only would this give her the opportunity to learn more about the count's relationship with Madeleine and with the Opéra Garnier Ballet, but Olivia felt drawn to Nathalie and wanted to know more about her and her life.

"There's a wonderful *pâtisserie* around the corner from our home. I'll send the cook to select some delicacies for us. We could have coffee and cakes. Perhaps tomorrow afternoon?"

"That sounds wonderful. Thank you, Countess."

"*Bon.* I'll have our driver pick you up at four o'clock."

"I'll be waiting. I'm already looking forward to it." She gave the countess her warmest smile.

* * *

Heads swimming with images of what they'd seen and heard, Steven and Olivia knocked on the apartment door. Burnished copper hair flowing freely over her shoulders, Evangéline came to the door wearing what resembled a surprisingly modern Moroccan caftan, black, with colorful threads decorating the neckline and sleeves. Olivia's earlier suspicion that Steven's mother had time traveled widely—and to future times—was getting some confirmation. *She would have done well in the sixties,* Olivia thought. *I bet Mom and Evangéline would have really hit it off. No wonder Steven's father fell for this gorgeous and exuberant woman.*

"My darlings! Come in, come in. Are you exhausted? Did you have a marvelous day? What did you do and who did you see? I want to know *everything.*"

Steven and Olivia laughed. Olivia, finding her voice first, said, "I see you're casual and comfortable this evening, Evangéline. If we're not expecting guests, do you think Steven and I could get comfortable too, in our own clothes? Only if we're staying in alone with you, of course."

"*Absolument*! I know how it feels to have to live in clothes of another century. *Allez, allez.* Come back when you've changed. There won't be anyone around this evening. It's only the Duclos family who live in the building, and they never come up here. As I mentioned, Monsieur Duclos is our travel agent. You no doubt noticed the sign on his shop downstairs when we arrived the other day? Madame is the building's *concièrge*. She takes in our mail, sweeps the front steps, and listens to all the gossip around our little courtyard. And, of course, you met Louis, their son and my assistant." She laughed. "Take your time. And in the meantime, I'll open a bottle of *vin rouge*."

Once again in their own clothes, they heaved a sigh of relief. Steven wore a pair of soft navy corduroy trousers, white shirt open at the neck, cream-colored cable-knit cardigan, and what he called his carpet slippers. Olivia was comfortable in her black jeans and cowl-neck pullover with a pair of thick, warm socks on her feet.

"I swear I'll never take something as simple as a pair of jeans for granted again," she said. "I'm looking forward to spending a relaxing evening at home with Evangéline."

"Me too. We haven't had much time to talk with her since we arrived. My head was spinning the first two days."

"I know what you mean. And I have to admit, I've been straining to understand all this rapid-fire French. You're so much better at it than I am."

"Being raised bilingual made all the difference. Besides, I think you're doing swell."

"What do you want to do about the murder board, Steven? We need to update it. It feels like our interview with Brigitte and Jojo was ages ago, not just this morning. What a day!"

"Yeah, it does. I want to know what you learned from the countess as soon as we have a chance. When we were in the carriage, I was trying to get a feel for the Comte de Chamfort. I kept thinking of what you said about feeling ill at ease around him."

"Why don't we make it an early night with Evangéline, and we can update the board later? Right now, I want to relax with a glass of that red wine she's opening."

"Sounds good to me!"

* * *

When the sun slid below the horizon, the temperature plummeted, making it feel like winter again. A fire blazing in the living room hearth rendered the apartment cozy and warm. Evangéline always maintained a low fire in the stove for cooking and heating water, so the kitchen, too, was especially comfortable.

Evangéline leaned back on one of the chairs circling the table, sipping her wine. Behind her, on the wooden shelf serving as a counter, sat a ceramic pitcher and five lidded jars reading *Farine, Sucre, Thé, Café,* and *Riz*. Olivia was familiar with the standard kitchen canisters and was surprised to see the one for rice. A stack of four multi-colored bowls, cups, and plates occupied the end of the counter, where a stoneware jar held a small collection of silverware.

"Something smells delicious," Steven said. "What's for supper?"

"A simple dish but heartier than a usual supper because it's so cold tonight—chicken *provençal*. It's made with tomatoes, garlic, rosemary, and olives. Louis brought us another fresh baguette this afternoon for dipping in the sauce." She brought her thumb and index finger together to her lips and made a kissing sound. "Simple but scrumptious. I'm also preparing—as you can see on my cutting board—vegetables and potatoes to roast."

"Can I help you, Evangéline?" Olivia offered.

"*Merci, mais non.* I'm almost finished. Maybe tomorrow. But, you can help me with something else. Can we speak English tonight? I'd like very much to practice."

Steven and Olivia both nodded. "Sure."

They relaxed in comfortable silence, enjoying their first glass of wine, as Evangéline cut the remaining handful of vegetables and threw them in a bowl. She tossed in some olive oil, salt, and pepper, then used her bare hands to mix everything together until the oil coated it all. After washing her hands, she joined them at the table, grabbing the bottle to refill her own glass. "That can sit until we're ready to put it all in the oven." She drank some of her wine, planted her feet on the floor, and leaned forward, eyes sparkling. "So, tell me about today. Were you able to interview those girls? Where did you have lunch? What did you do all afternoon?"

"Wowie, Evangéline, are you always this animated?" Steven asked. He couldn't remember his mother ever acting quite like this. She'd always been easygoing and calm, not so intense. Maybe she slowed down as she got older.

Sensing something in Evangéline's posture, Olivia said, "You go first. Did something happen today?"

"I have wonderful news." She looked like she could barely contain herself. She sat up straight and exclaimed, "I sold a painting! Actually, I sold *four!*"

"Awesome!" Olivia blurted out.

"That's aces!" Steven said. "But how did you manage that on a Sunday?"

"There's a man called Paul Durand-Ruel. He's been buying paintings from Edgar and Alfred—you remember Alfred Sisley from the moving pictures last night? And he buys from Claude Monet and Pierre-Auguste Renoir, too. From most everyone in our circle who's creating the new style of art. Well, I say new, it's been around for twenty years, but it takes time for a revolutionary style such as ours to take hold. It's called Impressionism. Have you heard of it? Monsieur Durand-Ruel sells the paintings in his gallery. Not only that, he likes to come to our studios to see where we work and examine what we have lying around. He wants to see how each of us puts our own stamp on the style. He takes a genuine interest. He loves our art." She took a breath and another drink of wine. "Edgar introduced us yesterday, and M. Durand-Ruel came here this afternoon. He's going to represent me. He's going to sell my work." Evangéline was giddy.

"Congratulations," Steven and Olivia chorused. They raised their glasses in a toast.

"To the woman who's going to take the art world by storm. Brava, *Maman*," Steven said.

Evangéline rolled her eyes at him and grinned.

"Well, our day pales compared to your news, Evangéline," said Olivia. "But, to answer your questions…." And she outlined their activities over the past eight hours.

"Have you ever met Brigitte and Jojo? They dance at the Moulin Rouge. Do they model for any of your artist friends?" Steven asked.

"No, I don't think so. You make them sound like silly schoolgirls."

"That was exactly my impression of them," Steven said. "What about the Comte and Comtesse de Chamfort? Have you encountered them? Do you know who they are?"

"No, I haven't met them, but I've heard of *him* from Edgar. Edgar doesn't like him or the others."

Olivia had to translate the name for a moment. Edgar. As in Edgar Degas. *Look at your amazing life, Olivia!*

"Why not? And what others?" Steven said.

"There's a group of aristocrats like Chamfort who call themselves patrons of the ballet. Edgar thinks they just like to hang around young girls. Well, to be honest, the ballerinas aren't all girls, although some are only fourteen or fifteen. Most are in their late teens or twenties. Edgar's heard that these men help the dancers get ahead in their ballet careers. And they buy them things. Clothes. A piece of jewelry."

"How does he know this?" asked Steven.

"The director and the ballet master at the Garnier gave him permission to sketch and paint the dancers. He's there during classes, rehearsals, and performances. He's seen those men lounging around, not doing anything but watching. Edgar has actually included some of them as anonymous, shadowy figures in a couple of his paintings. Listen, he doesn't actually *know*. It's more that he suspects. And of course, there are rumors."

"That explains the creepy feeling I got when we were with the Comte de Chamfort yesterday morning," said Olivia, then explained to Evangéline how she'd felt. "I hate to say this, but I wonder...*if the rumors are true*...exactly what do those men expect in return from the ballerinas? Ick! Maybe I'm being naive, but I hate to think the ballet's not what I always thought it was. Which is something beautiful and—I know how this is going to sound—pure. Those lovely dancers, in their fairy-tale costumes, telling wonderful stories. I feel like I'm ripping off the rose-colored glasses. It's like somebody told me there's no Santa Claus."

Steven patted her arm and gave her a commiserating look, then turned to Evangéline. "Do you know who the other men are? The ones Edgar's seen at the ballet?"

"The only name I remember is the Duc de Rochechouart. Thomas is his given name. You'll have to ask Edgar for the others, or perhaps your policeman friend, Etienne. I had the impression there were four or five of them. But listen, Steven, don't investigate *any* of these men without talking to Detective Berthot first. It's critically important!"

"Why?" Steven frowned.

"Because they're the cream of the aristocracy. The Rochechouart family is the oldest noble family in France. There would be terrible repercussions if it appeared you were questioning them as suspects."

Great! Steven thought. *Another complication in this already complicated case. Maybe I should have taken Olivia's suggestion to stay home.*

Evangéline rose from the table and put the chicken and vegetables in the oven. She turned and smiled at Steven. "I think that was a hungry, grumbling stomach I just heard."

And with no warning, for the first time, Steven felt like he was spending time with his mother. A warm feeling washed over him, and he settled back in his chair to watch her move about the kitchen.

It had been worth it after all. All the discomfort, all the hassle, leaving his beloved job with barely an explanation to the chief, dragging Olivia halfway across the world, and more than a century into her past. It had been worth all of it just to spend this one evening with the woman who was going to become his adored mother.

* * *

The simple meal Evangéline prepared was delicious and took him unawares—it was one of his favorite dishes that his mother used to fix for him. He mopped up the scrumptious sauce with pieces of the crusty baguette, torn from the loaf, which was then placed back on the tablecloth in traditional French family style. While they ate, their conversation took on a less serious tone—no leering ballet patrons, no murder investigations. They simply enjoyed the meal and each other's company.

After Evangéline opened a second bottle of wine, Steven said, "Evangéline, I have a few questions for you, if you don't mind."

"Of course. What are they?"

"I found two tram tickets at the bottom of the staircase where Madeleine died. One was for Vincennes, the other the Gare du Nord. Do you think there's anything significant about those destinations?"

She thought for a moment. "Definitely not the Gare du Nord. It's one of the busy train stations. Anyone and everyone uses it. And…I think the same for Vincennes. You'd take that tram to go to the park and the zoo. It's a popular place for families to visit. No, both places are common destinations. I don't think there are any clues there."

"Okay, thanks. Do you know anything about the relationship between Suzanne Valadon and Henri? Is she his model? Are they lovers?"

"Both, I think. Why?"

"Olivia overheard her say something last night that struck us as cruel, as well as inappropriate. And more important, suspicious. After Degas made his toast, and he and Henri started talking about how wonderful Madeleine was, Suzanne muttered under her breath, 'At least I have you all to myself now.' What do you think about that?"

"Suzanne never pays attention to conventions. She says what's on her mind and does exactly what she feels like. It's gotten her into trouble more than once."

"Did Henri spend an inordinate amount of time with Madeleine? Did Suzanne feel ignored or left out of his life?"

"No, I don't think so. She has her work and, of course, her son to raise."

"Oh! Is she married? She has children?"

"No, she's not married. We don't know who Maurice's father is, although we have our suspicions, but it's irrelevant. Maurice is a lovely boy and so talented. It looks like he may become an artist as well."

"I don't think I've ever heard of a painter by the name of Maurice

Valadon," Olivia commented.

"No, it's Utrillo. Maurice Utrillo. A friend of Suzanne's formally adopted Maurice so he would have a legitimate last name. It'll make his life easier. It was an incredibly nice thing to do."

"I see. So…the relationship between Suzanne and Henri…you don't think she was jealous of Madeleine or the time Henri spent with her?" Steven asked.

"You mean you're considering Suzanne as a suspect?" Evangéline's jaw dropped. "No, that's not possible. Are you serious?"

"It's certainly within the realm of possibility," Steven said. "And what about her relationship with Edgar Degas? When they arrived, I noticed she was holding onto his arm."

Evangéline laughed. "No, you're on the wrong track there. Suzanne and Edgar are very close. He was the first person to buy one of her drawings. He's been a mentor to her. Like a father, really." She shook her head. "No, you can't be considering Suzanne as a suspect. Even if she had been jealous of Madeleine, she'd never do anything as horrible and vicious as to push her down the stairs. It's too awful to think of."

Chapter Sixteen

Sunday night, in another part of Paris

They gathered in his library. Top hats and wool cloaks had been left with the butler. Wives had been left at home. Some guests had loosened their bow ties; others were comfortable as is. A servant had lit a wood fire in the large stone hearth, an antidote to plummeting temperatures and the return to winter weather. The crackling orange flames threw off light, casting a subtle glow, and the scent of burning logs filled the wood-paneled room. Floor-to-ceiling shelves lining three walls housed hundreds, perhaps a thousand, classic and recent tomes exquisitely bound in gold-embossed leather. Among many others, here were Corneille, Racine, and Molière, the seventeenth-century triumvirate; Aristotle, Plato, and Socrates representing the Greeks; the revolutionaries Voltaire, Rousseau, and Didérot; Proust, Hugo, and Balzac, certain to become future classics; and the group's favorite, Charles Baudelaire and his racy, exotic, sensual poems in *Les Fleurs du Mal*.

The butler had already arranged the bottles of whiskey and gin, brandy and liqueurs. He'd set out a magnum of Dom Pérignon in a silver bucket and some snacks: a bowl of shelled nuts, a plate of *gougères*, and a basket of crackers next to a bowl of caviar on ice.

As was their tradition for many years now, the four met at one of their Paris *hôtels particuliers* or apartments to privately celebrate the New Year. They would see one another, with their wives, at the New Year's Eve gala hosted by the Comte and Comtesse de Chamfort on Tuesday night, but for now, they would celebrate the arrival of 1896 and their long and lasting friendship privately. And this year, they would discuss murder.

After they had drunk several glasses of Dom Pérignon and enjoyed the caviar, the Duc de Rochechouart led his three aristocratic friends into the dining room for a sumptuous meal. As the servants entered and exited the room, bringing more and more dishes while removing empty or partially empty plates, the men discussed safe topics of conversation: Parisian politics, recently published books, trips they were planning to take, their predictions for the New Year, and recent scandals among the aristocracy. As soon as coffee and dessert were served and the bottle of brandy left on the table, the Duke told his butler they did not wish to be disturbed. The man quietly left the room, pulling the doors closed behind him.

"The police are investigating Madeleine's death," said the Comte de Chamfort, leaning forward and speaking in a near whisper.

"How do you know? I've heard nothing about that," said the Comte de Beauharnais, frowning.

"I was at the Garnier yesterday watching the class when that annoying old fool Berthot came in with an American detective."

"Why are the Americans nosing around?" asked the Duc de Rochechouart, the hand holding a brandy stopping on the way to his lips.

"That's what I wondered when Jean-Claude contacted me with a commission last night," said the Marquis de Polignac.

"What's this?" demanded the Duc de Rochechouart, his steel gray eyes flashing. "Have you done something without our discussing it first?"

"Only a simple warning, Thomas," replied the Comte de Chamfort. "I thought it was important to act quickly, so I suggested Benoît contact those low-lifes we sometimes use. The two men will send a clear message to the Americans that they should stay away from things that don't concern them. And…perhaps they should return home sooner rather than later."

"I see." The Duc de Rochechouart set down his glass and steepled his fingers in front of him. His gaze narrowed as he considered this new development. The others knew this look well. No one spoke. They waited. "There's no way the police can trace those men back to us?"

"No," said the Marquis de Polignac. "Absolutely not."

"I hate to add to our concerns, but my man in the Sûreté tells me the toxicology report on that other dancer came in," said the Comte de Beauharnais, looking around the table and catching each man's eye.

"After all this time?" said the Marquis de Polignac, edging closer to the table, frowning.

Beauharnais shrugged. "They discovered arsenic in the *chocolats* the girls ate."

"Who was the one that died? What was her name again?" asked the Duc de Rochechouart, selecting another sweet, popping it in his mouth, then delicately wiping the frosting from his lips onto his linen napkin.

"The one called MiNou. Ridiculous common name," sneered the Comte de Chamfort.

"I don't like it. These two events are too close together. It's dangerous. It could focus attention on us," said the Duc de Rochechouart.

"Will there be an investigation, Maxime?" asked the Marquis de Polignac.

"Yes, my source says the *commissaire* put Etienne Berthot in charge," the Comte de Beauharnais told his friends.

"That old fusspot! He's like a dog with a bone. He'll never let up. He'll dig as deep as he has to until he uncovers the truth," snorted the Comte de Chamfort, looking like there was a bad smell under his nose.

"Have they learned anything yet? Do they know how the chocolates got into the dressing room?" asked the Marquis de Polignac, taking a large gulp of his after-dinner brandy.

"Not that I've heard. They plan to start looking into it tomorrow. Berthot is going to interview the dancers at the Opéra Garnier," Beauharnais replied, sipping his coffee.

"I was beginning to wonder if your suggestion was the right choice to be our spy at the Sûreté," said the Duc de Rochechouart. "After all that money we've been shoveling in his direction, at least it's finally paid off."

"Yes, it's worth it now that we have some solid information," the Comte de Beauharnais said.

"And we have plenty of time and a warning. No one should attend the class or rehearsal tomorrow. I'd been looking forward to watching Gigi, but it's not worth the risk," said the Marquis de Polignac.

"I agree. And we're going one step further. I want everyone to refrain from observing the dancers for at least two or three weeks," said the Duc de Rochechouart.

"Right," the Comte de Chamfort said. "With the holiday approaching, anyone should understand that we have better things to do than hang around watching a bunch of insignificant girls working up a sweat. Our absence will not be noticed."

Chapter Seventeen

Monday, December 30, 1895

Paris, France

Evangéline had an early appointment to visit the art gallery owned by her new dealer. Paul Durand-Ruel had told her to come at eight-thirty so they could finish the paperwork before he opened. After breakfast with Steven and Olivia, she went to her room, where she chose her finest wool dress—a shade of purple that clashed so violently with her copper hair that she loved it and always made a point of wearing it on special occasions. She selected a warm cloak, leather gloves, and a muff, then stuffed a small sketch pad and pencils into her bag. Evangéline went nowhere without her sketch pad.

"*Au revoir, mes chers.* I'll pick up something to make for supper on my way home. Good luck with your interviews today. I'll see you tonight." Evangéline leaned over and kissed them on the cheeks, then left the apartment.

Since the gallery was near the Elysée Palace, she would need a carriage. She decided not to ask Louis to get one for her. Instead, she would stroll up to the Place du Tertre and engage one herself.

It was Evangéline's habit to go out early each day during the week, even if she had nothing pressing to attend to. She liked to walk the streets of Montmartre and breathe in the fresh morning air, greet friends and neighbors she encountered on the sidewalk, say hello to the shopkeepers who were setting up produce and wares for sale outside their front doors, and see who was up on the square painting or sketching. Sometimes there was the thrill of meeting a new artist.

Shutting the apartment door behind her, Evangéline descended the stairs and crossed the small courtyard. Madame Duclos was sweeping the area near the entrance.

"A bit foggy this morning, eh, Madame Duclos?" Evangéline said. She'd been unable to see the *concièrge* until she was practically on top of her.

"It'll be worse out in the *quartier*. Be careful, Mademoiselle."

Evangéline opened the wooden door to the street, closed it securely behind her, then stepped out onto the sidewalk.

"Oh my goodness," she exclaimed. It certainly *was* worse outside their little courtyard.

Overnight, a thick fog had enveloped the city. The familiar buildings across the street had disappeared. High on the hill, the top of the church under construction had vanished, and there wasn't a windmill in sight. Evangéline could barely see her hand in front of her face. *Well*, she thought, *this is an important appointment and surely the sun will burn off the fog soon. I'll just watch my step.* Turning left, she headed up toward the top of the *butte*.

Evangéline hadn't walked ten paces before the coach was upon her. The enclosed carriage pulled up to the curb, and a large masked man jumped out. He threw a rough hand over her mouth, grabbed her by the waist with his other hand, and thrust her into the coach. The driver cracked his whip, and the horses took off, snorting and throwing their heads back as they sped down the street.

At first, Evangéline was so shocked she felt paralyzed. People weren't dragged off the streets of Montmartre! Of course, you'd expect it down in certain parts of Paris, but not up here. It took her less than a minute to gather her wits and strike out at her captor. She made a tight fist and swung her arm hard in a backhanded arc. She heard the crunch of cartilage as her fist connected with the man's nose. He swore and grabbed her throat, pushing her back into the seat. Fumbling with his other hand, he pushed a sweet-smelling cloth up against her face. Evangéline tried to hold her breath, but it was too late. She slumped to the side.

Shortly after Evangéline had lost consciousness, the carriage pulled into a cul-de-sac. Along both sides of the alley, abandoned buildings stood in various states of disrepair. The driver secured the horses to a post on the broken sidewalk, pulled a key from the pocket of his tatty coat, and unlocked a door in one of the few shacks not boarded up. Taking her feet while his partner grabbed Evangéline under the arms, they lifted her out of the coach and carried her down the stone stairs into a cold, dark, damp cellar. They dumped her on a thin mattress on a cot pushed up against a wall.

The pair regained the sidewalk, locked the door, and left.

Chapter Eighteen

Steven and Olivia had finished their breakfast and were lingering over coffee when Etienne arrived, humming with excitement.

"You'll never guess what happened!" he said.

"You've got our attention," Steven told him.

"The toxicology report on the chocolates came in. I couldn't believe it. I was sure nothing was going to come of it. I had resigned myself to accept the fact we'd never know what happened. Evidently, it just took some time." He paused in dramatic fashion and stared at them. "It was arsenic. The dancer MiNou Bordeaux was poisoned. My boss officially opened a case, and I'm in charge. More importantly, our investigations are now connected. We have two dancers killed within months of each other. *And* they were both artists' models. That brings two very different communities together. This should be interesting."

"*C'est formidable*! That's terrific," Steven said. "We have a lot to tell you as well."

"*Bon.* Let's talk in the carriage."

"Can we stop to get our *Orient Express* tickets on the way?" Olivia asked. "We also need your advice on a hotel reservation in Bar-le-Duc."

"Yes, we'll do all of that. *On y va.* Let's go," said the Paris detective.

En route to the *Orient Express* ticket office, Steven and Olivia shared what they'd learned from their interview with Brigitte and Jojo, and also told Etienne about the carriage ride with the Comte and Comtesse de Chamfort.

"Well, well," Etienne drew the words out. "You've been busy. Olivia, you'll have a wonderful chance to learn more about the Comte de Chamfort when you're at their home this afternoon, but please be careful."

"The countess was lovely yesterday. I'm not worried. It'll just be...." Olivia had no idea what the French equivalent for *girl talk* was, so she simply said, "I'll be fine. Don't worry."

"*D'accord.* Now, let me tell you about the arsenic. The dancers received two boxes of chocolates, twenty-four pieces in each box. Two girls got sick to their stomachs but were able to return home that same night. Marielle DuPin was very ill and spent several hours in the *toilette.* And as you know, MiNou Bordeaux died. The rest of the girls were fine. Our toxicologist tested all the *bonbons* that remained. He found no poison at all in one box. In the second box, four chocolates each contained a small amount of arsenic; the other ten pieces had not been tampered with.

"We should remember that doctors often prescribe small quantities of arsenic for a number of ailments. It's possible the girls who became sick were already taking arsenic for something, and their bodies couldn't tolerate the additional amount. According to our toxicologist, MiNou Bordeaux must have been on an arsenic regimen and must have eaten at least three pieces."

"One thing strikes me right away," Steven said. "This poisoning appears to be random. As a plan to murder somebody, it's ridiculous to say nothing of unreliable. How would you know your intended victim was going to choose a piece containing the arsenic? *And* how could you be sure she would eat enough to die?"

"*C'est ça.* Exactly. It seems our killer didn't care who died. He or she was satisfied as long as some dancers got sick and someone died.

So, the question is…was it a warning of some kind? Did the killer want to frighten all the dancers? Or was it an attempt to frighten only one ballerina, and the poisoner knew she would understand the message was intended for her? Was it a show of power for one or all the dancers?"

"Good questions," Steven said. "The killer could have been sending a message. For example, I can get to you any time if I want to."

Etienne nodded. "I need to find out who had access to the dressing room other than the people who work at the Garnier. Did the perpetrator leave the chocolates in the room himself? I use the masculine, but, of course, it could easily be a woman. Did he or she give the boxes to someone and ask that person to deliver them to the dressing room? Were they sent by a messenger?" He sighed. "The first thing I have to do is speak to the director. We must suspend the morning class and be given full access to all the dancers for our interviews. They will not be happy about that, but it's now a case of murder. I'll explain this recent development, and I'll also tell him about your investigation. We'll arrange it so we can both question the girls. Perhaps small rooms for each of us, side by side. What about Mademoiselle?" Etienne asked, turning to Olivia. "Do you also wish a room of your own, or will you accompany Steven?"

"I think I can be of more use if I stay with Steven. I'll take notes and look for indications that someone's lying—you know I'm a journalist. I trained for this kind of thing. And I can always ask a question if I think of something after Steven has finished."

"Another thing…when we get to the questions about a relationship with one of the patrons, and whatever that may entail, the girls might be more comfortable talking with a woman. As a matter of fact, Olivia, maybe you should ask those questions," Steven said.

"Let's play it by ear." She turned to Etienne. "I'll be blunt for a minute. I hope you won't mind or be shocked by what I'm going to say."

He nodded for her to continue. "Believe me, Mademoiselle, I have seen and heard it all."

"Yes, I imagine you have. Okay, so we're talking as though we suspect that one or more of those men—the so-called patrons, the aristocrats—are doing certain things for the dancers in exchange for sexual favors. If we're right, there are four men that we know of, and there are dozens of dancers. Even if we're right about the four of them, many of the girls might not even be aware of what's going on. I think we should keep an open mind. Maybe those men are nothing more than voyeurs. Disgusting as it sounds. Perhaps some of them are truly good-hearted and want to help the girls, financially or in some other way. But, we should tread carefully, especially with the younger dancers. They could still be innocent and unaware of any nefarious goings-on."

"Well said, Mademoiselle. I see why Steven values your help so much."

"I know this isn't the French way, but you can call me Olivia if you want to. We're going to be seeing a lot of each other this week, I think."

Etienne inclined his head. "Thank you. And since I feel you are an equal part of our team, Olivia, if you would be more comfortable calling me Etienne, please do. As I said to Steven the other day, I believe we are going to be very good friends."

They discussed their strategies, where their interviews would overlap, and the questions that held the greatest importance for each of them. By the time they reached the office of the *Orient Express*, the two detectives and Olivia had a clear vision of the day ahead.

Etienne accompanied Steven and Olivia inside the rail company headquarters. Steven inquired about two round-trip tickets, leaving Paris on New Year's Day and returning late on Thursday, January 2nd. Money having exchanged hands, Steven asked for the clerk's advice on securing a hotel room in Bar-le-Duc for Wednesday night, which, of course, was a holiday. The clerk replied that, since Bar-le-Duc was a small town and not a tourist destination, he believed Steven would have no trouble finding a room. He suggested Steven ask at the train station when they arrived.

* * *

Mission accomplished, Etienne instructed Henri's driver to take them to the back entrance of the Opéra Garnier.

"I think you should both come with me, but wait in the hallway. I'll speak to the director alone. If he wants to meet you, you'll be nearby."

As they approached the director's office, a handsome young man exited. Etienne stepped aside to let him pass, then knocked on Gailhard's still open door as he entered.

Pierre Gailhard rose, shook Etienne's hand, and indicated a chair on the opposite side of his impressive desk. Etienne thanked the opera house director for seeing him, told him about the enquiry into Madeleine Gervaise's death, and explained Steven's role in the investigation.

"Monsieur le Directeur, I also have an investigation to run. And I'm sorry to say that case *is* directly connected to the Opéra Garnier Ballet. The Sûreté has received the results of tests performed on two boxes of chocolates that the dancers shared after a performance in late October. I know you'll remember that after eating some of the *chocolats,* several ballerinas became quite sick and, tragically, MiNou Bordeaux died."

Gailhard closed his eyes and shook his head, then, looking at Etienne, said, "I will never forget that terrible night."

"I can well imagine, Monsieur. The tests showed some of the remaining chocolates contained arsenic. Your dancers were poisoned. MiNou Bordeaux was murdered."

The director's jaw dropped, and he gasped. "But who...?"

"That's my job now. While the American detective, Monsieur Blackwell, asks questions regarding Madeleine Gervaise's death, I'm here to interview the dancers about the chocolates."

"*Bien sûr.* I am at your disposal."

Ten minutes later, Etienne exited the office and told Steven and Olivia everything had been arranged. "Monsieur Gailhard was distressed at the idea of a murder—to say nothing of two—connected to the Opéra Garnier Ballet. He remembers MiNou fondly and was shocked when I told him she was poisoned. Add that to Madeleine's murder, and the fact that Madeleine worked here for nearly two years, he can see the newspapers having a field day. Lots of bad publicity! He gave me *carte blanche*. Anything we want, we've got it. We're to wait here for one of the *gardiens* to show us to the rooms he's setting aside, and to make sure we have everything we need."

At that moment, the director's office door opened and a chubby man, immaculately attired, slid past them. He gave a brisk nod, then hurried down the corridor.

The man wasn't anything like Olivia imagined the director of such an important opera house and ballet company would look, although she didn't really have anything in particular in mind. Maybe she thought he'd be more dancer-like, slender, and romantic-looking. Instead, heavy lids hooded his deep brown eyes, and dark brows hung over them like cliffs. He had a large nose that met an equally large mustache, above a short beard that only covered half his cheeks. But he moved fast. Olivia had to give him that.

Etienne went on. "The director's going to speak with the ballet master. An assistant will bring the dancers to us one at a time, then escort them back after we've both interviewed them." He handed Steven several sheets of paper. "Here's a list of all the Opéra Garnier ballerinas this season. You'll see it notes the girls' hometowns, their

Paris addresses, and the roles they've played so far—whether they're a principal, a soloist, or are in the *corps de ballet*. I have the same list.

"*Eh bien*, Steven, as we said before, I'll concentrate on the poisoned *chocolats*, while you focus on Madeleine's murder. I'll inquire into what everyone saw or knows, with the initial idea that it was a perpetrator from the outside. But, I'm keeping an open mind. It could easily have been a ballerina. We've already heard something about the character of Marielle DuPin. Tripping another dancer to advance your own career is nasty and cruel. It's worth taking a close look at that girl."

The *guardien* returned and announced that the interview rooms were ready, then stepped aside to await further instructions.

Nodding his thanks to the man, Etienne turned back to Steven and Olivia. "Now, for my part, A la Mère de Famille chocolates are very expensive. One box alone would be a stretch for a dancer's budget, but two is unimaginable. Unless the girl came from a wealthy family—"

"Or had a patron," Steven interjected.

"Exactly. I'm going to get some additional background information on each girl's family circumstances from Monsieur Gailhard—he said he'd be back in a few minutes—then I'll start my interrogations."

* * *

It was a tiny room with pale gray walls, encircled by a chair rail around the perimeter, and rendered elegant by raised-panel wainscoting. Light from a small chandelier threw shadows from the high ceiling down onto a table and four chairs.

"I hope we can finish here before noon. I think talking with the dancers at the Moulin Rouge will yield more information. After all, that's where Madeleine was working when she died," Steven told Olivia.

"I agree. It makes sense to start here, though. The ballet dancers have to be here early for class. The Moulin Rouge dancers finish late at night, so I imagine no one expects them to show up until after lunch."

"If Brigitte and Jojo are any proof of that, I think you're right." Steven chuckled. Then the smile dropped off his face and he said in a serious tone, "Here's what I want to know: Did Madeleine have a relationship with the Comte de Chamfort and, if so, what was that relationship? Did she have a relationship with any of the other aristocrats? Were there any problems between Madeleine and another dancer? Did one of the ballerinas—besides Marielle—resent her? Why did Madeleine leave such a prestigious place for the less acclaimed Moulin Rouge? Imagine all the hard work she must have done and the time she put in over years and years to be accepted here, Olivia. Something serious had to have happened."

* * *

November 1894

Madeleine waited and waited and waited. After that exhilarating September morning, when she had partnered the ballet master in a tricky movement in the pas de deux *while Monsieur Petipa, the choreographer, looked on, she was sure it would be only a matter of time until* le maître *promoted her to soloist in this wonderful new ballet. After all, hadn't Monsieur Ballerat said her dancing had been astounding? Hadn't he told her he might promote her? Hadn't she impressed Monsieur Petipa with her skills? Wasn't this her moment?*

But weeks went by, and nothing happened. No one said anything. No one called her into their office with the good news. No one left a note in her cubby.

Finally, one morning after class, Monsieur Ballerat told the company they were ready to begin rehearsals for the upcoming ballet. He proceeded to assign the dancers' positions in the corps de ballet. He announced who would dance the solo part, and he congratulated the young woman who would continue to dance the role of principal ballerina.

Madeleine had been moved to the first row in the corps.

Months ago, first row in the corps had been her goal. Madeleine knew she should be thrilled. She should feel satisfied that, because of her hard work, she'd met her objective. But, after the high praise from le maître, she had built up her hopes and was already picturing herself as a soloist. Upon hearing the assignments, she was devastated. Her head spun, her heart pounded, and her body shook. She was so distraught that, as soon as they were excused, she flew from the room. Backstage in the dressing room, Madeleine pulled off her pointe shoes and tore off her rehearsal dress. She threw on her skirt and jacket, laced up her boots, and grabbed her cloak. Unable to speak, she ran out of the Opéra Garnier, consumed with anger and disappointment.

Rounding the corner, head down, she slammed into the Comte de Chamfort.

"Oh my goodness, Mademoiselle, please forgive me. Are you all right?"

Madeleine caught her breath and looked up at the man who had shown a persistent interest in her for months.

During most of September and all of October, the Comte de Chamfort, one of the aristocrats who hung around the ballet watching classes and observing rehearsals, had been pressuring Madeleine to accept an invitation to join him for a glass of wine or Champagne, to have supper with him after a performance, to allow him to buy her gifts.

Each time, she had said, Non, merci. But word got around, and Madame took her aside one morning before class.

"What is wrong with you?" Madame asked angrily. "You cannot treat Monsieur le Comte in this fashion. He is too important to the ballet."

Her face screwed up in confusion, Madeleine said, "What do you mean?"

"How do you think we stay afloat? Money does not grow on trees, my dear. We are always on the brink of collapse because the government doesn't supply us with sufficient funds. Le Comte de Chamfort and the others you see in the rehearsal hall keep the company going with their donations. Do you think they do it out of pure love for the ballet?" She snorted. "Of course not! They expect to get something in return for the thousands of francs they give us."

"I'm sorry, but I still don't understand," Madeleine had said.

"Oh, mon Dieu, what am I to do with you? Listen to me carefully, Madeleine. This is how the world works. Those good-looking, wealthy young men support us by donating the money we need. In exchange, they select a dancer who will be their...eh...companion until such time that they choose someone else. Le Comte de Chamfort will advance your career. In exchange for time spent with him, you can ask him to request that the ballet master move you to a soloist position, and later to a principal role. With the Comte de Chamfort as your champion, you will attain these achievements years faster than if you tried to do it on your own. Ask Gigi or Arielle if you need to know more. They seem happy with their arrangements.

"Now, the next time the count invites you for a glass of Champagne, you will say yes. Or I'm afraid your days at the Opéra Garnier may be numbered. Monsieur Ballerat cannot afford to indulge a young girl's whims."

Madeleine may have been naive about the way things were done in this great capital city of Paris, but she wasn't stupid. She understood fully well what Madame meant when she said Madeleine would be the count's "companion." She struggled with this new and shocking information. One day, she decided it would be worth it. The next, she was incensed that she was being forced to make this choice. Madeleine had come to Paris to be free from her father's demands and the life he had laid out for her. Free from Bernard, whom she did not love and did not want to marry. Free to make her own way in the world, free to dance. How could it be that in order to pursue her dancing dream, she would have to place herself under the Comte de Chamfort's control? It was so unfair!

For weeks, she had avoided making the decision, coming up with one smiling excuse after another, trying to keep the count at arm's length, not saying yes, but not exactly refusing his invitations either. Just putting him off.

Now it seemed the time had come. It seemed she was not in control of anything that mattered.

"Oh, M. le Comte, je suis désolée! I'm so very sorry! I wasn't looking where I was going."

Madeleine's entire body was shaking from her anger at the crushing announcement from le maître *and from the collision. My God! Of all people, she had to crash into le Comte de Chamfort.*

"It is nothing, my dear. But I see you are upset. May I invite you to lunch, and you can tell me all about it? If I'm not mistaken, you have no rehearsal this afternoon, and there is no performance tonight. No reason not to enjoy a little lunch." He smiled, and his beautiful face lit up. "You see, I do realize how you dancers eat. Or I should say how you don't eat."

In that brief instant, Madeleine decided Fate had intervened and was telling her that the way to soloist and, eventually, prima ballerina was through this man.

"You are most kind, Monsieur le Comte. Thank you. Yes, that would be lovely."

Chapter Nineteen

Steven and Olivia faced their first interviewee, a young dancer named Claudine Verlaine. In fact, she was so young that Madame insisted on being present during the questioning.

"She's just a child," the chaperone said. "Barely fourteen."

Olivia was stunned. She must be exceptionally good to dance at Opéra Garnier Ballet.

Steven began, "Now, Claudine, you're not in any trouble. Do you understand?"

"*Oui, Monsieur.*" It came out hesitantly, but she looked them in the eye. "Madame said it is about poor Madeleine?"

"Yes, we're working with the French police, looking into her death. Now, tell me how well you knew Madeleine Gervaise."

"Like I know all the dancers. We spend all of our time together. Every morning, every afternoon, and every night."

"Did Madeleine talk about personal things, like a boyfriend?"

"Most of us talk about everything in our lives. We have become each other's family, sisters, as well as friends. We're so far from home, you see."

"Did you ever hear her refer to a fiancé from home?"

"I heard her talking about him last summer. She said a man who thought he was her fiancé was coming to Paris to see her, and she would have to set him straight."

"What did she mean by that?"

"She didn't consider him her fiancé. She didn't want a boyfriend. She was only interested in dancing. Madeleine was worried because he was a man who didn't like taking no for an answer."

Olivia took this moment to bring up the aristocrats.

"Careful how you go, Mademoiselle. Fourteen is still a tender age. Even in France," said Madame.

Olivia nodded. "Claudine, do you know the rich men who are patrons of the ballet? They sometimes watch your rehearsals or attend the class, sitting off to the side."

Claudine shivered. If she hadn't been concentrating on the dancer's every move, Olivia might have missed it. Was it chilly in here for someone wearing a light-weight, sleeveless dress? Or did it signal something else?

"I know who you mean," she whispered.

"Do you know why they come here during the day?"

"I think they give money to the Garnier. I heard the Duc de Rochechouart talking with the director once. Monsieur Gailhard said the duke was generous with his donations. Maybe it allows them to watch rehearsals." Her brows lifted, her eyes opened wider, and she smiled, giving the impression that she wanted to be helpful.

"Do you know if any of the patrons have a special friendship with any of the dancers?" Olivia knew she was on shaky ground here. She had no idea how worldly this young woman was. In order to get this far at such a young age, she must be tough, but she could still be innocent of the ways of the world. And of course, Madame was sitting there scrutinizing every question they asked and each word Claudine spoke.

"Oh, yes." Claudine smiled. "The Marquis de Polignac is very fond of Gigi Pantier. We always hear him shouting *Brava* after a performance when she is a soloist."

"Does she usually dance that important role?"

"No, maybe two or three times. She was very excited." Claudine sighed. "I want to be a soloist someday."

Olivia smiled. "I'm sure you will. Do you know if Gigi and the *marquis* spend time together outside the Opéra Garnier? Perhaps he takes her to supper after the show?"

Claudine shrugged. "I don't know. After a performance, I am always too tired to pay attention. I go home to eat and sleep."

"Who do you live with?" Steven asked.

"She stays in the dormitory with the other young dancers," Madame replied, arms crossed across her chest, eyes narrowed.

"Have you ever met any of the patrons, Claudine?" Olivia pushed on.

Claudine's face lit up. "Oh, yes! Every fall before the season starts—I mean, the ballet season—there's a special dinner for all the dancers. Monsieur Gailhard invites the people who attend every premiere and who are well-known to the Garnier. And the patrons you're asking about, they always come. Everyone celebrates the new season with us. I met the Marquis de Polignac and the Comte de Beauharnais last autumn at the dinner. They are both very nice." She looked down and blushed, then murmured, "Handsome too."

"Did you ever see Madeleine with any of the patrons?" Olivia asked, bracing herself for another interruption from Madame.

"She spent a lot of time talking with the Comte de Chamfort. And I think she told me he bought her a pair of leather boots last winter. Hers were falling apart."

"Do you know if she spent time with him outside the Opéra?" Olivia asked.

Claudine hesitated and looked away, then wiggled in her chair to find a different position. "Umm…maybe."

"Why did Madeleine leave the Opéra Garnier Ballet, Claudine?"

Steven said.

"That's it. That's enough questions. Claudine knows nothing about Madeleine's private thoughts. Madeleine was some ten years her senior. Why would she confide in a child?"

And with that, Madame stood, pulled Claudine out of the chair and across the room. The door slammed shut behind them.

"It looks like we hit a nerve," Olivia said.

"I'd say so. It would appear Madame wants to keep the ballet's secrets."

"Or maybe, she didn't want Claudine to wonder about what having a patron *really* means."

"Yeah, could be. Claudine seemed comfortable with the Marquis de Polignac and the Comte de Beauharnais. She might even have a crush on one of them."

"It was when we mentioned the Comte de Chamfort that Claudine was uncomfortable. She knows something."

"Maybe we can get her alone sometime. And I'm adding Madame to our list, too. She definitely knows something."

"Who's next, Steven?"

"I want to talk with Gigi Pantier. We'll see if she's willing to tell us about her relationship with the Marquis de Polignac."

* * *

Etienne didn't have to wait long for Pierre Gailhard to return. As he dropped onto the wooden visitor's chair, Etienne thanked Gailhard again for his cooperation in both investigations.

"This list of the dancers employed now…." Etienne held up the sheaf of papers. "Is there anyone who was here at the beginning of December that's not on the list, M. le Directeur?"

"Only the two girls that you know about. Madeleine Gervaise left

158

in late October. And Marielle DuPin was fired two weeks ago for intentionally injuring a dancer. Everyone else is on the list."

"*Bon.* I need two more things. Is there a way to find out if any of the girls come from a wealthy family?"

"Absolutely. Most of our dancers cannot afford to pay for the ballet school. We offer a scholarship to those who meet our high standards. It's rigorous, I can tell you."

Suspecting the answer, Etienne asked nevertheless, "How do you fund the scholarships? Especially when so many of your dancers benefit from one."

"We're lucky to have several wealthy patrons who are quite generous. I am most grateful to those men. Actually, I think you encountered the Comte de Beauharnais leaving when you arrived."

"Yes, I thought that was him."

"The count is devoted to the ballet."

"I see. Returning to my question…who, if any of the dancers, is not receiving a scholarship right now?"

"Actually, I remember that the family of the girl who was fired, Marielle DuPin, paid for her. And, let me see…." The director of the Garnier squinted and looked off into the distance, gently pulling his mustache while he considered Etienne's question. "Yes. Yes. But let me double-check." He opened a drawer and pulled out a folder thick with papers, tied with a worn burgundy ribbon. "I have information here on each of our dancers." He leaned over and paged through the dossier until he found what he was looking for. "Here we are. Only one other girl's family pays her fees. Claudine Verlaine."

Etienne made a note that Marielle and a girl called Claudine probably had the money to purchase the chocolates. It sounded like Marielle had a motive. He'd have to question Claudine to learn whether she did as well.

"Thank you, I appreciate that. Finally, can you tell me how much money each dancer earns?"

Etienne knew immediately by the figures conveyed—even the greater amounts the more experienced ballerinas took in—that none of the dancers could afford the expensive chocolates. So, it was down to a rich *Papa* or a patron.

* * *

After Gigi Pantier made herself comfortable across from Steven and Olivia, and Steven had explained why they were there, he said, "We understand the Marquis de Polignac is a special friend of yours, Mademoiselle."

The difference in age between Claudine Verlaine and this young woman—she looked to be in her early twenties—made all the difference in the poise and self-confidence Gigi Pantier exhibited. She sat ramrod-straight, her hands in her lap, and smiled. "Yes, that's true."

"Can you tell us how you met?"

"*Le marquis* started watching the classes and rehearsals about two years ago. He was friendly with the other gentlemen who observe. One day, after a rehearsal—I was dancing in the second row in the *corps de ballet* at that time—he called me over. I had heard from one of the older dancers that if any of the patrons wished to speak with us, we must not insult them by refusing. They give a lot of money to the Garnier. The ballet always needs money." She rolled her eyes. "So, I went to him. He asked my name and how long I had been dancing. He told me he thought I was very good, and he didn't understand why I was not a soloist. He asked if I wanted to dance a solo part. Of course, I said yes. He asked if he could take me to supper." Again that Gallic shrug. "It is always helpful to have rich friends, *non*? I liked the way he looked, and he was very polite, so I said yes. We've become close friends."

Steven gave Olivia a nearly imperceptible glance. She asked, "I hope you'll forgive me for being blunt, Mademoiselle, but, before I ask my question, I want to remind you we're investigating the death of Madeleine Gervaise—"

"You wish to know what I'm expected to do for the chance to dance a more prominent role, for the suppers and *Champagne*, and for the exquisite dresses he gives me?"

Olivia nodded.

"Nothing at first, Mademoiselle. Benoît made it clear he was not like the others. He was a patient man, and he could wait…a reasonable amount of time. I know what it looks like from the outside, but I don't care. I came to Paris with nothing. All I had was a passion and the determination to dance. My family is not well-off. So I give my body to him once in a while. He doesn't take my soul. And for that, I have become a soloist and wear beautiful clothes. Some day I will be too old to dance. Or I will meet a nice man and fall in love and marry him. This is only for now. And it is worth it to me."

"Thank you for your honesty, Mademoiselle," Steven said.

"I only have one more question about your friendship with the Marquis de Polignac, Gigi," Olivia said. "Have you noticed a difference in the relationship over the past two years? Has the *marquis* changed in the way he treats you? Has he become more demanding? Less patient, less understanding?"

Her dark brows met in the middle. "It's very interesting that you ask me that. Yes. He's been expecting me to spend more and more time with him. We've argued about it." She stopped and looked off into the distance, as if debating whether to say what was on her mind. A subtle nod of her head indicated she had made up her mind. "I will also tell you Arielle has been complaining that the Duc de Rochechouart has been more persistent over the past few months. I don't know why they have changed."

"Can you make a guess?" Steven asked.

"Perhaps we are no longer a novelty and it takes more to satisfy them. Perhaps they are drunk with their power over us. Perhaps they are just bored with life." She gave that ubiquitous Gallic shrug.

"Those are excellent ideas. You're very perceptive, Mademoiselle. Now, turning to Madeleine Gervaise, we understand there was a relationship of some type between her and the Comte de Chamfort. Perhaps a friendship similar to yours with the *marquis*?"

"That one! I would not walk across the street to say hello. I do not trust him. But I must tell you, I know nothing for certain. Nothing, you understand? Madeleine never confided in me. She questioned me once about my relationship with the *marquis*, but she never told me why she wanted to know, and I didn't ask. The only thing I *can* say is that I heard them arguing more than once. I believe he wanted her company more often than she wanted his. That is all I can tell you."

By noon, Steven and Olivia had spoken with Amélie, Marie-Dominique, Eliane, Arielle, Vivienne, Juliette, Simone, and Liliane. They learned nothing more of interest or value.

"Let's have one more go at Yvette before we quit here," Steven said to Olivia. "We'll be able to find a restaurant open for lunch, even if we get there a little late."

Yvette Caron entered the room, already on edge. Apparently, the girls had been sharing their interview experiences when they returned to the rehearsal room.

"Please sit down, Mademoiselle." Steven did not smile at her. "We would like to follow up on a couple of things from our talk the other day."

Following Steven's lead, Olivia asked, "Yvette, what was Madeleine's relationship with the Comte de Chamfort?"

Her fists clenched in her lap, the dancer squeezed her eyes shut and said nothing for what felt like a long period of time. Finally, she opened them and stared at Olivia, then at Steven. "Please don't ask me that. These are powerful people. I need this job. Please." Her brow puckered, the corners of her mouth tipped down. "Please," she whispered.

"We can protect you, Yvette. No one—*no one*—will ever know we learned about it from you. Someone has already spoken of the relationship, so all you would be doing is filling in some of the blank spaces. Confirming what we already know."

Olivia leaned forward, smiled, and said a little more gently this time, "We need to know everything, Yvette. Your friend's death is highly suspicious. If the count had nothing to do with it, nothing will happen to him. I promise you, we will be discreet. Trust me. We know how to do this."

Yvette drew her lips between her teeth. Her hands worried on the skirt of her dress, moving back and forth as if she were washing them. "You *swear* no one will know? You *promise*?"

"Yes," Steven said, and Olivia nodded.

"He summoned her a few months after she joined the company."

"How does that usually work?" Olivia asked. "Do the men motion to the girl they're interested in, or do they tell someone that they want to speak to her?"

Yvette sat up abruptly. "You know about the others?"

"Yes, we know about the others."

"Oh! Well, it depends. If the man can get the dancer's attention, he will motion her to approach him. If not, he'll call to the ballet master or whoever is working with us at the moment. He'll say he'd like to talk with whoever he has chosen."

"Then what happens?" Steven asked. "How does that first conversation go?"

"Usually the man says something like he thinks we're a wonderful dancer and would we like to advance in the company. If we dance with the *corps de ballet*, he asks if we would like to be a soloist. If we dance solos, would we like to do that more frequently? Or do we dream of being the principal?"

"And in exchange for helping to advance your career…?" Olivia asked.

"It's gradual. It starts with little things. Perhaps a refreshing glass of wine after rehearsal. Or a light supper after a performance. Sometimes the first offer is of clothes or shoes. It's easy for us to say yes to a pair of leather boots or shoes. Then, eventually—" Yvette stopped as her face became beet red and she looked away.

"It becomes a physical relationship, *n'est-ce pas?*" Olivia said gently. The dancer nodded.

"And with Madeleine, how did it progress, Yvette?" asked Steven.

"She came to Paris to be free to dance. Her father was strict, always telling her what to do. When she was younger, he allowed her to take dance lessons, but after a while, he made her quit. He said dancing was frivolous and told her what her life was going to be. He said she had no choice, that she would do what all the other girls in their town did. When she was seventeen, he arranged with the family of a local boy for him to be engaged to Madeleine. She did not want any of that. She did not want the boy, and she did not want to be married. She told me she was like a caged bird at home. When she arrived in Paris, she felt like she could breathe for the first time in her life. She loved her father. She knew he was trying to do his best for her, but she needed to dance."

"It must have been very difficult for her," Olivia said. "So, Yvette, coming back to the arrangements here at the Opéra Garnier…."

"Nobody tells you how it works when you join the company. Madeleine didn't understand that she would have to spend time with the Comte de Chamfort in exchange for the things he bought her and the promotions he would arrange. She resisted at first; she refused his company. But the count is not a man to accept no for an answer. Someone must have explained it to her. One day, Madeleine went to lunch with him. Just like that!" Yvette looked straight at them, eyes wide in amazement. "I don't know why she changed her mind. But the Comte de Chamfort is also a possessive man. He is jealous. Over the past year, he's insisted on more of her time. They began to argue. He wanted more of her, and she wanted to give him less. But she couldn't break free. She was trapped. The ballet master yelled at her. And Madame told her this was the system, and Madeleine was too far in debt to the count to refuse." Yvette hung her head, then looked up and into their eyes. "That's why she left. She had to get away from the Comte de Chamfort. She became frightened he might hurt her."

"You've been very brave, Yvette," Olivia said. "We will never mention your name. We'll be careful how we proceed."

After the door closed behind Yvette, Steven and Olivia let out their breath.

"Wow!" she said.

Steven raised his brows. "It's pretty much what we expected. Although, I'm surprised the Comte de Chamfort was so obvious in trying to control Madeleine. I suppose each of the men approaches the situation differently."

"Remember, Gigi said the Marquis de Polignac demanded nothing beyond the pleasure of her company at first. He was happy with the time she wanted to spend with him during the early days of their relationship. It's only been recently things have changed. I get the impression these two aristocrats—Chamfort and Polignac—are quite different in how they behave and approach the dancers."

Steven nodded. "Let's get Etienne and discuss everything over lunch."

Steven and Olivia didn't have long to wait. The door to Etienne's room opened, and a dancer hurried out. She brushed by them and disappeared deep into the interior of the opera house. They entered the small room.

"We've finished here, Etienne. Would you like to take a break and have lunch with us?" Steven leaned across the table the French detective was using and whispered, "We found out about the relationship between Madeleine and the Comte de Chamfort!"

"Oh! Did you? *Formidable!*"

"Yes, we want to tell you everything we learned and hear how you made out. After lunch, we're going to the Moulin Rouge. I think that'll give us better insight into Madeleine's final days. Nini was very forthcoming. So were Brigitte and Jojo. Maybe the other Moulin Rouge dancers will be open with us as well. I especially want to talk with Marielle DuPin, the girl who tripped another dancer. It sounds like she's got the personality to harm her rivals."

"Good idea, *mon ami.* I know a little place not far from here." He told Gailhard's assistant he would be back in a couple of hours and that the room Steven and Olivia were using was no longer needed today.

* * *

The bistro was a long, dark, and narrow cavern and looked like it had been there since the *Révolution.* A man Steven decided must be the owner hurried to welcome them, kissing Etienne's cheeks and giving him a big hug. Etienne introduced Steven and Olivia as "a detective and his assistant from New York."

"Ah! My new American friends. Luigi Peppino, at your service." He pumped Steven's hand and kissed Olivia's. "Come sit at our best table, and I will bring you the most scrumptious items on our menu. Good Italian home cooking. You will see."

Trattoria di Napoli reminded Olivia of *Giovanni's,* where she spent many enjoyable evenings with Liz and Sophie. Red-and-white checked cloths covered the small tables scattered throughout. Despite the time of day, candles stuck in Chianti bottles dripped and sputtered, and some of the gas lights scattered at intervals were lit. Oil paintings of various sizes hanging throughout the eatery depicted the town of Naples, the coastline along the Tyrrhenian Sea, nearby Mount Vesuvius, and the legendary Isle of Capri. Olivia smiled at the memory of a boat trip she once took into the Blue Grotto caves, where the unique neon blue color of the sea was still vivid in her mind.

"I'm eager to see what Luigi chooses for us," she said. "I love Italian food."

A waiter hurried over with a carafe of mineral water, a bottle of red wine, and a basket of fresh bread. He'd barely turned to leave the table when a second waiter brought a platter of *antipasti*, a variety of meats, cheeses, and bruschetta with assorted toppings. Hungry after the busy morning, they each chose several items.

Steven took a bite of a bruschetta topped with tomatoes and basil and said, "Mmm, this is delicious."

"That's the same one I chose." Olivia took a bite. "Ooh, it is! I wonder if your friend will tell me how to make this, Etienne."

"I'll ask. No doubt it's an old family recipe." He chuckled. "Everything's an old family recipe here. He'll be pleased and proud by the compliment."

As they ate their way through the exquisite meal—the antipasti, spaghetti with a light Mediterranean tomato sauce, then a mouthwatering veal dish—the conversation turned to the two murder cases.

Steven told Etienne what Gigi revealed about her relationship with the Marquis de Polignac, and what Yvette finally confessed about the relationship between Madeleine and the Comte de Chamfort. He stressed that the count's behavior and Madeleine's fear of being physically harmed had caused her to abandon her beloved ballet career and leave the Opéra Garnier.

"Gigi said the Duc de Rochechouart had also become more demanding of Arielle. It seems like the aristos are increasing their pressure on the dancers. We asked her why she thought that might be," Olivia said, and told the Frenchman Gigi's idea of the aristocrats exercising their power over the dancers.

"Etienne, I wonder if you weren't far off the mark earlier when you spoke of someone wielding their power over the girls with the boxes of poisoned chocolates," Steven said. "Perhaps our two cases *are* connected. Maybe it's all about power."

"I want to know more about the other name on our list, the Comte de Beauharnais. The director told me Beauharnais—the man who was leaving the office when we arrived—is devoted to the ballet."

"So far, we haven't heard of a dancer connected to him," Steven said. "Maybe he isn't the private patron of anyone."

"If he has daughters, the arrangements at the ballet might be repulsive to him," Olivia added.

"Anything is possible," said Etienne. "But if he's disgusted by the arrangements, how can he stand by and let it happen?"

"Maybe he wants to keep an eye on things," Olivia said.

"Coming back to the behavior of the other three aristos," Etienne continued, "It looks like we might have a pattern here—enticement, then expectations and demands building to more expectations and more demands."

"And what happens when those demands aren't met?" Olivia asked rhetorically.

"Exactly," said Steven. "What did you learn about the chocolates, Etienne?"

"If we're looking at one of the dancers as the perpetrator, most of the girls receive a scholarship and wouldn't have had enough money to buy the *chocolats*. The exceptions are Marielle DuPin and Claudine

Verlaine. I couldn't see a motive for Claudine Verlaine, and she's so young. I don't see her conceiving a plot to poison her fellow dancers as a means to further her career. We already know about Mademoiselle DuPin's penchant for hurting someone she considers a rival. She's lucky the ballerina that she tripped didn't break a leg. She's my number one choice if the poisoner was a dancer. Based on what you just said, I'll speak with Gigi Pantier and Arielle Lambert again. Since both have relationships with the aristocrats, they could have asked for money at any time. They might have told the men they wanted to buy a new hat or gloves or anything, for that matter. Then, instead they purchased the chocolates.

"Now," Etienne continued. "If we're looking for someone outside the company of ballerinas, I haven't learned enough yet. Every time I asked someone to speculate and guess what might have been the reason such a thing happened, no one seemed to have any idea. None of the dancers I spoke with knew how the candy arrived in the dressing room. No one saw anyone walking through the corridors carrying two boxes of *chocolats*. Remember, the A la Mère de Famille packages are unmistakable and easily recognized. The orange and gold design on the boxes stands out like a beacon. No one could miss them. None of the girls opened the dressing room door to accept a gift from a deliveryman. Not one dancer offered even the tiniest bit of information. That in itself is suspicious.

"I spoke with the man who sits near the back entrance where we came in. He doesn't remember accepting delivery of the chocolates either. It makes me think someone inside the Opéra Garnier must have smuggled them in somehow."

"I agree with your thinking." Steven paused, then said, "Etienne, the aristocrats—our four manipulators—would all wear a cloak to a performance, wouldn't they?"

Etienne stopped his veal-filled fork midway from his plate to his partially opened mouth. "You, my friend, are brilliant! Yes, all four of them arrive at the ballet in their luxurious carriages, driven by loyal family servants in fine livery. These coachmen are trusted servants who drop off their charges wherever they are told and who will keep their mouths shut if anything unusual or even illegal occurs. The four men are always dressed in their finest silk top hats and cloaks. And the cloaks are easily big enough to conceal two boxes of chocolates."

Chapter Twenty

While Steven, Olivia, and Etienne were enjoying an Italian feast, Evangéline was waking up. She regained consciousness slowly. She was disoriented, light-headed, and unable to focus on her surroundings. She couldn't remember what had happened. Her head was pounding, like it had been rent in two. She wondered if she had been hit with something. She carefully touched a couple of spots, then brought her fingers in front of her face, but saw no blood. She tried to sit up but was so dizzy she fell back on the filthy mattress. Evangéline closed her eyes and took several slow, deep breaths, sending clean air through her body. She could feel the panic creeping in and knew she needed to keep it at bay. After a few minutes, she opened her eyes again. Thank God her vision was clearing!

She eased herself up into a sitting position. She could see clearly now and was both sickened and horrified by what she saw. Desperate to get off the soiled and repulsive thing she'd been lying on, Evangéline stood and did the best she could to brush herself off. She realized she was only moments away from vomiting and forced herself to stand still and take a few more slow, even breaths. She couldn't let herself make this disgusting hovel any worse. A scuttling along the opposite wall sent shivers down her spine. Naturally, there would be rats.

The room was tiny, more like a cupboard than a room, and had two narrow windows high near the ceiling. Outside one window, she saw the top part of a planter and thought it seemed to be sitting on the ground. She must be below street-level. She observed several rough wooden shelves attached to one wall, and a couple of empty canning jars lingered on the middle shelf. The floor appeared to be packed earth. The only piece of furniture was this horrible cot she'd been lying on. Evangéline wondered if she was in a fruit cellar. The place smelled musty, but not moldy. Why was she here? And where exactly was she? And who were those men? Because now she clearly remembered two men.

Standing in the middle of the shadowy room, Evangéline remembered closing the street door on the courtyard after leaving her apartment, then being enveloped by the fog, then the horses and carriage looming in front of her like some sort of mystical creature. She remembered the rough hands pulling her off the sidewalk and dragging her into the coach. She recalled the sickeningly sweet smell, then passing out. Chloroform! They had drugged her. But who had done this? And why? It must have to do with Steven's investigation. Well, that was a conversation they'd have later.

She hadn't gotten a good look at the driver, but a mental picture of her kidnapper came into focus. Thank goodness for her artist's observations. She knew she'd be able to sketch him as soon as she got out of here.

Evangéline heard the rattle of a padlock, and her head snapped toward the heavy wooden door. The creaking door was slowly opening.

Her heart beat faster. Her breath came in heaving gulps. She took a step back, wondering what she could do to defend herself. There was nothing to grab onto, nothing she could hit him with. Then she remembered the apartment key was in her drawstring bag.

Evangéline secured the bag on her wrist and clutched the heavy iron key between her fingers. She wouldn't go down without a fight. She'd claw his eyes out if she had to.

The door opened, and two men entered. Both wore black masks completely covering their faces.

"So, you're awake," said the taller one.

"Good, save us from carrying you out like we carried you in," said the husky one.

"Cooperate and we'll drop you off on the *butte*. Fight us and we'll knock you out again," continued the tall one. "And maybe do some damage to that pretty face of yours."

"You don't need to drop me off. I can walk home."

"But we don't want you to identify this place, do we?" sneered the husky man. "We're going to blindfold you. We'll put you in the carriage and drop you off like civilized people. Cooperate and you won't get hurt."

Loath as she was to let them touch her again, Evangéline hid her hand behind her bag so they wouldn't see the weaponized key and stood still as one of her abductors tied a (*hopefully clean*) cloth over her eyes. They led her up a short staircase, outside, and into the carriage.

This time, even though she couldn't see, Evangéline was awake and alert and was able to note the journey the coach took. She memorized a sharp left turn, a straight flat stretch of two or three blocks, then two right turns. She felt the subtle sensation of her body pressing more firmly against the back of the seat and knew the horses were pulling them up a hill. After less than ten minutes, the carriage swung around a corner and continued straight for what seemed like a long block.

The man seated next to her put his face up close to hers. She smelled bad breath mixed with garlic, cheap wine, and strong cigarettes. He snarled, "Tell those interfering American friends of yours to stop sticking their noses into things that don't concern them and lay off. Tell them to mind their own business and go home. This is your only warning. Next time, we won't be so nice. Remember, we can get you any time we want. We know where you live. We know where you go every day."

There was a knocking on the carriage wall. He reached across her, opened the door, and, using both hands, shoved her out of the coach as it leaned into a curve in the road.

Still blindfolded, Evangéline was thrust into an unknown void. Arms swinging wildly, she tried to grab onto something. As her body twisted and spun, she attempted to get her feet on the ground, but her skirts had wrapped her legs in a tight cocoon. After what seemed like minutes, but was only seconds, Evangéline struck a heavy iron post supporting a handrail. Her left side hit hard, knocking the wind out of her. She grabbed the blindfold, tore it off, and threw it to the ground. She found herself looking down from the top step of one of the tallest staircases in Montmartre. Thank God for that post! If it hadn't been there, she would have tumbled down a steep stairway that stretched more than a block below. Still leaning against the handrail post, although hovering on the edge of the top step, she felt her heartbeat slow and her breathing return to normal. She carefully scooted back, easing herself away from the precipice.

Evangéline reached up, grabbed onto the looped end of the railing, and tried to pull herself into a standing position. She staggered, still dizzy from the spin her body had gone into. She gripped the wrought-iron bar tighter, teetered on the top of the soaring incline, then regained her balance.

Naturally, by the time she could stand up, the carriage was long gone.

Evangéline straightened and brushed herself off. Her soiled cloak looked as though she'd been rolling around in the dirt, which, she silently conceded, she had been. Her hair had come out of the chignon she had so carefully designed this morning. What a fright she must look. Damn kidnappers!

Remembering that filthy cot, she promised herself she would throw this cloak out and buy herself a new one. The thought of ever wearing it again made her feel sick.

Evangéline moved away from the staircase to a safe spot on the sidewalk, pulled her sketch pad and a pencil from her bag, and quickly drew everything she could recall about the two horses, the coach, the driver, and especially the man who had been inside the carriage with her, her abductor. At least that was something she could give to Detective Berthot.

She looked around and spied a street sign—white lettering on the bright blue porcelain background—displayed on the edge of the building at the corner. She had lived in Montmartre for several years now and knew the village well. She knew exactly where she was. The massive construction project for the new church was to her right. All of Paris stretched out below and beyond the hill to her left. She was on rue du Cardinal duBois. Around the bend and down the street sat the Place du Tertre. Surely one of her artist friends would be there today and could help her.

When Evangéline arrived at the Place du Tertre, she realized she had no idea what time it was. She only knew she had set out early this morning to get a carriage to take her into town for the meeting with her new dealer. She needed to get word to Paul Durand-Ruel and let him know why she had never arrived this morning. She surveyed the artists and painters working at their easels and on sketch pads and saw no one she knew. Then, on the opposite side of the square, she spied a familiar figure walking in her direction. Husky, dark blond, bearded. Her friend Alfred Sisley carried his easel folded under one arm and a wooden paint box holding his supplies in the other hand. She hurried to him.

"Alfred," she whispered, hand on her chest, panting, trying to catch her breath, "I'm so glad to see you. I need to talk to someone. I'll buy you a glass of wine."

Taking in her nervous and disheveled state, and noticing that she was breathing hard, Sisley frowned. He shifted his belongings, grabbed her arm, and led her to a nearby café. "Of course, my dear Evangéline. Whatever has happened?"

They chose a table in the darkest corner of the tiny café. Evangéline ordered a carafe of *rouge*.

"You are not going to believe what just happened to me," she exclaimed, then told him of her harrowing experience.

Sisley's jaw dropped, and his eyes widened. He reached out and covered her hand with his. "Evangéline, I don't know what to say. That's monstrous. But why? Why would a complete stranger abduct you, then let you go later? You say he didn't try to take your purse or interfere with you. And thank God for that!"

"Do you remember meeting the Americans who were with me at the Lumière brothers' showing the other night? They're detectives from New York. Henri hired them to investigate Madeleine Gervaise's murder."

"*Sacré*! And these miscreants threatened you to scare them off?" Sisley gulped his wine. "And to think I was wandering around looking for something new to paint while you were undergoing that unspeakable ordeal. How can I help you?"

"I need to get word to Paul." Evangéline told him about her missed meeting. "If that messenger we sometimes use is on the square today, I can send word with him."

"I'll find him for you. Stay here. I'll be right back."

His chair scraped across the rough floor, and Alfred Sisley disappeared out the front door. Evangéline leaned back in her seat and thought about what she wanted to do. A bath. First, she needed a long, hot bath to wash the grime and disgust off her. Then she would go out and shop for supper. Cooking always made her happy and drove everything disagreeable out of her mind. After that, she did not want to leave her apartment for at least one whole day. She needed the comfort of her home to get rid of the horrible feelings that still clung to her skin.

Tonight, she would tell Steven and Olivia everything, and they would decide what to do next.

Chapter Twenty-One

Etienne was beginning to think the affair of the poisoned chocolates had nothing to do with the ballerinas at the Opéra Garnier. Except, of course, as victims. Nevertheless, when he returned after lunch, he went through the motions. By four o'clock, he had finished questioning the remaining dancers. Amélie, Eliane, Arielle, Marie-Dominique, Vivienne, Juliette, and Simone told him nothing he didn't already know. *Time for the staff*, he thought.

He found Monsieur Ballerat, the ballet master, and Monsieur Petipa, the choreographer, in the rehearsal hall working out a problem with the pianist.

"Excuse me, gentlemen." He introduced himself and explained why he was there. "Did any of you witness someone deliver two boxes of A la Mère de Famille chocolates on the night you debuted *Swan Lake*? It was the same night several dancers became sick and MiNou Bordeaux died."

All three men explained they were on the stage, in the wings, or, in the case of the pianist, in the pit from about thirty minutes before the show to some twenty minutes after the final curtain.

This didn't surprise Berthot. He could think of no reason why the ballet master or the choreographer would sabotage their own company, and he couldn't come up with anything related to the pianist that made any sense. He thanked them and left.

For the next two hours, Detective Etienne Berthot prowled the Opéra Garnier, talking with carpenters, electricians, and general maintenance employees. He spoke with the guards at all the entrances and the workers in the ticket booths. He procured a list of names and addresses of the ushers from Monsieur Gailhard, the director. This he would pass on to one of his men to be investigated tomorrow.

Time to get back to the office, Etienne thought. Sometimes, when he set aside a problem and concentrated on something else, the answer, or at least a path forward, would present itself.

* * *

Outside the *Trattoria di Napoli*, Steven and Olivia climbed into the waiting carriage, and Henri's driver brought them to the Moulin Rouge.

The thin, white-haired man they'd seen three days ago opened the door in response to Steven's pounding. Today, he was dressed in dusty, baggy work clothes.

"*Bonjour*, Marcel. Do you remember us? We came here on Saturday with Detective Berthot."

A strong-smelling cigarette hanging out of the side of his mouth, Marcel stuck out his hand to shake Steven's as he pulled back the door to let them in. "*Oui, les Américains*. Nini is on stage working with some dancers on a new number. I'll take you."

"Thank you, but if you have a minute, I'd like to ask you a couple of questions first."

"Sure." He blew a cloud of smoke up and over Steven's shoulder. The small entry reeked.

"Is there a particular entrance the dancers use when they arrive and leave the cabaret?"

"Yes, Monsieur Zidler wants them to use the back door. You have to go down the alley over there to the right." He pointed to a spot a few steps from where they stood. "It's narrow, and it's easy to miss if you're not looking for it. When you get to the back, you go through a gap between the two buildings, and you're in the courtyard behind the Moulin."

"Do you leave that back door unlocked, or does someone let them in?"

"I let them in. I always know ahead of time when people are due to arrive for a rehearsal or a show. I've got a list of all the performers—the dancers, the acrobats, the clowns—whoever it is. I sit inside the door and check 'em off my list when they get here and when they leave for the night. Everybody has to sign in and sign out."

"Marcel, do you still have the list for last Sunday night?" Steven shot Olivia an expectant look, brows raised, eyes bright.

She held up crossed fingers.

"Sure, come to my office and I'll show you. Then I'll take you to Nini."

"Office" was using the term broadly. It was no more than a closet-sized cubicle, but he did have a small desk and chair, and a calendar on the wall. He took a screwdriver, inserted it in a tiny opening at the bottom of a wall-mounted lamp, and turned it. He grabbed a box of matches, lit one, and placed it near a small opening. The gas light sprang to life.

Marcel opened the top drawer of his desk and pulled out a cheap notebook. Starting at the end, he flipped back several pages. "Here you go. Monsieur Zidler wants me to keep my notebooks for a year, then when he says it's okay, I throw them out. Every week, he checks to see who showed up late for work and which girls stayed after the show. That's when they'd likely be talking with the customers. Maybe getting the men to buy them a drink or two. That's good for business, you know."

Olivia looked over Steven's shoulder, and they read:

Sunday, December 22, 1895.
Rehearsal: None.
Show:
Brigitte Allard arr. 18:30 dep. 1:30
Jojo Moreau arr. 18:30 dep. 1:30
Madeleine Gervaise arr. 18:40 dep. 3:45
Marielle DuPin arr. 18:45 dep. 3:48

In the space to the left of each name was that person's signature, confirming their arrival time. Near or overlapping the departure time were the employee's initials. There were over two dozen names representing people Steven and Olivia hadn't spoken to yet, some they hadn't even heard of. They noticed that all the performers arrived between six-thirty and seven in the evening and left at some time after one in the morning. They paid special attention to the fact that Marielle had departed only minutes after Madeleine on the night Madeleine was killed.

"What time does the show start, Marcel?" Olivia asked.

"The first one is at twenty-one hours. And the second performance starts at twenty-three-thirty." Olivia mentally converted the times to nine p.m. and eleven-thirty p.m. "Each show lasts two hours. Everyone gets a half-hour break between shows."

"Marcel, can you tell me if there are any men who came to the club who paid special attention to Madeleine Gervaise?"

"I'm never in the cabaret when there's a show going on, Detective. Monsieur Zidler wants me guarding the back entrance and keeping track of his employees' comings and goings. Nini can tell you about the gentlemen who are regulars."

Entering the theater, they saw Nini had abandoned the dancers to practice on their own, so Marcel led them to her office. Nini was lounging on the couch, drinking a glass of red wine, wearing a loose floor-length cotton dress that resembled an Oriental dressing gown, scarlet with bright flowers and leaves trailing down to her ankles. Steven and Olivia chose the same colorful armchairs as before.

"*Oooh! Les Américains!* Welcome back, my darlings. How is the investigation into my dear Madeleine proceeding?"

"Slowly, but we are gathering information. I think we're getting closer, Nini," Steven said.

"*Bon!* That's what I like to hear. How can I help you today?" She swung her legs off the couch and planted her feet on the carpet. The wine-colored fabric that covered the sofa resembled chenille with its thick pile. Nini leaned over in anticipation of Steven's questions. The scooped neck of her robe gaped open, providing a clear view. The dance instructor wore no corset or bra. Embarrassed, Steven looked away.

"Can you tell me if there were any men who paid special attention to Madeleine?" he asked her.

"*Mais oui!* Maybe a dozen or more. My Madeleine was very popular. Perhaps it would be better if you and Mademoiselle came to a show, and I pointed them out. I could introduce you to any of them if you wanted."

"That's a good idea. But I'd like to have a list of names in my notebook as well."

"All right." Nini provided the names of a dozen men. Steven asked about their circumstances. Were they well-off? Did they belong to the middle class? To the aristocracy? How long had they been coming to the Moulin Rouge, and did they visit on a regular basis? How did they interact with Madeleine? Did they buy her drinks, take her out to late-night suppers, buy her expensive gifts? Did any of them make a nuisance of themselves, or worse?

More than half an hour later, Steven had some sketchy notes that he thought made a good starting point.

"*Merci bien*, Nini. This'll give me a place to begin. Have you noticed anybody new lately? Someone who only started coming to the performances in the past month or two, and perhaps came often? A man who showed a particular interest in Madeleine, I mean."

The dance instructor screwed up her face and looked off in the distance. She took two gulps of her wine and thought some more, then nodded her head. "Yes, there was a new gentleman in the group of Madeleine's admirers, now that you mention it. His name is Gaston something or other."

"So, you noticed him talking with Madeleine after the shows?"

"I think so. He certainly *tried* to engage her. You should ask Brigitte or Jojo, though. They'll know better than me."

"All right. What can you tell me about him?"

"He's taller than average, although not a giant. He's fairly slender, and he has brown hair—full and shining. He constantly runs his hand through it, like he's proud of it. He won't be going bald any time soon." She chuckled. "He's probably in his forties. Although I have to tell you, I'm not good at guessing anyone's age. He's well-dressed, but he doesn't strike me as upper class, if you know what I mean. Maybe he's someone who's come into money or who's learning how to act with money he recently earned. He always wears a top hat. He looks pleasant. He smiles and seems likable." She drained her wine glass.

"Nini, you are amazing!" Steven exclaimed. "I wish all my witnesses had a memory as good as yours. It would make my job a lot easier. How is it you're so observant?"

"These are my girls, Monsieur. I am responsible for them. I care for them. Naturally, I pay attention to the men who pay attention to them. Remember, though, all of this could mean nothing. As I said, he's been hanging around, but I don't know if he ever invited Madeleine out or if she went anywhere with him after a performance."

"I understand. We'll take your advice and talk with Brigitte and Jojo," Steven said. "What about a customer who isn't as likable as this Gaston? Has anyone been bothering any of the girls? And Madeleine, in particular, of course?"

"Oh dear, now that's more difficult. If someone drinks too much and gets rowdy beyond our acceptable limits, we throw him out. But, remember, we *are* a cabaret, and men do like to drink. We tolerate a lot. But we have employees who roam the floor each night. If someone is bothering one of the girls, harassing her, bullying her, or if he continues to touch her and it is not welcomed, he will be thrown out and not allowed to return for some time. We have to protect our girls, Monsieur. We take that very seriously. Again, you should talk to Brigitte and Jojo. They're usually around after the performances and, of course, they were close friends of Madeleine's. I'm sure she would have told them if someone was stalking her or being troublesome." She grabbed a bottle of wine from the small table near the sofa and poured another full glass. "Oh, my goodness! I'm so sorry. Where are my manners? Would you care for a drink?"

"No, thank you," Steven said. "We'll talk with Brigitte and Jojo now. Are they here this afternoon?"

"They should be on stage practicing." She rose from the couch, went out into the hall, shouted for Marcel, and returned to Steven and Olivia.

Marcel stuck his head in the room, then went to fetch the two young dancers as instructed.

When Brigitte and Jojo appeared in the doorway, Nini rose and said, "*Le Détective* Blackwell and Mademoiselle Watson wish to speak with you again, girls. Come in." She turned to Steven and Olivia. "Use my office. I want to check on the rest of my troupe, see how they're coming along with the new steps."

* * *

After the dancers had settled on Nini's couch—Olivia thought they could be sisters, except for Jojo's southern accent—Steven asked, "Did you notice anyone new hanging around Madeleine during the past few weeks?"

Brigitte and Jojo looked at each other as if trying to read the answer on the other's face. Then Jojo said timidly, "She had many admirers. But lately, yes, there has been someone in particular. The man in the top hat."

"Oh! Gaston," said Brigitte. "His name's Gaston Visière. He drives a carriage."

"Do you know who he works for?" asked Olivia.

"No, but it might be that big new store called Le Bon Marché. He told us about it. It's a *grand magasin*," said Brigitte.

"So, this man Gaston," Steven said. "You've seen him spending time with Madeleine?"

"Yes, he was one of her favorites," Jojo said.

"But, don't forget Gaston likes us too, Jojo."

"Yes, that's true." Her eyes lit up, and she nodded her head, her blonde curls bobbing. "He brought a friend one night, and they took Brigitte and me to supper after the performance. It was wonderful."

"Tell us about Gaston," Olivia said.

After Brigitte and Jojo described the man as generous—*You wouldn't believe how much our supper cost!*—handsome, and very nice, Steven and Olivia starred his name in their notebooks.

"Do you know if Gaston ever took Madeleine out for supper?" Steven asked.

"Yes, he did," Jojo said.

"Two or three times," Brigitte added.

"What about somebody who was bothering Madeleine?" Steven

asked. "Had anyone been pestering her? Stalking her? Following her and not taking no for an answer?"

Again, the dancers consulted each other's faces for a clue.

"Well, there was someone last month, but he hasn't been in the Moulin since Bruno threw him out," Brigitte said.

"Tell me about that man," Steven said.

"Big and dumb," said Jojo.

Brigitte nodded and made a face. "That's about it. He was a few years older than us, maybe in his late twenties. Rough looking and rough acting. He didn't speak well. He didn't have any manners. One night, I saw him grab Madeleine's arm and try to drag her to the bar for a drink. She managed to pull away from him, and after that, she avoided him. Another night, though, he tried it again. That's when he got thrown out."

"Can you remember exactly when that was?" Olivia asked.

"Not long after she started working here, so early November," Jojo said.

"So, if I understand you ladies, two men paid special attention to Madeleine in the past couple of months. Gaston Visière and the big dumb guy."

Brigitte and Jojo giggled.

"*C'est ça.* Right," said Brigitte.

"Do you have any idea what the big guy's name is?" Steven asked. "Or where he lives or works?"

Both dancers shook their heads.

"And you haven't seen him in the cabaret since Bruno threw him out?"

"*Non,*" Jojo said.

"I think Mademoiselle Watson and I would like to meet your friend Gaston and talk with him. Does he come here on certain nights? Does he have any kind of routine?"

"I haven't paid attention to that, Monsieur," said Brigitte.

Jojo shrugged. "Me neither."

"Do you know who the Comte de Chamfort is?" Steven asked.

"Oh, yes!" they chorused.

"Did he come to see Madeleine?"

"Only once, right after she started dancing here," Brigitte said.

"What was Madeleine's reaction to him?"

"She wasn't happy to see him," Jojo said. "She left right after the last performance that night. Never went out on the floor at all. She told us he was the man who bothered her when she was at the Garnier. She wanted nothing to do with him."

"So they didn't have drinks together? She didn't leave with him?"

"Definitely not. She avoided him."

"Ladies, thank you very much for your help. Mademoiselle Watson and I will return tonight if we can. Hopefully, your friend Gaston will stop in and we can talk with him." Steven consulted his notes. "Now, can you send in Marielle DuPin, please?"

"*Désolée, Monsieur.* Sorry. Marielle isn't due back until tomorrow. She went home for Christmas," said Brigitte.

* * *

A gentle snow was falling late Monday afternoon as Marielle DuPin strolled through Chartres, her hometown. She passed the cathedral with its uniquely different spires reaching toward the clouds and continued down a narrow winding street past medieval brown-and-white timbered houses set at odd angles along the way. This was her final night at home, the last night with her family before returning to Paris, to the Moulin Rouge, to dance.

What a wonderful holiday it had been! She enjoyed the warmth of their hearth and the love of her family—her indulgent father, *Maman,* who was a wonderful cook, and her younger brother, who was now a young man and had outgrown his childish pranks. But perhaps more than that, Marielle reveled in knowing that when she returned to the Moulin, no one stood in her way any longer. Her hated rival, Madeleine Gervaise, was dead.

Marielle knew she'd never top famed dancers Jane Avril or La Goulue—they were too well established, at least for now. But they were getting old and worn. One of these days, no one would be interested in looking at them. So, Marielle adjusted her goals accordingly. Her aim now was to dance so well and attract so many admirers who would spend money at the cabaret after the performances that Nini would *have* to create a special number just for her.

Marielle turned back for home, buoyed by happy thoughts of her future at the Moulin Rouge.

* * *

Snow was falling in Paris, too. It caught in the deep charcoal manes of the chestnut-colored horses as they trotted up the hill, pulling the coach that carried Steven and Olivia back to Evangéline's apartment.

"I don't know about you, Steven, but my brain is buzzing with too many names. *Again!* I'm glad I have my appointment with the countess this afternoon. Coffee and pastries are exactly what I want right now. I'm going to empty my mind of everything we heard today and relax. I'll start fresh later."

"We did learn a lot. I'm not sure yet what's going to be important or who we'll need to concentrate on. But in every case, at least at home, I reach a moment where it all falls into place and I know—I can see how it happened, who the perpetrator was, and why they did it. I'm going to relax too, then I'll add the new material to the murder board."

188

Olivia nodded. "I'm looking forward to hearing how Evangéline's meeting with her new dealer went this morning. I'm so happy for her. I wonder if this is her big break."

Chapter Twenty-Two

They arrived at Evangéline's apartment in the December dusk. Gas lamps flickered along the narrow street, creating halos of light atop the black poles. When Henri's driver pulled up to the curb at the courtyard entrance, Steven got out of the carriage and helped Olivia down.

"Monsieur, can you get a message to the police detective we've been working with?" he asked the coachman.

"*Bien sûr.*"

"Can you tell him we learned a great deal today and, if it's at all possible, could he meet us at the Moulin Rouge tonight before the first show?"

The driver tipped his cap and pulled away from the curb.

"That was a good idea," Olivia said. "You know, I thought contacting people was hard in your time, Steven, but it doesn't compare to here. I never appreciated my cell phone more than I do now."

Steven opened the wooden door into the courtyard and gestured for Olivia to enter first. By the light of additional gas lamps, one set near the front door of each of the buildings bordering the square, they saw Louis playing with a ball, throwing it against a wall, and catching it again. They said hello and continued into Evangéline's building. Out of courtesy, they knocked on her door before entering.

Unlike the lit street and courtyard below, Evangéline's apartment was dark.

"Maybe she's gone out again," said Olivia. "Could you light one of the lamps?"

A muffled sound reached their ears.

"What's that?" Olivia whispered. She heard the scraping sound of the wooden match, then the room came into focus as Steven lit a lamp near the door. "That's better."

A movement on the couch caught their attention.

"Evangéline!" Olivia exclaimed.

Huddled under blankets at one end of the sofa, Evangéline struggled into a sitting position. When Steven lit another light, Olivia could see Evangéline's eyes were red-rimmed, as though she had a cold or had been crying.

Olivia rushed to the couch, dropped next to her, and grasped her arm. "Evangéline, are you all right?" She stopped and shook her head. "Stupid question. Sorry. Of course, you're not."

Steven hurried over and threw himself onto his knees in front of Evangéline. "Are you hurt? What happened?"

"I'm okay now. It's over. I think when it was happening, I kept everything inside of me. I had to be strong, you see. When I got home, I took a bath and then went out shopping for our supper. After I returned, I started playing it all over again in my mind…and, well, I suppose all the emotions leaked out." She ran her fingers through her long copper hair and shook her head as if trying to dislodge a bad memory. "Here, Steven, grab that bottle of wine off the table and pour us a glass. Olivia, add some coal to the fire, please. I'll tell you everything."

Although anxious to hear what had happened, they did as she asked.

Evangéline sighed. "I'm so happy you're home! I didn't realize it affected me so much."

Steven and Olivia had never seen her like this. Their anxiety increased.

The fire caught, and the flickering light that filled the hearth made the living room feel warmer, safer. Steven set the wine and glasses on the low table in front of the sofa. Olivia handed a glass to Evangéline, then one to Steven. He inserted himself into the space between Evangéline and the arm of the sofa, as if he couldn't bear to be far from her. She smiled and shifted closer to Olivia to give him room, then she grabbed his hand and squeezed, smiling that beloved, familiar smile.

"Now, tell us what happened," Steven said.

"Two men kidnapped me this morning."

Steven and Olivia gasped. "What?!"

Evangéline hurried to add, "I wasn't attacked. They didn't do anything to me, if you know what I mean."

"Thank God!" Steven said.

In a measured tone, Evangéline told them everything that occurred from the moment she stepped out onto the sidewalk in the thick fog, to when the masked man threw her out of the carriage at the top of the stairs on rue Cardinal duBois.

"That's it," he said. "We're stopping this investigation right now. We'll go home. I will *not* put you in any more danger. What if you hadn't caught the post supporting that railing? What if you had fallen down those stairs? You could have hit your head and been knocked out. You could have been killed like Madeleine."

Evangéline began to protest.

"No. Absolutely not. That's it. We're done. We'll celebrate the New Year with you, then Olivia and I are going home. We'll explain to Henri, and he'll just have to accept it. I'm sure he *will* accept it when he hears what they did to you."

Olivia had never seen Steven so upset. "I agree one hundred percent, Evangéline. We won't put you in danger. Think of what they could do the next time." She shuddered and squeezed Evangéline's hand. "It's been wonderful meeting you, getting to know you, and spending time together. We wanted to help your friend Henri, but Steven's right. Nothing is worth you being hurt. Investigation closed!"

"I appreciate these sentiments from both of you. Really, I do. But don't you see? It's more important now than ever to keep going. You're obviously getting close. The killer's afraid you'll get closer. He knows you'll find the truth. We need to get Detective Berthot here and discuss it with him. I can send Louis. And before you say no, remember there's a place where I can go—a place where they'll never find me—until this is over."

"First of all," Steven said, "I agree we need to talk with Etienne. Do you want me to call down to Louis? He's playing in the courtyard."

"Yes, thank you."

Not a minute passed when they heard a knocking and saw a blond head peeking around the slowly opening door.

"*Bonsoir*, Mademoiselle."

"Louis, go up to the square and engage a carriage to take you to the Préfecture de Police. Tell the driver to wait. Ask for Détective Etienne Berthot. Tell him we have an emergency and you have a carriage to bring him to us." Evangéline struggled to disentangle herself from the blankets and went to get some money from her purse. "Here, this is more than enough for the carriage. Keep the usual amount for yourself, *chéri.*"

"Right away!" The child spun around and flew out the door. They could hear his boots clattering on the stairs.

"Now, *mes chers*, look what I have to show the police." Evangéline picked up her sketch pad and returned to the sofa. She flipped past several pages, then showed them the drawing of a man. "As soon as I caught my breath and got my feet on solid ground, I made this sketch. This is the man who took me."

"You're amazing!" Steven exclaimed, regarding her with unabashed admiration. "This will be a huge help to the police."

"Evangéline, you said you could go someplace where those men couldn't find you. Where is that?" Olivia asked.

"Well, my first choice—and the easiest—depending on how long I'd have to stay there, would be this very apartment, but in *your* time, Olivia." Evangéline looked triumphant, as though she'd offered the most brilliant solution.

Steven's and Olivia's jaws dropped.

"Why are you both looking so surprised? It's the obvious answer. I can easily stay there. We keep the apartment empty in all time periods in case we need to use it. The three of us could spend our evenings together here in 1895—I wouldn't be at risk with both of you here. And as long as I have my art supplies, I can stay in 2014 during the day for as long as I need to."

Steven and Olivia looked at each other, faces scrunched up in indecision. He spoke first. "I don't know. Let's wait to see what Etienne says."

The clock on the mantle chimed four o'clock.

"Oh no! I have to go meet the countess," Olivia exclaimed. "Her driver will be here any second. Should I tell him something happened? That we have an emergency, and I'm sorry, but I can't leave?"

"No, this is a chance for you to discover information about the count that I'd never be able to," Steven said. "I'm sure you won't be long. An hour, maybe? When Etienne gets here, Evangéline will tell him what happened. When you get back, we'll all decide what to do. Together."

Evangéline nodded. "He's right, Olivia. Go. We'll be here when you return. The very least we can do is offer Etienne something to eat. You can help me prepare supper. I'll teach you the secret to making caramelized onions." She gave Olivia a warm smile.

"All right." Olivia grabbed her cloak and headed toward the door.

"Hold on," Steven called out. "I'm going to wait with you in case the kidnappers are lurking out in the street. I want to make sure you get into the Chamforts' carriage safely."

***

When Olivia arrived at the Chamforts' Paris home, the butler escorted her into a comfortable pale apricot-and-gold sitting room, made even richer looking by the shimmering flames in the fireplace. The Comtesse, in a charcoal gray silk dress that matched the darkening sky, was standing at a floor-to-ceiling window, gazing out at a snow-covered lawn. She greeted Olivia warmly, taking her hands and saying how glad she was Olivia could come. She led her to a small round table set with a crisp white linen cloth, fine porcelain cups, saucers, and plates, and a silver coffee service.

"Oh, Countess, this is lovely," Olivia exclaimed.

The Comtesse de Chamfort poured rich black coffee into a delicate cup and handed it to her guest. "I realize it is quite against what is generally accepted in Paris society, but perhaps we might use each other's first names since we're alone here. I've heard that is more common in America. Is it true?"

"I'd like that, Countess. Actually, at home, I believe it depends on one's station in life. But I would be happy to have you call me Olivia." Olivia hoped her smile reached all the way to her eyes and that the countess understood it was genuine.

"It'll be our little secret, Olivia. My given name is Nathalie." She indicated a two-tiered plate laden with exquisite desserts. "Please, help yourself. Cook chose the most delicious pastries for us."

After they each selected a pastry, Nathalie peppered Olivia with questions about her life in the United States. As Olivia answered, she thought of what she could ask to learn more about the count and his proclivities. Finally, there was a break in her hostess's enthusiastic interrogation. Walking a thin line between would be acceptable in 1895 and what she really wanted to know, she began with, "How did you meet your husband, Nathalie?"

"Our parents knew each other because of the vineyards our families own. They're near each other in the Loire Valley. I suppose you could say we moved in the same circles. I saw Jean-Claude at gatherings during my childhood and at parties when I was older. Eventually, his father and mine arranged our marriage."

"Oh, I see." Olivia was surprised to hear of another arranged marriage, although she realized she should have anticipated it. Earlier this month, when she had accompanied Steven to a Christmas party in his time at a Great Camp in the Adirondacks, they learned that their host and hostess's marriage had been arranged. Evidently, it was common in the late nineteenth century on both sides of the Atlantic.

Yet another reason to be thankful for living in 2014.

As Olivia enjoyed the *café* and *pâtisseries*, Nathalie continued to probe for more details about life in America, and specifically Olivia's life. Olivia did her best to satisfy her new friend's curiosity. She thought, though, the countess was getting the better bargain. She needed to get going and start asking questions so she wouldn't return to Steven empty-handed.

"You know, Nathalie, as interested as you are in life in the United States, I'm fascinated by your life as well. To be honest with you, I love working. I'm not sure I would be happy staying at home. I like being busy, having something to do."

"I stay busy at home. We have a lot of parties and dinners. Naturally, we have a cook and a staff of servants who prepare the food and maintain the house, but I do all the planning." She laughed. "I can tell you that arranging the seating charts can be a challenge. People are always having their petty little squabbles. One must be up-to-date and avoid seating certain people near each other." She sipped her coffee. "Then there are the children. It was easier when they were at home. I was always occupied doing something with them. Taking them on picnics in the summer and ice-skating in the winter. Nanny was wonderful, but I enjoyed spending some time with them every day when they were small. Sometimes I played with them after their nap or joined them when they had a meal. Often, I read to them at night. Both boys are in boarding school now, you see. Of course, they came home for the Christmas and New Year holidays, but they'll go back soon. With them gone, there isn't as much to do." She paused, gazing off into the distance, then added, "It can be tiring, having nothing to do."

Olivia felt the countess's sadness. She would hate living in this time when women's lives were so restricted. And being rich wasn't all it was cracked up to be, either.

Wanting to get the conversation back on track, Olivia said, "You were saying that your children are away at school now that they're older. I imagine that gives you more time to spend with the count and to get together with your friends like we're doing this afternoon, *n'est-ce pas?*" Olivia smiled.

"Jean-Claude is always very busy. At the Opéra Garnier Ballet and at our home in the valley. Naturally, he has to keep an eye on our workers to be sure they tend to the vines properly and then, after the harvest, to oversee the wine-making."

"It sounds like he's gone a lot. That must be difficult."

"Yes, but I do have a very special friend. We're lucky to be able to see each other, talk, and share a meal quite often."

"You know, Nathalie, sometimes I think all we need is one special person in our lives."

* * *

Olivia heard the door open and turned to see the Comte de Chamfort enter the room.

"Ah, yes! I had forgotten you invited our charming American friend for coffee this afternoon, my dear."

He strode to where Olivia sat and held out his hand. She offered hers, and he bent slightly to kiss the air above it.

"Your beautiful wife is a most gracious hostess, M. le Comte," Olivia said.

And naturally, you couldn't refuse Nathalie's invitation. Spying on me in my own home, eh? I wonder what my unsuspecting wife revealed during your little tête-à-tête. What shall I do with you? They say keep your enemies close. Let's see...how can I accomplish that? Yes! This is a unique opportunity to learn more about the investigation into the chocolates, the dancer who died, and the investigation into Madeleine's death. I must not let this chance pass me by. The party! I'll insist they attend the party, and the four of us will keep an eye on them. There will be many chances to learn more tomorrow night.

"You must allow us to show you an even greater example of French hospitality, Mademoiselle. We are having a supper party tomorrow night to celebrate the New Year. We would be honored if you and Monsieur Blackwell would come."

"Oh, yes!" exclaimed the countess. "Do say you'll come, Mademoiselle."

"Thank you so much," said Olivia. "It would be a privilege to join you. Steven will be thrilled when I tell him."

"*Bon!* That's settled then. Until tomorrow evening," said the count with a slight bow. He turned on his heel and left as abruptly as he had entered.

* * *

Nathalie stood at the front door, watching the carriage pull away. She lost sight of it when the drive curved and the coach disappeared behind a stand of trees. The countess gave a tiny wave, although she knew *l'Amércaine* could no longer see her.

During the past hour, Nathalie had found herself envying this free woman with her independent spirit and love of work. She tried to imagine what it must be like to feel that untethered. Although her father had been forward-thinking and had educated her well, he had been locked into the mores of their time and never questioned the idea of an arranged marriage. So now she was under Jean-Claude's control, and she didn't like it any more than when her father had ruled her life.

What must it be like to be free? Free to do what you wanted, to make your own decisions, to have real meaning in your life. Freedom. Such a lustrous word. Like a shiny new coin. Nathalie remembered back to her childhood when she and her best friend roamed the woods and ran in the garden. She supposed there had been freedom in that, but it would take a lot more than walking through the woods and running in the garden to feel the exhilaration now.

No matter how hard she tried, Nathalie simply could not conjure up an image of herself not being connected to Jean-Claude. It wasn't even worth the time to think of leaving him and starting a new life on her own. What would she do? How would she live? She had no work skills. She hadn't even raised her own children. She sighed. At least she could throw a successful New Year's Eve party tomorrow night.

Everyone who was anyone was coming. The staff had put up beautiful holiday decorations, and the house was redolent with the scent of pine boughs and wreaths. The Christmas tree, that German trend that had become so popular over the past years, looked magical with its twinkling candlelight and sparkling glass balls. Nathalie knew the supper she had arranged for the gala would impress even the most fastidious of tastes. And the gift she had chosen for the King's cake was stunning.

Another New Year. How time flew by. She'd lost count of the number of New Years she and her friend had celebrated in secret. Nathalie hoped that sometime in the next few days, they'd be able to spend some time together and toast the New Year privately.

She turned away from the front door and softly closed it.

* * *

As the carriage transported Olivia from the Chamforts' Paris residence, her mind was buzzing with everything she had heard and experienced during the past hour. *Poor, poor Nathalie! What a miserable life she must have. Kids off to boarding school, husband never around. And her husband probably a creep to boot. Thank goodness she has one close friend. I wonder if I'll meet her at the party tomorrow night. Tomorrow night! Wait until Steven hears how we're celebrating New Year's Eve! We'll have a chance to observe the count more. Hmm, I wonder how Chamfort treated Madeleine. Not great, if the way he treats his wife is any indication.*

* * *

March 1895

After that first lunch with the Comte de Chamfort, Madeleine wondered if, somewhere deep inside, she'd always known that one day she would have to surrender to the way things were done at the Opéra Garnier Ballet. She'd always been the kind of person to keep certain things private, to avoid discussions about personal matters. But, after her lunch with the count— Jean-Claude, as he had instructed her to call him—Madeleine had sought out Gigi Pantier.

Madeleine had watched how Gigi manipulated her relationship with the Marquis de Polignac and noticed that she seemed somewhat in control. Yes, Madeleine wanted to advance in her career, but not at the cost of losing herself or her independence to someone like the Comte de Chamfort. The question was: Could she do both?

Gigi had been understanding but had not minced words. She let Madeleine know exactly what was, eventually, expected. She'd told Madeleine she would be able to drag things out a bit, but that, at some point, she'd have to capitulate. She must ask herself if it would be worth it.

In the beginning, it went well with Jean-Claude. She explained that she needed a little time to get to know him better, to feel comfortable. He was patient and understanding. In her mind, Madeleine composed a schedule of activities she could use, things she thought of as "steps," in order to prolong the inevitable. During December, she allowed him to take her for several meals, a stroll arm-in-arm along the boulevards to look at the Christmas decorations and lights, and a ride in his carriage bundled up in furs. In January, she let him kiss her after three late suppers. In February, he treated her to a special Valentine's Day dinner, complete with Champagne, caviar, and a dozen roses.

But by spring, Jean-Claude was becoming impatient, so Madeleine steeled herself and gave in, all the while remembering what Gigi Pantier had told her. "He might take my body, but he doesn't take my soul. I'm using him as much as he's using me. I'm in control."

After it was over, Madeleine didn't really know how she felt. On one hand, she had given away something special that she'd always thought she would give her husband, if she ever had one. On the other hand, she thought perhaps people had made a big deal about an act that seemed so very natural.

Jean-Claude was exceptionally handsome, tall, blonde, and muscular. He reminded her of that painter she used to see on the streets of Montmartre, the one who died last year. Gustave Caillebotte was his name.

When they were together, Jean-Claude treated her like a princess. He was attentive, kind, fun, funny, and adoring.

If this was her path to the top, she decided, it was worth it. To his credit, Jean-Claude gave her everything—and more—than she'd expected.

By summer, Madeleine was promoted to soloist.

* * *

Some forty minutes after Olivia had left Evangéline's, there was a banging on the apartment door. Steven jumped up from the couch and opened the door to their friend Detective Etienne Berthot.

"I came as quickly as I could," he panted, having run up the flight of stairs. "What's the emergency? Where's Mademoiselle Watson? Did something happen to her?" He looked wildly around the living room. "I'll never forgive myself if—"

"No, Etienne, she's fine. Please, *calmez-vous.* She's having coffee with the Comtesse de Chamfort. Something *did* happen earlier today, but the danger has passed for now."

Evangéline rose from the sofa and held out her hand. "*S'il vous plaît,* M. Berthot, come and sit down. Join us for a glass of wine. And I'll tell you about my frightful experience this morning."

Etienne's brows shot up onto his forehead, and he dropped into an armchair. He took a gulp of wine, then said, "What happened?"

Evangéline told him that when she'd stepped out into the fog, a man grabbed her, then threw her into a coach and knocked her out. She told the policeman about waking up in what she decided had been a type of fruit cellar, about the filth and the rats. She left nothing out. Finally, she relayed the message from the kidnappers.

Etienne listened, quietly absorbing every detail. As he was about to question her to elicit more information, she stood and reached for a sketch pad on a small table nearby. Returning to the couch, she showed him the drawing of her kidnapper.

"Well, I'll be damned!" Etienne exclaimed. "It's *Gabriel Glissant*. 'Slippery Gabe' is what we call him. Looks like he's graduated from petty theft."

"How do you know it's him?" Steven asked.

"It's that big mole under his ear. Mlle Neuilly, if you hadn't noticed that mole, we'd still be in the dark. Did you get a look at the man doing the driving?"

"No, when they first took me, the driver had his hat pulled low, so I didn't see anything. Then, on the way back, when I was more clear-headed, they were both wearing masks that hid their faces. This one, your 'Gabriel Glissant,' was taller than the driver and of medium build. His partner was about my height but quite husky. Oh! I just remembered. The driver had a bit of an accent. Maybe Spanish. Like someone who came to this country when he was a child. His French was very good, but there was a slight trace of an accent."

Etienne shook his head in wonder. "I'll bet that's Carlos Garcia. He hangs around with Gabriel and his crew."

"How dangerous are these men, Etienne?" Steven asked. "Is Evangéline safe staying in her apartment?"

"I've never known them to kill anyone or cause any real damage. The most we ever arrested them for is theft or beating up some unlucky soul *before* they robbed him. But, I will say this…these boys are for hire. It would not surprise me to discover that one of our aristocrats paid them to do their dirty work."

They spent the next half-hour going over more details of the kidnapping, Etienne probing further and further. Steven opened a second bottle of wine, and still they talked. Just when Steven thought there was no more to be learned, he heard the door creak open and looked across the room to see Olivia enter the apartment.

"You're home," he exclaimed, rushing to greet her. Not caring what

Etienne might think, he pulled Olivia into a hug and held her tight. "I've been so worried." He whispered so the others couldn't hear. "It felt like I'd sent you into the lion's den where all kinds of terrible things could happen. I regretted letting you go the minute you left and every second you've been gone. I'm so sorry, Olivia. I should have never encouraged you to go. If anything had happened to you…." He tightened his hold on her. "We're not splitting up again while we're here."

"Oh, Steven. I'm sorry you were worried, but it was fine. Really. We had coffee and pastries exactly as the countess said we would." She hugged him back. "I was perfectly safe."

"Not if the Comte de Chamfort is our killer, and he thought you were there to trick him into some kind of confession. Or if he thought you were snooping around looking for clues."

"The count wasn't home…well, until I was about to leave. I think he had forgotten Nathalie invited me."

"Nathalie?"

"Yes, she suggested we dispense with the conventions while we were alone and use each other's first names. Pretty bold, huh? She's got a rebellious streak. I like her. Although I feel sorry for her. I think she's unhappy."

"I'm glad you like her, but I don't care how unhappy the Comtesse de Chamfort is. There's a chance her husband is our killer. Or at the very least, the poisoner of those chocolates. What did you say about him not being there until you were leaving?"

"Come back here and tell us what you're talking about," Evangéline called.

"Steven's afraid I might have put myself in danger at the Chamforts' house," Olivia told her.

"If the count was responsible for Mademoiselle Neuilly's kidnapping and thought you'd ignored the warning to abandon the investigation…

yes, maybe," Etienne said. "But let's not get ahead of ourselves. There are concrete steps I can take now that I've seen Evangéline's wonderful drawing."

Evangéline stood abruptly. "I think that's enough of this depressing and frightening conversation for now. I'm going to prepare our supper. Then, later, after we're nourished and relaxed, we'll talk more. Come, Olivia, you can help me." Halfway to the kitchen, she stopped and turned to Etienne. "And since you're a guest in my home and about to have supper with us, I think it's time we dispensed with formalities. My name is Evangéline."

The Frenchman nodded and gave a little bow. "And would you do me the honor of calling me Etienne?"

While Steven and Etienne discussed policing techniques in New York and Paris, and shared some of their memorable cases, Evangéline instructed Olivia in preparing a simple dish made with chicken thighs and caramelized onions. They also cooked rice and opened a jar of stewed tomatoes, a gift from a neighbor last fall.

"I'm surprised we've been having such big meals in the evening, Evangéline. I thought lunch was your main meal."

"Yes, that's true. But I know you and Steven are used to a substantial supper at home. And I think he needs food after the difficult days you're enduring." She turned toward the living room and called out, "*A table!* Come on, you two. Olivia, put the rice in that blue bowl, please."

"I didn't realize how hungry I was," Steven said after several bites. "This is wonderful."

"No matter what we end up doing with this investigation or how long we stay, I hope Evangéline will give me a few more cooking lessons," Olivia said. "She makes everything seem so easy, and it tastes like a gourmet dish."

As they were finishing their meal, Olivia said, "I have a surprise for everyone…the Comte de Chamfort invited Steven and me to a New Year's Eve party and supper tomorrow night."

Evangéline's brows shot up to the top of her forehead. *"Oh, là, là.* Mingling with high society. You should go. Henri'll be thrilled you received this invitation. You'll have access none of us has, even with Henri being a member of the aristocracy. He never associates with them. Maybe you'll discover something to confirm Edgar's suspicions, too. I'm certain some of the ballet patrons will be there. They all must know each other. People of that class only associate with each other. They're probably good friends."

"I agree," Steven said. "I hope you said we'd go."

"Mais oui." Olivia grinned.

"Olivia, this is an incredible opportunity. I don't know how you did it, but, *Brava,* my dear," Etienne said. "Here, both of you, write down these names. These are the men who spend their time watching the ballet dancers, the supposed patrons." The policeman made a face. "They're all aristocrats from important French families. Ready?" He listed the names and titles. "Le Duc de Rochechouart, first name Thomas. Obviously, you will never call them by their given names, but you should have the information. Le Marquis de Polignac, Benoît. I don't know anything about him. Le Comte de Beauharnais, Maxime. Remember, we saw him at the Opéra? He dotes on his two daughters. You already know Le Comte de Chamfort, Jean-Claude."

Steven and Olivia recorded the names in their notebooks.

"The one you need to be especially careful with is the Le Duc de Rochechouart. He belongs to the oldest aristocratic family in France. Rochechouart is a powerful and private man. And…he has a reputation for being ruthless. It's said he can look you in the eye with a smile as he slides in the knife. Tread very carefully. He will likely not even design to speak with you." Etienne raised his brows and gave them a look, the meaning obviously the same in French as in English.

"I might have a better chance than Steven to find out what they really do at the ballet," Olivia said. "I bet they underestimate a woman's intelligence and skills."

Etienne chuckled. "I imagine you're right. *Bonne chance!* Good luck!

The discussion returned to Evangéline's kidnappers, Madeleine's killer, and what they should do next.

"I'm going back to the Sûreté. I promise you I will arrest those two men within the next twenty-four hours. I know where they hide out and what streets they work. And I'll find out who hired them. We have plenty of snitches on our payroll at the Préfecture," Etienne told them. "Evangéline, tell me again the exact words they said to you."

"They said I should tell my interfering American friends to lay off and stop sticking their noses into things that don't concern them. They should mind their own business and go home. They said this was my first warning. They can get me any time they want because they know where I live and where I go every day." She shivered. "I believed them, Etienne."

"My first concern is for Evangéline's safety," Steven said. "If there were two of them today, there must be more in their gang. It doesn't matter if you lock up Gabriel Glissant and Carlos Garcia, Etienne. The person or people who hired them will hire others if they want to continue their threats. I'm afraid things could escalate. What if they hurt Evangéline the next time? Or hold her prisoner for days? What if the Comte de Chamfort *is* involved with the kidnapping and decides he doesn't like the fact that Olivia was at his home today? He could interpret that as us thumbing our noses at him, and Olivia could be the next kidnapping victim. I don't like any of this!"

"Let's take a step back and look at what we're dealing with here," said Etienne. "First of all, we have the poisoned chocolates. But *I'm* investigating that case. Gabriel Glissant and his pal Carlos specifically mentioned 'those interfering Americans.' They didn't say a word about me. So, let's put the poisoning case aside for a moment. Somehow, the kidnappers knew you were investigating Madeleine's death, Steven. It makes sense the killer or someone close to him hired them. So, let's focus on Madeleine's murder. You and Olivia have been asking questions at both the Moulin Rouge and the Opéra Garnier Ballet. I believe the killer is connected to one of the dance groups," Etienne said.

"I agree. If the connection is at the Moulin Rouge, the killer could be a member of the dance company, one of the staff, or a customer who frequents the cabaret. And if he or she is connected to the Opéra Garnier Ballet, it could also be one of the dancers or staff, but instead of customers, I'd say we're looking at one of the aristocrats," Steven said. "I don't see how a dancer would have enough money to pay the kidnappers or have the knowledge to hire them. How would she know where to find men to pull off a kidnapping and make threats?"

"*Exactement.* And I don't think a staff member at either dance place is responsible for killing Madeleine because of what you just said, but also because I see no motive. Nini cared for Madeleine and valued her place at the Moulin. Remember, she often chose her for various roles and special positions on stage above the other girls," Etienne said. "And at the *Opéra*, Madame hovers around those ballerinas like a mother hen. She may have hardened her heart to the way the aristocrats use the dancers because she recognizes the need for their money to keep the ballet going, but I believe she cares for the girls in her way."

"*D'accord.* And I'll go one step further, Etienne. I'm leaning toward the killer being connected to the Moulin Rouge because that's where Madeleine worked for the past two months. I think if the connection lies with the Moulin Rouge, it involves one of their frequent customers," Steven said.

"I know we said the dancers probably wouldn't know how to find someone to kidnap Evangéline and couldn't afford to pay a kidnapper.

But we don't know if some of them receive money from their families, or what kind of families they come from. Not all of them can be poor girls from good families," Olivia said. "I keep thinking about Marielle DuPin. She tripped a fellow dancer, knowing she could cause severe damage. Who knows what she's capable of? We know nothing about her background. For all we know, she has a brother or a cousin or a father who's a crook and would have helped her do anything she asked."

"You're right, Olivia," Etienne said. "Actually, she was not on scholarship at the Opéra Garnier. Her family paid her ballet school fees. For now, though, let's set Marielle DuPin aside until we have a chance to talk with her."

Steven nodded. "Until then, we agree that the killer, as well as the person who hired the kidnappers, is most likely a customer who frequents the Moulin Rouge or an aristocrat at the Opéra Garnier...or possibly Marielle DuPin."

"We *must* gather more information on that girl," Etienne said, then looked at Evangéline. "I have one last question. Do you have any idea where you were held prisoner? I know you said they knocked you out when they took you and blindfolded when they released you, but...any idea at all?"

"Yes, maybe. As you say, on the way back to the *butte,* I was awake. I tried to pay attention to the turns and when they threw me out of the carriage—"

Steven winced.

"—at the top of the staircase on Cardinal duBois, I jotted down the directions I memorized. Of course, I can't be sure, but I think it must have been to the north of here, near the fortifications. Perhaps near Clignancourt, although I don't think we went through the toll booth."

The French detective slowly nodded his head. "That makes sense. There's an area there with plenty of abandoned buildings, shacks, and sheds. I'll have a couple of my men take a look. You didn't leave anything behind, by any chance, did you?"

"You mean crumbs like Hansel and Gretel?" Evangéline laughed. "I'm sorry. I never thought of it. That would have been a good idea."

Steven felt a sense of hope. Etienne was sure he knew who the kidnappers were, and he knew where and how to find them. It wouldn't be long before he broke them and they gave up the information the police needed: Who had hired them to kidnap and threaten his mother? That would put them one step closer to the person who murdered Madeleine Gervaise.

"Etienne, I know that in police work, we all have our own methods of getting to the heart of an investigation and discovering who the perpetrator is. For me, the key is organization that I can see. I set up a murder board. I write down all the facts of the case and our observations from the crime scene and from every interview. And I note the connections and relationships of all the people involved, even if they're not at the center of things. A few days ago, Olivia and I set up a makeshift murder board next door in the apartment where we're staying. If you don't object, I'd like to update it now with the information we got today. Then I need to just *think* about everything. Sometimes when I sit and stare at the board, I see things I didn't notice before. Does that make sense to you?"

"Yes, it does. My old partner used to work like that."

"While you're at the Préfecture setting your investigation into the kidnappers in motion, Olivia and I can try to make some inroads into this case and narrow down our suspects. What do you say?"

"That sounds good. I want to find Gabriel Glissant and Carlos Garcia and get them in an interrogation room as soon as possible. Who knows? We may discover more than we expect to."

"What about Evangéline?" Olivia asked.

"Don't worry about me for now. They will not come back for a day or two. I'm sure of that. They'll lie low. And if the police arrest them, it'll take whoever hired them a couple of days to hire more people to come after me. I believe I'm safe until the New Year. And after that…well, I know a place I can go where they would never find me."

Chapter Twenty-Three

After Etienne left, Evangéline said she wanted to do some work in her studio. "Even though it's dark out, the gas lamps will do. I can still accomplish a few things. And it'll calm me."

"Are you sure you want to stay by yourself tonight? I can sleep on the couch if you'd like," Steven said.

"*Merci, chéri, mais non.* I feel safe here. Besides, it's my home." She wrapped them both in hugs and kissed their cheeks. "I'll see you in the morning. Go update your murder board. Do some thinking. Remember, poor Madeleine is counting on you to find the truth."

* * *

After getting into comfortable night clothes, Steven and Olivia tackled the murder board.

"How do you want to begin?" she asked.

"Let's start at the top of the suspect list. Both the young dancer, Claudine, and Madeleine's roommate, Yvette, said Madeleine told Bernard she did not want to be engaged to him. Or possibly to anyone. She wanted her freedom."

"I wonder if that's the bottom line to this case, Steven. Madeleine Gervaise wanted to be free from Bernard *and* the Comte de Chamfort."

"That's a good thought." He made a note: *MOTIVE FOR ANYONE: Freedom?*

"Another thing those two men have in common is they don't like taking no for an answer. Why don't you star Bernard and the Comte de Chamfort?" Olivia said.

Steven followed her suggestion and noted both men's penchant for insisting on getting their own way.

"Right. Now, based on what Evangéline told us, I'm putting *Unlikely* next to Suzanne's name. Evangéline knows her well and I trust her judgement. I'm convinced we're looking at a man connected to the Moulin Rouge or the Garnier Ballet, Olivia."

"I think you're right. I know we're going to talk with Madeleine's father this week, but I really can't get excited about him as a suspect. It feels wrong. Maybe I'm prejudiced against the aristocrats for their sense of entitlement, but they spring to mind before anyone else when we talk about the Opéra Garnier. I think we hit the jackpot with the ballet dancers this morning. I'm amazed by everything they told us about the duke, the *marquis*, and the counts." Olivia flipped some pages in her notebook. "Steven, if these aristocrats are so important, maybe even untouchable, how is Etienne going to interview them?"

"There's always a way to get information out of people. He'll know what to do."

Steven paged through his notebook until he reached his notes on the interviews with Claudine Verlaine, Gigi Pantier, and Yvette Caron. Those were the moments when they gained the most significant information. He reread what he'd written, then returned to the murder board.

Under **SUSPECTS**, he added **THE ARISTOCRATS**. He noted the dancers were afraid of the men's influence, fearing they would lose their jobs if they spoke to the police. Because Steven believed this was critical, he underlined and starred the sentence. He listed the aristocrats' names in descending order of their importance in the ranks of nobility, the dancers with whom they had a relationship, and the descriptions of the men and their relationships with the ballerinas. When he finished, it looked like this:

Le Duc de Rochechouart (Thomas) Arielle's patron. Becoming more demanding and insistent over time. No apparent connection to Madeleine. Powerful. Ruthless! Since he's the most important aristocrat of the group, is he the leader? Would he act to protect the privileges the aristos enjoy? How far would he go to safeguard their position at the ballet?

Le Marquis de Polignac (Benoît) Gigi's patron. Young and handsome. Patient at first. Is more demanding now.

Le Comte de Chamfort (Jean-Claude) Was Madeleine's patron. Gigi repelled by him. Yvette terrified of him. ***He's the reason Madeleine left the Garnier Ballet.***

Went to see Madeleine at the Moulin Rouge. She wasn't happy to see him and left right after the show. She didn't want anything to do with him. Avoided him.

Did he pursue her at the Moulin Rouge? Did he threaten her before or after she left the Garnier Ballet? Is he violent? Did he follow her the night of her death? Would he employ someone to do his dirty work? What does he gain by Madeleine's death???

Le Comte de Beauharnais (Maxime) No known relationship with a dancer. Claudine comfortable with him, says he's nice. Young and handsome. Has daughters and is devoted to them.

How can he be involved in the patron scheme when he has young girls of his own??

"That looks good," Olivia said. "I like your questions. It occurred to me…we spent all that time with the count and countess yesterday on the carriage ride. I never asked what you thought of him. You've got a good sense of people. You should add your own impressions to the murder board."

"I will, and I'll add yours too. At first, I thought he'd want to know how we were doing with the investigation. I was sure he'd try to ask some subtle questions. But he talked about everything *but* the case. He's smart, well-educated, personable, and interesting to talk with. He's devoted to his family *château* in the Loire Valley and his vineyards. I was surprised he actually works. I thought aristocrats just lazed around. Their place here in Paris is what you'd call a second home. Their main residence is a castle near Amboise." Steven laughed. "Can you believe it? People still live in castles in this day and age."

"Yeah, but it's not 'this day and age.' We're in 1895, not 1934," Olivia said.

"Oh yeah, right. Gee, do you think I'm getting used to it here, Olivia?"

"Not really. Or maybe in a temporary way. We should assimilate while we're here because if we come across anyone who's particularly sensitive to people, we want to give off the vibe that we belong."

"You and your vibes. That expression always gets me." He leaned over and kissed her. "I'll be glad when this is over and we can go home."

"Me too!"

"Okay, enough of a break. Back to work, partner," he said. "So, thinking back, I remember the count did ask me once how we were making out with the case. He made it sound like a polite question, something he could ask about my work while he was going on about his vineyards. I told him it was early days, and we were gathering information. He's quite clever, so it might have been a bluff. I hate to say it, but I'm not sure. He's a wily character, Olivia."

"I got that impression, too."

"Listen, you said you felt uneasy near the Comte de Chamfort at the opera house Saturday. Did you feel the same on the carriage ride?"

"No, but I wasn't really paying attention to him. I was more focused on the countess."

"I keep forgetting to ask you…what's she like? Between yesterday's ride and your coffee and cakes today, you must have a pretty good feel for her."

"She's well-educated and smart. She's cultured and interested in art, literature, the theater, music, and the ballet. She told me they attend the premiere of every ballet and they enjoy attending musical evenings at several different concert halls. Now, here's something interesting. At one point, Nathalie leaned in close and whispered that she likes to know what's going on with the new styles of art and music that are happening now—as though it were illegal or something she shouldn't do. She said she went to hear Debussy's debut of 'Prelude to the Afternoon of a Faun' last year. She made it sound like a daring adventure."

"Maybe she *is* a bit of a rebel."

Olivia shrugged. "The only other thing I'd add is I think she's lonely."

"Why do you say that?"

"It was the way she talked about her husband's involvement at the ballet. I got the impression he spends more time there than with her."

"That's interesting. We haven't considered any of the aristocrats' wives. What do they think about the time and money their husbands spend on these dancers? Olivia, that opens up a whole other line of inquiry."

"Oh no! Like we don't already have enough suspects! Let's go back to our notes and be done for tonight."

"Agreed. But now I'm even happier we're going to the party tomorrow night. Maybe you can get some of the wives talking."

Olivia groaned.

"Let's go over what we learned from Nini, Brigitte, and Jojo," Steven said.

"Right." Olivia consulted her notes. "More than a dozen men were fans of Madeleine's, but the customers who took her out are probably the important ones, right? Because they could have gotten close enough on the staircase to push her. "

"Yes." Steven nodded, reread his notes, then added the following information to the murder board under the heading **SUSPECTS**:

Gaston Visière

Fan of Madeleine at the Moulin Rouge. Took her out to supper 2-3 times.

40 y/o Tall, slender. Thick brown hair. Good-looking.

Well dressed. Wears top hat.

Generous. Likable.

Drives carriage. Maybe for Le Bon Marché.

One of Madeleine's favorites. Did she reject him when he invited her a 4th time?

The "big dumb guy"

Find out who he is.

"I thought it was funny when Brigitte and Jojo told us about the quote, big dumb guy." Olivia laughed. "Are you serious about listing him, Steven?"

"He harassed Madeleine, and Bruno threw him out. I'd bet anything the fella was mad and felt humiliated. It wouldn't surprise me if he was still angry. He sounds big enough to throw Madeleine down the stairs. Even though she would have wanted to keep her distance from him, it's a possibility. We can't overlook him, Olivia."

"Yeah, you're right. Those are good points. I must be getting tired if I think it's funny."

"We've had a long day. I'm tired too."

"Let's leave the board for now and go to bed. We'll look at it in the morning with fresh eyes. And remember, Steven, Marielle DuPin comes back to town tomorrow. We can finally meet this legendary mean girl."

Chapter Twenty-Four

Tuesday, December 31, 1895

Paris, France

New Year's Eve day dawned cold and blustery. Big fat snowflakes swirled in the wind outside their rattling windows. Steven and Olivia dressed in warm clothes and went next door to Evangéline's apartment.

Steven knocked, and the door was flung open by a tall, dark-haired man they had never seen.

"Who…?" he began.

Then a flash of copper hair, and Evangéline came running across the living room. She eased the man aside and cried, *"Bonjour, mes chers.* Come in, come in." She was beaming.

Evangéline took the man by the arm and introduced them. "My Théo has come home just in time for the New Year. What a glorious surprise last night! I probably should have told you so you wouldn't worry about me being alone, but it was late. I didn't want to wake you."

Steven and Théo shook hands. Olivia said hello.

"We're all family, Théo. You must call them by their first names."

Evangéline hurried off to the kitchen, and they heard the sounds of china and silverware. Olivia joined her and together they put bread, butter, jam, a basket of croissants, as well as a jug of milk and the *cafetière* on the table.

"Oh! You got croissants today," Steven exclaimed.

"Yes, I thought we deserved a treat."

While they enjoyed a leisurely breakfast, Théo asked Steven about his work as a policeman and questioned Olivia about being a reporter and living in America. He was a good listener and seemed genuinely interested, asking questions and making appropriate comments at all the right moments. Occasionally, he would touch Evangéline's arm, smile, and gaze into her eyes.

When it was Steven's turn to inquire about Théo's line of work, Evangéline's beau grew excited. It turned out that he, too, was an artist and had been in London setting up his first gallery show in England.

"It was my first time out of the country," he told them, his face and voice animated. "I wanted Evangéline to come with me, but she said she couldn't. Now, I understand why. It's very generous of you to help with this investigation."

Keeping to the story they'd agreed on, Steven said, "We were already on our way here. I'm more than happy to help."

"Tell us about your trip to London," Olivia said. "It sounds exciting."

"It was *magnifique*! I took the train to Calais, then crossed the English Channel by boat. It was like being in the middle of the ocean. So rough and wild! Then, when I arrived in Dover—you should see the white cliffs…*incroyable*!—I took a second train to London. I had more than a dozen paintings with me, all carefully packed in crates. I must confess…I was so relieved when I unpacked everything at the gallery and saw that all my canvases had survived the journey unharmed." He turned to Evangéline. "My love, I want you to go back with me for the opening. I leave again on Sunday."

Evangéline turned to Steven. "Do you think you'll have solved the case by then?"

"It doesn't matter. You should go. It's a wonderful opportunity. But I have to say, I need to get back to my job soon. We have a small police station, and my fellow officers depend on me. I can't be away for too long. I need to solve this case!"

"What are your plans for today?" Evangéline asked.

"Olivia and I only have one interview to conduct. A dancer named Marielle DuPin. I have her address, so we'll question her at her apartment. Etienne's picking us up at ten. After that, we plan to go to the Préfecture. We'll have a chance to interrogate those two men and find out if Etienne's made any progress on that other matter." He raised his brows at her, wondering if she had told Théo about her awful ordeal yesterday.

Understanding, Evangéline said, "Théo knows. I told him last night."

Théo frowned, shaking his head as he blew out his cheeks with a deep sigh. "I cannot tell you how distressed I was to discover what my Evangéline endured while I was gone. I plan to stay with her in the apartment every minute. If she goes out, I will accompany her. Even more now, I must persuade her to leave Paris and return to London with me."

"Etienne seemed pretty sure he'd have the kidnappers in a cell by today. He knows who they are and where to find them. I think she's safe," Steven said.

"I will not take any chances. I have a gun and it will be on my person every moment we are out of the apartment."

Evangéline shook her head. "You worry too much, *chéri*. I'll be fine." She turned to Olivia. "Now, let's talk about your party tonight!" She addressed Théo, "They've been invited to the New Year's Eve gala hosted by *le Comte et la Comtesse de Chamfort*!"

"Oh, my goodness! You are associating with the top levels of the aristocracy. How did that come about?"

Olivia told him about their first encounter at the ballet rehearsal, how they accidentally ran into the count at the Lumière brothers' show, then the coincidence of meeting on the Champs Elysées, and his returning home after her coffee and pastries with the countess. A long, slow whistle accompanied his raised brows. *"Là, là!* I will look forward to hearing all about it tomorrow."

"Now, Olivia, we must find something special for you to wear," Evangéline said.

"I loved the gold dress you wore Saturday night. Do you think I might borrow that?"

"Mais oui! It will look fabulous on you. Come, let's go try it on. And we'll pick out shoes and some jewelry too. By the way, Théo, I've let Steven wear some of your clothes. He did not bring the right things with him." She cast a look at Steven and Olivia, telling them clearly that Théo knew nothing of her time-traveling life.

Théo shrugged. "Of course, my dear. Take whatever you need, Steven."

"Evangéline, what are your plans for tonight?" Olivia asked as they walked to the bedroom.

"Théo and I will toast the New Year together here at home. He's been gone more than a week, and I've missed him dearly."

"I can understand that. When I don't see Steven for a day, I miss him."

"Yes, we'll go out to the shops later and buy our favorite foods and champagne for our own little party." She opened the wardrobe doors. "Now, let's get you settled for tonight."

* * *

By ten-thirty that morning, Etienne, Steven, and Olivia were knocking on Marielle DuPin's apartment door.

"Steven, I'll introduce us, then turn over the questioning to you, *d'accord?*"

"Sure. By the way, are you familiar with the 'good cop, bad cop' technique?"

"If it is what it sounds like, yes."

"*Bon.* If she gives us any trouble, how do you feel about being the bad cop today?"

"Sounds like fun. I accept." Etienne grinned, his tired, lined face showing a flash of his younger, more free-spirited self.

The heavy oak door opened a crack.

"Yes? Who are you?" asked a beautiful blonde.

"*Détective* Etienne Berthot with the Sûreté, Detective Steven Blackwell from New York, and his *assistante,* Mademoiselle Olivia Watson. Are you Marielle DuPin?"

"*Oui.* But I'm in a hurry. I must get to the theater soon."

"The sooner we start, Mademoiselle, the sooner we'll finish and you can go," Etienne told her.

"What is this about?" She opened the door another inch, but still barred their way.

Olivia noticed the designer-made dress, as well as the gold necklace around her graceful neck.

"We're investigating the death of one of your colleagues, Madeleine Gervaise."

Marielle DuPin visibly relaxed. "Oh, I see. All right then. Come in."

She led them into a small living room furnished with a good quality couch upholstered in a rust tone, two armchairs—one covered in a leopard print and the other in gold fabric—side tables, a coffee table, and a small desk against one wall. As there was only one window and the sky was dark, sconces lit the room. Crackling flames danced in a large fireplace, helping to illuminate the space but also creating shadows as they warmed the apartment. Olivia enjoyed the scent of burning wood, another indicator that Marielle DuPin was well-off. Coal was cheaper.

Marielle sat up straight in the gold brocade chair, her deep purple dress creating the appearance of royalty and making the chair seem like a throne. Etienne commandeered the end of the sofa nearest her, while Steven took the other chair, and Olivia sat at the far end of the couch next to the French policeman.

"I understand you were able to go home and spend Christmas with your family, Mademoiselle. Where do they live?" Steven asked, smiling, intending to put her at ease.

"Chartres. Do you know it?" Dark brows above rich brown eyes lifted ever so slightly. A small cat-like smile touched the corners of her mouth.

This one is used to using her charms on men, Steven thought.

"Oh, Chartres is a beautiful city," Olivia said. "How lucky you were to grow up there."

Marielle inclined her head in Olivia's direction as if she were Marie Antoinette acknowledging a less-worthy subject, but she said nothing. Evidently, she had decided Olivia wasn't important enough to merit an answer. Or perhaps it was because Olivia was a woman. Steven thought the dancer likely preferred to interact with men, whom she believed she could manipulate.

"When did you leave Paris for your holiday?" Steven continued.

"I took the eleven o'clock train on Tuesday morning, the twenty-fourth." Then she added unnecessarily, "Christmas Eve day."

"Did you hear about Madeleine Gervaise's death before you left?"

"Yes, I had forgotten something at the Moulin on Monday night and went back early Tuesday morning to retrieve it. Marcel let me in. He told me the news."

CHAPTER TWENTY-FOUR

"How did you feel about that?"

"What do you mean?"

"Well, the brutal murder of a fellow dancer, a colleague, someone you knew. A young life cut short. Were you sad?"

"I was shocked. But Madeleine and I only worked together. We were not friends. We were not close, so no, I did not feel sadness."

"Why did you choose to be a dancer, Mademoiselle?"

If Steven's question surprised Marielle DuPin, she didn't show it. "I must dance. It's my life," she replied in all seriousness, as though it was a basic truth and should be obvious.

"And your father didn't object to your dancing at the Moulin Rouge?"

"My father is very forward-thinking, Monsieur. He owns a bookstore and meets all kinds of people with many philosophies on life. He would never stand in my way. He respects all the arts."

"I see."

Before he got to the more critical questions, Steven tested the truth in Marielle DuPin's answers. He wanted to know if she thought she could get away with lying to them. He chose some questions to which he already knew the answers.

"Did you work Sunday night, Mademoiselle?"

"Yes. I work almost every night."

"What time did you leave the cabaret on Sunday?"

"As soon as possible after the last show. I had a drink with a middle-aged couple I had not seen before at the Moulin—they were celebrating their wedding anniversary. Nini always encourages us to meet the customers and make them feel welcome. But that night, I was tired, so I excused myself as soon as I could. I changed my clothes and left."

"When would that have been?"

"Sometime around three, I think. Maybe a little after."

"Did you see Madeleine leave?"

"No, I wasn't paying attention to her or anyone else. I wanted to get out of there and go home."

"I imagine that to return here to your *appartement*, you might walk in the same direction as Madeleine would on her way home."

"I don't know where she lived."

"Didn't you sometimes see her when you were walking home?"

"No. I rarely walk home. One of my admirers usually gives me a ride in his carriage. Although, not that Sunday night."

Okay, Steven thought, *enough of the easy stuff.* He pretended to consult his notebook as he let the silence draw out for several seconds. Then he leaned forward and captured her gaze with a granite stare, refusing to let her look away. "I understand you were fired for deliberately tripping a dancer at the Opéra Garnier Ballet."

"How dare you!" Marielle stood up quickly, those beautiful brown eyes flashing. "I will not be insulted in my own home. That's it. I'm finished answering your questions. What right do you have, anyway? You're not even French. You have no jurisdiction here."

Etienne stood up and took a step in Marielle's direction. He looked down on her, his face an angry storm. He whispered, "Sit. Down."

Olivia shivered at the menacing tone in his voice.

The dancer dropped back down in her chair, but her eyes shot daggers at the two policemen.

She's one tough cookie, Steven thought. *I think Etienne would scare* me *under certain circumstances.*

"I am all the authority you need, Mademoiselle," Etienne said quietly. "Now, you are going to tell us about that day when you *deliberately* tripped a fellow dancer and were fired. Why did you do it?"

"What does that have to do with Madeleine's death?" Marielle asked stubbornly, sliding back in her chair, as if trying to put as much distance as possible between them.

Etienne had regained his seat at the end of the couch near the dancer. He leaned forward, grabbed the arms of her chair, and pulled it to within inches from where he sat. He slowly inclined his head until their foreheads nearly touched.

"You don't seem to understand how this works, my dear." He spoke in a soft, chilling voice. "We ask the questions. You answer them. Don't make me repeat myself."

Steven could see Marielle warring with herself. This woman was clearly used to dictating how things went in her dealings with men. He had to admit, though, Etienne was frightening right now, and Steven was amazed she wasn't cowering. Finally, Marielle spoke.

"She was always getting better roles than me. I only wanted to give her a sprained ankle or something so she wouldn't be able to dance for a week or two. I wanted *le Maître* to see what I could do."

"Didn't you consider you might cause a serious injury? Perhaps even life-altering? That young woman could have fallen and broken something that would have prevented her from ever dancing again."

"No, it never occurred to me." Under her breath, barely audible, she murmured, "She wasn't very good, anyway."

All three heard her and were shocked at her callousness. Marielle DuPin seemed not to value the lives of others. It wasn't much of a stretch to believe her capable of murder.

"It's our understanding you also resented Madeleine Gervaise for getting better roles and positions in the dance company than you did. You strike me as a vindictive woman, Mademoiselle," Steven said. "I can easily see you following Madeleine out of the cabaret and pushing her down those stairs. You're strong enough. You hated Madeleine, didn't you?"

"I didn't go near her," she spat. "I don't know when she left the Moulin on Sunday night."

"Let's talk about *chocolats*, Mademoiselle," Etienne said, suddenly switching gears.

The effect of that statement was immediate. Marielle froze, but

Steven noticed her jaw tremble. *Ah ha. She knows something about those poisoned chocolates.*

Etienne obviously noticed it too, because he said, "You were seen, Mademoiselle. It was you who put the boxes of tainted chocolates in the dancers' dressing room."

"I have nothing more to say." Marielle stood. "You will leave now. I have to go to work." She went to the door, opened it, and waited.

Etienne followed her to the threshold. He reached over and slammed the door shut.

"Marielle DuPin, I am taking you in to the Préfecture de Police for further questioning. You are under suspicion of the murder of MiNou Bordeaux and the attempted murder of the dancers at the Opéra Garnier Ballet by arsenic poisoning. Get your coat. Now!"

* * *

The coach carrying Etienne, Marielle, Steven, and Olivia clattered through the elaborate golden gates into a cobblestone courtyard, surrounded on three sides by the imposing justice center. One of the oldest buildings in Paris, the Palais de Justice made up one part of the complex that also housed the Sainte-Chapelle and the Concièrgerie, the enormous medieval prison where *révolutionnaires* held Marie-Antoinette before sending her to the guillotine at the Place de la Concorde. The driver let them off at the entrance to the Préfecture.

They entered the building and found themselves in an enormous open chamber. The stone walls were easily three feet thick, and the ribbed, vaulted ceiling rose over twenty feet in the air. A uniformed officer stood behind a massive wooden counter, a large lined book open in front of him. Etienne took one of the fountain pens and wrote his name, rank, and the time he had arrived. Underneath, he wrote Steven's and Olivia's names with the note that they were guests of

Detective Inspector Berthot. Finally, he added that he had brought in one Marielle DuPin, a dancer, for questioning regarding a murder and poisoning. He handed Marielle off to a second officer, instructing him to put her in a cell.

"We will speak to you later, Mademoiselle. In the meantime, I want you to think about your future and what it could mean for you if you cooperate…and also what it will mean if you make this *difficile*." He stepped back and nodded to his colleague. "Take her away."

The policeman half-led, half-dragged Marielle DuPin to an enormous oak door with elaborate metal hinges and a box mounted near the side with a heavy iron key in the lock. He led her over the threshold and threw the door shut behind them. The crash reverberated in the large space, and Olivia felt the echo resonate inside of her. She imagined centuries of these heavy prison doors slamming behind thousands of people who knew they would never be released. It must have been terrifying. She was sure Marielle was terrified now.

Etienne took them to his office on the second floor. It was pretty much what Steven expected. It looked like the nineteenth-century version of his own office at the Knightsbridge Police Station. The French policeman sat behind a large wooden desk piled with newspapers, folders, and papers. Three wooden file cabinets lined one wall opposite a bank of windows that let in a small amount of weak light. It had stopped snowing by the time they'd reached the Préfecture, but heavy clouds still covered the sky. Etienne gestured toward two chairs in front of his desk. "Have a seat. Olivia, let me take your cloak."

Etienne called to the officer seated at a desk outside his office. "Jean-Louis, did they track down Gabriel Glissant and Carlos Garcia yet?"

Jean-Louis stepped into the doorway. "No, Monsieur. They're still looking. It seems Gabriel is being his usual slippery self today."

"Let me know as soon as they bring them in, please."

The man gave a small salute and returned to his post.

"So, Steven—and Olivia, too—what do you think of our little interview with Mademoiselle DuPin? Is Marielle the purveyor of our poisoned *chocolats*?"

"She's probably the one who put the boxes on the table in the dressing room, and if she didn't actually put the arsenic in the chocolates, she knows who did. She could have had a partner...but I'd say she was working alone." Steven grinned. "By the way, congratulations on a masterful coup back there. I liked how you told her she was *seen*. Good guess!"

The French detective made a face. "Sometimes we get it right."

"Etienne, when you changed the questioning from Madeleine's murder to the poisoning, Marielle's reaction was noticeable. I was surprised she lost control, though. Up until that point, I thought she was going to be hard to break," said Olivia. "It was astonishing." She grinned. "Like Steven said, that was a good move."

Etienne chuckled. "I've learned a thing or two about interrogations, Olivia. Some day, I'll tell you about the difficult ones. Now, Steven, do we believe she is our poisoner, but not Madeleine Gervaise's killer?"

"I think so, but I know when you question her, you'll cover everything."

"*Bien sûr*. I'm going to let Mademoiselle DuPin sit in the holding cell for several hours. Hell, I might even leave her until tomorrow morning. If I approach her too soon, I'll be wasting my time. I want her begging to talk to me. I'm going to stay here in the office for the rest of the afternoon. I'm sure my men will bring in Evangéline's kidnappers today. They can't hide from us for too long. We know all their hideouts. I want to be ready to talk with those two. I'll jot down some questions for my interviews with Gabriel and Carlos, and also with Mademoiselle DuPin. It would be nice to have both cases wrapped up before lunch tomorrow. I might be able to spend some time at home on New Year's Day. Put my feet up, enjoy a fire, read a book, actually see my wife, children, and grandchildren." Etienne remembered the early days of his career. He'd always thought he'd have more time with his family as he rose in the ranks. But then, crime had exploded in the capital city, and here he was in his fifties, working harder than ever. "What are the two of you going to do now?" he asked.

"I think we'll go back to the apartment. I'd like to update our murder board and organize the questions we're going to ask Bernard Fournier and Madeleine's family when we get there," Steven said.

"Shall we plan to meet here around nine o'clock Friday morning?" Etienne suggested.

"*D'accord*. I'll send Louis with a message confirming we're back. I hope everything goes well and we'll be able to return Thursday night."

They stood, and Olivia grabbed her cloak. Steven reached out a hand to the French policeman. "Good luck with your interviews, *mon ami*. And I wish you a very Happy New Year. May 1896 be a wonderful year for you."

"And for you, my friends." He came from behind his desk, hugged them, and kissed both of them on the cheeks. "Have a safe journey. We will meet soon. I'll be eager to hear all about your party with the Comte de Chamfort and his aristocratic friends. Keep your eyes and ears open. You never know what bits of information you'll pick up."

Chapter Twenty-Five

New Year's Eve 1895

Paris, France

When Olivia slipped the gold dress over her head, it slid down her body like liquid. Gazing at herself in the mirror, the enormity of attending this evening's party struck her, and her breath caught. A whirlwind of emotions—excitement, awe, fear, and joy—enveloped her. She longed to discuss everything with Liz and Sophie. Talking with her two best friends was always the right thing to do.

Although she was excited to attend the New Year's Eve gala at the Count and Countess's Paris home, Olivia was still in awe of her newfound ability to travel into a different time. It was hard to believe she was actually here with Steven in 1895, soon to be 1896. She also had to admit that she was somewhat afraid for the evening to get underway because tonight she was on a tricky mission. A two-fold mission.

On a professional level, she was helping Steven with the case. In that regard, she was determined to gather information on the four aristocrats: the powerful and ruthless Duc de Rochechouart, the

Marquis de Polignac, the seemingly unattached Comte de Beauharnais, and their host, the Comte de Chamfort. She had no idea how she was going to do this or what information she'd be able to discover, but she was going to give it her best shot. Olivia was keenly aware of how important it was to keep in mind that women in 1895 acted very differently from women in the twenty-first century. She would have to be subtle, clever, and rely more on her observational skills than on her reporter's flair for questions. Olivia thought she had a good chance of learning about the four men from their wives. She knew it would be critical in those conversations to pay attention to how the women talked, acted, and interacted. As long as she behaved in the proper and accepted manner, she was sure she'd be able to glean a lot from them.

On a personal level, and for no other reason than because she liked her, Olivia wanted to know the countess better. She knew she'd probably never see Nathalie again after tonight, but still, she felt drawn to her. The countess was under the control of her husband and bound by the mores of society, yet she had shown some defiance. Olivia sensed this woman possessed complex layers and hidden depths to her personality. If they could spend some time alone during the party, it would be almost like talking with a friend, and might help the ache of missing Liz and Sophie. They could delight in the women's gowns, which were surely going to be fabulous. She could compliment Nathalie on her home décor, and perhaps the countess would show her around the *hôtel particulier*, something they'd not been able to do yesterday because the servants were preparing everything for tonight.

Finally, Olivia felt joy in having this time with Steven and sharing these incredible experiences. Since they arrived last week, Olivia realized she hadn't been plagued by her usual worries of their impossible situation. In Knightsbridge, not a day went by without her being sharply aware that she was falling deeper and deeper in love with Steven. She knew there was no good resolution to their dilemma. How could they possibly have a normal relationship when in his time she hadn't been born yet, and in her time he was already dead? Olivia felt sick every time that thought ran through her mind. Would they have to decide soon? How much longer could they go on like this?

Steven entered the room, interrupting Olivia's musings. She turned at the sound of his shoes on the wooden floor.

"Wow, you look great!" she said. "A tuxedo and top hat were made for you."

"And you, *ma chérie*, look stunning. I wish I could take a picture."

"I was just thinking that. I'm so bummed I can't have my phone."

"Well…you do have your phone, remember? You needed it and you'll need it again when we're back in Paris in your time and when we go home."

Olivia's jaw dropped, and her eyes widened. "Oh, my God! I completely forgot it was in my overnight bag. Are you telling me, Steven Blackwell, that you think I should smuggle my phone to this party tonight? Seriously?"

"Well, you did it once. Remember the first time you left our house in my time? We went to the Three Lords for supper and you snuck pictures all night long. No one saw you or was in the least suspicious. I bet you could do it. At the very least, we could take pictures of each other now, so we'd have something when we get home." He wiggled his eyebrows. "What do you think? Are you game?"

"I can't believe how bold you are right now. Paris must be having some kind of effect on you."

"You don't think I'm usually bold?"

"You're brave and super smart and loving and lots of other wonderful things…but to spit in the face of time travel. I'm not so sure. You've always been the more careful, reasonable one."

"Yeah, that's true…but let's at least take pictures of us now. Bring your phone with you, and you can decide later if there's a chance and you want to take it."

Olivia went to the chair where her travel bag sat. She checked her phone's battery and was thrilled to see some of the charge remained.

Steven and Olivia took photos of each other in their exquisite gala outfits, then Olivia took a selfie of them together. He pulled her into his arms and said, "Olivia Watson, no matter what city or what century we're in, I love being with you." He pulled back slightly so he could look at her and went on. "See the influence you've had on this 1930s fella? Before I met you, I would *never* have said anything like that. But it's true."

"I love being with you, too. There's nowhere I would ever rather be."

They stood and kissed for what seemed like a very long time.

* * *

While Steven and Olivia were getting ready for the New Year's Eve gala, Etienne was organizing a group of trusted officers to head out into the streets of Paris to find and bring in Gabriel Glissant and Carlos Garcia. He suspected the two miscreants would be practicing their villainous trade near the restaurants in the Quartier Latin this evening, picking as many pockets as they could as holiday revelers let their guard down, distracted by too much wine and the New Year celebrations. All the officers knew Gabriel and Carlos well, having chased them down and arrested them numerous times.

"I'd like us to go out in pairs," Etienne said. "Thibault and Louis, start at the Pont Royal, go up rue du Bac, and when you hit the boulevard St.-Germain, slow down and take your time. There will be a lot of house parties taking place in the *appartements* as well as celebrations in the *restaus*. Denis and Baptiste, I'd like you to begin at the Pont Neuf, then go up rue Dauphine until you reach St.-Germain. You know that's a wide and busy street. It'll take all four of you looking for our two kidnappers. And don't forget all the little side streets." He turned to his right-hand man. "Jean-Louis, we'll start at the beginning of the boulevard St.-Michel down near the *quais*. I want to comb through the Boul'Mich. There are all those cafés for people who are going to do more drinking than eating tonight. They'll have their pockets stuffed with francs."

Etienne had been leaning against his desk and now straightened up. "We know Gabriel and Carlos have become permanent fixtures in the *Quartier*. If you don't see them on your first pass, go over the same streets again. And remember, blow your whistles as loud as you can, and hopefully one of us in another group will hear you and come to your aid. I've alerted the cops on the beat and told them we'll be searching, so they'll keep an eye out while they're doing their duties as well. If you blow your whistle, someone will surely hear you and sound theirs to get the chain going. I want those two scoundrels in the cells before the clock strikes midnight."

* * *

Etienne and Jean-Louis had been strolling up and down the Boul'Mich for over two hours when Etienne spotted their quarry entering rue St.-Séverin. He elbowed his friend. "See them? Over there on the left. They just turned onto St.-Séverin."

"Naturally, going into the rabbit warren."

Etienne chuckled. "Well, we always enjoy a challenge, don't we, Jean-Louis?"

Call it a rabbit warren, a spider's web, or a maze, the area of the Quartier Latin where the two villains were headed was a confusing labyrinth of twisting, turning alleys and passageways, some barely wide enough for a man's shoulders.

Holiday revelers filled the streets, singing, calling out to friends, blowing noisemakers. Gas lights flickered in long, narrow bistros and tiny cafés barely large enough to hold a hundred people. The year 1896 was getting off to a great start.

Etienne and Jean-Louis followed their targets, deeper and deeper into this ancient hamlet, which sat on top of the Catacombs, home to thousands of corpses. Etienne always felt a shiver run down his spine when he entered this maze of tiny *ruelles*. He wouldn't be surprised if the streets were full of ghosts, just waiting to take you by surprise and slide an icy hand along your cheek.

The two policemen raced after the kidnappers, moving quickly but taking care not to be seen. Etienne wanted to get as close as possible before they pounced on them. They were at the point of nabbing their quarry, and he didn't want to lose them.

Gabriel must have heard their running footsteps, because suddenly he looked over his shoulder and spotted them. "Cops!" he shouted to his partner. The pair took off, Etienne and Jean-Louis at their heels. Now they could blow their whistles, alerting the rest of the team. And blow they did. Gabriel and Carlos sprinted faster, down an alley, around a corner, through a tiny lane, around another corner. One optimistic bistro owner had set tables and chairs on the tiny patch of sidewalk in front of his establishment. Several tables were already occupied. The villains didn't miss a step. They sideswiped two tables, sending glassware crashing and wine spilling to the ground.

"They're heading toward the Seine," Etienne shouted to Jean-Louis, his breathing becoming more difficult as they ran on. *I'm too old for this*, he thought.

The policemen put on a burst of speed. Finally, when they could almost reach out and grab a jacket flapping in the breeze, the miscreants slipped down the tiny rue du Chat qui Pêche.

Le Chat qui Pêche was the most minuscule of streets, the narrowest of alleys, so insubstantial it was barely there. It was where the scoundrels made their first mistake. They'd thrown themselves into this tiny alleyway without looking first—and they should have known better.

A small wooden cart pulled by a donkey, filled with New Year's revelers who'd misjudged the narrowness of the *ruelle*, had gotten stuck. The passageway was blocked.

Etienne peered over the shoulders of Gabriel Glissant and Carlos Garcia and saw the merrymakers were already climbing over the front end of the cart—some onto the donkey itself—and spilling out into the lane. He and Jean-Louis had better hurry, or the kidnappers would join them and be gone.

Jean-Louis ran ahead of Etienne and grabbed Gabriel's jacket from behind. Etienne quickly backed up and out of the way to give Jean-Louis room to act. Jean-Louis dragged Gabriel Glissant out of the passageway and threw him to the ground, then shoved his knee onto his back. Etienne hurried into the space and grabbed Carlos Garcia before he had a chance to jump onto the donkey cart, then dragged him out of rue du Chat qui Pêche.

The entire operation took less than two minutes. The policemen handcuffed both criminals and towed them down to the *quais*, and across the bridge to the Préfecture de Police.

Chapter Twenty-Six

The coach carrying Steven and Olivia entered the grounds of the *hôtel particulier* between tall, black iron gates and continued down a long graveled *allée* past groves of bare-branched trees, scattered pines, and frozen, manicured gardens. Their driver swung around a curve, bringing them into a carriage sweep and to the front entrance of the Comte de Chamfort's magnificent mansion. The residence was ablaze with light. The count had been one of the first in the capital to install electric lighting, and it was still a wonder to his friends and associates.

A footman in full livery stepped to the carriage and opened the door. He placed a wooden block under the edge of the coach, helped Olivia down, then moved to the side. Steven disembarked, took Olivia's arm, and they ascended the wide marble stairway. The heavy, carved oaken doors were flung open, and, as they entered the grand foyer, they heard the sounds of an orchestra playing. Olivia felt a tremor of nerves hopscotch through her stomach. What in heaven's name was she doing in this palace? And how was she ever going to pull off the charade? Not only was she not used to socializing with high society, she was not used to masquerading as a woman who lived more than a hundred years ago. *Olivia, how do you get yourself into these situations? Okay, breathe. You can do this.*

On one side of the imposing entry, a curved stairway led to the second floor—Olivia could see the dip in the center of each marble step where hundreds, maybe thousands, of people had trodden over the centuries. On the opposite side, a massive gilded mirror hung over an antique Louis XV burled wood bombe chest with intricate ormolu drawer pulls. In the middle of the space, a large round table similar to the style of the dresser held an enormous crystal vase filled with red and white flowers and assorted greenery.

The tuxedoed butler took their cloaks and Steven's hat, handed them to another servant, then led them up the sweeping staircase to the ballroom. After asking who they were, the butler announced their names in a deep, sonorous voice.

Olivia thought they'd walked into the Hall of Mirrors in the Palais de Versailles. The ballroom was lit by a dozen crystal chandeliers whose electric lights shimmered and reflected in the mirrors lining one wall. Floor-to-ceiling windows, set in arched alcoves, filled the opposite wall. Everywhere she looked, Olivia gazed upon decorative painting worthy of a Michelangelo—inside the alcoves surrounding the windows, on the ceiling, and on every available wall space. Her first thought was whether she had dressed appropriately. But when she saw what other women were wearing, she sent up a silent prayer thanking Evangéline. The gold dress was perfect.

Olivia barely had time to take in more of their opulent surroundings before the Comte and Comtesse de Chamfort glided over to welcome them. The count was predictably attired in a tuxedo, and the countess in a vibrant red velvet gown. As Olivia noticed the countess's makeup, she realized Evangéline had once again nailed it. Like Olivia, Nathalie wore face powder, rouge, and red lip color. She had also darkened the mole near her mouth, reminding Olivia of Marilyn Monroe once again.

The count shook Steven's hand and nodded to Olivia, calling her Mademoiselle. The countess inclined her head to Steven and took

Olivia's hands. She leaned in and whispered, "I'm glad you came. I so enjoyed our conversation yesterday. I've been looking forward to talking with you again tonight."

"Thank you, Countess. I'm thrilled to be here."

"Let me introduce you to some friends," said the Comte de Chamfort. He and the countess led Steven and Olivia to a small group of two couples.

The Duc de Rochechouart was well built and had movie star looks: dark hair, heavy brows over gray eyes, and a chiseled jaw. But his arrogance and sense of entitlement shone through, making him seem shallow, someone Olivia had no desire to befriend. And, of course, she remembered Etienne's comment about smiling while sliding in the knife. She shivered.

His wife, however, appeared to be the opposite, both in looks and in personality. She smiled broadly when presented to Olivia, her green eyes sparkling with flecks of gold. She was plump and quite short, so that Olivia had to bend slightly in order to hear her. The duchess's silver gown, with its metallic threads, complemented her ash blonde hair.

The other couple was the Marquis de Polignac and his wife. The *marquis* enjoyed the classic "golden boy" looks. He was tall, slender, and had blond hair and deep blue eyes. A few silver hairs showed in his goatee, giving him a distinguished look. He seemed friendly and smiled at Steven and Olivia when they were introduced. He placed his hand on his wife's lower back and proudly presented her. The marquise's rich auburn hair caught the light from the chandelier above and shone. Her rich brown eyes sparkled as she nodded and smiled, showing small white teeth.

Olivia had never been good at guessing people's ages, but she thought both couples were somewhere in their forties.

At first, the duchesse and the marquise seemed content to let their husbands talk with Steven. They stood quietly next to their respective spouses while the duke and the *marquis* asked the usual questions about what it was like to live in America and what kinds of crimes Steven had to deal with in his job. After a few minutes, the Duc de Rochechouart excused himself, taking the duchess with him. Olivia was sure he believed he was above people like her and Steven, and had forced himself to speak with them for the shortest amount of time possible, and only out of a sense of politeness. An obvious disdain for them had been evident during the brief conversation.

As soon as Steven and Olivia were alone with the Marquis de Polignac and his petite wife, the conversation flowed more easily. Olivia turned to the marquise and asked her how she and her family had celebrated the Christmas holiday, mentioning that Christmas was her favorite time of the year. Olivia then moved to the topic of the Polignac family—two boys and a girl—and listened to the proud mother for a good five minutes. Getting her to discuss her children had been a good move, because the marquise now seemed comfortable enough to ask Olivia how she and Steven had met *le Comte et la Comtesse de Chamfort.*

This was the opening Olivia had been looking for. "Steven and I were interviewing a dancer at the Opéra Garnier Ballet as part of our investigation."

"Investigation? You mean *le Détective Blackwell* is working here in Paris?"

"Yes, we're working with one of the detectives at the Sûreté, investigating the death of a former ballet dancer named Madeleine Gervaise."

La Marquise de Polignac blinked her beautiful eyes once or twice and said, "We? Do you mean that you work with the detective?"

Olivia smiled. "Yes, I do." Then, reminding herself that she was having this conversation in 1895, she added, "I know it's not common, but I really like it. And there are certain circumstances where I can make a difference." After the marquise nodded thoughtfully, Olivia asked, "I understand that your husband, *le marquis*, is a patron of the ballet. Do you also enjoy attending the performances?"

"Oh yes! We attend each premiere and frequent the opera performances as well."

Before Olivia could dig deeper into the *marquis's* relationship with the ballet, the Comtesse de Chamfort joined them.

"Are you enjoying yourself, Mademoiselle?" Nathalie asked Olivia.

"Yes, thank you. *La Marquise de Polignac* and I are having a lovely conversation. And I must tell you, Countess, your home is beyond anything I could have imagined. It's beautiful."

"Thank you. Would you like to see some of the rooms? I just had the wallpaper redone in the dining room. It is most agreeable."

"Yes, I would. Very much."

The countess turned to her friend, the marquise, and said, "*Ma chère Marie-Françoise*, please excuse us while I show our American guest around a little."

Marie-Françoise tilted her head in acquiescence. "*Mais, bien sûr.*"

* * *

September 1895

The first six months with the Comte de Chamfort were like a dream for Madeleine. They got along beautifully and actually grew to like each other. He was patient when she was too exhausted to see him after a performance. And she understood how much he was helping her career, so she pushed herself to go out with him on those nights when all she wanted was to go home alone.

Despite Jean-Claude's patronage, Madeleine had never stopped working hard, continually driving herself to improve. She was confident that any day now her technical skills would qualify her to dance the principal role in a ballet. And with Jean-Claude's support, that day would become a reality.

One afternoon in early fall, quite by chance, Madeleine encountered Jacques Tailleur, son of the woman who hired her as a seamstress when she'd first arrived in Paris. She hadn't seen him in more than a year. They hugged and kissed each other's cheeks, then went arm-in-arm for a coffee. Madeleine thoroughly enjoyed their visit.

If only she had known what it would cost her.

That night after the performance, Jean-Claude waited for her, as usual, in the hallway outside the dressing room. Exiting the room, she turned to him and went up on tiptoes to kiss his cheek, but he grabbed her arm and pulled her down the corridor, striding so fast that she struggled to keep up. He said nothing when they went out the back of the building. He said nothing as he shoved her into the carriage, then climbed in after her.

As the coach lurched forward, he turned on her, anger sparking in his eyes. "I saw you today," he growled.

"What do you mean? Where? Why didn't you call out to me?"

"You were kissing another man. Then you went arm-in-arm with him into a café. What do you think you're playing at, Madeleine?"

"Oh, Jean-Claude, that was only Jacques. Do you remember I told you I worked for a seamstress when I first arrived in Paris? He's her son. I hadn't seen him in over a year. So we had a coffee to catch up. That's all." She was so relieved that it had been a misunderstanding.

"I don't care if it was the great Napoléon himself. You do not kiss other men in public. Do you understand me?"

"But, he's like my brother, Jean-Claude. It meant nothing. I would never, ever cheat on you. You must know that by now."

He gripped her arm so tightly that she cried out in pain. "You will not be seen in public with another man. I don't care who he is. Do you hear me?"

"Yes, Jean-Claude," Madeleine whispered. "I'm sorry I upset you."

Jean-Claude had never shown her his temper, and now that he had, Madeleine wondered exactly how much he was in control of it. Would he lash out at her again? Would he actually strike her? And would he know when to stop?

From that day, their relationship changed. Jean-Claude became more demanding. He was rougher, at times cruel. Gone was the laughing, considerate lover. In his place, an unreasonable, angry man.

Madeleine didn't know what to do. It was a strict, though unwritten, rule that a dancer did not leave her patron. Quite the other way around. How long before Jean-Claude tired of her? How long must Madeleine endure this unforgiving servitude?

As the weeks went on, and Madeleine frantically searched for a way out, another situation reared its ugly head at the Opéra Garnier Ballet.

There was a dancer in the corps named Marielle DuPin. If Madeleine was driven, there was no comparison to Marielle. While Madeleine worked hard and followed the rules, was courteous and friendly to everyone, Marielle made no friends, lied, cheated, and conspired to move ahead as fast as possible. The golden prize, of course, was to dance the principal role, and Marielle DuPin didn't care who she had to trample to get there.

Although it was unintended on her part, Madeleine often found herself a step ahead of Marielle. If Marielle danced in the third row of the corps, the ballet master assigned Madeleine the second row. When M. Ballerat promoted Marielle to the second row, it was only after he had moved Madeleine up to the first. Until Madeleine became the Comte de Chamfort's companion, all of this was pure accident. Naturally, Marielle didn't see it that way.

Then, odd things began happening. One night after applying her makeup, Arielle returned to her costume to find that the threads in a seam had loosened. Another night, a ribbon on one of Gigi's pointe shoes had gone missing. A month later, a hole had mysteriously appeared in Yvonne's stockings. Only last week, Madeleine couldn't find the lucky charm she always pinned inside her skirt. Someone had launched a campaign to upset Madeleine and the dancers in the corps de ballet. *She assumed it was Marielle.*

Though Madeleine had her suspicions, Marielle was clever, and no one could accuse her or prove that it was she behind the incidents. Madeleine began to wonder how far Marielle would go.

The stress caused by Marielle's antics, combined with Madeleine's anxiety that Jean-Claude was going to hurt her, was building to an unbearable intensity. Madeleine feared she might be in real danger, and no matter how much she loved the ballet, it was not worth dying for.

* * *

The Comtesse de Chamfort led Olivia down the marble stairs into the foyer and began a brief history of the house. Talking as they glided over the deep-piled runner in the main hallway, they reached a set of double doors. The countess pulled open the pair of pocket doors, revealing a formal dining room. Blue paper adorned with floral wreaths circling stone bridges and follies covered the walls. A long table with a dozen chairs occupied the center of the room. Soft light twinkled in the chandeliers overhead.

"Oh! I can see why you like your new wallpaper. It's beautiful," Olivia said as she tried to come up with a way to pursue an impression she'd had Sunday and hadn't had the opportunity to follow up on yesterday.

On Sunday, when Olivia asked the countess if she had known Madeleine, she got the distinct feeling that Nathalie, as she now thought of her, was not happy with the time her husband spent at the Opéra Garnier Ballet or with the dancers. Olivia knew she had to be careful. She and the countess had just met and were not friends. The count and countess were also of a higher class than she and Steven, and that mattered in Paris right now.

Then Olivia thought *dining room, family dinners.* It was a small avenue, but one she couldn't pass up.

"Oh, Countess, I can picture your beautiful family around the dining table for dinner every night. It must be wonderful to live in such lovely surroundings."

Reacting without thinking, the Countess de Chamfort gave a small snort. Olivia's suspicions were confirmed: all was not well in the Chamfort family.

The countess must have realized that she had given something away and quickly said, "When they were younger, the children ate in the nursery with their nanny, so it was only Jean-Claude and me at dinner. Now, he is often away. He spends a great deal of time on his charitable work at the ballet and, as you know, he sees to our vineyards. I'm usually on my own." Olivia watched her adjust a false smile on her lovely face. "Of course, after a busy day, it's lovely to have peace and quiet. It's unusual, but I enjoy reading while I have my dinner."

Hoping to endear herself further to her hostess, Olivia said, "I used to live alone, so I always read when I had my meals. I grew to like it. And I know what you mean about having the peace and quiet to relax and enjoy the meal."

The countess gave her a smile that reached all the way to her sad eyes. "You're very kind, Mademoiselle." She raised her arm and indicated several pieces of deep cobalt blue porcelain showcased in a spectacular cherry hutch, black-edged with elaborate scrollwork. "You might be interested in some of the Limoges we've acquired. I especially enjoy using the blue-and-white plates with the gold edges. They look lovely in candlelight...." She wandered over to the French windows and gazed out.

Olivia wondered what Nathalie would have seen out that dining-room window had it not been dark outside. Wide steps on a terrace or two leading to a lush lawn? More manicured gardens? Perfectly sculpted topiary? Gravel pathways? A fountain whose clear water gurgled in the spring and summer months?

But it *was* dark out. Heavy snow clouds covered the moon and the stars, rendering the night pitch black. Olivia knew the countess was looking inward. At her life. At her past.

"The gardens are lovely in the spring."

Olivia began to respond, but realized the countess was still talking. She almost missed what came next, Nathalie was speaking so softly.

"I was an only child, but I grew up with the gardener's son. We were the same age. We played together on the lawns, along the paths, in the woods. Hide and seek. Throwing and catching a ball. I had a hoop and stick that we took turns with. He was better than me." She gave a low chuckle. "I don't know how that could have been over thirty years ago. In some ways, we seem more real than my own children do. With their nanny and their boarding school."

Olivia didn't know what to say.

The countess shook her head and turned back to Olivia. She smiled—genuinely, this time. "Look at me. Becoming nostalgic. You must forgive me. I don't know what came over me just then."

As they continued their tour down the long corridor, passing several closed doors, the countess recited the names and dates of the Chamfort ancestors represented in the many framed portraits lining the walls. Olivia heard a muffled flush, and a door to her right opened. A gentleman in one of the ubiquitous tuxedos exited. *Good to know where this is*, she thought.

At the end of the hallway, the countess pointed out her husband's study. She made it clear to Olivia that, although they could take a quick peek, they dare not cross the threshold. A fire crackled in an ornate fireplace, warming the room, making Olivia long for an office like this at home. A large partners desk sat in front of a tall window, a burgundy-colored Chesterfield sofa and two club chairs—all leather— occupied the space near the hearth, and a drinks cart holding crystal decanters and expensive-looking bottles of liquor stood in one corner. The countess laughed and said, "I'm not allowed in there. It's my husband's domain."

Hoping to lessen the countess's obvious embarrassment, Olivia joined in her laughter and said, "It's the same in America. Men like their private spaces."

* * *

As Olivia and Nathalie climbed the staircase to return to the ballroom, a clock somewhere in the depths of the mansion chimed. The countess said, "Right on time, they're going to serve supper now."

Olivia had kept her eye on the Comte de Chamfort earlier and did so again during the elaborate meal. Liveried servants served oysters, caviar, salmon, *foie gras*, and more, and kept the guests' glasses filled with several wines.

Olivia enjoyed her conversation with her neighbor to the right, the Comtesse de Beauharnais, a stunning honey-blonde whose hair was lightly streaked with silver. She'd barely spoken the question "I understand you have two daughters?" when the countess's face lit up and she proclaimed her and her husband's devotion to their girls.

The meal ended with the traditional *Galette des rois*, the King's cake. The Comtesse de Beauharnais leaned toward Olivia and whispered, "Be careful in case you get *la fève*. You don't want a broken tooth to start the New Year."

"La fève? Qu'est-ce que c'est? What's *la fève*?" Olivia asked.

"Traditionally, it was a bean, but Nathalie's cook puts a small glass marble in the batter instead. Whoever finds it in their piece of *gâteau* wins a prize."

"Oh, that sounds like fun. Thank you so much for warning me. It would be easy to break a tooth if you didn't know."

Olivia leaned over and whispered the warning to Steven.

To her amazement, Olivia saw a small, round piece of glass when she first slid her fork into the slice of cake. Thrilled that she hadn't bitten down on it, she said, *"Voilà la fève. Je l'ai trouvée.* Here's the *fève.* I found it."

Everyone set down their forks and clapped, shouting, "Brava!"

The butler brought a small, black velvet jewelry box and placed it next to one of Olivia's wine glasses. At the head of the table, the Comtesse de Chamfort said, *"Félicitations, Mademoiselle. Ouvrez-la.* Congratulations, Mademoiselle. Open it."

Olivia untied the white silk ribbon and gasped when she saw what was inside. An exquisite gold pin sparkling with jewels rested in a satin nest. Two flowers, their petals made of glittering, multi-faceted red stones and tiny diamond-like gems, sat above the stem, which was encircled with vines and leaves encrusted with dark green jewels. Olivia held up the pin for everyone to see. The gems caught the candlelight and glowed even more richly. Olivia had no idea if these stones were real, but the pin was stunning.

"I don't know what to say, Monsieur le Comte and Madame la Comtesse. It's absolutely beautiful. I will think of you every time I wear it."

The guests applauded once again, then returned to their dessert and coffee.

Shortly after, the butler approached the count and whispered something in his ear. Several servants arrived with more bottles of Champagne and filled each flute.

"Let's count down together, *mes amis,"* said the Comte de Chamfort.

Olivia had forgotten it was New Year's Eve. "Oh, it must be almost midnight," she said to Steven.

Chairs scraped across the parquet floor as the men and women around the table stood, each with a glass of Champagne in their hand. Olivia heard the call of a trumpet from the orchestra, which had been playing at a low volume during the meal. This must have been the signal because everyone began to count backwards. *"Dix, neuf, huit, sept, six, cinq, quatre, trois, deux, un...Bonne Année!!"* they shouted, raising their glasses. All along the table, the guests touched their neighbors' flutes with their own, the sounds of tinkling crystal resonating and mixing with wishes for a good and prosperous 1896.

"Vive la France!" called out the Comte de Chamfort.

Their guests answered the call and raised their glasses to France.

* * *

The orchestra wasted no time before they resumed playing. The floor soon filled with couples dancing the waltz.

Olivia whispered to Steven, "I need to go to the bathroom."

"Should we ask someone where it is?"

"I already know. I noticed it earlier when the countess was showing me around."

"Okay, I'll wait here. Let's dance when you get back."

He watched her walk away.

* * *

Olivia paused at the doors to the ballroom and looked back at the party-goers. The colors of the women's gowns looked like an impressionist painting as couples twirled around the dance floor. The swirling tones of sapphire, scarlet, emerald, and plum created one of the most beautiful scenes she'd ever witnessed. Wondering if the count and countess were dancing, she searched the crowd and realized the Duc de Rochechouart, the Comte de Chamfort, and the Comte de Beauharnais were not there.

Olivia made her way down the curved staircase, holding onto the gold-brushed banister so as not to slip on the smooth marble steps. As she approached her destination, she heard voices coming from the count's study, one door farther down the hall from *la toilette*. She searched for a place to hide. *Where were the alcoves when you needed one?* Deciding to check the restroom first to be sure no one was in there, she carefully opened the door. The tiny room with the toilet and a small sink was empty.

Olivia could still hear the men's voices. Obviously, they thought no one would be here on the main floor at that moment—there were probably facilities she didn't know about closer to the ballroom. She decided to stay in the hall but keep one hand on the doorknob. She could listen and watch the study door, which had been left ajar. If the voices became louder, as though someone were approaching the door, or if there was the slightest movement of the door, she'd be able to dash into *la toilette* with no one the wiser.

"What happened with the artist woman?" asked a deep voice that sounded familiar, though Olivia couldn't place it.

"It all went according to plan."

Olivia recognized the Comte de Chamfort. That made sense. After all, it was his house, his study.

"They didn't hurt her, did they? We don't need any more problems right now." The deep voice again.

"No, they grabbed her off the street as she was coming out of her apartment, then dumped her in a cellar they knew about."

A new and unfamiliar voice asked, "Didn't she struggle? How did they get her to stay in the coach?"

The Comte de Chamfort answered. "They knocked her out with

chloroform."

"How long did they leave her in the cellar?" The unfamiliar voice.

"A few hours. Then they took her back up on the *butte* and threw her out of the carriage."

"I thought you said they didn't hurt her."

"They didn't. Maybe she got a bruise or two, but nothing serious. It could have been a lot worse. They could have killed her," the Comte de Chamfort said.

The deep voice spoke again. This time, he sounded concerned. "But Benoît has control of those two hoodlums, doesn't he?"

"He says so." The Count de Chamfort seemed to have all the information.

"What about this business of the American policeman investigating Madeleine's death?"

It sounded like the owner of the familiar voice, the one Olivia still couldn't identify, was the leader of the group. She'd already made the assumption that the three aristocrats who were missing from the ballroom must be the three voices coming from inside the study. Since she recognized the voice of the Comte de Chamfort, and she knew Benoît was the Marquis de Polignac, the other two voices must be the Duc de Rochechouart and the Comte de Beauharnais. But which was which?

That's it! Olivia hadn't spoken with the Comte de Beauharnais, only his wife, and had no idea what his voice sounded like. The deep voice must belong to the Duc de Rochechouart, who had been reluctant to talk with her and Steven earlier, who was in charge of the aristocrats. And it made sense, she thought, remembering that both Evangéline and Etienne had told her and Steven the duke's family was old nobility and very important.

"I don't know anything about that. My spy at the Sûreté tells me they're treating Madeleine's death as murder. And they're investigating the chocolates poisoning that happened back in October as well." Olivia now knew that this was the Comte de Beauharnais speaking…and he had placed an informant in the police department. *What a hypocrite! He was the father of two daughters. How could he be involved with these creeps and their disgusting arrangement at the ballet?*

Le Duc de Rochechouart spoke again. "We didn't have anything to do with that, did we? The *chocolats?*"

"No, not as far as I know," said the Comte de Beauharnais.

"Well, let's keep it that way. Tell Benoît to call off his dogs. No more kidnapping. No interference until we see how things progress. I don't want to draw attention to us. We don't want to ruin our nice little arrangement at the ballet."

"I'll take care of it tomorrow, Thomas," said the Comte de Chamfort.

Olivia had heard enough and did not want to tempt fate. She tiptoed into the WC and quietly closed and locked the door. After she finished, she placed an ear against the door, closed her eyes, and strained to listen for any sounds through the thick oak. Nothing. She slowly opened the door and peered down the hallway. It was empty.

Olivia realized she would be in grave danger if one of these three men were to see her re-enter the ballroom at that moment. They'd wonder where she'd been, and that was one small step to suspecting that she had been listening in on them. She shuddered. *You're in over your head on this one, Olivia,* she told herself.

Fortunately, when she arrived back at the gala, the orchestra was taking a break and a large group of people stood chatting near the doorway, blocking her from view. Olivia was able to sneak in unnoticed. She found Steven standing where he said he would be. She grabbed his hand and led him to an isolated spot where she told him everything she'd heard.

* * *

Close to one-thirty in the morning, Steven whispered, "What do you think about going home soon?"

"Yeah, I've had enough. I saw some people leaving, so it must be okay. I don't want us to be the first ones."

"Let's find the count. We can thank him and say good night."

The Comte and Comtesse de Chamfort were exiting the dance floor when Steven spotted them. He held out his hand to the count and gave a small bow to the countess. "We can't thank you enough for your gracious invitation to this wonderful party. We'll always remember this evening and how we began the New Year."

"And I'm speechless about the beautiful pin!" exclaimed Olivia. "I'll always think of you when I wear it."

"You're most welcome. We've enjoyed having you here. By the way, your driver spoke with our butler a little while ago. Apparently, there was an emergency, and he had to leave. Of course, you must take our carriage. Gaston will drive you home."

"That's very generous. Thank you." Steven spoke for both of them.

Downstairs in the foyer, having received their outer apparel from a servant, Steven and Olivia were ready to depart the Chamforts' mansion. They took two steps in the direction of the front door, then paused to allow the couple in front of them to exit first. The man, having had too much to drink, pushed one of the doors too hard, causing it to slam against the wall. When the door hit, a key fell from the lock. It bounced and landed near Steven's foot. He picked it up.

"Oh, my good sir," exclaimed the drunken man. "I am so sorry."

"It's nothing," Steven said. "I can easily put it back in the lock."

He held up the key so Olivia could see it, turning his head so no one could see and raising his brows. "Take a good look," he whispered as he stepped around her.

The butler quickly intervened. "My deepest apologies, sir. I can do that."

"It's nothing. By the way, this is a beautiful key. We don't have anything like it in America. It's like a work of art."

The butler gave a slight bow as he inserted the key back into the lock and said proudly, "Yes, all the keys on the estate have that same design."

A liveried servant stood at the top of the staircase, ready to help, but they declined. Steven gave his arm to Olivia, and they descended the red-carpeted steps.

A carriage pulled up from a spot where it had been waiting, and a slender man about Steven's height jumped from the driver's seat. *"Bonsoir, Monsieur et Madame."* He greeted them with a smile. As he tipped his top hat and gave a slight bow, the light from the lamps by the front door hit his shining, thick brown hair. Something clicked in the back of Olivia's mind, but, at the moment, she was focusing her attention on not tripping as she stepped onto the wooden block and into the luxurious carriage.

The driver confirmed the address with Steven, and they took off into the night.

Chapter Twenty-Seven

Wednesday, January 1, 1896

Paris, France

Olivia was excited about what she'd overheard on New Year's Eve and convinced Steven they had to tell Etienne before they left Paris. "I don't want to wait until Friday, when he could be looking into this. Besides, he needs to know right away there's a spy in the Sûreté." They asked Evangéline to send Louis with an urgent message.

When Evangéline knocked on the door of the Duclos family's apartment, the *concièrge* answered. *"Ah, Mademoiselle! Bonne Année à vous."* She reached out and kissed Evangéline on both cheeks.

Evangéline returned the New Year's greeting and the kisses. "Madame Duclos, could I send Louis out with a message? I'm sorry. I know it's a holiday, but it's important. I'll pay him twice the usual amount and he'll be able to travel in a carriage."

"Oui, bien sûr." She turned back into the apartment and called out, *"Louis, Mademoiselle Neuilly a une mission pour toi."*

Evangéline explained that she needed *le Détective Berthot* urgently and emphasized that speed was of the essence. Louis should hire a carriage up on the Place du Tertre, then go to the policeman's home first, as he was likely not at the Sûreté on New Year's Day.

Etienne arrived as Steven, Olivia, Evangéline, and Théo were finishing their second cup of coffee.

"*Bonne Année à tous*! Happy New Year to everyone! I understand you have an urgent matter to discuss. However, I must tell you I was planning to come anyway. I have marvelous news," he told them. "We arrested Gabriel Glissant and Carlos Garcia last night, and we've got them locked in a cell. Evangéline, you have nothing to fear now. It's safe for you to stay in your apartment. And, of course, go outside whenever you wish."

"That's wonderful! Thank you." Evangéline turned to Steven and Olivia and added, "Now, you can go off to Bar-le-Duc and not worry about me."

"Etienne," Olivia said, "I have a lot of information for you—and one item isn't good." She told him about the conversation she overheard last night in the Comte de Chamfort's study.

"You took quite a risk, Olivia, but it paid off." He smiled at her, his eyes lighting up with admiration and affection. "So, if I understand you correctly, the Duc de Rochechouart appears to be the leader of the aristocrats. The Marquis de Polignac hired the kidnappers on behalf of the group. The Comte de Beauharnais has placed a spy in the police department—we'll soon find him, never fear. And the Comte de Chamfort is the one who channels all the information to the group." He nodded, thinking silently for a moment. "So…we know the aristos were behind the kidnapping. They intended to intimidate Detective Blackwell so he would stop his investigation into Madeleine Gervaise's death. And we now know for certain Evangéline is safe from further harm because the Duc de Rochechouart does not want to risk their comfortable arrangement at the ballet. I'm not surprised the aristocrats don't want us looking into their relationships with the dancers." He raised his brows and grimaced. "And, according to what you heard, Olivia, they had nothing to do with the poisoned *chocolats*."

Etienne stared at Olivia. "I must say I'm overwhelmed and greatly impressed by the amount of information you've uncovered. *Brava!* Steven, you have an amazing partner in your work. You're a lucky man."

Steven squeezed Olivia's hand, then said, "I have something for you as well, Etienne." He retrieved the key from his pocket and asked, "Do you remember my showing this to you?"

"*Bien sûr.* The key you found at the bottom of the staircase where the poor girl was killed."

Steven told the policeman about the guest bumping into the door and the key dropping to the floor. "I held it in my hand, Etienne. I'd swear it was the same design."

"And the butler said that all the keys for the Comte de Chamfort's property were made in the same style?"

"Yes."

His mouth slightly agape, Etienne shook his head. "Again, I must repeat myself…I am overwhelmed with the amount of information both of you attained last night. *Incroyable!*"

"What will you do next, Etienne?" Steven asked.

"I'll meet with my boss, *le Directeur Général*, and bring him up to date on everything. First, with regard to the hiring of the kidnappers, we'll need to tread lightly because of the Marquis de Polignac's position—and, of course, the position of the other three as well, since he arranged it for the benefit of the group. I'll continue with the poisoned chocolates case while you go on with your investigation into Mademoiselle Gervaise's death.

"Because we want the aristocrats to continue cooperating with us, I think I can persuade *le directeur* to look the other way for now. We don't need to address the actual hiring of Gabriel Glissant and Carlos

Garcia at this very moment. Those two won't give up the name of the person who employed them. They'll take the responsibility and be out of jail in a few months since Evangéline wasn't seriously injured. And thank God for that!" He turned to Evangéline. "I hope you understand. I know you went through a terrible ordeal, but we need to put all our energy into finding our two killers first. We can always go after the Marquis de Polignac later."

"*Bien sûr.* I should let you know I'm going to London on Sunday with Théo for the opening of his show. We'll probably stay several days."

Etienne acknowledged her with a nod. "Next, concerning the keys… certainly the Comte de Chamfort had a motive for killing Madeleine—she accepted his gifts, then refused his attentions. Later, adding insult to injury, she left the Opéra Garnier Ballet. His ego must have had a difficult time accepting that. Men like Chamfort are accustomed to always having their way. Also, and we don't know this yet, but he could be a man of temper. He may have become angry at the manner in which she treated him."

"I hate to cause a problem," said Olivia, "but I imagine several of the Comte de Chamfort's employees would need a key to do their jobs. One of them could have killed Madeleine for any number of reasons that we don't know yet."

"Of course, you're right, Olivia. My work in the next twenty-four hours is cut out for me." The French policeman stood. "Now, we should be off to the train station if you are going to catch the *Orient Express.*"

* * *

260

October 1895

In late October, after weeks of long hours and demanding rehearsals, the company presented "Swan Lake." It debuted to a standing ovation lasting ten minutes. Everyone involved with the company, from the lady who cleaned the floors to the prima ballerina, was thrilled. Everyone but Marielle DuPin, who was still seething at being kept in the second row of the corps.

The dancers rushed back to the dressing room to change and relive their favorite moments of the night. On the low table in front of the sofa sat two beautiful boxes of A la Mère de Famille chocolates, their orange and gold design glowing in the gas lights. The girls were thrilled at such a treat and hurriedly opened both boxes.

In less than thirty minutes, two became so sick they could barely stand, but after some time were able to return home. Marielle DuPin became violently ill and spent several hours in the toilette. *MiNou Bordeaux enjoyed two delicious pieces but after swallowing the third chocolate, fell to the floor in a fit. She died an hour later.*

Luckily, Madeleine had chosen not to eat any of the chocolates and had returned home unaffected.

There was no performance the following day. The time off gave Madeleine a chance to face her situation. Exactly how badly did she want to stay at the Opéra Garnier Ballet? Things with Jean-Claude had reached a breaking point, and she had to acknowledge she was afraid of him. He hadn't hit her yet, but she feared any day now he could lose control and lash out. She no longer knew who he was.

As if that wasn't enough, there was the incident with the chocolates last night. When her roommate had returned from the Garnier and recounted the horrifying incident of the chocolates and poor MiNou's shocking death, Madeleine knew the time had come for her to decide. She was no scientist, but it seemed a logical conclusion that someone had tampered with the candy. Four people ate several pieces of chocolate. Three became ill, one died. The dancers who took one or two pieces were fine. She ate none, and she was fine.

Had the chocolates been poisoned? Had Marielle gone to that extreme? Did the ballet have enemies, and had an enemy somehow inserted poison into the candy? But why? Who would have done such a thing? Had they been meant for her? Was Jean-Claude behind it?

After a late breakfast, Madeleine went for a walk. What should she do? What were her options? One thing Madeleine knew for sure: she didn't want to die for the ballet—either by Jean-Claude's cruel hand or by an anonymous poisoner. She had to leave.

Madeleine entered a small park a few blocks from her apartment in Montmartre and sat on a bench to think. Suddenly, everything was too much. Her life was spinning out of control, and she felt overwhelmed by an impossible decision. Madeleine broke down crying.

"Hey, it can't be that bad, can it?" said a sweet voice.

Madeleine looked up into the smiling faces of two young women about her age, a blonde and a redhead. One sat on either side of her.

"I'm Brigitte," said the girl with flaming red hair. "This is my roommate, Jojo."

Madeleine sniffed, took out a handkerchief, dried her eyes, and blew her nose. "Madeleine. Nice to meet you. And, yes, it is that bad."

"Tell us," said Jojo. "It'll feel good to get it off your chest."

So Madeleine told them almost everything.

As she finished her story, and Brigitte's and Jojo's eyes grew large, Madeleine said, "So I have nowhere to go if I want to keep dancing. I don't know what to do."

"Does it have to be the ballet?" Brigitte asked.

"What else is there?"

The two women grinned. "The cancan," they chorused.

Jojo patted her hand. "Come with us. You'll be safe at the Moulin Rouge."

* * *

While Olivia had known some of what to expect, Steven was agog at the sheer luxury of the *Orient Express*. Since today was a holiday and the trip would only take three hours, they chose to spend the time in the bar car. They sunk onto rich crimson velvet seats and drank Champagne while listening to a pianist playing a shining black, baby grand piano. Around them, the highly polished wooden walls, with their decorative inlays and Lalique glass panels, reflected light from sconces mounted between large windows, oversized for panoramic viewing. Crystal chandeliers along the sculpted ceiling above sent beads of light dancing in the champagne flutes.

As the train chugged through eastern France, steam from the locomotive drifted back over the cars, mixing with increasingly heavy snow. The thick carpets and exquisitely embroidered drapes muffled the sounds of the engine pulling this marvel. Steven and Olivia gazed out the windows, thrilling in the view as they passed towns and villages with their half-timbered houses and rust-colored roofs nestled amid forests. They caught glimpses of church spires and castle towers. Olivia spied a river at one point, its surface frozen solid. It reminded her of ice skating on a local pond when she was a kid.

Steven set his champagne flute on the table between them and reached for a snack. An assortment of fancy canapés—tiny shrimp, oysters, caviar on toast, among others—rested on Limoges plates. Wiping his fingers on a linen napkin and taking another sip of his drink, he asked Olivia, "Do you remember when Etienne first told us about Bar-le-Duc? He said something like, 'The area used to be ours, but now it's theirs.' Do you know what he was talking about?"

"Yes, over the centuries, there have been a couple of wars that France lost. They had to give Alsace and Lorraine to either Germany or Prussia, depending on what year it was. By my time, the territory had gone back and forth four times, I think. I know France got it back after World War I and—" Olivia stopped. Steven didn't know about World War II.

When they'd first met, he'd been adamant when he told her he didn't want to know anything about future events. She had always respected his wishes and wouldn't say anything now. But, to think that here they sat enjoying a leisurely train trip through eastern France, where they would spend the next two days not far from the German border, and in less than five years in Steven's time, this part of the world would be embroiled in one of the worst wars in human history. The thought of what was to come pierced Olivia's heart.

Steven's comment shook Olivia out of her reverie.

"So it sounds like we're actually going to Germany today, or maybe Prussia."

"I think so."

"Hey, we didn't do this last night." He raised his glass and clinked hers. "Happy 1935."

"And Happy 2015 for me."

They laughed.

"Okay, that was weird," she said.

"Do you mind discussing the case while we're alone?" He glanced behind him to make sure no one had taken the seats. "There are some threads I'd like to pull."

"Sure."

"Good. So first, I want to talk about Marielle DuPin. Think back to how she acted when we arrived at her apartment. When she realized Etienne and I were police, she didn't want to let us in. Then, as soon as he made it clear we wanted to question her about Madeleine's death, she threw the door wide open and invited us in."

"You're right. I noticed it at the time, but you started asking questions, and it fell to the back of my mind." Olivia leaned in closer to him. "She relaxed too soon, Steven. Do you think it means she didn't kill Madeleine?"

"I do. She's guilty of something, but it's not Madeleine Gervaise's murder. I'd say poisoning the chocolates is just the thing she would do. Remember, only weeks after the candy incident, she was fired for tripping another ballerina. I think Marielle DuPin is a spoiled brat who always wants to be number one and is used to getting her own way. Those two incidents—the poisoned chocolates and the tripping—are almost like temper tantrums. As serious as they were."

"She might not have imagined anyone would die because of the candy, Steven. Maybe she knows people take minute quantities of arsenic for medical reasons, and she thinks it's safer than it is. She probably didn't have any idea that some dancers had already reached their safe limit and that one or two pieces of candy would make them so sick...or kill someone."

"True. So, for now, let's dismiss Marielle as Madeleine's killer." Steven set his glass down and reached for his notebook. He thumbed through, pausing every few pages to read, then said, "I don't see any of the other dancers—either at the Opéra Garnier Ballet or the Moulin Rouge—as serious suspects. According to Nini, Brigitte, Jojo, and several other girls, Madeleine was likable. Remember, you also told me her landlady said she was pleasant and friendly. So, at both dance places, she did her job, showed up on time for rehearsals, stayed after the cabaret shows when she could because that's what her boss wanted, went out with her friends when she could afford it, and was a good roommate. It sounds like all she cared about was dancing. That leaves us with the four aristocrats: the duke, the *marquis*, and the two counts. I think we're going to eliminate Bernard pretty fast tomorrow morning. I'm still convinced the motive has something to do with one of the dance places." He popped a toast with caviar in his mouth.

"Eavesdropping on the aristocrats' conversation last night was aces,

Olivia. Really swell! It seems like the Duc de Rochechouart is their leader. He was the one who kept asking questions. He didn't place a spy in the Sûreté. He didn't hire the kidnappers. I say he keeps his distance, and he keeps his hands clean. He's the master puppeteer. We may find out later that he told someone to hire a thug to kill Madeleine, but he certainly did not do the hiring. Why would he? According to our interview with Gigi Pantier, it sounds like he's occupied with Arielle. We have no information that links him to Madeleine."

"And remember, the duke's family is one of the most important families in France, Steven. Killing someone would put his family in an unacceptable position. He'd avoid that if there was any other way. Maybe he'd order a murder, but why Madeleine? Like you said, he wasn't her patron. I don't see a motive for him. Especially since Madeleine wasn't even at the Garnier anymore. I think he'd be sure to stay at least one step away from any criminal activity."

"I agree. Even though Etienne said he's ruthless, he probably reserves that kind of behavior for his business interests. Let's take him off our list. If new information comes to light, we can always put him back. Now, the Comte de Beauharnais has his hands full with reports from his spy at the Préfecture de Police. It sounds like that's his principal activity and contribution to our group of aristos. We haven't found out if he's a patron of one of the dancers yet. Maybe he's not involved with anyone."

"Right. And although he goes along with the group, maybe the fact that he has young daughters is simply too distasteful for him to participate in their scheme at the Garnier. What about the Marquis de Polignac? He hired the kidnappers, Steven. He must have some kind of connection to the…" She made air quotes. "…underworld, for lack of a better word. I mean, think about it. If I wanted to hire somebody to kidnap or kill someone, I wouldn't have a clue where to start. And if I did somehow find a name, why would that person trust me with a job that could land him in jail or the electric chair? And how would he know I had the money to pay him?" Olivia took a sip of her Champagne, then frowned. "I'm disappointed in the Marquis de Polignac. I should know better by now, but looks can be so deceiving."

Steven raised a brow. "So, the Marquis de Polignac is your type, huh?"

"No! You're my type and you know it."

They laughed, and Steven leaned over to kiss her. Still uncertain of the social mores of the time, he bussed her cheek and did it quickly, just in case.

"So that leaves our friend the Comte de Chamfort," he said.

"Or one of his employees. That's it! I can't believe I forgot to tell you." Olivia exclaimed, trying to keep her voice down. "Last night, there was something about the Chamforts' driver that rang a bell. I was concentrating on not tripping when I climbed into the carriage and didn't pay much attention. Do you remember the description of one of Madeleine's admirers at the Moulin Rouge? Nini said Madeleine's new admirer was a man named Gaston."

Steven found the page in his notebook. "Sure, a carriage driver called Gaston. Taller than average, brown hair, brown eyes. Pleasant. Smiles a lot." He paused. "I see where you're going, but that describes about half of the male population, Olivia." He chuckled. "It describes me!"

"No, I mean yes, but wait. There was something in particular that Nini said. She made a point about his hair. She said it was full and shining. Do you remember? She laughed and said he wouldn't be going bald any time soon. Last night, when the count and countess's driver bowed to us, he took off his hat, and the light from the lamps at the front door made his hair look shining and thick. He ran his hand through it, then gave us a big smile. Henri's driver has carted us around for almost a week now. Have you *ever* seen him smile, even a little? Why did this guy smile at us?"

"I don't know, Olivia. It seems pretty thin. Do we know the Chamforts' driver's name?"

"When we were getting ready to leave, the Comte de Chamfort told us that Henri's driver had to leave in an emergency. Then he said, 'Gaston can take you home.'"

Steven thought back to their final moments at the New Year's Eve gala. He pictured the four of them—the count and countess, Olivia and himself—standing by the door to exit the ballroom. He recalled the conversation. His jaw dropped.

"You're right. But wait a minute. If the Comte de Chamfort planted his driver at the Moulin Rouge so he'd become a familiar admirer of Madeleine's, building up her trust in him, then killing her, why in heaven's name would he offer Gaston to drive us home?"

Chapter Twenty-Eight

Wednesday, January 1, 1896

Bar-le-Duc, France

After leaving the *Orient Express* and connecting to a local train, Steven and Olivia arrived at the tiny station in Bar-le-Duc shortly before noon. Steven grabbed their shared suitcase, and they stepped off the train into the swirling snow, wind, and cold.

"Let's get some advice from one of the rail workers, Olivia."

They walked to a counter and explained to a man in a dark cap and long, baggy blue jacket that they needed to find a place to stay for the night, and they also wanted to eat lunch. The railroad employee smiled and said there was a small hotel not far from the station and that it boasted a good restaurant. He gave a shrill whistle, and a man bundled up in a heavy coat rushed to the counter.

"Pierre can take you. And Happy New Year to you!"

It was a simple donkey cart with two wheels and one animal to pull them. Pierre set their case and the rope-tied box with Madeleine's belongings in the back, then helped Olivia up onto the seat. He instructed Steven to jump in next to their luggage while he walked alongside the cart, controlling the donkey with a whip. Olivia was glad the animal appeared to be smart and was obedient, so Pierre didn't need to use the crop.

They rounded a curve where one building disappeared into the next one, built so close together Olivia couldn't see any space between them. As they bounced along on the uneven road, she looked up and noticed gusts of wind catching smoke from the many chimneys that marched from one roof to the next. After less than ten minutes of travel, Pierre led the donkey to the front of a plain gray building with a bright blue door and shutters. He helped Olivia down from the high seat while Steven hopped out of the back of the cart with their suitcase and cardboard box. The driver doffed his wool cap and wished them *une Bonne Année.* Steven paid the man, and they entered the small hotel.

Reserving a room for the night was quick and easy. Steven registered them as Monsieur and Madame Blackwell—Olivia turned away to look at a painting on the wall so the clerk wouldn't see her smirk. After Steven had signed the register, the clerk turned to a group of pigeonholes behind the reception desk and extracted a heavy iron key. Handing it to Steven, he told them how to reach their accommodation.

The room was charming and warm, thanks to a fire in the grate. They left their traveling bag on the bed and returned downstairs to the restaurant for *le déjeuner.*

While they enjoyed their pork roast, sauerkraut, and potato salad, Steven said, "It's already after one. By the time we're finished with lunch, the only thing we'll be able to do is visit the local police station. At least we'll get that out of the way. We need to report to whoever's in charge. Etienne gave me a letter of introduction explaining why we're here and vouching for me. If one of their officers can take us around tomorrow, everything'll go faster and we'll be able to make the train back to Paris."

"I know we have to cross our t's and dot our i's, but it almost feels like a waste of time coming here. After all, we're pretty sure our killer is in Paris, right?"

"Yes, but we have to keep an open mind. Pretty sure isn't enough. We need to run down every clue and tie up every thread. You never know what we're going to find. Everything we think we know could boil down to nothing more than supposition and guesswork. I've seen it happen, Olivia. I had a case once where we were all positive we knew who the killer was. All of us! Will, Jimmy Bou, the chief, and me. We were so sure. Then, all of a sudden, the entire investigation got turned on its head. Someone confessed. And when he told us how and why he committed the crime, it was crystal clear. We wondered what we had been thinking. I don't want to make any mistakes here. Especially with the aristocracy involved. Besides...," he grinned and reached across the table to squeeze her hand. "...this trip gives us a private interlude together."

She giggled. "What's gotten into you? Interlude?"

"Just enjoying our holiday." He fluttered his eyebrows.

She grinned. "Okay...so, back to business...we're thinking it's Gaston, right? I say we have two choices. One: he killed her for himself. He became obsessed with Madeleine—granted, it was a pretty short time for that to happen, only two months, but even so—and he couldn't have her, so no one could. Maybe he was angry because she let him take her to dinner two or three times, then when she rejected him a fourth time, he lost it and pushed her down the stairs."

"Right." Steven continued Olivia's hypothesis. "Or two: Gaston killed her on behalf of his employer, the Comte de Chamfort. We already know why *he* might want her dead. French society is very class-conscious right now. I imagine it would be easy for an important person like the count to persuade a so-called lowly employee to do his bidding. He could have told him that Madeleine was a tramp and had threatened his family for some made-up reason. He'd only have to provide a vague explanation. Actually, I don't think a person like the count would explain much at all. He might have said she was blackmailing him and that it had to stop. Or he simply could have paid Gaston such a large amount that he couldn't say no."

"An offer he couldn't refuse," Olivia said.

"What?"

"Remember that Mafia movie we watched a few months ago? *The Godfather*?"

"Oh, yeah. Right." Steven ate the last bite of his meal and set down his knife and fork. "Mmm. That was delicious." He took a drink of mineral water. "Having said all that, we don't want to get ahead of ourselves, Olivia. We don't even know yet if the Gaston who's a customer at the Moulin Rouge is the same fella as the Gaston who's the Comte de Chamfort's driver."

* * *

While Steven and Olivia's train was pulling into Bar-le-Duc, Detective Etienne Berthot was beginning his interrogation of Marielle DuPin at the Palais de Justice in Paris. He had decided to let her sit overnight in a cell, a horrifying experience for anyone, let alone a woman who'd had an easy life thus far. Etienne knew the bravado she'd shown at her apartment was just that, a false face, a disguise, lies woven together to create camouflage. He was looking forward to tearing that away, to seeing what really lay below the surface.

Etienne had an officer bring her up to one of the many interrogation rooms after he knew she would have been given a piece of bread—no butter, no jam—and a weak cup of coffee. He let her sit for an additional half hour. Then, settling his face into the mask *he* normally wore when questioning a suspect, he opened the door.

Marielle DuPin stood underneath a high window with heavy iron bars, looking up at the sky. She turned when he entered. He could tell she wanted to spit at him. Or maybe gouge his eyes out. Her night in jail showed on her face, in the slump of her shoulders.

"Please sit down, Mademoiselle," he said.

"You win, Detective. If I cooperate and tell you everything about the *chocolats*, will you let me go? I cannot spend another night in that cell."

"Tell me everything and we'll see."

"I never meant to kill anyone. I would not do that. That's a line I would never cross."

"Why did you poison the candy?"

"I wanted to make some girls sick so I could be prima ballerina that week."

"How did you get the money to buy, not one, but two boxes of A la Mère de Famille chocolates? They're very expensive."

"I have money. My family sends me an allowance every month. I saved up."

Ah! She planned this, thought Etienne. *That changes everything. It was premeditated.*

"So, you didn't enjoy the patronage of an aristocrat who supports the ballet?"

"Patronage?" She sneered. "Indentured servitude is more like it. Those poor girls—and I mean poor in every sense of the word—were forced to dance to a very different tune after one of those men began buying them things, or after they insisted that *their dancer* be given an advantage in a particular ballet. Yes, they give a lot of money to the Opéra Garnier Ballet, but those girls pay the price for it." She briefly closed her eyes and shook the image away. "No, Detective, I had no association with any of the aristocrats."

"So, you bought the chocolates. Did you never think that one or more of the dancers might be taking an arsenic treatment of some kind? That they were already ingesting a controlled dosage and that even the smallest amount could do serious damage or kill them?"

She looked surprised, then hung her head. "No, that never crossed my mind. I thought they would become ill and Monsieur Ballerat, the ballet master, would choose me to be the principal for several nights."

"You took a hell of a risk, Mademoiselle." Etienne shook his head. "I must speak with my supervisor, but I can tell you that even with an accidental death—and this crime was clearly premeditated—you will surely spend time in prison."

Etienne stood and left the room. He heard her sobbing as he made his way down the hall.

***

After their delicious *déjeuner*, Steven and Olivia asked the waiter for directions to the local police station and were pleased to discover it was only a short walk from the hotel. It had stopped snowing, and the village sparkled like a Christmas card, enveloped in a blanket of pristine snow.

Steven presented the letter from Etienne, and they waited while the chief of police read it.

"I have heard of *le Détective Etienne Berthot*. He has the reputation of being a superior policeman. How can I help you, Detective Blackwell?"

Steven explained the interviews he needed to conduct the following day.

"I imagine it would expedite things, and certainly make it easier for you, if one of my officers were to take you to the desired locations," the chief suggested.

"I would be most grateful, Monsieur. We were hoping to catch the train back to Paris late tomorrow afternoon."

"*Bon*, that's settled then. Someone will pick you up at your hotel at nine o'clock in the morning. That gives you an early start, and Bernard will have finished with his baking by then, so he should be in a cooperative mood."

Chapter Twenty-Nine

Thursday, January 2, 1896

Bar-le-Duc, France

Officer Friedrich Dulaine waited outside in the carriage when Steven and Olivia entered *La Pâtisserie Fournier*.

Olivia took a deep breath and gazed over the displays. "Oh my God, Steven, I feel like I died and went to heaven. I *hope* it's not this guy. How could a man who makes all this incredible stuff be a killer?"

"All this incredible stuff" was rows upon rows of delicate *tartes, mille feuilles, clafoutis, Napoléons, macarons, gâteaux opéra,* and on and on. Olivia couldn't even identify most of these delicacies.

"I'm bringing as many as I can carry back to Evangéline, Steven. We'll have a tea party tomorrow."

A husky young man of average height, with messy brown hair, rich brown eyes, and a small clipped beard, stepped through a door into the shop. He was wiping his hands on his white apron. *"Bonjour, je peux vous servir?* Good morning, can I help you?"

Steven identified himself and Olivia and presented a letter from the local chief of police, proving he had the right to ask questions.

"You are Bernard Fournier?"

"*Oui, Monsieur.* This is about my poor Madeleine, *n'est-ce pas?*"

"Yes. I only have one question for you, M. Fournier. When did you return to Bar-le-Duc from your trip to Paris last week?"

As Steven began asking his question, a bell tinkled behind them, and the shop door opened. An elderly woman wrapped up in scarves and a heavy coat said, "I can tell you that. It was Sunday evening at six o'clock."

"*Ah, Mme Hauschild.* Happy New Year to you," Bernard rushed to hold the door open for the woman.

"Detective Blackwell, Mademoiselle, Madame Hauschild owns the haberdashery across the street. Madame, these are police officers investigating our Madeleine's death." Bernard sniffed and wiped his eyes.

She patted his arm. "Time, *mon cher* Bernard, give it time. Time will soften your grief."

"Madame…," Steven picked up his questioning, eager to get the information and move on to the family. "…how is it you can be so sure of the hour Monsieur Fournier returned?"

"I had just closed my shop. My neighbor was coming later for supper, so I came here to buy something for dessert. I was deciding between two tartes and some macarons when Bernard entered with his suitcase. He was all alone, and so very sad. His face held much sorrow. I asked him where Madeleine was, and he said he never had a chance to speak with her. He never even saw her. She wasn't home, and she wasn't at her dance rehearsal either. He couldn't find her, so he returned home."

"I finally realized that when she said she didn't want to marry me, she meant it. I thought she would tire of living in the capital—so crowded, so busy, and so loud. I was sure she'd want to come home again. But, I was wrong," Bernard Fournier said.

"You must have just caught the train to have arrived here at six."

"Yes, I had to run. But there was no point in staying in Paris and wasting money on a hotel. I knew it was finished between Madeleine and me. I came home."

"Thank you for your time and your honesty," Steven said. He doffed his hat and turned to leave. With one hand on the doorknob, he looked back and said, "You have my sympathy, Monsieur Fournier."

* * *

In the carriage, on their way to Madeleine Gervaise's parents' house, Olivia said, "I felt sorry for him, Steven. His head was filled with big dreams of his and Madeleine's future together. He really did love her." She shifted her parcels. "By the way, thanks for waiting so I could buy the pastries."

He nodded. "I agree, but, remember, people have killed out of love for centuries. Probably since the beginning of time."

Officer Dulaine drove the carriage to a modest stone house a mile outside town. A black wreath hung on the front door. Olivia was not looking forward to questioning the family about their deceased daughter and sister.

It took no time for Olivia to feel the pain that inhabited the Gervaise home. She felt like she couldn't breathe, as though the walls and ceiling were closing in. Grief filled every crack and crevasse, covered every surface, and hung in invisible blankets. Photographs were turned face down on the mantel. The mirror above was covered in black crepe so that Madeleine's spirit wouldn't be trapped. Olivia hoped Steven would hurry through his questions so they could leave and be out in the fresh air again. Then, as soon as the thought entered her mind, guilt washed over her. *She* could walk out the door and enjoy the rest of her day. This family was imprisoned in their suffering, and would likely remain so for a long time.

As Steven had suspected, no one in the immediate family could shed any light on Madeleine's murder. Her father visibly struggled to hold it together, to not break down. His eyes glistened with unshed tears. From the way he spoke, he had forgiven his daughter for dancing at the Moulin Rouge long ago. Olivia did her best to explain that the cabaret was not what Monsieur Gervaise thought it was. She hoped it helped. When Steven presented the box containing Madeleine's belongings, her mother became so distraught—sobbing, shaking, appearing close to fainting—that one of her daughters had to help her into her bedroom so she could lie down.

Madeleine's two younger sisters could offer no additional information. Since their revered older sister had left for Paris, they had been disappointed to receive few letters. They offered the missives to Steven and Olivia to glance through, but begged that they be able to keep them. After a quick perusal, Steven could see there was nothing to help with the investigation.

This was a family in deep grief, trying with little success to come to terms with the murder of a beloved daughter and sister. Steven could not in good conscience drag out his interview any longer. After a difficult hour, they took their leave.

* * *

"Officer Dulaine, do you think we can catch the train to Paris?" Steven asked when they climbed into the waiting carriage.

"Oh, easily. I'll take you to the hotel to pick up your things, then we'll go directly to the station. You'll have a bit of a wait. But you'll be having your supper in the capital."

Chapter Thirty

Friday, January 3, 1896

Paris, France

Friday morning dawned clear, but the temperatures had dipped below freezing. It was one of those days when it was too cold to snow. It was the kind of day that felt like home, making Olivia long for her familiar routine and prompting Steven to tell her he was ready to go back to Knightsbridge. To their life. To their house.

Evangéline and Théo provided each of them with an extra pair of socks and warm cashmere scarves to wrap around their necks and faces. Standing at the doorway as Steven and Olivia were about to leave for what they hoped would be the final day of the investigation, Evangéline and Théo wished them good luck, adding that they were sure the case would be finished by the time Steven and Olivia returned home tonight.

"I *know* today's the day you'll solve it! We'll have a celebration supper," Evangéline declared. "And we can have the fabulous desserts you brought back from Bar-le-Duc. I confess I wanted to taste one for breakfast."

Having sent Louis to let Henri know they had returned to Paris and had an appointment with Etienne at the Préfecture de Police this morning, Steven and Olivia knew their driver would be waiting. They'd also told the boy to inform Henri the case was nearing an end.

* * *

Etienne was nearly hidden behind his paper-and file-laden desk when an officer escorted Steven and Olivia to the detective's office. "*Ah, bonjour, mes amis!* *Merci,* Jean-Louis. Please have some coffee brought up for our guests." He turned to Steven and Olivia. "Come in, come in. I have much to share with you. How was your trip? Fruitful or a waste of time?"

"Both," Steven said as he helped Olivia out of her cloak and hung both his and hers on hooks behind the door. "We've eliminated Bernard Fournier, the former and unwanted fiancé. As you know, we were pretty sure he'd be cleared, but now there's no doubt. We found an eyewitness who saw him at six o'clock Sunday afternoon. She stated she was in the *pâtisserie* when he walked in with his suitcase, only moments off the train from Paris. He was already back in Bar-le-Duc by the time Madeleine was murdered, Etienne. And, naturally, I checked for later train schedules. There was no other train from Bar-le-Duc to Paris until Monday morning, well after Madeleine had been killed."

"*Bon.* It is as we anticipated. But to do a thorough job, we know we have to go through the motions and not simply assume. And the family?"

"We found no suspicious behavior whatsoever. Quite the opposite, in fact. They're devastated. Madeleine's mother couldn't even sit and talk with us. One of the girls had to help her to her bed."

"Etienne, it was so bad you could *feel* the sorrow in that house. It was awful," Olivia told him.

"That's the thing about these cases that always gets me." He thumped his chest over his heart. For a moment, Steven wondered if Etienne's eyes had actually glistened. "I don't know how a parent can live through the death of a child. Especially when it's murder. I think I would lie down and wait to die." He shook his head and cleared his throat. "Enough of that." He took a drink of his coffee. *"Eh bien,* I'm glad to tell you we've solved the case of the poisoned chocolates. I persuaded Mademoiselle DuPin—Marielle—to confess. She tried to make me believe she only wanted to make some of the dancers sick enough so they wouldn't be able to perform. She thought if enough of them were ill, the ballet master would choose her to dance the principal role. She swore she thought no one would die. Only that they'd be out of commission for a few days. Sick to their stomach and the like."

"And were you convinced?" Steven asked, suspecting the answer.

"Not really." That Gallic shrug again.

Olivia realized she'd miss that when she and Steven were home. She'd become fond of the French policeman.

"But it's irrelevant. There will be a charge of manslaughter. The crime was premeditated because Mademoiselle DuPin saved her money in order to buy the two boxes of *chocolats.* I told her she'd likely spend time in prison because, frankly, I didn't want her to become hysterical. She'll probably face the guillotine."

Olivia gasped.

Etienne held her gaze with fierce, dark eyes. "You met Madeleine's mother, Olivia. You saw the effect Madeleine's death had on her. Now, imagine how MiNou Bordeaux's mother must feel. What would she think about this punishment?"

"I don't know, Etienne, but it won't bring her daughter back. I think a killer would suffer more if he—or she—spent the rest of their life in prison. Execute them, and certainly the anticipation would be horrible, but when it actually happens, it would be quick. Almost merciful. Having witnessed the unspeakable grief that Madeleine's mother was going through, I think a killer should suffer."

He smiled at her. "Well, you're in good company, Olivia. Voltaire and Victor Hugo agreed with you. I will tell you I don't think about it at all. It's not my job to decide the punishment that a killer or a thief, a kidnapper or any other villain should receive for their crime. If I permit myself to become emotionally involved, it would hinder the way I do my job." He took a final drink and pushed his coffee cup aside. "Now, to the business of the kidnapping. We're still holding Gabriel Glissant and Carlos Garcia. Our penal code allows us to keep them for a while since kidnapping is a major crime. Let us focus all our efforts and attention on catching and arresting Madeleine's killer."

"Etienne, I owe you an apology," Olivia exclaimed. "I discovered something else and completely forgot to mention it the other day."

"More than everything you overheard from the conversation among the aristocrats?" The Frenchman's eyes widened, and his heavy brows rose.

"Yes." And she laid out the factual information, as well as her suppositions, about Gaston, the Comte and Comtesse de Chamfort's carriage driver.

"At the very least, it warrants an interview," Steven said.

"No question. We'll go get him *immédiatement*. I am relieved to say this will be much easier than if we needed to question the count or countess. Their driver has no particular privileges or status."

* * *

A short while later, two carriages pulled into the circular drive of the Comte de Chamfort's mansion. One carried Etienne, Steven, Olivia, and Jean-Louis, the Frenchman's second-in-command. The other coach transported three additional *policiers*. Each of the five French police officers was armed. Steven was not.

Before they left, Etienne explained it could compromise their case if he gave Steven a gun. However, he'd said, there was no reason the American detective and his *assistante* could not accompany them and observe.

"You'll appreciate, Steven, that we must do nothing to risk a successful prosecution, if the driver Gaston is indeed our man."

"Of course, I completely understand. I would do the same if I were in your shoes. Thank you for allowing us to be there at what I hope will be the resolution of this case, Etienne. Olivia and I are eager to return home."

"You are very welcome. After all, you've done most of the work on this investigation. I couldn't possibly keep you away from what I, too, hope is the end. You've been generous in helping Henri. He's a lucky man to count both of you as friends."

Cautioning Steven and Olivia to hang back, Etienne, with Jean-Louis at his side and the three additional policemen behind them, took the large brass knocker and banged on the oaken door.

After a moment, the door opened. The tall, usually restrained, butler allowed his facade to slip for a moment. Eyebrows shot up, and his mouth gaped at the group of uniformed police officers. However, he quickly regained control and said he would see if *le Comte de Chamfort* was available for *la police*.

Etienne didn't wait for an invitation to enter the manse. They all trooped in as the butler disappeared through a doorway on the far side of the large foyer.

Olivia thought how different it looked from the brightly lit, glittering entrance hall they'd seen on New Year's Eve. Today, the space was dark but somehow filled with shadows, reminding her of the *chiaroscuro* effect in some paintings. She hoped the gloom didn't portend a disastrous result in their investigation.

The Comte de Chamfort, brow furrowed, his mouth in a frown, strode across the marble floor. "What's the meaning of this, Berthot?"

"Good morning, Monsieur le Comte. We are here to take your driver, Gaston, to the Préfecture for questioning."

"Why?"

"We believe he may have been involved in Madeleine Gervaise's death."

"What? The dancer? Why in heaven's name would he? I doubt he even knew her."

"We'll let you know when we have more information, sir."

"Now, wait just a minute. You can't just take this man. I need him. I have things to do today. You don't even sound certain that Gaston did it. Why can't you wait a few days? Perhaps next Tuesday. I believe I can plan to stay in and won't need him."

"It doesn't work like that, Monsieur le Comte. The citizens of France don't dictate when and how the police do their jobs. I apologize for any inconvenience, sir, but we must take Gaston now. If—and I say *if*—after interviewing your driver, we decide he had nothing to do with the death of the young dancer, we will release him immediately, and he can return here to perform his duties for you."

Unnoticed by anyone throughout this exchange, as though she had floated in on a cloud, the Comtesse de Chamfort appeared on the far side of the foyer, nearly invisible in a dark navy dress. Instead of joining them, she stayed on the edge of the darkness a step beyond the threshold of a doorway. She said nothing. She made no noise. She simply glared at her husband.

A slight rustle of the countess's silken skirts caught Olivia's attention, and she glanced across the entrance hall. Although Nathalie's features were cloaked in shadow, she thought the countess seemed shaken. Had Nathalie suspected that Gaston killed Madeleine? How would she feel, having been driven around Paris by a murderer? Had she known about the true relationship her husband had with the dancer? Had she wondered if the count asked—or more likely commanded—the carriage driver to commit murder?

As Olivia tried to make out Nathalie's face in the dark, a glimmer of light from the still-open door caught the countess's features. Suddenly, Olivia realized the countess wasn't shaken. She was angry. She was practically shaking with fury.

At that moment, the Comtesse de Chamfort took a step into the foyer. The sound of her shoe on the hard marble floor echoed in the space, and everyone turned to look.

The count smiled a nasty, mocking smile. "Well, well, well. What have you and your chauffeur been up to, my dear?" he asked.

It was the moment everything changed.

"You bastard!" the countess cried, her eyes flashing with rage. "How dare you ask me what *I* have been up to? You and your damn dancers. One after the other after the other. Time and time again, you humiliated me. It wasn't enough to cheat on me. No, you had to prowl like a tomcat in an alley. You couldn't even pick decent girls. You had to choose *dancers*!" She spat out the word. "You cheapened our life. You made a fool of me." She took another two steps into the foyer. "And your total obsession with your precious Madeleine…it was too much to bear."

The lovely, sad, lonely countess—the woman whom Olivia had enjoyed meeting and had liked so much—appeared, at this moment, mad. She seemed to have lost all sense of her social standing and the etiquette that required. She only seemed aware of her husband.

"You are despicable. I should have told Gaston to kill *you* instead of that dancer. Well, I won't make the same mistake twice. I've had enough, Jean-Claude. You've pushed me too far."

In total indifference to the presence of six policemen, Nathalie pulled a gun from the folds of her dress, aimed, and shot her husband where he stood. The count screamed as he spun around, the bullet hitting his shoulder. He turned back to her, bent over, clutching his bleeding arm, his black eyes narrowed, pain and fury mixed on his face. "How dare—"

And before he could complete the sentence, before Etienne could reach her and knock the weapon to the floor, the countess shot him a second time.

This time, the bullet went into his chest. The Comte de Chamfort fell back onto the marble floor. A crack resounded as his head hit the unforgiving surface.

As the count was falling to the floor, Etienne raced across the room and grabbed the gun from the countess's hand. "Handcuffs, quickly," he shouted, pinning her arms back as she stood defiantly still.

While an officer hurried with the handcuffs, Jean-Louis ran to the fallen aristocrat. He tore off the count's jacket and opened his vest and shirt. The first shot had indeed gone into his shoulder. Although it was bloody, that one could wait. The second bullet had lodged close to his heart. Jean-Louis was glad the fall had knocked the count unconscious because when he leaned in and put pressure on the wound in his chest, the man would have screamed in agony.

Having heard the commotion, the butler reappeared.

"Quick," Steven shouted, "get some clean sheets."

To his credit, the man left and returned in an instant with two large white sheets. He helped Steven and the police officers tear them into strips while Jean-Louis rolled up the count's jacket and tried pressing it against both wounds. When they'd torn enough pieces, Steven helped Jean-Louis wrap the improvised bandages around the count's torso and shoulder, finally staunching the blood flow.

After placing handcuffs on the Comtesse de Chamfort, Etienne handed her to one of his officers, instructing him to keep her off to the side of the foyer and not allow her to escape. "Go find the driver, Gaston," he instructed Jean-Louis and his other two men. "Be careful. He may be armed."

"He'll likely be taking care of the horses," the butler told the policemen. "Go out the front door here and turn right toward the trees. Alongside the woods, you'll see a path leading to the stables in the back."

Olivia walked over to Nathalie. "Where are your children, Countess?"

"In the country with Jean-Claude's parents until next week."

"That's good."

"Don't judge me, Mademoiselle. You really have no idea," Nathalie said, her face a mask.

"You're right. I don't. And I *don't* judge you, Countess. I just feel sad."

Chapter Thirty-One

Ten minutes later, the policemen returned with a subdued Gaston Visière. It appeared the driver had resigned himself to his fate: his head hung, his shoulders slumped, and his feet shuffled as he tried to keep up with the police officers. He looked up when Etienne spoke and saw the Comtesse de Chamfort, also in handcuffs and being held by a *policier*.

A look passed between them.

Olivia caught it. *What was that? It was intimate...and sorrowful. Could it be? Could the driver be the special friend the countess was talking about the other day? What had the count meant when he'd said "your chauffeur?"* Olivia couldn't imagine how a relationship between Gaston and Nathalie could possibly work in this complex Parisian society, where your station in life meant everything. On the other hand, if he were the gardener's son that she'd grown up with....

Olivia was sure she'd seen a flicker of regret flash across Nathalie's face. A slight coming together of her brows. A sagging of her cheeks.

However unlikely, Olivia knew there was something between them.

Etienne arranged for one of the count's workers to drive a carriage, taking Gaston and a police officer to the Préfecture de Police. Another of the Chamforts' servants drove the count, who had regained consciousness and was moaning in pain, and an officer to the hospital in a second carriage belonging to the estate. Jean-Louis and the third policeman accompanied the countess in the police carriage, while Etienne, Steven, and Olivia returned to his office in the conveyance in which they'd arrived.

* * *

When they reached the Préfecture de Police, Etienne barked orders at the officers at the entryway. They were to take Gaston Visière and the Comtesse de Chamfort to the cells. He would summon them presently when he was ready for the interrogations.

Neither prisoner had uttered a word since the police handcuffed them at the Chamfort residence.

Back upstairs in his office, Etienne dropped into his chair, motioning for Steven and Olivia to sit as well. Then he called for a pot of coffee. "It'll help me think," he told them.

"I know you and Steven are the experts, Etienne, but I wondered if you noticed the look Gaston and the countess exchanged when your men brought him in?" Olivia asked.

"No, I must have been looking somewhere else. What was it?"

"It was intimate. Nothing like the way a servant would regard his employer. It was the look between a man and a woman. They know each other, Etienne. I'd swear that Gaston and the countess have known each other for a long time. *And* known each other well. No words were needed, but a message passed between them. That look spoke volumes."

"I wonder how they could have known each other."

"I think I know the answer to that." Olivia told Etienne and Steven about the countess's reminiscence in the dining room on New Year's Eve. "She was showing me some rooms in the mansion. We stopped in the dining room, and she went to the window while I was examining some china. She stood there, gazing out. It was completely dark outside. She couldn't have actually seen anything. Then suddenly, she spoke so softly, I almost missed it.

"She told me about her childhood, how she grew up with the son of her family's gardener. How they spent every day together, playing and attending lessons with her tutor—before you ask, yes, the boy was included. She was completely lost in the past. I had the impression that she longed for it. That she preferred it to her present."

"You think the carriage driver, Gaston Visière, was the little boy she grew up with," Steven said.

Olivia shrugged. "It would explain things, wouldn't it?"

"Remember the count's reaction when we arrived, and you told him we needed to talk with Gaston, that we suspected him of being involved in Madeleine Gervaise's death?" Steven asked.

"He was genuinely shocked. He had no idea of a connection between Gaston and the murder. The count did *not* order his driver to commit murder. I am sure of it," said Etienne.

"It must take an incredible amount of trust and convincing to get someone to kill for you. If they grew up together—and it sounds like they were, for all intents and purposes, brother and sister—they'd believe in each other, depend on each other, and look out for each other. If they've had this relationship for over thirty years, their bond and the trust between them would have grown even stronger over time. The countess might not have needed to give him a reason." Steven looked off toward the small window. Clouds filled the sky. They'd see no sunshine today.

"You know," Olivia began, "I spent a fair amount of time with the Comtesse de Chamfort this week. Sunday in the Bois de Boulogne, Monday afternoon at their home when we had coffee, and Tuesday evening at the party when she showed me around the mansion. I think she's an unhappy and fragile woman who can no longer endure the pain and sadness her husband caused her. Her emotions are in shreds.

I think it's exactly what she said—that he pushed her too far—and she broke."

"I think Olivia's on the right track. The count's behavior drove her to two extreme actions: telling her driver to kill her husband's mistress, and shooting her husband herself," Steven said.

Etienne nodded. "Yes, but it doesn't excuse her. Murder is murder, and attempted murder is as serious." He thought for a moment. "We'll speak with the driver, Gaston Visière, first. He looked like he was ready to talk when we were at the manse." An officer entered carrying a tray with three cups, a pot of coffee, cream, and a bowl of sugar. "*Merci*, Jean-Louis. Would you send someone down into the kitchens to bring us some lunch? I think we'll question our prisoners on a full stomach. It's already after noon."

* * *

An hour and a half later, Etienne, Steven, and Olivia gazed across the table at Gaston Visière.

"Tell us about it," said Etienne.

Gaston Visière struggled. He swallowed a lump in his throat. His eyes filled with unshed tears. His hands clenched, then loosened. His jaw trembled.

"Nathalie was born into the Fonblanque noble family. My father was the head gardener for the Comte de Fonblanque on the estate the Comte de Chamfort now owns. I was an only child, and Nathalie had no brothers or sisters. We were born within months of each other. My mother died giving birth to me. Nathalie's father, the count, didn't want to lose my father because he did such beautiful work. The count was ahead of his time in his thinking. He instructed Nathalie's nanny to take care of both of us. I realize that is unheard of, but, growing up, we knew no different. Since we were so isolated there, we spent all our time together playing, running, exploring the woods, and even learning. Nathalie's tutor was told to include me.

"Nathalie's mother died when she was fifteen. Despite the privileged life the Comtesse de Fonblanque had, she was always sad. Nathalie would give her little gifts and tell her lovely stories. She would try to make her laugh, to make her happy for a short while, but it never lasted. She committed suicide one summer when Nathalie was away visiting her grandparents. Nathalie was never the same after that.

"When the Comte de Fonblanque arranged Nathalie's marriage to the Comte de Chamfort, she insisted I come with her. I was the only person who really knew her, who understood how she thought and felt. I was the only friend she had, a friend who cared for her. The Comte de Chamfort did not know the true nature or depth of our relationship at that time. He is not broad-minded, but he wanted to please his future wife. He said I could work for him as a carriage driver. Naturally, Nathalie and I have had to act a certain way, but when the count is away—and that is often—we spend time together. I drive to an inn outside of Paris where we share a meal and a bottle of wine. We can talk the way we used to. We confide in each other. We are each other's strength."

"So, you were well aware of the arrangement the Comte de Chamfort has at the Opéra Garnier Ballet," Etienne said. It wasn't a question.

"The pig! He didn't appreciate what he had at home. He does not deserve her."

"You love her," whispered Olivia.

Gaston raised his eyes and softly smiled. "Since before I could walk or talk. I would do anything for her."

"It seems you did," Steven said.

The carriage driver hung his head. Then he straightened up and said in a defiant tone, "She was right, you know? In the foyer, when she said I should have killed him instead. I was stupid. That's what

I should have done. I could have freed her from the never-ending humiliation. We would have been free to be together. We could have moved away where no one knew us. Started a new life together." He was quiet for several moments.

Etienne said nothing, letting the silence fill the small room.

"Will I be executed, do you think, Monsieur?"

"Yes, I should think so."

"Can I see her before…before it happens? To say goodbye?"

"I'll do my best, but I can't promise."

"Thank you. Just once more. Then I'll be able to face what fate has in store for me."

* * *

Etienne, Steven, and Olivia returned to Etienne's office.

"I wanted to cry for that man. I don't know about both of you, but I feel drained from the emotions in that interview," said Olivia. "Is it always like that?"

"Not usually," Steven said. "At least not for me. I've only had one or two final interrogations that were as hard to listen to as that one."

"I know he killed someone, but I can't help feeling sorry for him," Olivia added.

"You can't think like that, Olivia. Many people have unhappy lives, or try to help a friend. But they don't commit murder. There is no excuse for taking the life of another human being. None."

"I know, Etienne. You're right, of course. And when I remember the grief Madeleine's family is suffering, I know he must be punished." She turned to Steven. "Do you remember the research on madness that I did a few months ago for a client?" She paused. "I do research for professors and writers. I own a small business," she told Etienne.

"Oh!" Etienne said, amazed once again at Olivia's skills and initiative.

"I learned that many aristocratic families in Europe pass down a condition from one generation to another. It's called porphyria. It's a type of madness. It might explain the countess's complete change of personality that we witnessed in the foyer of their house."

"It may explain her actions, Olivia, but it does not excuse her, and it will not save her. She convinced one man to kill for her, and she tried to kill another," Etienne said.

"When do you want to question her, Etienne?" Steven asked.

"Let's wait a few minutes. I'm going to stretch my legs and take a short walk. You two relax. Ask Jean-Louis if you need anything. I'll be back shortly."

As soon as Etienne was out of hearing distance, Olivia turned to Steven. "Steven, I don't want to watch the interrogation with the countess. I can't. I really liked her. I feel so sorry for her. It's too sad."

Steven took in her drawn face and realized he had never seen Olivia affected like this. He reached over and took her hand. "Why don't we go back to the apartment? I don't need to be here anymore. This is Etienne's case now."

Her face lit up. "Oh yes! Thank you for understanding." She leaned over and kissed his cheek.

Etienne returned to his office shortly.

Steven stood. "Etienne, *mon ami*, we're going to leave the countess—and tying up those threads with Gabriel Glissant and the aristocrats—in your capable hands. You don't need us here taking up space. We'll go back to Evangéline's and make our plans to return home. My boss will be wondering why I've been gone so long." He chuckled, extending a hand to Olivia, who rose and reached for her cloak.

The French policeman came from behind his desk and grabbed Steven's hand in both of his. "*Je vous remercie infiniment.* I thank both of you very much. When you first arrived, my hands were tied, but little by little, you showed *my* boss there were reasons to investigate. I'm glad we're getting justice for the poor girl." He turned to Olivia and enveloped her in a big hug. "If the two of you ever decide to move to Paris, let me know. We could use you at the Sûreté." He gave her a warm smile that reached all the way to his dark eyes.

"It was an honor working with you, Etienne," she said. "And a great pleasure getting to know you. We'll think of you often."

"I hope Paris crime will slow down for you in 1896, Etienne, so you can enjoy your beautiful family more. Especially those grandchildren!" Steven said. "And as Olivia said, we will think of you often, my friend. It has indeed been an honor."

"I wish you both a *bon voyage*. I hope you can rest on the ship on the way home. I've heard the North Atlantic can be rough in the winter. Hopefully, you'll have a smooth journey."

If he only knew, Olivia thought.

* * *

Outside in the courtyard of the Palais de Justice, Steven suddenly stopped walking. "I've got an idea."

"What?"

"It's going to be dark soon. Let's go over to the Eiffel Tower and see it all lit up. We may never get back here—at least not for a while, and certainly not in 1896. Besides, I'd like to sit and do nothing. We both need a break."

"Excellent!"

Steven hailed a carriage and gave the coachman their destination. When they pulled up to the near-deserted plaza between the Trocadéro and the tower, the driver jumped down from his perch and opened the door. Steven helped Olivia down, then paid him. They strolled to a bench near a line of trees and sat, comfortable together, neither feeling the need to talk right away.

The plaza was emptying, as the few remaining visitors caught carriages to take them home for their supper and an evening around a warm fire with their families. The weak winter sun slipped behind the city skyline, cloaking the capital in darkness. Suddenly, up and down the Eiffel Tower's four legs and center core, thousands of gas lights were lit, transforming the structure into a magical, sparkling beacon.

"Ooh!" Steven and Olivia chorused.

They were the only ones left in the plaza and felt as if they had discovered a secret spot.

Steven put his arm around her and squeezed. "It's like our own private showing."

After some time, Olivia said, "I hate to say it, but it's getting awfully cold, Steven. My toes are numb. Let's get a carriage to take us back to Evangéline's. If Théo is out and she doesn't have company tonight, I'd love to put on my own clothes and relax with a glass of wine and dinner."

"That sounds swell. But I want to say something first."

The tone of his voice made Olivia turn and examine his face. "What's the matter? Is something wrong?"

He turned so they were face-to-face. "No, not at all, but I want to tell you something." He caressed her cold cheek. "I love you, Olivia. With my whole heart."

"Oh!"

"The time we've spent here, away from home, away from our normal lives, far from our friends and the fellas at the station, made me realize that being with you is the most important thing in my life. I don't know how I would have managed here without you. And I don't mean solving the case. I mean getting through every day in a strange place. I love being with you, but I realized I also rely on you. You make me feel like I'm never alone. You always have my back. I can count on you no matter what happens. We might never be able to have a regular relationship…like a marriage and children…but I want you to know that you're the one for me. All I want is for us to be together any way we can."

Olivia felt her jaw dropping a bit. Her mouth opened, but no words came out. She cleared her throat. "I cannot tell you how much time I've spent agonizing over how we could work it out to be together. Every time I started imagining a different scenario, I realized it wouldn't work for some reason. Steven…." She put her hands on his face. "I love you, too. With my whole heart. I feel exactly the same about everything you just said. You're it for me. Forever. All of a sudden, I don't care anymore how we do it, how we figure it out. I want to be with you. That's it."

He stood and pulled her up with him. Wrapping his arms around her, he kissed her long and deep, not caring who might be watching, not caring whether this was acceptable behavior in 1896.

Chapter Thirty-Two

When Evangéline opened the door and waved them into the apartment, Steven and Olivia were thrilled to learn Théo had gone to visit his brother overnight, and the three of them would be alone for the evening. Evangéline's beau knew nothing about her ability to time travel or who Steven and Olivia really were. Without him, they'd be able to talk freely. They told her the case was over, and Olivia asked if she would mind if they changed into their own clothes. Of course, Evangéline understood their desire to be comfortable.

"While you're changing, I'll take your plane tickets to Monsieur Duclos downstairs at the travel agency. I'll cross over to Olivia's time, which is now 2015. The twenty-first-century Monsieur Duclos is actually a great, great—I don't know how many greats—grandson of Louis, my young assistant. Naturally, they have to keep the agency in the family. I'll show him the open-ended tickets and have him make reservations for you on the first available flight out of Paris."

Olivia felt a moment of panic, and it must have shown on her face, because Evangéline said, "Don't worry. You won't have any problem going home. Remember, you can *always* return to your own time. It doesn't matter that you arrived in 2014 but will return in 2015."

Olivia let out a deep breath. "Okay, good. Thanks."

"That's a swell idea, Evangéline," Steven said. "But make sure we have enough time to see Henri before we leave. I want to tell him about the investigation. He deserves to know everything. Or at least as much as he wants to. I need to give him the money that's left. And I especially want to thank him for being so generous and allowing us to use his driver every day. That made a big difference."

"He'll appreciate that. I'll try to get your tickets for Sunday."

Evangéline accompanied them to their accommodations next door and retrieved their plane tickets. They all met up again in her apartment a half hour later. "You have reservations for Sunday morning at ten-thirty. That leaves us tonight to be together, just the three of us. Tomorrow we'll meet with Henri so you can tell him about the investigation."

Evangéline had left the gas-lit sconces around the living room on low, so the ambience was cozy and intimate. As they relaxed, glasses of wine in hand and a fire warming the area, Steven and Olivia told her how the investigation came to a close earlier that day.

"That poor woman, suffering like that. And that poor man. To love someone your whole life but not be able to say it or be together openly in public…how very sad," Evangéline said. "I hope these stupid rules of society change someday." She took a drink, and the flames reflected in the ruby liquid made it look like a sparkling magic potion. "I'm glad you solved the case, but I'm going to miss both of you."

"Evangéline, I can't tell you how thrilled I am that we had this time together," Olivia said. "Steven missed you so badly. He's talked about you all year. I deeply regretted that I hadn't had the chance to know you. Now, I do. And I'm so very happy."

"I am too, Olivia. And I'm glad to know Steven won't be alone. He has you."

Steven and Olivia were seated on the sofa across from her, perhaps closer together than they had been all week.

Evangéline looked from one to the other. "What's going on with you two? If you don't mind me asking. Did something happen today?"

They smiled at each other.

"It's okay. You can tell her," Olivia said.

"We committed to each other tonight—officially."

"You've seemed committed since the first moment I met you. Steven, how many women do you know who would risk travelling back in time more than one hundred years to help their beau with what must have looked like an impossible investigation? My goodness! She didn't even blink when I asked you to come here. And how many men would trust their girlfriend to work on a case in a situation as dangerous as this? You two are tied together. I could see it immediately."

They both grinned.

"Well, we made it official today," Steven said.

"Yes, we don't know how we're going to manage it, but we agreed that we're going to stay together. Somehow. No matter what," Olivia said.

"It seems to me you're already managing it. You'll figure out the rest as you go. That's what we all do." Evangéline tossed off one of those Gallic shrugs and stood. "Now, Olivia, how about your last cooking lesson? I can't let you leave without knowing the most important basic of French cooking—*une sauce béchamel*. We're going to use it to make a delicious mushroom soup tonight. We'll heat the baguettes so they'll be warm and crispy. Of course, we'll have salad and cheese.

"*Absolument*! That sounds perfect." Olivia grinned and followed her into the kitchen.

Chapter Thirty-Three

Saturday, January 4, 1896

Paris, France

Saturday night, Evangéline, Steven, and Olivia joined Henri de Toulouse-Lautrec, Suzanne Valadon, and Edgar Degas at the Lapin Agile, the historic cabaret high on the *butte* in Montmartre. A scarce few red-shaded gas lights glowed in the tiny music hall, creating shadows and a sense of camaraderie. They sat crowded, elbow-to-elbow, on rough-hewn, wooden benches around heavy, wooden tables, their closeness creating not only physical warmth on this bitterly cold winter night but also an intimacy because of the nature of their conversation.

The three artists were eager to hear the resolution of the two cases. After calling for glasses of absinthe and bottles of *vin rouge*, Henri asked Steven to tell them what happened and how he and Olivia figured it out.

Suzanne was delighted and laughed wholeheartedly when Evangéline told her she was nearly a suspect. "Ha! I don't mind being notorious, but I'd rather it be for love, not murder."

After Steven finished, they were silent for several long minutes.

Then Henri raised his glass and said, "To Madeleine and MiNou, two beautiful souls whose lives were cut short." They all drank to the dancers. Then he lifted his arm again and added, "To our American friends, Monsieur Blackwell and Mademoiselle Watson, without whom we would never have known the truth. Thank you."

At that point, the music began, and everyone was happy to lose themselves in song. There was hooting and hollering throughout the cabaret, solo performances, and group sing-alongs. Père Frédé, the manager, grabbed his guitar and played songs popular with the crowd. Two men entered the room, saw Henri and his friends, and waved. Seeing Olivia's raised brows, Henri leaned over and whispered, "My friend Paul Gauguin. He's an artist as well."

"Ah," she gulped.

"That's Emile Zola with him. He's a writer. And an exceptionally good man. He speaks his mind. Which, of course, we can do *here*. The Lapin Agile is a place for free talking. For everyone. Not like many places in Paris."

Olivia sighed. The night couldn't get any better. She squeezed Steven's hand and leaned back against the wall, soaking up the experience.

Since they were leaving tomorrow, Olivia had risked bringing her phone. Toward the end of the evening, after glasses of absinthe—cut with water and poured over sugar cubes—and several bottles of wine, and while everyone was distracted by Père Frédé's playing, she palmed it and took several pictures. They were all too drunk to notice the flash or to care. She quickly stuck it back in her little draw-string bag and rejoined the singing.

* * *

Evangéline left Steven and Olivia at the door of their apartment, saying she would have breakfast ready for them early so they wouldn't miss their flight.

"After you leave tomorrow, I won't see you again until after I marry your father, Steven. We're only allowed one time for something like this. And of course, I won't be able to tell you about this past week. We can't share the future." She hugged him tight, not letting go for several long seconds. "I'm going to love being your mom." The love on her face and the warmth glowing in her eyes made Steven feel like he truly had his mother back in that moment. It had all been worth it. Everything inside him settled into place, and Steven knew he could move on now without her.

Evangéline turned to Olivia and wrapped her in a big hug. "Take good care of him, Olivia. It's up to you now. I'm only sorry I won't have the chance to know you longer and better. But I'm so very happy that you have each other." Her eyes filled with unshed tears. She grabbed their hands. "And remember…everything will work out."

Not the end.

A Note from the Author

Murder at the Moulin Rouge is a work of fiction. Although some characters in the story were real people, as far as I know they never said or did any of the things I have them say or do. I've included the birth and death dates for several of them in the Cast of Characters. Except for Evangéline Neuilly, who is fictional, all the artists mentioned were real people. Some additional real-life people who made their way into the novel as minor characters are: Auguste and Louis Lumière, Marius Petipa, Paul Durand-Ruel, Père Frédé, and Nini, although Nini was a dancer, not the house mother-dance instructor who appears in the book.

Henri de Toulouse-Lautrec revered Edgar Degas, who influenced his work more than any other artist. Degas was older and established in the art world when Toulouse-Lautrec was beginning his career. Although they knew each other, and certainly spoke occasionally and ran into each other, they were not good friends as I portrayed them.

Every time I write a book, I research the time frame when my story takes place, looking for real-life events that I might be able to incorporate into the novel. This time I hit the jackpot when I learned about the first-ever public movie screening hosted by the Lumière brothers. I *had* to make sure Steven and Olivia attended that historic event! If you would like to watch the films they saw that night, here's the link: https://www.youtube.com/watch?v=b9e74DoGwhs

The Lapin Agile is an institution in Montmartre. It's been a meeting place for artists and music lovers since 1860, and they still present shows four nights each week. The Lapin Agile stands out among other music halls for many reasons, but the one I find most interesting is the quantity of original art hanging on the walls of the small cabaret—there's barely an inch left uncovered. As you sit at rough wooden tables on hard oaken benches, the lamps draped in red, you're surrounded by works of art by Picasso, Utrillo, Toulouse-Lautrec, and others. I encourage you to google the Lapin Agile to find out more, and if you visit Paris, make a reservation and go see a show. It's so much fun!!

As I was researching this novel, I had the rose-colored glasses ripped off when I learned about the involvement of the aristocrats at the Opéra Garnier Ballet. I was both sad and infuriated to discover another institution had been corrupted by that type of behavior. In addition, I had always considered myself an observant admirer of art. I completely missed the hints Degas put in some of his paintings!

Another surprise was the Paris Morgue and the fascination Parisians had with death in the late 1800s. For more information, check out the Paris morgue at https://www.edwardianpromenade.com/amuse ments/the-morbidity-of-the-paris-morgue/

All the locations mentioned in the story are accurate—you can actually google the addresses to see where some of the characters live—with the exception of the staircase where Madeleine is killed. I replaced the double staircase on the rue des Saules with a taller, steeper one nearby.

Finally, if you're interested in seeing the clothes the characters wear, Olivia in particular, I've posted pictures on my Facebook Author page https://www.facebook.com/WriterCarolPouliot/?view_public _for=101607075003213. I also include photos of the clothes in my monthly newsletter. You can sign up at https://www.carolpouliot.co m/.

Acknowledgments

Once again, I have been privileged to work with four incredibly talented Beta readers whose dedication and insights made *Murder at the Moulin Rouge* better. My heartfelt thanks to Jon Anderson, Mickey Hunter, Marylou Murry, and Sue Scheeren Watchko. I loved discussing all the details with you. You guys rock!

As I mentioned in a recent newsletter, one of the things I am not good at is the back cover copy. Thank you to fellow "sleuths" Jen Collins Moore, Tina deBellegarde, and Lida Sideris for rescuing me as always.

Merci à Yves and Vincent at the Lapin Agile in Paris for making me welcome and letting me in early so I could take pictures. (You'll find a number of the photos I took on my Facebook Author page and in my Newsletter.)

Thanks to Denise Donato and Anna Cotter for listening to me talk about this book for the past two years!! And for offering terrific thoughts and suggestions.

Thank you to Tina deBellegarde for always being there and having my back. It wouldn't be any fun without you.

Thank you to Shawn Reilly Simmons for your wonderful notes. You always nail it! And to Deb Well for a million little (and big) things.

A book isn't doing any good if it sits on a shelf and no one reads it. It takes dedicated booksellers, librarians, and reviewers to get the word out. A lot of people have helped me along the way, and continue to support my books. I am deeply grateful to you.

Finally, a huge thank you to everyone who has read and continues to read The Blackwell & Watson Time-Travel Mysteries. I'm grateful for your interest, for helping spread the word, and for the reviews you've posted. I hope you enjoyed this latest addition to the series. *Merci!!*

About the Author

A former language teacher and business owner, Carol Pouliot writes the acclaimed Blackwell and Watson Time-Travel Mysteries. With their fast pace and unexpected twists and turns, the books have earned praise from readers and mystery authors alike. Carol is a founding member of Sleuths and Sidekicks, Co-chair of the Murderous March Mystery Conference, and former President of her Sisters in Crime chapter. When not writing, Carol can be found packing her suitcase and reaching for her passport for her next travel adventure. Learn more and sign up for Carol's newsletter at http://www.carolpouliot.com.

AUTHOR WEBSITE:

https://www.carolpouliot.com/

SOCIAL MEDIA HANDLES:

https://www.facebook.com/WriterCarolPouliot/?view_public_for=101607075003213

https://www.bookbub.com/authors/carol-pouliot

https://www.instagram.com/carolpouliotmysterywriter/?hl=en

https://www.goodreads.com/author/show/15907927.Carol_Pouliot

https://www.pinterest.com/cpouliot13/
https://www.sleuthsandsidekicks.com/

Also by Carol Pouliot

The Blackwell & Watson Time-Travel Mysteries
Doorway to Murder (#1)
Threshold of Deceit (#2)
Death Rang the Bell (#3)
RSVP to Murder (#4)

www.ingramcontent.com/pod-product-compliance
Lightning Source LLC
Chambersburg PA
CBHW032340310726
48973CB00007B/1786